Ginger and Ice

Joanne Elves

DEDICATION

To those who love to hold a book and turn the pages by hand.

CHAPTER ONE

Tuesday. That meant hills.

Meagan leaned into another hill, cursing how her legs and her lungs hurt. "Hills are my friend. Hills are my friend," she chanted like a mantra through her heavy breath. Her track coach from a decade ago drilled it into her that hills were excellent for strength and speed. Speed and strength were things she was reluctant to lose, but she still hated her weekly hill repeats.

Someday, all this running is going to pay off in something other than cheap medals, she thought as she pounded up another hill.

Her run began at the YMCA, located on the banks of the Bow River, which meandered through the heart of her hometown, Calgary, Alberta. The trail began with an easy warm-up on flat terrain and then it was up Crescent Hill, which took her out of the valley. It wasn't an easy climb, nor were the six repetitions.

The route followed the paved paths and the dirt trails created by dog walkers and cyclists. She'd make it to the top, trying to catch her breath without stopping. Then plunge down the next trail to the river. Whatever path came next was her path back to the top.

Some paths were long and gentle, others were just plain nasty. By the sixth slog up the hill, 40 minutes and six tough kilometres were behind her. With her heart pounding and her breathing deep, sweat was dribbling through her loose thick braid of red hair and down her neck and spine, soaking her light shirt and sports bra.

She turned at the top for the last time with a smile on her face. Done! The run down was relaxed, as was her pace back to the Y. She was preoccupied thinking about what route she would run tomorrow for a faster tempo run and didn't sense someone coming up behind her until the person was very close.

She listened to the stride – and relaxed. After so many years of running trails, she could tell a seasoned runner's stride.

A tall man loped up beside her, waved with a gentle flick of his fingers as he passed her, but without looking directly at her face.

What little breath Meagan had left, stopped. This man, who was now breezing ahead of her was not only the fittest but the best-looking man she had seen on the river pathway in a long time. With every stride, he gained distance on her, but she wasn't going to let him out of her sight – not yet at least. Besides, a little distraction was a good thing.

Even though the calendar had not flipped to November yet, winter was already biting at their heels. Lucky for Meagan however, a warm Chinook wind had everyone – including the guy who passed her, dressed for summer.

His legs were long and strong, and slightly tanned. Strong calf muscles offered a good kick when he strode ahead. His thighs did seem a little big for a serious runner though. *He must be cross-training,* she thought.

Her mind wandered as she surveyed his back. *A beautiful yield sign, broad strong shoulders, maybe he is a swimmer or a gymnast. Na, he's probably 30. Nobody is a gymnast at 30.*

His arms swung relaxed back and forth, pulling him further away with every swing. She picked up her pace again to keep watching him run, but he turned off as she ran straight towards the YMCA. *Well,* she thought, *that was a nice change of scenery.*

She pushed the stop button on her watch, slowed to a walk and strolled over to the edge of the raised concrete flowerbed to stretch her chronically tight leg muscles. She raised her right leg just as the tall man walked up beside her. His voice caught her by surprise, almost making her lose her balance.

"Good run?" he said, as he began a stretch regime too.

Meagan was stunned. He was talking to her!

"Ah, yeah, just short today, did the hill drill." She hoped he'd realize that's why she was so easy to pass and why she looked so ragged. *Funny,* she thought to herself, *I must look like a soggy rag doll with my sticky hair and sloppy shirt. What could be so interesting about me?* On the other hand, the glow of sweat on his face and body made her blood flutter in her veins.

"How about you?" she asked, so he would talk again.

"I went short too, but a lot easier. I went to that old fort, crossed the bridge and came back by the Zoo. No hill work unless you include the overpasses."

Meagan smiled at his joke. "Obviously, you're not from Calgary if you called it the old fort."

"Nope, just here for a few days from Boston. But man! If it's this hot all winter, I'm staying!"

Meagan shook her head from side to side. "Oh, don't get fooled. This doesn't happen every day. We get heaps of snow and endless bouts of freezing days."

"Well, to run without a hat and mitts in winter is awesome. I'll make sure I go again tomorrow to take advantage of this."

She changed legs to continue stretching. "Oh, if the weather holds and you want a beautiful trail with great hills, run the Douglas Fir Trail."

"What's it like?" he said, as he stepped closer.

Her heart raced and she stumbled over her words. She put both feet on the ground to concentrate on her words and his face. He actually seemed interested in her and didn't notice the lack of makeup, bags under her eyes or the straggly hair. He looked into her eyes as she spoke, which made it even harder to talk.

"You start here and head west," she said, as she pointed west and with arms and hands turning and rolling with her description. "When you come to the train tracks, cross through the fence and go up. It's a beautiful trail. You can't hear the traffic or see any of the city because the trees are so thick. In the summer the moist smell of the forest is intoxicating, but right now it's a bit cool because it's so shady and the snow can be slippery. You run up and down trails for about twenty more minutes until it bumps into the train tracks again. You can come back the same route but I usually hit the river path and run that back. It's one of my favourites."

"Can you do it tomorrow morning?"

Meagan was stunned by his bold, but delightful offer. She was about to answer, but he continued.

"I'm sorry, I should know better than to be so rude. You don't even know me. Are you stopping here? I'm staying at the Sheraton," he said, as he waved at the Y and then to the hotel next door. "Do you have time after your shower for a coffee?"

"Yeah, I do," she said, without giving herself a chance to come up with an excuse why not.

"Great," he said, as he put a hand on her shoulder. He gave it a gentle squeeze and started to walk off, "I'll be back right here in…half an hour? Can you?"

"Sure," she said, still motionless as he walked away. Her brain clicked back into gear and she skipped quickly over to him. She held out her hand. "I'm Meagan."

He laughed, smiled and clasping hers with both of his said, "I'm Chris."

"See you soon Chris," she said, with a smile, then she turned away thinking to herself in a panic, *Shit! Only half an hour! I can't even touch beautiful in that short of time.*

She lunged up the steps three at a time; not noticing the burning muscles in her thighs.

The rest of her stretching was cast off as she tossed her running clothes into a sweaty heap and bolted to the showers. The spray came on and she leaned into the steamy beads letting the water rinse off the sweat and mud from the thawing trails. She tried to hurry and plan how to get beautiful, but her mind kept wandering over to the Sheraton and him. *He must be getting into the shower now too. I wonder if his chest hair is thick like the hair on his head,* she almost said out loud. Embarrassed by her thoughts she grabbed the shampoo and started to lather far too much soap into her hair. As the suds rolled over her breasts her mind went back to the Sheraton.

I wonder if he is thinking of me, she laughed out loud and said, "I hope his thoughts are as impure as mine."

Meagan's eyes flipped open as she realized the old ladies from the aquatic class were now in the showers with her. A few were staring at her.

"Aw crap!" she said, as she turned the water cold. "Did I say that out loud?"

The closest lady smiled in acknowledgement.

She quickly left the showers vowing to keep her mouth shut until she left the locker room.

She took thirty-five minutes…probably because of her mental steamy shower scene.

Meagan bolted out the doors with her red duffle bag over her shoulder, looking the best she could considering the clothes she brought for the day were not exactly first date threads. The Carhart canvas work pants did fit her nicely and if anything, the old marathon race shirt under her fleece would give them a topic to talk about. A bulky fleece was enough to keep her warm that day - but she did wish it would show her figure a bit more.

Much to her delight, Chris was walking across the plaza. He waved when he saw her. *Perfect timing!* she thought. And he was perfect…but dressed slightly nicer than she. A crisp golf shirt was tucked into dark pleated pants over a six-pack of abs she could see through the fabric. A suit coat draped over his arm and expensive leather loafers replaced the runners. Unlike her bulky black ironman watch, the gold watch wrapped around his wrist glittered in the sun.

The wind was whisking her long hair and Chris watched it bounce as she ran to him. As she stopped, he reached out and touched her strawberry locks.

"Your hair is beautiful. It's all I noticed as you skipped down the stairs," he said, as he rubbed it between his fingers. "In The Bahamas, you would stop traffic."

He quickly let go, embarrassed and said, "So, where can we find a cuppa joe?"

She was stunned for a minute by his boldness, but she was also thrilled and thought, *The Bahamas! Where did that come from?*

Quickly recovering, she answered, "In the market, there is a cafe where we can grab a coffee and if you like, we can sit out here on a bench in the sun."

"Sounds fine," he said as they started for the market.

With large dark roast coffees in hand, they found a dry bench near the duck pond. She made sure she didn't sit too close even though the soft scent of his shaving cream made her want to nuzzle his neck.

They talked about the weather, the trails along the river, the ducks that overwinter on the pond, choices in runners, favourite movies and food.

"Speaking of food, do you realize we have talked right into noon?" he said, as he glanced down his watch.

Meagan finally noticed the world around her. People were pouring out of the office towers towards the shops and hot dog vendors and the river trail. He was so captivating and handsome. She still didn't know why he was in Calgary or what he did for a living. One thing though, he did sound single. Never did he mention a *"we."*

She smiled and started to get up. "Time flies when you're having fun."

"I'd love to invite you out for lunch, but I have to be somewhere at 1:00, but do you know me well enough to take me on that run tomorrow?"

"I'll try, but I don't know if I have the legs for it after this morning," she said, somewhat apologetic.

He surprised her when he smiled and said, "I followed you for a few minutes before I passed you and I can tell you, you have great legs."

"Hey, you aren't supposed to size a girl up as you pass her. Just for that, you are in the lead on the trail tomorrow. I'll be at our spot in front of the Y at 8:00 waiting for you."

Chris took her hand for the second time and held it. "That sounds fine, Meagan, I'll be ready. Now I gotta get going."

With that, he gently squeezed her hand and walked away. Again, her thighs were burning, but this time it wasn't muscle strain, and the throbbing was way higher.

CHAPTER TWO

Meagan dashed to her truck, tossed her bag in the backseat and grabbed her cell phone. Chris was going to be on time for his meeting, she had already missed hers!

The phone was answered quickly and with the aid of call display, the greeting was not pleasant.

"Meagan – why didn't you turn your phone on earlier? I have been trying you all morning!"

It was Ginny, Meagan's assistant who hated not having a tight rein on Meagan. It drove her nuts when Meagan left her cell phone in the locker when she ran.

"And a pleasant good morning back," said Meagan, not acknowledging the rant.

"Brent Dickens has been trying to reach you. Aren't you supposed to be at his job right now?" She was right, but Meagan didn't care this time.

"Sorry, I wondered why my phone wasn't ringing. I didn't realize it was off 'till now," she said lying. "Be a bud would ya? Call him. Tell him I'm coming with sandwiches."

"Okay, when will you be back here?"

"I don't know, I promise to leave my phone on now and I'll call you when I'm done. 'kay?"

"'Kay." Ginny's feathers were smoothing out now that the phone link was replaced.

With fresh sandwiches, juice and more coffee, Meagan pulled into the job site and parked next to a new-loaded Lexus SUV. The owner of the blinged-out beast and acreage was Brent Dicken, a partner in her father's law firm. Meagan loved Brent like an uncle. He realized when Meagan was young she had a creative head and inspired her to chase her own dreams in architecture.

Unlike Meagan, her older brother Ben, followed their father into law and being firstborn – listened to their domineering mother and joined their dad's firm – at least for a while. He left after he was accepted to the bar to start up a company with friends from school. Their mother was disappointed but somehow accepted that far better than Meagan stepping out on her own.

The day Meagan graduated from university she opened her own office and Brent was her first client. Oddly, she built or renovated three houses for him and not even a kitchen reno for her own parents.

Brent was building a new home in the country for his current wife. In the twenty or so years she had known him, he'd gone through more wives and mistresses than most people go through new cars. But, it kept her gainfully employed every time a new love came on the scene.

As Meagan piled out of her truck with lunch and blueprints, Brent came through the opening where a 12-foot-high bay window would soon be placed.

"Well, it's about time you showed up! I'm starving. What did you bring to eat?" he said, as he grabbed the lunch bags to lessen her load. Meagan was thankful the sentence was laced with sarcasm and not anger.

"I'm so sorry, Brent. I lost track of time downtown. Have you been waiting long?"

"Nope, I barely got here myself."

Meagan was visibly relieved as they walked into the main part of the house. She talked to a few of the carpenters as Brent cleared off a space on what would be an enormous island in the kitchen. They chatted about the family and the business in between bites. After lunch, they would start on the blueprints and how they should change his house – again.

Meagan absently rubbed her aching calf muscle. Her neglected stretches were coming back to haunt her.

"Pull a muscle running today?" asked Brent as he peeled back the lid on his coffee.

"Naw, it's a chronic thing. I should have stretched but I was side-tracked."

A vision of Chris running by her, made her smile but she shook the image away quickly. She didn't need Brent prying any further. She jumped off the wooden box she was perched on, grabbed her coffee and said, "Come on, let's see what changes we need to make to this place before they finish the walls."

Meagan tossed the garbage while Brent leaned over the latest edition of the concept sheet. He was easy to please and loved everything she did but his new wife wanted to show some control.

"Monica sent me with a new list of changes," he said, as he pulled a wad of ripped magazine pages from his briefcase.

Meagan wasn't surprised to see the pile of paper and mentally she groaned. Monica rarely came to the site to see how the last changes were going. Instead, she would peruse design magazines and find ideas she wanted to be incorporated into the mansion, rip the page from the book and give it to Brent. Meagan tried to be accommodating, but the changes were starting to affect the structure of the building and they were approaching the drywall stage.

She shuffled through the pages. The changes were going to cost Brent more money and her time. That meant another long night of sifting through samples of tile catalogues and carpet colours, but at least it wasn't structural this time.

"Okay, I don't know how the teal tile will go in the front hall, but I'll see what I can dig up. I'll go over this tonight and bring new samples tomorrow."

"I'll bring lunch," said Brent, trying to sweet-talk her.

Lunch isn't what she wanted. What Meagan wanted was the evening to primp before she met Chris for the run in the morning.

She woke to a beautiful morning; the predawn light made the fresh layer of snow look blue. When the sun did come up the snow would look crisp. Meagan, however, did not feel crisp at all. She was up until 2:30 a.m. digging through samples of dirty tiles and dusty carpet.

She quickly rolled out of bed, tossed her hair into a tight braid, swallowed some juice and ran out the door with a banana to eat on the way to the Y. The hope of looking her best was shattered again.

Meagan didn't know why, but she really wanted to impress this guy. It was foolish considering he was from out of town and she didn't even know what he did for a living. Realistically there was no way a long-distance relationship was worth all this – but since short distance relationships weren't working either, she might as well give it a try. What's to lose?

It was 7:58 a.m. when she reached the stairs. It was still below zero, so she wore running pants, a thick shirt and mitts. She kept looking up at the hotel windows and danced around to stay warm. She constantly reached down to pull the tights down over her exposed ankles, which was the only time she hated how tall she was.

He still wasn't there at 8:15 a.m. and she started having doubts about him coming. *Maybe he is a blowhard like the rest of them,* she thought to herself. *He probably already saw me and my get-up from his room and ran the other way.*

She looked up at the hotel windows once more. There was no frantic waving by anybody in any of the windows. As she sighed and turned to start her run, Chris looked out his top floor window again, but she did not see him.

She had only run a few minutes when suddenly her heart jumped into her throat at the sound of his voice.

"Hey! Wait up! Meagan!"

Meagan looked back and there he was, sprinting towards her. She forgot all about controlling her heart rate as it pounded harder at the sight of Chris running towards her.

Christ, he's even better looking from the front! she thought.

As he got closer, she could see he was rather a mess, worse than her. The shadow on his chin showed he hadn't shaved, his body wasn't moving as spry as it did yesterday, and his sunglasses seemed to be hiding something more than protecting his eyes from the still absent sun. Still, he was fantastic to see running, towards her.

"I thought I was being stood up," she smiled as he joined her. They continued running making it hard to study his face further.

"I'm sorry," he panted. "I saw you waiting just before 8 and then my phone rang. I could see you standing there from my room. I was hoping you'd look up and see I was stuck on a call. I pushed my luck – didn't I?"

"I didn't see you, I guess I looked up at the wrong time, at least you knew which way to run to find me."

"Okay now that I found you can we slow down? This pace will kill me!" Chris said as he pulled back on her arm.

His touch made her tingle. As usual, Meagan started out too fast and that usually cost her in the last part of run. She slowed down and he took his hand off her arm.

"There, I should be able to handle this," he said.

They matched stride, heading towards the trail she described to him.

"So, are you up to a hill run this morning?" she asked to break the silence that overtook them while they settled into an easy pace.

"Actually, it was a bit of a rough night. I'm not sure I can push up a hill."

Meagan was puzzled. *How could a businessman from out of town have an exhausting night?* she thought to herself then decided to ask.

"What did you do last night to beat you up so badly?"

He paused before he answered. "I got beat up."

Meagan stopped moving, "What!"

Chris laughed and pulled on her arm to get her moving again. "Are you a hockey fan?"

"No, not really, why?" Meagan's mind was racing, "What does hockey got to do with you being rolled?"

"I wasn't rolled," he said laughing. "I'm a defenceman in the NHL and last night I ended up in a fight on the ice."

"Oh my God, were you hurt bad?"

"Only my pride. I think I bruised some knuckles, and my eye is a bit of a mess – but I'll live."

"Why didn't you tell me you're a hockey player?"

"I don't like to advertise, I guess. That way when I meet people who don't recognize me, I can relax and not worry about impressing them."

Meagan couldn't decide if she was impressed or not. Hockey was definitely not one of her favourite sports, especially because of the fights. But it explained why he was in such incredible shape. She was still fantasizing about his physique, but seeing it bruised didn't appeal to her.

They kept running towards the hills, the path dipped under the bridge and climbed up steeply again.

"Oh no," he said. "Does this mean you don't like hockey players?"

Her silence was interpreted as rejection.

"Oh! Oh no, not at all! I've never met a famous athlete before and now I'm afraid you'll think I'm a dope because I've never heard of you before. Shit, I don't even know what a defenceman does for the team."

She didn't mean to show her ignorance, but she blurted it out before thinking. She should have kept her mouth shut and looked it up later.

"So," she continued, afraid of his response. "Does this mean you leave town today?"

He paused before he answered, "Yeah. We play tomorrow night in Edmonton. Then we go home for a while. Our lives revolve around the rink during the season. Most days we are skating. I like to get a run in as much as possible too."

Her heart stopped fluttering like a schoolgirl and crashed into the pit of her stomach. She knew he was from out of town when they met, but she hoped he'd be here longer and from somewhere closer than Boston. She tried not to sound dejected or too hopeful when she continued talking.

"When do you come back? Maybe we can go for a run again next time."

"We don't play Calgary much during the season. Then it depends on which teams make it to the playoffs. We are only a month into the season so if Calgary plays well and we play well, we will be here during the playoffs. I have a feeling though that after this run, you won't want to see me during the playoffs!"

"Oh, don't be so sure," she said, as she slowed the pace further. "I'm not exactly in top form today either. I got beat up too – but it was a roll of carpet around midnight."

He laughed, "Now what do you do for a living to have a roll of carpet assault you?"

As she explained her career as a project manager, they turned off the main path into the trees on a narrow loose gravel trail covered in a light layer of new snow. Only a few other runners had left tracks before them. The cool air in the trees was intoxicating and cleansing. She could see a smile creep across his face. The trail gently began to roll, and the conversation ceased.

Meagan was analyzing his ability and he was handling the hills nicely, so she turned onto a steeper trail.

"Whoa now, Missy," he said, as he gasped for air. "Are you trying to kill me?"

"Sorry! You were doing so good, I thought you were all right. Are you hurt somewhere else?" Meagan wasn't breathing too hard yet. She was surprised by her strength today considering the amount of sleep she had.

"No, damn it! You're beating on my pride!" he gasped.

"There's the top," she pointed. "We'll turn back from there."

He nodded, so she ran ahead. There was no room to run beside him and she wanted the opportunity to see him run again. She figured there was no way a relationship would blossom from this, so she might as well get one last good look at him.

She picked up her pace and even though the path was slippery, lunged to the top. When she turned around – he was right behind her. He wasn't as slow as he said! *Damn those fast-twitch muscles of a hockey player!*

Within two strides he wrapped his arms around her, almost knocking her over. She was shocked by the show of affection.

"Three more seconds and I would have passed you!" he said, as he worked at catching his breath. They stood there grinning at each other, arm in arm.

"If I wasn't breathing so hard – I'd kiss you," he added.

Meagan smiled, her chest heaving from the excitement. "I'll wait."

Chris chuckled and took his sunglasses off to wipe the sweat from his brow. She winced when she saw how swollen and colourful his left eye was.

"How can you see through that thing?"

"I can see beautifully," he said, as he looked at her. He took a slow breath, gently tilted her chin up, and gave her a slow kiss.

Oh my God! thought Meagan. *Never in a million years did I ever expect to be canoodling a hockey player at the top of this trail.*

He moved his hand from her chin and brushed the loose strand of hair off her face as he finished the kiss with a smile. His eyes were locked on hers.

"You are so beautiful. I wish you lived in Boston."

"I wish you played for Calgary."

"Do you like to travel?"

"As much as possible."

"Do you think this is the beginning of a beautiful relationship?"
She laughed at his use of a corny phrase and that he kept using beautiful.
"Maybe."
With that, they kissed again, losing their breath to each other.

The run back to the Y was over too quickly. They chatted the whole way back as easily as they did the day before. If they weren't running Meagan was sure he'd have his arm around her shoulder and they would be strolling slowly.

They stopped in front of the stairs and Meagan was at a loss as to what to do or say. What was going to happen? How would they ever see each other again let alone start a relationship! She decided to let Chris break the ice.

He reached down and took her hand in his.

"So," he said slowly.

"Yeah..." she said back as slow.

"How are we going to make this work...start for that matter?"

"That's what I was thinking."

He caressed her fingers in his big, calloused hands, "Could you come up to Edmonton?"

"I'd love to, but I am so swamped. I have commitments to keep."

"Come on...please?" he whined like a little boy as he pulled her closer

"You stay here," she said, a little disturbed that he thought her commitments were of less value than his.

"What? The mighty hockey player miss a game?" he said sarcastically. "You're right, we have to find a time to meet properly, maybe even have a date. Maybe, something where I don't have to chase you."

Meagan reluctantly let go of his hand and reached into the tiny pocket in the front of her pants to pull out a folded business card.

"I was hoping you'd want to stay in touch so I, um, brought along a card. My cell number and email are on it too, so you don't have to go through my excellent, but somewhat nosy assistant."

He took the card and read her name, "Meagan Dunphy, President. Wow, you didn't tell me you are in charge of the business. I'm impressed."

"Awe, don't be. It's not that big a deal. When I start franchising across the country, then you can be impressed."

They stopped talking, a lump of nerves was welling up in Meagan's throat. She looked at him, put her hand carefully on the swollen half of his face and gently kissed him on the other cheek.

"Take care of that mug of yours," she said, stepping away.

He smiled and said, "I'll try, but I get paid the big bucks for taking the hits."

"Can't ya duck?"

"Maybe I should," he laughed. "can I call you when I get back to Boston?"

"I'd like that."

It took all her willpower, but she turned and ran up the steps. When she went through the door, she looked back. He was watching her go in. He waved at her, holding her card tight in his hand.

She was beaming ear to ear as she passed the entry desk.

The attendant working at the desk said, "Good run today, Meagan?"

"The best ever, Tony. The best!"

CHAPTER THREE

All the effort she put into finding samples and redrafting the plans paid off. The meeting with Brent went great. Monica showed up and even more surprisingly, liked her concepts. It looked like that job would finish smoothly, as long as her tradesmen continued to do their best.

Meagan had a fantastic crew of people working for her. In a short period of time she had acquired some of the best talents in the industry.

Contractors were loyal to her, maybe because she was loyal and honest with them. Many people, including her parents, thought she was crazy to go out on her own at such an early age.

"Go to work for one of the big companies first," lectured her father. "Use their funds and reputation to learn from your mistakes."

Meagan didn't plan on making any mistakes that she couldn't fix. There had been a few but not career-ending blows, or anything life-shattering that is until she met her ex-boyfriend, Stephen.

Stephen...not Steve. Stephen Simpson was everything her parents wanted in a son-in-law and she was everything in a wife that Stephen wanted. The problem was she didn't want what either party wanted. Just like when Meagan said she didn't want to be a lawyer, it was her mom that was most upset of them all. There had been no formal engagement, but her mother already knew who would cater, who would sing, where it would be and who would be on the guest list.

Unfortunately, for her mom, Meagan didn't want to be invited to that wedding and broke it off with Stephen. That was when she stopped going home for the Sunday night dinner/lecture series.

On Thursday, Meagan was working long into the night out at Brent's country home. As she turned her truck towards the brightly lit city, she searched the radio for some good tunes. Suddenly the voice of a hockey commentary came blaring through her dashboard.

"And it's Barton, handing it off to Chellow, Chellow takes it down the ice, passes to Lomprey, he scores!"

"Holy shit! The game!" Meagan shouted at the dash. "How could I forget? Shit!"

She checked her watch. "It's gotta still be the first period... or is it quarter? Jeez I gotta learn the game!"

Her boot pushed the gas pedal harder; it was forty-five minutes to her house, but only 15 to her brother, Benjamin's.

She parked in front of a beautiful new two-story brick home. The landscaping was minimal compared to the stately homes on either side. The house, however was stunning. Well, she thought so because she designed and built it.

Meagan bolted up the snow-covered lawn, leaping over the frozen stunted shrubs and rang the doorbell. The house was dark from the front, but she knew he was home by the barking and shouting coming from the back.

Ben opened the door and a large golden retriever leapt into Meagan's chest.

"Megs," said Ben, "Nice to see you, come on in."

She was already in and still playing with the dog.

"Soda! Get off!" shouted Ben as they walked down the hall. "I was watching the game, Wanna watch?"

"Sure."

"Really??? Wanna beer?"

"Sure," she said again as she turned into the den where the giant screen TV dominated the room. She stopped dead in her tracks. There *He* was, larger than life on the screen. It was intermission and *He* was the interview. As Ben handed her a beer she said, "What a shiner." Not really to Ben, but he took it as so.

Chris's eye was still bruised and swollen. If she were alone, she would have put her hand up to the screen and gently touched it again.

"Oh yeah, he took that in a fight the other night here. Man, that was a bad hit. I'm surprised he can see."

Ben had turned the sound down but turned it up to listen since she was showing interest.

The announcer was questioning Chris on the fight.

"So, Chris, the doctors gave you the green light tonight. Were you worried about your vision?"

"Yeah, Ron," said Chris as he wiped the sweat from his brow, "Johnson hit me pretty hard. I didn't see that one coming and it swelled up so bad. I couldn't see out of it 'till about noon yesterday."

"Are the doctors confident you won't lose any vision?" asked the announcer.

"Yeah, but I gotta watch out for a while, it might be sensitive to another hit."

"Are you going to stay away from the fights?"

"No, I'll listen to some good advice I got," said Chris, smiling.

"And what's that?"

"Duck!"

The announcer and Ben started to laugh, and the commercials came on. Meagan smiled to herself. *Holy crap,* she thought. *He's actually thinking about me.*

"Meagan? Meeeeeaaagan...are you listening?"

Ben sat down on the leather sofa and was talking but she didn't hear a word.

"Where are you?" he said, looking at her still standing where she first came in.

"Benny, I told him to duck," she said, not knowing whether she should confide in him, but she was bursting with the secret.

Ben stared at her in disbelief. "Get outta here!"

She sat down on the oversized chair, took a swig of her beer and smiled as she swallowed.

"I met him on the path and offered to take him on a trail run," she said, rather nonchalantly.

"You don't even know this guy and you went for a run on deserted trails through the trees?"

"I met him Tuesday."

"Before the game or did he pick you up after the game?"

"No, of course I didn't go to the game. He ran past me down by the Y and we started to talk."

"Are you crazy? Did you know he was Chris Burrows?"

"I thought he was a businessman. I probably wouldn't have talked to him if I knew he was a hockey player," she said laughing.

"Are you going to see him again?" Ben asked.

"I hope so, why?"

"So, I can! Do you know how famous he is?"

"No, actually, I was hoping you would fill me in. Is he any good?"

"Shit! Are you ever out of touch! He is one of the most famous players on the ice today. He's probably the highest-paid defenseman in the league and the highest-scoring defenseman even though he has the highest amount of time in the penalty box this year. He has a contract with Boston for another five years. If his body can stand the beating, he will retire at 35, one rich goon."

"How do you know all this stuff?" she said bewildered by his knowledge.

"Gez, Megs, Google the guy or read the sports page! Any time he plays he is on the cover."

She couldn't stop herself from asking, "Is he single?"

Her brother laughed, "Burrows is single but there are always gorgeous blondes dangling from his biceps. When everyone knows you make about 10 mill a year, that's going to happen. And that's why I'm sitting here, alone on a Friday night, waiting for my sister to order a pizza. I don't make the mills as a lawyer!"

"Yet! And it's Thursday," Meagan added to his sentence as she got up and went to the phone to order a pizza as the game resumed play.

She returned to her seat and watched the game with an interest she never had before. Suddenly watching grown men on skates chase a cold hard round chunk of rubber was interesting.

Whenever number 28 jumped over the boards and onto the ice her eyes were glued to his jersey. She couldn't see his face or his shiny black hair under the helmet and wished the damn thing wasn't on so she could see his features. But when he was slammed into the boards and the booming sound of his helmet crashing into the glass echoed through the TV, she was glad he had the helmet on.

At the next set of commercials, Ben asked, "Are you going to see him again?"

"I don't know. I hope so. But I really shouldn't get my hopes up. You said there is always a chick on his sleeve that probably melts whenever he speaks. Really, what chance have I got?" she said, somewhat forlorn.

"Just as much chance as the next girl. Maybe he really wants an overworked, underpaid red-head who can out-run him and build him a damn nice house."

Meagan didn't answer. The doorbell rang and Ben, along with the barking dog went down the hall to get the pizza. Meagan went into the kitchen and brought plates, napkins and more beer into the den. They settled in to watch the game.

The announcer on the TV was going nuts, calling the play, but it all confused Meagan. *Red line, blue line who gives a shit!* is all Meagan could think as she tried to understand. Finally, the rising voice yells, ".... Burrow scores!!!!"

"He didn't score with you, I hope!" said Benjamin, rather firmly.

"Oh, Ben! How do you make love running trails when there is a fresh layer of snow? she said, defensively but fantasizing that it sounded like a great idea.

She stayed and watched the rest of the game and left after the three stars were announced. Of course, Burrows was listed.

Meagan drove home glowing, listening to the radio commentaries ramble on about the game. She parked her truck and took as many samples, binders and boards as she could carry into her garage/storeroom. Her house was in a trendy part of town but was worth less than half of the house she built for her brother. It was a small two-story with a walkout basement she fixed up with a minimal amount of over-costs.

The main floor was the kitchen and the living room with the walkout basement devoted entirely to office space. Upstairs was her private space, a small spare room, bathroom and her large bedroom and bath. Someday, she planned to move the office to another location and take back her house. Until that time came, however, the cramped space would have to do.

She walked through the walkout basement door, dumped her purse and computer bag on the workbench before heading back out for the heap of approved samples. When she got upstairs to rinse her go mug in the kitchen sink, she glanced at her phone that had spilled from her bag, the message light flashing.

That's weird. I've had it with me the entire evening, she said to no one in particular. She pushed through to retrieve the message.

"Hi Meagan, it's Chris here...from the run. I'm just back to the hotel and ummm, thought I'd phone and see if you caught the game tonight. Um, well, that's all. I guess you are out. I'm heading off tomorrow, so I'll try calling you some other time. Oh, thanks for the run. I felt great tonight."

The recording beeped and the electronic voice said, *"Thursday, 11:06 p.m."* That was five minutes ago. She missed the call when she went to retrieve the samples. Meagan couldn't call back, she didn't know where he was staying, and the phone number was listed as "Private Caller." She was upset about missing his call but fell to sleep knowing he had called and would call again.

CHAPTER FOUR

Friday morning, Meagan woke early. Chris kept popping into her dreams, as did the looming meeting she was heading to that morning. And that meeting was far more important than a crush on a hockey player.

Along with all the other architect firms in town, she was attending a meeting to bid on the designs of a new grouping of hotels. The Cottonwood chain of boutique hotels was planning five new mountain lodges. Today's meeting would introduce the concept to the architects, and they would have to come back with designs, costs and timelines. From those bids, the company would award the job. If it were awarded to her, her little company would suddenly be in the big leagues.

She rarely searched out her best clothes, but today she wanted to look like she was already a class establishment. Glancing through the dry cleaner bags hanging at the back of the closet, she found her navy-blue suit. The plastic fell to the floor as she slipped into the skirt.

Her mother's voice rang through her head *"Always have a decent suit that has been tailored to show off your God-given assets."*

"Yeah, that way," echoed Ben, *"if you can't land the job on your work skills – they will hire you because of your fantastic legs!"*

As she studied her image in the mirror, she hoped it wasn't her legs that would get her the job. She wanted to win this on her own. "But," she said to her image, "If my legs get me through the door, at least I'm that far. I guess a girl's gotta do what she's gotta do – except sleep with the boss."

She went down to the office where Ginny and Walt, her favourite stonemason were going through the order for one of the jobs on file.

"Whew wee, Meg! You going to an interview or a funeral?" asked Walt, as he saw her come through the door.

"Oh, haha," she said sarcastically as she grabbed a mug of coffee. "The

Cottonwood meeting is today. If we get it – you'll be expected to call me by my full name then."

"What...Meag-an?" he said, as he jumped out of jabbing range. She didn't dare poke him for fear of spilling coffee on her suit.

She left the office with what she thought would be ample time, but a fender-bender on Crowchild Trail plugged her route, making her arrive with only minutes to spare. She parked her tattered workhorse among many other SUVs in the parking lot out front, recognizing some of her competitors by their vehicle and of course, by the names plastered on the cab doors. She calmed down as she rode the elevator, but her heart sank as the doors opened into the lobby of the Cottonwood Hotels office.

The first person she saw was the only man that could make her crumble. He hadn't seen her yet, but she knew it was him by the slope of his shoulders and the cut of his expensive suit.

It was one of her university instructors – Carl Russell. Just the name made her teeth grind. He was a good instructor, but he based most of his lecture material on his own works – forgetting to even mention the greats like Frank Gehry, Jean Nouvel or Norman Foster. Thinking of himself as a "ladies' man," he flirted with the women in his class and it was rumoured he eventually lost his position at the university because of that. Of course, he quit before any accusations could ruin his career.

Meagan knew they weren't just rumours. She was the one who made the accusations. The creep called her in for "extra tutorials" saying he saw potential in her work, but she needed to work out a few kinks. She didn't know what her "kinks" were, but because she was as gullible as the next female student – she went to see him.

After a few meetings, it was very apparent to her what the hell was going on. The *extra help* as he called it was his disguise of offering better marks for sexual favours. He tried to persuade her and after some extremely embarrassing advances, she warned him she would press charges.

Carl didn't think a young "simple" redhead would have the guts to challenge such a powerful professional both at the university and in the community. When he continued to press her into having sex and groped her – she called her father's firm to represent her. When Meagan confronted Russell in front of the dean, Russell accused her of slander and stormed out. The dean, (who knew her father and the family's reputation of integrity) didn't say anything to Meagan. He nodded knowingly and told her it would be handled.

Russell finished the semester, leaving the school before the "rumours" could ruin his reputation. When he handed out the final papers, he held tight to hers as she reached for it.

"You might as well go get knocked-up by that boyfriend of yours so that you will do something of value because your stupid concepts will never make it in the real world," he hissed through his teeth. "Or, I'll make your life hell."

Well, she got out and he did make life hell. Just like in school, she lost out any time he was bidding on the same job. He always had that look in his eyes like he knew something she didn't know. Probably years of experience and a reputation as a great architect had lots to do with it. And, that he was simply an asshole.

As she walked into the room, he turned and as soon as they made eye contact, there was that insulting look.

"Well, if it isn't Miss Dunphy," he said, sounding a bit like he said dumpy instead. "Are you representing a larger firm today? This is probably out of your league. Have you done anything larger than a donut shop yet?"

As usual, her tongue tied into a bow hitch and words stumbled back down her throat. All she could say was, "No, I'm here on my own. And yes, I have done bigger than a donut shop."

She grabbed the spec folder and quickly walked across the room to avoid the man. Meagan couldn't understand how a professor could be so juvenile. But then again, he wasn't a professor and really never was.

She took an empty seat next to a man she had never seen before, making sure she was on the end of the row so Russell couldn't bother her anymore. She fumbled for a pen and settled in to peruse the thick kit.

Holy shit, she said to herself, *this is going to take a lot of effort.*

She heard and smelt Russell sit down behind her. His cheap aftershave hadn't changed in years. He was talking to someone next to him in a hushed voice she was sure he wanted her to hear. She begged her ears to not listen.

"Ladies and Gentlemen," said a tall middle-aged man in a deep blue suit. "If you could all take a seat, we can start this discussion shortly."

The meeting went on for two hours. During that time, three different spokesmen from Cottonwood got up to speak, each tossed more restrictions onto the growing list. Meagan could sense many people in the room were becoming agitated and discouraged by the strict guidelines. But she learned a long time ago that's when she should pay greater attention. She could feel the competition slipping. Maybe just maybe, this was going to be her turn.

When the meeting was adjourned, she stayed seated, hoping Russell would leave ahead of her. Her plan failed.

As she stood to leave, he was right behind her.

"You know Miss Dunphy," Carl said in a somewhat sympathetic voice as he reached out to guide her by the elbow past the chairs. "This might be a little over your head. If I recall from class, bids were not your strong point. Maybe you should stick to subcontracting."

Meagan's lip curled and she twisted slightly to shuffle his hand off her elbow. As she was about to tell him to mind his own business, a waiter bumped him from behind. Carl was caught off guard and lunged into Meagan. To keep herself from landing on the floor with him on top of her she quickly dropped all her belongings and steadied him. His papers fell with hers.

All three of them bent over to pick things up. The waiter continually jabbered his apologies, which was a good thing so Carl couldn't continue to insult Meagan.

When everything was sorted, Meagan was fuming and embarrassed. Instead of saying a thing, she gathered herself and left.

Driving back to the office Meagan's mind raced with the *I shoulda said this! I shoulda said that!* Somehow that man always ruined her day.

When she got back to the office, Ginny was the only one there and that suited Meagan just fine. She stomped up to her bedroom and quickly changed back into her regular work clothes, hanging the suit back under the plastic.

Passing through the kitchen she grabbed the stack of mail and the bid package or what was left of it. When all the material fell to the floor at the meeting, she scooped it up as quickly as possible. It was a mess. She decided to use the kitchen table to sort it all out.

She had everything – the sitemaps, the synopsis of the company and their corporate philosophy, the contour map, a copy of the architectural guidelines and two duplicate sheets on how the buildings should follow the structural imagery of the 1930s.

Two?

She must have picked up Russell's copy too. She read the contents list and she had everything plus the spare which ironically had the website where it could be found listed electronically. Laughing to herself, she placed everything in a tidy pile. "If he can't figure it out, then that's too damn bad."

By the time she went back into the office with the mail and the bid package sorted out, a few more of her employees had come back to the office. Brian and Jennifer were two young architect interns, fresh out of school and both worked like dogs. Thankfully, they were happy being paid kibble. They were bent over their workstations, hopefully billing the clients for productive work.

Out of all her employees, the small, rather round Dianne was the only person she would confide in and at this point she needed someone who she could vent on about Russell. The two were inseparable at university, but today her desk was void.

"Where's Dianne?" Meagan said to Ginny as she settled into her chair.

Ginny looked puzzled, "I don't know. She didn't say where she was going."

"What's she working on today?"

"I dunno," said Ginny, and then with a confused look on her face, "Have you ever noticed, every once in a while, she gets quiet and sorta slips in and out?"

Meagan looked at Ginny with a raised eyebrow and smirk. "What do you think, is she having an affair? I doubt that. I'm sure she can't keep a secret like that from us. Hopefully, she is drumming up business."

The phone rang, and Ginny reached for it. The conversation about Dianne was over.

Meagan cleaned off her desk, making room for the Cottonwood package. She had six weeks to come up with an idea that would blow their socks off and put her on the map. This time she wanted to make sure she didn't screw up. Thankfully, Mr. Defensemen was still only wishful thinking. Between watching over her office staff, keeping Brent's house on schedule and dreaming up the resort to beat all, she was going to be busy. Maybe if she got the contract, she would learn to play hockey.

The weather turned ugly and cold, typical for Calgary, making it easy to stay inside and thrash out some ideas. The only social dates she kept were with her running buddies who ran through any weather and any lame excuses.

It was 8:30 a.m. on a slushy Monday morning and the girls were headed out the door of the Y. Each one complained about the weather, sore knees or lack of energy. But as soon as they hit the path, the stride quickened, and they were off for the regular 10-km tempo run.

They were a sight to see. All five of them matching stride, in the tight bright cluster.

Emma was the fastest and the smallest. When the wind was strong, the others would threaten to put rocks down her tights to stop her from blowing away. Robin only made it half the time because of her job which kept her tied to the desk. Gloria, a slim ex-track star was strong and great for pushing everyone to be there. And then there was Lizzie, Meagan's oldest friend in the group and who Meagan tucked in behind the group with. Whenever those two ran out front, the pace was always too fast at the start.

"So, Meagan," said Emma, after they finished comparing the week's mileage. "How come you haven't been out much? Is there a new man or a new job?"

Meagan laughed through her heavy breathing. "Gee, they're both on my agenda! Do I have to choose?"

"No," Gloria added, "Be selfish and take them both. Is there something juicy we should know about?"

The other four women were all married with babies planned soon. It would make them all happy to see the last of their group happily hitched.

They were all so serious about their running that they figured children should be planned for the same time span so they could continue training together.

Meagan could never keep secrets from her friends and decided to tell them about Chris and the contract. They all knew of Carl Russell and his ruthlessness, but the hockey player was far more interesting.

"You met Chris Burrows? Holy shit!" said Gloria, laughing in wonder. "And you didn't even know who he was. That guy is definitely worth checking out. If you don't show some serious interest, there is a line-up of chicks that will."

"Thanks, Gloria," said Meagan. "But don't go buying dresses for the wedding yet. All I did was run with the guy. He probably has girlfriends in every town and the one in Calgary didn't show up. He's way out of my league. Don't you think he'd rather have a beautiful blonde sitting at the edge of the rink idolizing his every move instead of someone like me who's staring up at the rafters wondering what the snow load factor is?"

They all laughed, but Lizzie pulled Meagan back from the self-doubts.

"Maybe…" she said. "Maybe he isn't that shallow and is interested in a beautiful redhead capable of taking care of herself."

"Yeah," added Robin, as she poked her head out from behind Gloria, "Maybe you'll be a yin to his yang?"

Meagan smiled at Lizzie and silently mouthed the words, "I hope so."

As they turned the corner and started the journey back to the Y, Meagan fell silent. Maybe they were right. Maybe Chris was looking for a bright girl and not the high maintenance blonde. Maybe it was time to learn about hockey. But first, she had to finish the Cottonwood project.

CHAPTER FIVE

Meagan worked well into the night on most evenings. Sketches, samples and paint chips littered her office and upstairs into her home-space. Her morning meetings with the other designers and architects in the office were short with little input from her. They were all working hard on smaller projects. Home renovations in Mount Royal, second homes near Bragg Creek and food kiosks at the malls were not the million-dollar jobs, but they kept the payroll on schedule. She'd pull the team together on the Cottonwood project as soon as a concrete plan was in her head and on paper.

One day, Meagan sat at her drafting table twirling her pencil and stared at a piece of paper covered in doodles. Her ideas were coming together, but that morning everything had ground to a halt. Ginny quietly tapped on the door jamb and came in carrying a bright bouquet of spring flowers.

"Wow! Are these for me?" she said surprised. "I never get flowers."

Ginny said, "It's your name on the card, but I can easily scribble mine on."

"Not a chance, Chicky, hand them over!" Meagan shut her eyes and inhaled the aroma. "God, they smell like the west coast."

"Who are they from?"

"I hope not the banker!" she said, as she peeled back the flap of the envelope. She read the note to herself, smiled and tucked it quickly back into the envelope. "Gee, it's from Burrows. I thought he forgot about me."

Ginny smiled and started to walk out of the office. "The way your cheeks are blushing, I'd say you haven't forgotten about him either."

Meagan cleared a spot on the corner of her desk and placed the vase down. She admired the flowers. They were a stunning collection of tulips, freesia, daffodils and Gerbera daisies. She sat down and reread the card slower this time.

"*Hey Meagan,*" sprawled someone's sloppy, but legible handwriting. "*I saw flowers all over Vancouver and thought of you – as I have a lot lately. I'm in Vancouver for a few days for a game. Then I have an afternoon game Sunday in Calgary. I've got two tickets on hold at the ticket office for you. I hope you'll be able to join me for dinner after the game. Is it a date? I'll call you tonight.*
Chris"

"A real date with a hockey star – what will my mom think?" she said to herself.

Her phone rang. She looked down at the call display. It was her brother, so she picked it up quickly.

"Hi Ben," she said cheerfully.

"Hey, you sound happy. Did you snag the Cottonwood deal already?"

"No," she giggled. "Almost better. Want to go to the game with me on Sunday? I was just given two tickets."

"Who would be crazy enough to give you two tickets to a hockey game? Wait! It's Boston on Sunday. Did Burrows send them?"

"Yes!" she giggled again. "He sent flowers too!"

"Wow! But you can't show up with a guy. What will he think?"

He's calling me tonight to confirm. He wants to go out for supper after the game. I'll let him know I'm coming with you," she said, but then quickly added, "but you're not coming out for supper."

"At least let me hang around the dressing room door and meet him," he said laughing.

"It's a deal."

The rest of the day went surprisingly quickly. Maybe it was the smell of the flowers; maybe it was the thought of watching Chris at the game on Sunday or maybe the schoolgirl delight knowing that a boy who is interested in her was going to call tonight.

Ideas started to flow onto the paper of grand staircases, stained glass windows, and slate floors with riverbeds in stone, woodwork and colour scheme. The lodges were going to be breathtaking. Suddenly she had the ideas that would win her the bid.

Her train of thought was interrupted by Dianne standing at the door.

"Meagan. What has got you so captivated?"

Meagan glanced at her watch. It was already 5:30 p.m. Then she looked past Dianne and saw that everyone else was gone.

"Holy, I didn't realize it was so late. I guess I got into the Cottonwood stuff and time flew by. How did your day go?" she asked as she stretched and walked away from the drafting table. Dianne, in-turn, walked towards the table and started to glance over Meagan's drawings with a keen eye. She didn't answer the question. Instead, she started asking her own.

"These are interesting. Nice ideas," she said, as she slid the rough drafts across the table.

"Do you like them?" said Meagan, seeking approval from someone who had always told her the truth on all her designs.

"Yeah, very novel. What's with the retro look?" queried Dianne.

"The specs requested the look be 1930s. Neat eh? What would a Muskoka chair look good in front of?" she asked in a theoretical voice.

Dianne quickly said, "Oh, hummm, clever thought." Then, noticing the flowers quickly changed the topic. "Who sent the flowers?"

"That hockey player I ran with that one day. He's invited me to the game and dinner on Sunday."

"Oh, lucky you," she said, smiling. "I hope you like hockey."

"I guess I'll learn. But right now, I gotta get out to Brent's and see how the house is coming. Are you leaving soon?"

"No, my desk is a mess, you get going and I'll lock up," said Dianne.

Meagan grabbed her "BRENT" portfolio and headed for the door. "Thanks for the compliment on the ideas. I'll pull the team onto it tomorrow."

And with that Meagan headed to Brent's estate in Bragg Creek. Dianne went to her desk and picked up her phone.

There was a light snow falling as she left the darkened city. Meagan's mind danced from Chris sending flowers, to Brent's house, to the fresh ideas laid out on the drafting table. She was glad Dianne liked them.

Dianne had been a friend since first year of university. They both had great ideas and worked as a team harmoniously. What Meagan lacked in fine details Dianne shone in. But in larger detail presentation and really – the rest of the business though, Meagan handled it with confidence. That's why when she decided to go out on her own right after graduation, she asked Dianne to be part of her team. Of course, they both loved architecture, but their private lives were vastly different. While Meagan spent every spare minute being active, Dianne preferred a book, or binge-watching tv.

The two worked together very well doing small renovations and mall kiosks. When they started landing more contracts, Meagan added Ginny to the staff to handle the office while they were out on job sites. Ginny had no clue how anything worked architecturally but her ten years of service in the Canadian Navy as a ship administrator had her running a tight ship at the office too.

Only a few months ago, Meagan brought on the two intern students. Thankfully, a government grant was introduced to pay their wages because she couldn't. But if she got Cottonwood, she was determined to find a way to keep them on.

The days leading up to Sunday rolled slower than a glacier for Meagan. Chris called Thursday night like he said he would, and they talked forever about almost anything. It seemed like they were finding more and more things in common than Meagan thought. Now it seemed like getting to know him was a good idea.

On Sunday, Ben met Meagan a few blocks from the hockey arena and then they drove in together so they could park close to each other in the parking lot. When she pulled in beside his car Ben looked over at her, then at her truck, then back at her.

"Excuse me beautiful stranger but I'm here to meet my sister who never wears makeup or brushes her hair. Did you steal her truck? I'm sure that's hers."

Meagan got out and as he continued to size her up said, "Knock it off Ben," - as she pressed the creases out of her jeans - "...but do I look alright?"

She went shopping the night before and bought a new light brown mock turtleneck to wear under the new bomber style suede jacket her fluffed hair cascaded over. She thought the brown would show only mild support for the other team. Her new pants hugged her legs, making them look longer and her taller.

"When you want to, you can make that red hair lure in and capture a man's heart," said Ben. He smiled at her to convince her he was telling the truth. Their relationship had always been of friends first and siblings second. Meagan could only remember a few times in their childhood when he bothered her enough to wish he were somebody else's brother.

They strolled into the complex with plenty of time to pick up the tickets at the "Will Call," then wander over to get a beer and a bag of popcorn.

"Let me see where the seats are," said Ben.

Meagan threw some popcorn in her mouth and handed him the tickets she had stuffed in her coat pocket.

"Whoa, nice!" he said, smiling. "You know where these are?"

She shook her head left to right with a scowl and mumbled through the popcorn, "Ben, I've been here twice!"

"Right behind the home bench. I bet he got you these so he can hear you cheer for Calgary all night!" he said jokingly.

"Gimme the tickets!" she said, as she grabbed them back. "You be nice – or you don't sit with me."

"Sorry," he said, still laughing at his joke.

They made their way down the steps to their seats and settled in. Other people around them must have been season ticket holders because they were all talking like old friends. The lights dimmed and the music blared with the team theme song. Suddenly the announcer's voice blared over the canned tunes, "And now, YOUR CALGARY FLaaaa." His voice drowned under the cheers.

One by one, the team in red and white blasted onto the ice and the crowd cheered louder as the heroes' blades sliced the fresh sheet of ice. With every player, Meagan's tummy got tighter. She was so nervous, she quit eating the popcorn Ben was working hard to polish off.

Then the announcer got to the opposing team. The crowd didn't cheer nearly as much but when an outstanding player came out there were extra cheers. Then the voice said, "Number 28, Chris Burrows," and there he was.

Meagan stopped hearing the noise and zoned in on Chris. He had his helmet on and his hockey stick held casually in his hand. He stepped on the ice and glided swiftly and smoothly like he was born with skates on. He made the mandatory swoop around the ice, not even looking to see her. Meagan's heart sank. She watched him settle onto the team bench only 3 metres away.

Chris picked up his water bottle, raised it towards his face but stopped and turned his head to look directly at her. He smiled a deliciously warm smile and nodded his head in a gentle greeting. She beamed back and returned the nod. They held each other's gaze for what seemed a long time to Meagan. He slowly turned back to drink and refocus on the pre-game rituals. She could feel all the stares from the season's ticket holders that witnessed the friendly exchange and suddenly blushed. The turtleneck made her sweat.

After the puck dropped, the men on the ice flew after the frozen little orb like their lives depended on it. Actually, with how much hockey players make, their livelihoods do depend on their interactions with the puck. Chris played his share of the game. On and off the ice he went. He'd wait for the signal and jump over the boards to pick up where the last player left off.

The scoring in the first two periods was evenly matched at two each. Each team was playing well. Minutes before the second period was about to end, a fight broke out in the far corner and in the middle of it was Chris.

The crowd went nuts on their feet cheering on the two men. Chris was the bigger player and was ripping the shirt right off the other guys back. There were a few fists thrown at each other, but Meagan couldn't see if any connected.

"Please don't get hurt," she pleaded softly under her breath.

The refs peeled the men apart and both were sent to the penalty box for a roughing penalty. Chris sat down directly across from where Meagan was sitting. He picked up the water bottle and looked straight across at Meagan. He could see her look of concern and smiled at her. Both of them stopped watching the game and looked at each other. Players and linemen would skate past, but neither noticed or, cared. They were the only two people in the arena that counted. Even with his white helmet, sweaty hair and face and scuff marks on his chin from the fight he was still as handsome as the first morning she saw him, maybe more now in a rugged way.

"Meagan," Ben was yanking on her sweater to get her attention. She finally turned and looked at him.

"What?"

"Leave him alone."

"What, I'm just sitting here," she said, trying to look back.

"Leave him to do his job. The coach will have his neck in a noose if he doesn't watch the game."

"Okay," she said, as she looked back at Chris. He was still looking at her. She smiled then looked up at the clock. Thirty seconds were left on his penalty. She looked back at him and he was looking at the clock too. When he looked back at her they both smiled and nodded again. Then he went back to concentrating on the game.

"There, are you happy now," she said smartly at her brother.

"Yes, but not as happy as the coach."

There were only a few minutes left of the second period. The players chased the puck uneventfully until the horn blew. The teams went back to their dressing rooms and the fans all dashed for their 20-minute chance to smoke, pee or get more beer, which is where Ben wanted to go.

"You want one?"

"Naw, but I'll come with you."

They got his beer and strolled through the thick crowd of fans. Meagan was amazed to see many with their faces pointed towards television sets hung from the pillars. Of course, it was games from other parts of the continent beaming out. What else would it be – cooking classes?

Just before the third period started, Meagan quickly dashed into the ladies' room to see if she still looked okay. She was hoping he would smile at her through the glass again. She was still giddy from the first one.

When she got back to the seats, Ben was in deep conversation with a beautiful blonde girl who was in her seat. The woman rose when she saw Meagan coming down the steps.

"Hey, Meagan. This is Debbie Banks. She is an articling student at our firm. She thought you were my girlfriend," said Ben.

"That's a laugh. I'm only his sister. Do you want proof?" she said kidding her brother. "I'm not a lawyer, but if you'd like some advice, I'd stay away from..."

Ben interrupted. "I'll see you at work? Maybe we could go out for lunch, so MY SISTER, won't try advising you on anything."

Debbie said, "Sure, I'd like that. Nice to meet you, Meagan."

"Same here," said Meagan. "He's not that bad. I just like bugging him."

Debbie smiled at the teasing then went back up the stairs and Meagan sat down. "So, you never told me about her before."

"She's new."

"I think she is nice. Seriously, you should ask her out so none of those other single leaches at the firm catch her first."

Ben started to nod then stopped. "What do you mean – other leaches?"

The music started to blare. Meagan pointed at her ears and mouthed words like she couldn't hear.

The first lines came spilling onto the ice while the rest slid onto the benches. Chris was out on the ice, so the flirting smiles would have to wait.

It didn't take long before Calgary scored bringing them ahead by one. The fans went wild. Chris's team started to look defeated. Chris was on and off the ice many times playing as hard as he could. Suddenly Boston scored and the game was tied.

With only two minutes left in the game, Calgary was awarded a penalty giving the opposing team a man advantage. Chris jumped over the boards to play his position. He charged down to the Calgary end, bumping players away from the puck. It flies off a stick straight at him. He spins around and taps the puck to a teammate who slaps it through the goalie's legs. He scores! Both men throw their hands holding their sticks high in the air while the free hand pumps a clenched fist in celebration.

His team was up 4-3 with less than a minute to play. Chris skated back to the boards and rolled over and onto the bench. His game was over. Meagan watched the remainder of the game without looking at him. He was in his glory with his teammates and she didn't want to ruin it for them by making him do the "smiley thing" at her.

"Well, aren't you lucky," said Ben, as they got up from their seats to join the deflated home team fans as they inched up the crowded steps.

"Why?"

"Because now you get to go out with a happy winner instead of a sore loser," said Ben.

She had to admit, a conversation would be easy with a guy who just did one of the greatest plays of the game.

CHAPTER SIX

Instead of waiting around the dressing room door like awkward groupies, Ben and Meagan said they'd meet Chris in the lounge at the entrance of the building. With Calgary being defeated, the crowds weren't hanging around to celebrate so it wasn't hard to find a seat at the bar.

As they sat on the tall stools. Meagan's cell phone rang. The display said, "Chris B."

"Hello, Meagan here," she said into the phone with a look of concern written across her face.

"Meagan, it's Chris."

Oh no! she thought. *He's cancelling!*

"I wanted to tell you I'm going to be 10 extra minutes. I have to talk to a reporter from your newspaper."

"Oh, that's okay," she said very relieved.

"Will you wait?"

"Of course."

"Thanks. I'll hurry," he said and ended the call.

Ben looked at her, "Is he still coming?"

"Of course," she said again.

By the time Chris came bolting through the door, he was a half-hour late. The frantic look on his face showed he was concerned about keeping them waiting. Showing no sign of fatigue from the game, he moved swiftly across the room. Meagan slid off the barstool and stood up. He didn't even say hello, he wrapped her in a big wonderful strong hug. Ben sat with his eyes bulging, wondering if there was more to their relationship than she let on.

"I'm so sorry," he said as he hugged her. He let go of the tight embrace but still held her in his arms. "The stupid reporter couldn't spell Burrows."

32

Ginger and Ice

"It's okay, really. Um, this is," she said as she turned his body so he would notice her staring brother, "this is my brother, Ben. He is your biggest fan in Calgary."

Chris took his arms off Meagan and shook Ben's hand, easily enveloping it. "I've heard about you. Meagan said you are coaching her in the fine art of watching hockey. Do you play?"

"Yeah, just a men's league," Ben said blushing.

"Hey if I'm in town some night you play, let me know and I'll be a sub-in. But don't tell anybody it's me till after the game. If we lose - I don't want them to know I was there."

They all laughed, and Chris turned back to Meagan. "Wow. It's been so long since I saw you. The phone doesn't do you justice."

"Um, I made reservations and I think we are running late. Do you mind if we head out?"

"Not at all," said Chris. "I'm starving. Are you joining us, Ben?"

Ben put up his hand in protest. "Not a chance. She would kill me! I'm sure we will meet again."

They got to the cars – which by this point were almost the last two in the lot. The two men shook hands and Ben got in and drove off quickly. Chris and Meagan got into her truck and as she started the engine, Chris reached out and took her hand, pulling her close to him. "Now that the chaperone is gone, I'd like to kiss you," he said softly.

They kissed a nice proper peck and with foreheads still touching, Meagan said, "Hello, I'm so glad to see you."

"Me too," he said softly and brought his lips on hers for a slow sensuous romantic kiss. The light scent of his shaving cream lingered in her nose. It had been a long time since she'd enjoyed that sensation.

Meagan took Chris to a restaurant she had designed. She hoped Lance, the owner would be there to make her look far more important.

The hostess was showing them to a table in the middle of the crowded restaurant, but Lance walked in at the right time and came over. He took the menus from the girl and said he would take care of his friends.

"Meagan," he said giving her a light peck on the cheek. "Where have you been? It's about time you came in to see how well the place turned out."

"Thanks, Lance. This is my friend, Chris. I thought I'd take him out for a good steak."

"Hi Chris," Lance said as he shook his hand. "You played a great game today."

"Oh, you were there?" asked Chris.

"Yeah, the restaurant has season tickets to share amongst the employees, but I tend to take the Boston tickets for myself."

"You're not going to have the chef burn my steak because we won, are you?" asked Chris, with a look of concern.

"Are you kidding, I know how hard you throw a punch!" he said, as he pulled out a chair for Meagan at a secluded corner. "And by the way, since when were you a hockey fan, Meagan? I thought all you did was run?"

Meagan sat down blushing and looking straight at Chris — lost for words. "I guess I can learn to appreciate other sports even if running isn't involved."

Lance smiled and said to enjoy the meal and left them alone.

"Boy, everybody knows you," said Meagan.

"Yeah, this sports star thing can be a blessing or a curse. So...," said Chris as he looked around the restaurant, studying the décor, "Did you have any part of making this place? It's great."

Meagan was thrilled he liked it. She was pleased with how it turned out too. "I did. Lance hired me a few years ago to do some small renovations to another of his restaurants and I guess he liked my work, when this came up, it didn't even go to bid. He just asked if I could do it."

"Speaking of bids, how is the bid package going?"

"Oh, man, you don't want to hear, do you? All I do is eat, sleep and drink that project."

"No, really, I do want to know. What's the concept going to be?" he said earnestly.

"Well, I do think I've got a great idea coming." And with that, she started a long explanation of her ideas and how the colours and concepts were coming along great. She told him how it was mostly her ideas still, but she would bring in the team tomorrow. They were all to have studied the specs and be ready for the big powwow.

As she spoke a bottle of wine appeared with a note saying it was complimentary from Lance. They lifted the glasses of dark red wine and Chris said, "To you, Meagan. You make coming to Calgary worth anticipating."

The glasses touched like a gentle kiss and Meagan smiled at Chris, overwhelmed with the compliment.

"So, tell me about yourself, Meagan Dunphy. I know you like to run and what you do for a living," he said, with a smile leaning across the table to be closer to her. "Is Ben your only sibling or will I meet more?"

"No, that's it. He's older than me by a few years and thankfully has always been on my side."

"What do you mean by that?" he asked.

"Oh, dad wanted me to grow up and join him in his law firm like Ben had to and mom wanted me to marry a rich lawyer like she did. Whenever dad took me to the office to see what he did, instead of watching the litigation stuff, I was busy redesigning the building. I tried to like law and even took a few courses in university to see if I could do it, but it was useless. I'd rather design the office than sit in it.

"Dad seemed to take the news that I wasn't joining the team pretty good, but mom has never gotten over the thought that I'd consider architecture as a career instead of having the rich wife career. Ben didn't last at dad's firm too long, he figured if I could venture out without being disowned, so could he."

She stopped to take a sip of wine and noticed the salad sitting in front of her. Chris wasn't eating his yet, he was busy listening to her. "I've talked enough, tell me about you now. How many siblings am I going to meet and how come you are a hockey player?"

She took her fork in her hand and started to eat and study his features. His curly black hair caught the light perfectly and had her instantly wondering what it looked like against a pillow. She quickly refocused on her fork.

In-between mouthfuls he told her his history. "I'm from Seattle actually. That's where most of my family still is. I have five brothers."

"Six boys! Holy cow, your poor mom!"

"No kidding. I'm the second of the lot and dad died when I was in high school. Poor old mom had to raise all of us by herself. She didn't have a chance at remarrying. Who would take on six boys?"

"How did she do it? She has to be amazing," Meagan said, astonished at the story.

"Oh, she is amazing. Dad died on the job, so the insurance covered a lot of our living expenses. Mark, my oldest brother finished high school and went to work as a landscaper right away to help pay for things. A farm team already picked me, so as soon as high school was done, I was sent off to train and live with a family in Colorado. That way both of us could send money home to mom. Mack and Derek are all out of the house now, just Dave is at home and he graduates from high school in June. All of my other younger brothers either have a university degree or are working on it. Dave is set on taking engineering next fall."

"What does your older brother do?" she asked, concerned that he lost out on a career.

"Oh, I'd say he does pretty fine. His company grew and grew and now it's one of the largest landscape companies in the Pacific Northwest. He has over 200 employees year-round and then it's crazy during the summer. All of us have done time working for Mark. That's probably why everyone wants a degree."

"Boy, your mom won't know what to do with herself when Dave moves out. Has she got any plans to put her feet up and take a break?"

Their main courses showed up. A huge steak dinner with a mountain of vegetables was placed in front of Chris. She ordered the Ladies' Cut, but it still was going to be far too much.

"That's one of the reasons I picked up land in The Bahamas. I wanted to build a nice recreational property with a little guest bungalow for either her or a guest to stay in."

"Oh yeah," said Meagan through a mouthful of potatoes. "You mentioned The Bahamas before."

He smiled looking at her hair, "Yeah, I said the Bahamians would love your red hair."

She blushed, remembering the first encounter outside the Y.

"A few years ago, I was travelling with a friend through the Caribbean, trying to stay away from the mega-resorts. We landed on the island of Eleuthera and I fell in love with the landscape and people instantly."

Chris kept talking about the colour of the ocean, the endless pink sand beaches, the warm breezes and how remote the island was, but Meagan wasn't listening as much as she should have been. She was drinking in his features and watching how the candlelight flickered off his strong jawbone.

"The property I'm building on now is on the Atlantic side, which is a little rougher water. If I want calm beaches, I'll build the place on the other side and flip between places," he said.

Meagan suddenly paid attention and thought what he said didn't make sense. "You have property on both sides of the island?"

"It's only a mile across," he said, knowing she thought it sounded weird. "The island is 100 miles long and at the widest, it's a little over a mile wide. At one point, it is barely the width of a car. That spot is called the Glass Window Bridge."

"Glass Window?"

Chris's eyes twinkled with animation as he continued what seemed to be his favourite topic other than hockey. "It was called that way back when the sailors and pirates controlled the seas. They'd be sailing the rough waters of the Atlantic and could see through this arch separating the north and south islands. Through the window, they could see the calm smooth waters of the Caribbean, but knew they had to fight the Atlantic for another 30 miles before they could cut through a narrow channel called the Current Cut."

"There are no pirates now – are there?"

"Not of the swashbucklers and captains with parrots and peg legs. The pirates now are meaner and ruthless, smuggling drugs into the States using stolen yachts and high-tech machines."

"Boy, you really know your stuff!" she said, captivated by his excitement. "It sounds inviting, yet scary."

"Maybe you should come see it with me?" he said, quietly.

"Maybe I will," she said, blushing again.

The dinner went by far too quickly. They spoke and laughed like they had been friends forever. Meagan was surprised they could find so much to talk about considering their diverse backgrounds and interests that seemed poles apart.

Chris casually glanced at his watch and his shoulders sank. "Meagan," he said sadly. "I gotta go. Coach gives us a curfew and we have to abide or pay the fine."

Meagan looked at her watch and realized it was 11:45 p.m. She knew she was going to be exhausted in the morning, but her heart told her to enjoy it. Chris quickly paid the bill and they headed out the door.

As they walked, Chris put his arm around her chilled shoulder and squeezed her gently. She leaned into his body feeling like the world was all hers.

The hotel was only a few blocks from the restaurant and as they came through the last set of lights, Chris told her to pull to the side of the street.

"Meagan," he said, as he took her hand in his again. I, I don't know how to say this – but I really want to keep seeing you. I don't know how this long-distance thing is going to work, but I'd like to give it a try."

She was so afraid he was starting to give her the kiss-off but was overcome with relief when he said he wanted to keep seeing her. She looked at his deep dark eyes and smiled. She didn't answer with words. Her left hand reached up and gently caressed his smooth cheek, gently pulling him closer for a very, long sensuous kiss.

When she pulled up to the entrance to the hotel, a few other players were also slipping in under the curfew deadline. As the vehicle came to a stop, a few teammates noticed Chris riding shotgun.

"Aren't you glad we stopped around the corner?" he said, as he waved at his teammates through the front windshield.

"Yep," she said smiling. "They might be worse than a mom!"

"Yeah, but they don't talk as sweet!" he said, laughing as he got out. The door slammed and he joined the stream of players, waving as he went.

CHAPTER SEVEN

Everybody she bounced her ideas off thought the designs were exactly what Cottonwood needed. Meagan was proud of the bid package she and her faithful team were putting together. Brian was fantastic with colours and textures and brought countless schemes to the table until everybody agreed unanimously. Multi-pierced Jennifer, on the other hand, brought fixtures and furniture together. And, when presentations were set together, you'd think a single mind thought up the conglomerate.

Jenn and Brian smiled at each other when Meagan ranted about the skills they were beginning to master. Meagan caught a look at the smiles and felt like there might be an office romance starting to bud. That didn't bother her and oddly, she wasn't envious. Even she was starting to think a little romance was a good thing.

The only person who didn't seem to contribute whole-heartedly was Dianne and it upset Meagan. She remembered the day halfway through the design stage when she walked into the photocopy room and Dianne didn't notice her at first. Dianne was busy sliding papers and drawing across the glass screen. The light flashed in her unblinking stare as she concentrated on her task. Meagan was confused as to why preliminary drawings for Cottonwood were being copied by Dianne when that portion of the job wasn't her responsibility.

Meagan walked up beside Dianne.

"Hi."

"Oh! You scared me! What do you want?" Dianne said quickly, as she covered what she had been copying.

Meagan moved the papers so the drawings were exposed. "Why are you copying these? You aren't on this part of the project."

Dianne grabbed them again and tried to sound sweet, but her

nervousness shone through. "Brian asked me to...um, do some for him...he's swamped you know," she pushed the clear button, gathered the copies and swiftly left the room. Ginny came in at the same time.

"Meagan, there you are. You have a call waiting," said Ginny.

Unfortunately, Ginny blocked Meagan's view so she couldn't see if the copying was dropped on Brian's desk. It did seem odd that a senior designer would do the grunt work for the young intern. Maybe Dianne had an eye on the young guy too and that was her way of trying to get noticed. Meagan shrugged off the odd behaviour but was still curious as to Dianne's slow progress. After the phone call, she quizzed Dianne on her involvement but also wanted to know if anything was bothering her.

"How is the entry going?" Meagan asked lightly, as they met at the coffee machine.

"Er, fine," said Dianne as she poured a cup of coffee.

Dianne was cold to her friend and tried to get past Meagan without making eye contact.

"Can I see your ideas?" asked Meagan, trying not to sound annoyed.

"Sure, let me toss this on my desk and I'll be in to see you," Dianne said as she moved quickly to her station.

Over an hour later Dianne came in with what looked like jumbled ideas she had just jotted down. Her sketches were in the same pen as the notes and there were no computer layouts. It felt like lame ideas regurgitated from their early days in university.

Meagan decided to confront her. "This isn't what I was expecting from you, Dianne. I don't feel like your heart is in this project. Is there something bothering you?"

Dianne was instantly defensive. "I'm doing the best I can Meagan. Are you accusing me of slacking off?"

Meagan didn't want a confrontation, so she blew her question off quickly. "I'm not accusing you of anything Dianne. I hope in a few days your designs are as good as you used to,...I mean, usually produce. Maybe you should come up with your best two and do them up properly and present them later," she said smiling, hoping to calm Dianne down.

It didn't work. Dianne glared at her, spun on her heels and stomped out. She thundered through the room, slammed everything on her desk, pulled out her chair and flopped herself down. A minute later she grabbed her purse, shoved her chair under her desk and headed for the door.

"I'm gone for the day, Ginny," she said without even looking at her.

Ginny looked back at Meagan who was peering out of her glassed-in office and questioned, "PMS?"

They both shrugged their shoulders and got back to what they were doing.

The next day Dianne came in with her ideas laid out beautifully. She was back to her normal self, so Meagan didn't take the altercation any further. Dianne's participation in the project, however, seemed to be done and whatever was bothering her seemed to have worked itself out.

The late-night calls with Chris continued and it did seem like a spark was turning into a flickering fresh flame. Meagan was enjoying the fact there might be a chance of a romance. It wasn't going to be easy with him living in Boston and her in Calgary, but somehow, they would make it work.

Some days, she would catch herself staring out the window, planning how she would uproot her business and relocate to Boston where her fresh western-influenced ideas would be the rage. Other times, she visualized the look on her mom's sculpted face as she announced she was tossing her life away to move in with a big burly hockey player.

That idea always brought her wandering mind back to the present and back to the drafting table where it should be.

One night during one of their lengthy conversations on everything from brick styles to Zamboni improvements, Chris sprang an idea on Meagan that made her catch her breath.

"After you get this contract you are working so hard on – and before you sink your teeth into the construction, why don't you take a little holiday with me and see my place on Eleuthera." His voice sounded like he had been practicing the question for some time and he didn't add anything to it.

He let the idea sink in for a while, "Meagan?" he said, "Are you there?"

"Yes. Wow, what an offer. I think I deserve a break," her voice was slow because her mind was busy undressing him on the pink sand beach. She shook her head to stop the vision "Yeah, I'd like to do that. Can you get away?"

The excitement in his voice was audible. "If the pucks line up for both of us, we could meet for a few days during the All-Stars break in late January."

"That sounds like a great idea. It's been so long since I've gotten away. I think I've got enough air mile points to get a ticket," she said, thinking out loud about how she would afford the trip.

"My treat," he said laughing. "You don't need to cash in your points."

"Chris, I don't need you paying for my flight either. I can pay for it you know," said Meagan, a little hurt by what she thought was a male pride thing.

"I'm sorry, what I meant is you can use my good-guy points. I have enough to go to the moon and back. I'd gladly let you use mine. It's not coming from my pocket."

"Oh, sorry. I get a little defensive sometimes."

"I'm the defensemen. That's my job," he said, laughing at his own joke.

Meagan giggled along.

"I'm coming in for a game Friday night and we don't have to be anywhere until Sunday. I know this is a bold question but, could I invite you to go to Banff after the game Friday night and come back Sunday morning. I just have to get to L.A. by 6 p.m."

Meagan's heart stopped. *This weekend ... away with Chris?*

The thought was tantalizing. "I'd love that," she said in a whisper, her throat had suddenly gone dry. There was a small awkward pause in the conversation. Maybe both of them were thinking about the same thing. Like how this might take their relationship to a new and more serious level of commitment. It was a thought that thrilled Meagan.

"I don't know anything about Banff, other than there are bears and a big old castle. Can you make the arrangements for me?" Chris finally said, breaking the silence.

"Sure," she said, laughing at his reference to the castle. "It's the Banff Springs Hotel, not a castle. I'll see if I can get us a room."

"Great. Why don't you get your brother to come to the game with you on Friday and we can leave from there? I can score those tickets easy."

"Bringing Bro to the game will be easy. Getting him to not follow us to Banff won't!"

"Is he worried about you?" Chris asked concerned.

"Nooo. He'd be following his hockey hero," she said, laughing again.

"You are a funny girl, Meagan," he said warmly. "I'll email you the info about the tickets."

"Okay."

"It's a date then, see you Friday after the game."

"Don't take any hits that night, okay?" She was concerned about nursing a punched-out hockey player instead of seducing a date.

"I'll try."

They both hung up the phone. Meagan shut her eyes and drifted into fantastic images until she fell asleep.

Next morning, she was on the internet trying to secure a room for the weekend at 'The Springs,' but the normal route was impossible. The hotel seemed booked solid and the rack rate was dizzying.

"I'll have to call in a favour I guess," Meagan said aloud. She started thumbing through her messy collection of business cards.

The Fairmont Banff Springs Hotel was the oldest, most luxurious resort in the mountains and it had gone through millions of dollars of renovations. Lucky for Meagan, she did a few minor ones last year and still had an IOU owing from the manager.

As she waited for Darren to answer she hoped he'd reme of reduced rates on accommodations.

"Hey Meagan, good to hear you are taking a weekend off. Are you coming for a retreat or is someone coming along?" Darren said, a little too curiously.

"Ah, yeah, I have a friend coming into town from Boston and I thought The Springs would impress him."

"A HIM? I better kick someone out of the royal suite then," he said, teasing her.

"No don't do that. A normal room is fine," said Meagan, blushing over the phone.

"Don't worry. I'll get something ready for you for two nights."

"Thanks, Darren. Now I owe you one."

"You won't after you see the bill!" he said laughing. "I won't be here this weekend, but I'll call you next Monday to make sure it was satisfactory."

She secretly hoped his favour would include that "good-guy"rate.

Chris emailed to say there were tickets held in her name and she returned the email with the good news about the hotel reservations. She checked the weather and it looked like a Chinook blowing warm air was coming to town. It looked like the weekend was going to be perfect. All she had to do was concentrate on work and running until then.

The next morning, Meagan met with the girls for a run. Robin and Emma were missing for the day, so the trio headed west, their breaths looked like locomotive steam chugging behind them as they settled into their tempo. It was crisp and a light snow covered the path, hiding potential ankle breaking black ice, but all of them had run enough kilometres to know how to recover quickly when their footing goes out.

"So, is everybody ready for the Frozen Toes on Sunday?" asked Lizzie as they came out from under a bridge.

Meagan forgot all about the annual race when she booked the weekend. Obviously, she would rather be snuggled in bed with Chris than standing at a start line freezing her ass off with a bunch of scrawny runners, but she didn't want to tell the girls of her first rendezvous with the hockey player.

"Do you guys want to meet in the club lobby?" said Gloria.

"Yeah," puffed Lizzie.

No answer was coming from Meagan.

"Megs, can you make it?" said Gloria.

"I, um, can't. I totally gapped and forgot about it and double booked myself," she said sheepishly.

"How could you forget Frozen Toes? What could possibly be better than that brunch?" asked Gloria.

"I'm going to Banff with Chris," she blurted out.

There was silence for only a second and then the teasing and catcalls started. Meagan started to blush, so she picked up the pace.

"You little sneak. If it weren't for the race, you wouldn't have told us!" said Gloria laughing sadistically.

"You're right. I didn't want you guys jumping to conclusions."

The girls started laughing even harder.

"Oh, baby! That's exactly what we are doing! And those conclusions look great!"

"You won't be mad if I miss the race then?" asked Meagan.

"Hell no! We just expect all the details on Monday morning," said Gloria.

They calmed down and quit bugging Meagan, so they could finish their run. Meagan and Lizzie looked at each other and Lizzie raised her gloved hand with her fingers crossed. She smiled and nodded vigorously.

Meagan had a quick shower at the club and headed back to work.

She was pretty happy with the bid work and wanted to start preparing the final presentation. There was still well over a week before she had to submit, but as always, she set her own premature deadlines so if anything popped into her mind after it was ready, she still had a chance to alter the bid. When she got to the office, the mock-up was finished and sitting on her desk waiting for her approval from the drafting team.

The versions of the hotels were detailed to perfection in the computerization. Even the little people walking in and out with tiny little skis balancing on their shoulders looked happy to be there. Meagan couldn't have been more pleased and gathered everybody into her office to look at the model on the big screen.

They all came in and said all the right things. It was the first big project for the two young designers and their pride shone. They beamed as they showed off all the details to Ginny and Dianne. Even Mel, the drywall contractor came in and added his two cents of glowing praise. Surprisingly, Dianne gave a few critiques that seemed out of place in the jovial crowd and left the room. Everyone was too happy to pay any attention to her comments and lack of enthusiasm.

Meagan spent the rest of the day organizing the bid package but left just a bit early so she could go shopping for the weekend. She wasn't about to go to a hotel with a guy and pull out her ratty flannel pyjamas that were safety-pinned together. She wanted to pick up something but was perplexed as to what she should get.

She strolled the entire mall. Sexy? See-through? Barely there? More flannel? Feathers? No.

Almost out of frustration, she settled on a cute set of boxer shorts and a rather low-cut T-shirt to match. She laughed at herself in the hoped she wouldn't spend much time in the outfit.

Friday rolled around and Meagan was a mess. She was both

nervous at the same time.

Just as she wanted to leave, Dianne came into her office.

"Hey," she said as she flopped into the only soft chair in the office. "Got plans for the night?"

Meagan was beside herself. "Actually, I do!"

"Hey," Dianne said slowly, "Is it a home game tonight against a certain team from Massachusetts?"

"That's right," Meagan said, almost singing. "Ben and I are going to the game, then Chris and I are going to Banff for the weekend!"

Meagan was so pleased, she didn't notice how much Dianne was squirming in her seat.

"Sooo, you leave right from the game?"

"Yep."

"Staying both nights?"

"Yes! How scary! I haven't gone away with a man for so long – I don't think I know how to act!"

"Oh Meagan, relax," said Dianne. "What could possibly go wrong? It's about time you guys spent some quality time together. When do you think you will come back to the city?"

"I dunno, he has to be at the airport for a one o'clock flight, so depending on how well we like each other, I'll be back anytime way before that or just after one," replied Meagan.

Dianne laughed, and got up to leave. "Well, I guess I won't invite you out for a beer tonight then. Sounds like the competition is too hot. Have fun and I'll see you Monday morning. Try to wipe that silly grin off your face by then, would ya?"

"Not a chance. I feel great. Cottonwood is looking terrific and a guy likes me – a great looking guy at that. Life is good," she said with a confidence she hadn't felt in years.

Shortly after their conversation, Meagan started shutting down the office. Everybody was gone except her and Dianne.

"You working late?" she said as she slipped into her coat.

"Well, now that I don't have anything on tonight, I'll hash out some ideas," she said looking up from the computer. "I'll lock up."

"Thanks. I'll see ya later."

"Break a leg," said Dianne, as she watched her boss leave.

Dianne's gaze went down to her computer screen as the ping of an incoming email announced its arrival. She saw who it was and smiled.

Dianne quickly read the short note and replied with, *"Don't worry, the dope and the puck are gone all weekend. Plenty of time."* Then, she pushed send and said aloud, "Megs, you are such a trusting dope."

Dianne played a few games of solitaire then turned off the lights, locked the door and left for the night. Meanwhile, Meagan was merrily driving to the game, positive that whatever frump Dianne had been in for the last few weeks was behind her now and her old buddy was back.

Ben was waiting in the parking lot and they walked into the crowded building, picked up their tickets, beer and popcorn and walked down to the same seats as before. Unfortunately, they were too late to watch the warm-up; the Zamboni was already sweeping over the ice making the surface as smooth and shiny as a plate of glass.

When the visiting team hit the ice, her eyes were riveted on number 28. This time as he swooped back to the bench, he looked for Meagan. When they made eye contact, he smiled and raised his gloved hand to wave. She waved back and once again the nearby crowd searched to see who the lucky girl was to be selected for the wave. Meagan blushed and quickly turned to speak directly at her brother.

"This attention is really weird," she said, feeling heat in her cheeks from blushing.

"Gee Meagan, I think if you are going to continue seeing this guy, you will have to learn how to deal with it," he said sincerely. Looking straight into her eyes he continued. "No really. I mean it. You will be envied, admired and hated by a lot of people. If you get serious with Chris – you better find someone who can help you deal with the attention."

Meagan didn't answer. She nodded and thought hard about what Ben was saying. She looked around them at some of the beautiful women sitting in the first few rows and wondered if they were players' wives and girlfriends. She stared at two who were deep in conversation. They were picture perfect. Drop-dead gorgeous right down to the French manicured fingernails and designer loafers. None of the wives at this level would need to work. If she married Chris, would he expect her to give up her career so she could hang out with the other wives?

Meagan shook the image out of her head and gave herself a mental shake. *What am I thinking?* she thought to herself. *We have known each other for a few months and we've had like one real date, and here I am, trying to figure out our marital problems.*

The puck dropped, and the game was on. This game felt different than the one she attended before. The Calgary players seemed mad or revengeful.

Unprovoked a Calgary player grabbed Chris by the shirt and nailed him with a punch. Gloves and sticks were flying as helmets skidded across the ice. She refused to stand but the people around her stood up. She looked up and of course, there it was on the Jumbotron above the rink. Two guys were beating on Chris. Suddenly his feet came out from under him.

Sixteen thousand fans groaned as he hit the ice hard. Chris c

CHAPTER EIGHT

The two Calgary players glided away from Chris's crumpled body. The trainers from both teams leap over the boards and race to his side. Ben instinctively put his arm around Meagan's shoulder while they both stare up at the screen.

Unhurried, the players skated around the heap on the ice, picking up the scattered equipment. Slowly Chris started to move. The trainers got him standing, but he was bent over in pain.

Meagan kept her hand over her mouth so she wouldn't say anything – but she was screaming in her head, *Please be okay! Please be okay!*

As if he heard her, Ben starts to babble. "Don't worry, he'll be okay. It looks like his ribs took a good hit – but, but… he should be okay."

Chris slowly stood straight, but he was holding his arms across his chest. He looked like he was on the verge of blacking out again, but they carefully pushed him along towards the visitor's bench. The fans begin to cheer. Meagan could barely swallow, let alone clap or cheer.

As Chris went past Meagan, he looked up and tried to smile. She still had her hand over her mouth, so she gently blew him a kiss and tried to smile back.

The game resumed as if nothing had happened. Ben turned to Meagan and said, "What do you want to do?"

"I don't know. Puke? I don't know him well enough to go rushing anywhere. Maybe he is okay?"

"Let's just try to watch the game and see if he tries to call you."

Meagan pulled her phone out of her pocket and set it to vibrate and kept it in the palm of her hand.

A few minutes later the horn blew to signal the end of the first period. As the crowds emptied into the concourse, Meagan's phone started to dance in her hand.

"Hello?" she said quickly.

"Meagan, it's Chris."

"Oh Gawd, are you okay?" she said, almost crying.

"I'll be fine. Man, those guys really wanted me out of the game, huh?"

"You aren't going to keep playing – are you?" asked Meagan.

"Naw. The doctor wants me to get an X-ray to see if anything is punctured or broken."

"Is there anything I can do?" she asked.

"Stay there and watch the game – if you want? I should be back in time to go to Banff, that is if you'll still go with me."

"Of course I will, but should you?" she said, hesitating.

"I'll meet you guys in the bar after the game and we can assess the situation then. How's that?" he said, already sounding stronger.

"That will be fine," Meagan said.

Ben had been standing in the aisle waiting for the verdict. They started walking up the stairs.

"They are taking him for X-rays, and he will call or meet us in the lounge after the game," she said, feeling better now that she had talked to him. Seeing him in a heap scared her. How many other times would she have to sit through that she thought?

The game went on and on and on. Without Chris on the ice, it was just another boring game of hockey.

Boston won again. This time Meagan didn't care.

When they walked into the nearly deserted lounge, Chris was waiting at the bar where they had sat last time. A few fans were surrounding him asking him if he was okay.

When Chris looked up and saw the concern on Meagan's face as she came down the stairs he said, "Excuse me, I better go. There's someone coming in who's mad I got in a fight! This might get uglier." he said with a smile.

Meagan walked up but didn't touch him. She was holding back tears. Never had she seen a fight like that where someone she was falling in love with was getting a senseless beating. He knew this was new to her and it would be hard to take. He gently pulled her into his chest and let her cry.

"I'm okay. I'm okay," he said as his large hands rubbed her back to comfort her.

She wiped away the tears but said, "If you are so fine then why do you have this giant brace strapped around your chest?" She could feel it under his sweater.

"Okay, I'm not okay. I bruised a few ribs, but I'm fine," he said. "All I need is a good night's sleep and a few doses of Motrin and I'll be ready to play on Sunday. Do you guys want to stop for a beer?"

Ben knew he wasn't allowed to hang around. "No, I gotta go. I'm glad to see you're okay though. Too bad you missed the game. Calgary didn't stand a chance tonight."

"Ahhh," said Chris, "Sounds like you are starting to cheer for the other team."

"Shush. Don't tell anybody or I'll be tarred and feathered before I get to my car," replied Ben, with a laugh.

The two men shook hands and Ben smiled at his sister and then left them alone. Chris and Meagan looked at each other and Chris started to smile a great big grin. Meagan couldn't help but smile back.

"I was scared."

"I know. I'm sorry. When I was lying there, all I could think about is how you must feel. My mom used to go through the same thing."

"Did she get used to it?" asked Meagan, looking for assurance that it would get better.

"No."

"How does she handle it?"

"She doesn't watch the games anymore. Come on, let's go."

Holding onto the bar with one hand, Chris slowly dipped down to reach his duffle bag that was sitting on the floor.

Meagan tried to break gently at the traffic lights so as not to bother Chris's ribs. The last set of lights on the west edge of the city was a welcome sight in the rear-view mirror. As she set the cruise control Meagan started to relax. It was now 10:30 p.m.; it would be midnight for sure before they pulled into Banff. *So much for the sexy pjs tonight,* she sulked to herself.

Just like the day of their first run, Meagan was too quiet for Chris.

"Meagan," he said softly, putting his hand on her shoulder. "It's part of my job."

"What?" she said puzzled.

"The fighting. It's an aspect of the game I have to live with. I love playing hockey, it's my life. If I choose not to fight, my career ends prematurely."

Meagan stared at the highway as it dipped at Jumping Pound Creek and rolled up over Copithorne Ridge – both landmarks she had driven by numerous times. The moon was brilliant, shining a beam on every cow standing silently in the snow-covered field. Meagan was frantically searching for the right words, so she wouldn't ruin the relationship or crush what she believed in.

"I...I realize that, but I don't like it. That's probably why I've never liked watching hockey. Violence scares me. I can't imagine hitting someone and I don't want to be hit either."

"That's not the only part of the game," he said, defending his sport while taking his hand off her shoulder.

"I know, but doesn't it bother you getting hurt all the time?"

"This doesn't happen every game. Usually, the padding takes the hit. And honestly, fighting is moving out of the game. It's not like the old days."

"Do you like hitting the other players?" she said, revising her question and desperately afraid of the answer.

"It's something I do for the game — but it isn't a part of my nature. I don't fight outside of the rink and I don't plan to throw another punch after I retire."

She could see the conviction in his eyes when she glanced over at him. "It's not as much that you are throwing the punch, it's that you are being hit. I don't want you to never get up."

The conversation was not going in the right direction and they both knew it. The hockey fighting could cost them their relationship and neither wanted that.

Chris touched her cheek softly with the back of his hand. "Please don't hate me because of the fights."

Meagan reached up and held his warm hand on her cheek. "Please don't hate me because I don't like the fights."

He smiled and nodded. That discussion would have to wait or maybe it would never happen again.

It wasn't long before the exit ramp for the town came along. With the full moon, Chris was able to see the towering silhouettes of the rugged blue mountains. The conversation turned to the topography and the shadows.

Main Street Banff was generally a bustling place with tourists from all over the world busily buying trinkets or warmer clothes to battle the cold weather. At midnight though, it was skiers and snowboarders coming out of the taverns and restaurants.

The road crossed the Bow River and wound towards the Banff Springs Hotel.

"So why is it the Banff Springs?" asked Chris, as he read the signs pointing them in the right direction.

"Oh, a couple of rail workers back in the late 1800s stumbled across a cave where a hot spring was leaking out of the mountain. The rail company saw it as a gold mine to attract people to the mountains, so they built this hotel and since then, the hotel and the town have grown and never looked back," said Meagan, reciting the story she learned in high school. Then in her best baritone voice emulating Sir. William Van Horne added, "If we can't export the scenery, we'll import the tourists."

Chris looked sideways at her and shook his head.

"Come on! Didn't I sound like an old English dude?"

"Nope."

The looming hotel grew as they got closer. With the full moon popping in and out behind passing clouds, it seemed to be very European. The only thing missing was the fog.

Meagan pulled up to the front entrance and slipped the engine into park. A valet opened Chris's door and said, "Chris Burrows!"

"Hey, howzit going?" said Chris, trying not to sound hurt as he moved his legs to get out. His muscles had stiffened sitting in the car.

"I saw the game. Are you okay?" asked the valet.

"Yeah, I'll be fine," he said.

Meagan was already squeezing past the valet to give Chris a chance to get organized without an audience. "Would you like to grab our bags? There are only two in the back," she said, smiling and moving the valet towards the back.

She quickly turned around when the valet was at the back and gave Chris an arm to pull up on. She could see the pain written all over his face. She bit her tongue instead of lecturing him on the fine points of her side of the fighting argument.

Chris palmed the eager valet some bills and asked him to park the truck for them.

Arriving at midnight meant there were no lineups at check-in, so within minutes the valet had them up to the room. Parking the vehicle could wait – talking to a hockey hero couldn't. The whole way up the elevator and down the hall, the youth chatted about the game, spouting off statistics and opinions. Chris and Meagan let him go on. It looked like Chris had fans everywhere. He kept his arm around Meagan's shoulder as if in love, but by the weight she was holding up she knew it wasn't just love.

"Thanks, man," said Chris, as the door flung open to their room.

"If I sneak my phone in tomorrow, can I get a picture of us together?" he asked shyly.

"You bet," Chris said, shutting the door as quick as possible.

Meagan had already moved into the expansive room. It was one of the premier suites she had helped redesign and she was admiring the final product. It was the size of three regular suites with a separate bedroom and bath. The colours, fabrics and furniture were fantastic. Over by the floor to ceiling window was a wine bucket with a bottle of white wine chilling and beside it, a tray of cheese and fruit courtesy of the manager.

Chris regained his composure and came into the room. Cold sweat was forming on his forehead. The pain was creeping through the painkillers.

Meagan turned and looked at him. He could tell by the look on her face she was proud of something.

"Did you design this?" he asked, taking in the surroundings while easing his coat from his shoulders.

"Yeah," she said almost giddily. "It was one of the first things I did out of school. I didn't see this room done though. I think it looks great. I didn't know it was…"

She looked at him across the room and stopped talking. He was just standing there looking at her and not where her arms were waving. "Are you okay?" she said.

He walked to her and stood as close to her as physically possible. He took her hands in his and brought them to his lips and kissed them both. "The room is lovely, but the moon is casting you in a sexy glow."

She looked into his eyes and slowly moved her hands up to his face and drew his lips onto hers. The kiss was electric. He put his hands on her ribs with his thumbs brushing the base of her breasts sending waves of desire through her body. Her hand touched his forehead and she pulled away at the touch of the sweat.

"Holy cow! Are you in shock?" she said, as her senses came back. His face was very pale.

She pulled his hands away and moved him quickly to the sofa to sit down knowing if he passed out he would hit the ground worse than he did at the game.

Meagan dashed to the mini-bar and poured a big glass of water and came back.

"I'm fine. I'm fine," he protested. "But I could use the painkillers the doctor gave me.

"Where are they?" she asked.

"My jacket pocket," he said, as he drank some of the water.

Meagan quickly gave him the vile of pills and sat down beside him. He swallowed a few and smiled as he handed her the empty glass.

Meagan brought the tray of fruit and cheese closer. "Maybe we should slow down. Do you want a glass of wine?"

"Yeah, good idea," he said. He winced as he shifted his weight to get more comfortable.

Meagan went to the wine bucket and pulled out the wine to inspect the label. "This looks nice. I'll pour a couple of glasses."

As she went about opening the bottle and before pouring the wine she looked over at Chris. He had leaned his head back and shut his eyes. She only poured one glass, sat down next to him and had a few sips. As he started to relax, the pain softened from his face. She looked at it and started counting scars and stopped. Instead, she admired the jawbone, the perfect lips, the dark eyebrows, the earlobes…she had to stop. Nothing was going to happen tonight.

When she figured the painkillers were working, she put down her glass and stood up.

"Chris," she said gently. "Chris. Let me help you to bed."

His eyes flickered as he moaned. "Oh no. This isn't what was supposed to happen tonight."

"I know," she said smiling as she moved him towards the bedroom "You should see what I was going to wear to bed."

He stopped and shut his eyes as if in pain. "Now that hurt!"

"Don't worry, I'll be here tomorrow," she kissed him on the cheek and left to bring in his bag. She gave him a few minutes then came back in. He was standing there in his boxers trying to undo the chest brace.

"Are you supposed to sleep with that on or off?"

"Off. But I can't get the Velcro, why would they put it on the back like this?"

"So I can be in control," she said, with a hint of meanness in her voice.

The brace fell to the floor exposing the most stunning male chest Meagan had ever had within reach. She ran her hands down his muscular chest but stopped short fearing she would hurt him.

He said, "Why did you stop?"

"Because – can you believe it, I'm afraid I'm going to hurt...a defenceman." She stepped back smiling and said, "I'm going to finish my wine. I'll let you get settled and then I'll be in."

"Meagan," he said, as she moved towards the door. "Thanks for being so understanding."

She smiled back at him and shut the door.

Meagan finished her wine with a couple of chunks of cheese and a few green grapes then turned off the lights. When she walked in, he was sound asleep. A marching band could do loops through the room and he would have slept through it. She slipped unnoticed between the sheets on the far side of the king-size bed and fell asleep instantly.

CHAPTER NINE

On cue, Meagan woke up at 6 a.m. Chris was still asleep and she didn't want to disturb him. She quietly slipped out of bed and into her running gear. A quick note to let him know she didn't abandon him was left on the nightstand. She was sure she could get a good run in before he woke up.

From the main entrance, she ran down the steps to the golf course hidden under a thick blanket of snow. She had run enough races in Banff to know she could easily get in an hour by running to the end of the golf course then dodge out onto the Goat Creek Trail...that is as long as other people had been out to trample it since the last snowfall.

It was a great morning for a run. The air was still and very crisp. The sun was still a long way from peeking over the summits. Her breath hung behind her in the frozen air as she broke into her favourite pace. The resident herd of elk on the fourth fairway watched her but knew she was of no threat. Hunting in the national park is forbidden and the herd knew it. As she ran along the fairways she considered taking up the game. *Maybe I should learn the game and find a golf pro to date instead. They don't fight – do they?* she laughed to herself.

Meagan looped the golf course and started up the Goat Creek trail. Cross-country skiers had a set track and hikers had trampled down a trail too, but it was tough to run. After a kilometre of arguing with the uneven footing, she turned back. She decided to pick up the pace instead of going the extra distance.

By the time she got back to the hotel she was sweating and exhausted and a little chilled. She hadn't brought enough warm clothes for mountain running. Walking briskly through the lodge, she finally noticed all the Christmas decorations that festooned the common areas. With Cottonwood taking up so much time, she totally gapped on thinking about the season only a few weeks away. She picked up a copy of the newspaper and headed for the elevator.

As the elevator slipped past the lower floors, she flipped through the paper looking at the headlines. When she saw the sports section, she stopped cold. Looking back at her was a picture of herself on the cover.

"Local girl nets Burrows," stated the big black bold print.

"Mom's going to shit!" she moaned out loud.

The elevator doors opened, and she walked down the hall and quietly entered their suite. There were no sounds, so she placed the paper on the table and glanced in the bedroom. Chris had rolled over but was still asleep. Meagan walked past him into the bathroom and shut the door.

The bathroom was her favourite place in the room. She spared no expense in designing it. The thick shale-tiled floor was heated which felt great on her cold wet feet. The over-sized shower was two walls of clear glass and two of the same shale as the floor. She stepped in and turned on the water. Jets of water came from the stone walls and the ceiling. The stall was so big that a small stone bench sat at the end where a person could sit and be hit by the pounding water from all sides.

Meagan cranked up the heat to warm up her frozen body causing the glass to steam up. She stood there with her eyes shut with her face in the stream of droplets, oblivious to the movement in the room.

Chris opened the shower door and Meagan spun around to see him coming in. He stopped in his tracks as if waiting to be invited the rest of the way in.

She knew her mouth was wide open because water was flooding off her tongue. She quickly shut her mouth as she extended her hand towards his. He reached out and enveloped it as he stepped in and swung the door shut with the other.

They moved together and wrapped their arms around each other and hugged for a soothing long time. The water snuck between their bodies, lubricating and warming as it slid. Meagan's head was leaning against his chest; she moved her face slowly to feel the tingle of his chest hair against her cheek.

He pulled away just far enough to lean down and kiss her lips with a wide-open mouth. She responded and kissed him deeply. Meagan's heart was racing, far faster than during the sprint she just came from and her breathing was shallow. His hands moved from her back and he easily cupped her slippery breasts. He tried to bend his head to kiss her nipples but he flinched, his bruised ribs were too tender. Meagan gently pushed him towards the seat and sat him down in the heated spray. His lips were right at nipple height. She straddled his legs as he pulled her close to enjoy her perky nipples. She held the back of his head pulling him onto her breasts. She was moving over him, moving back and forth as if music was dictating her beat. She was anticipating what came next.

Slowly she moved further and further down until he was totally in her. His hands moved from her breasts and grabbed onto her hips. His firm hold guided her up and down. The water beat on the back of her head and sprayed over her shoulders. He leaned back enough to be looking straight up at her eyes but they were shut. Her head tilted back as she arched and bucked to the rhythm of the music thrashing through her veins. The beat got faster and harder until he pulled her down hard and kept her there. She wrapped her arms tightly around his neck and froze, enjoying and sharing the exhilarating sensation.

They were both breathing hard but slowed quickly. The water was still pounding on her back. Chris opened his eyes and looked around him. Reaching the soap; he lathered her back, then her arms and then around to her front. He cleansed her, gently rubbing her entire body. They stood up so he could rub down her legs then her feet.

She took the soap from his hand. To gladly reciprocate she walked behind him to reach up and rub his large muscular back. She was careful as she moved to his front so as not to rub too hard where the bruising of the ribs shone through his skin. The hair on his chest lathered as she made large circles over his pecs. She lathered her hands and slowly worked down his chiselled butt. She rubbed his rock-hard legs to finish off.

Not a word was spoken the entire encounter. Chris finally took the soap from her hand and put it back in the dish.

"That…was by far the best morning shower I have ever had," he said, as he held her in his arms under the spray. Then he laughed, "I have never been so dirty and so clean at the same time!"

They sat in the spray for a few more minutes, neither of them wanted their first lovemaking to end. Eventually, the water was turned off and wrapped in thick fleece robes they flopped on the bed together.

Meagan was on her back looking up at him, smiling. Then she said, "Your ribs. Don't they hurt?"

He was propped on one elbow while the other hand moved wet locks of red hair off Meagan's forehead. "Maybe great sex is the cure. They feel pretty good actually."

"It was probably the heat of the water," she said scientifically. "I need to design more showers with benches."

Chris reached down to the belt holding Meagan's housecoat and slipped it open so she lay there exposed.

"I'm pretty sure it was the great sex…on the bench."

Meagan smiled naughtily up at him and untied his belt too.

It was nearly noon when they finally emerged from the hotel room – both smiling from ear to ear. Meagan was famished and needed to eat if she thought she was going to continue at that rate of lovemaking. As she stepped into the elevator her cell phone in her pocket started to ring. She looked at the phone number on the display and moaned. "It's my mom," she said staring at the number.

"Aren't you going to answer it?" Chris said puzzled.

She flipped the ringer into vibrate mode and stuffed it in her pocket. "I forgot to show you the newspaper. I'm on the front page of the sports section."

Chris laughed out loud. "That's hilarious. What's wrong with that?"

The phone stopped ringing.

"Mom obviously saw the picture and the caption linking her daughter to a hockey player. She won't be happy with any man I see unless he is partner material at my dad's firm."

"Tell her I'm a lawyer in the off-season," he said as he gave her a loving shoulder check.

Meagan smiled at Chris but deep down she knew she was going to hear it. *Crap, I'm almost thirty and my mom still has control over me.*

When they reached the lobby the valet from the previous night was waiting for them.

"Chris?" he said, with his phone in hand. "How's your stay? Is there anything I can do to make it better?"

Chris quickly went into celebrity mode and was charming to the valet. "Hey man, what's your name? I'm sorry I didn't catch it last night."

"Jordan," said the beaming young man.

"Jordan, hey listen, can you line me up a cab that will drive us around town for the day? I don't want my girlfriend to have to find parking spots. If you can line that up, I'll get the office to ship you an autographed jersey."

Jordan's eyes popped, and his jaw dropped. "Not a problem!"

He started to dash off, but Chris grabbed him by the sleeve. "Wait, don't you want to use that thing?"

Chris was pointing at the phone.

"Oh, oh yeah right."

Meagan was standing there the whole time and took Jordan's phone and took a bunch of shots. She figured she better play along like a nice girlfriend. *Ya never know when the media will be taking photos to splash where your mom might see it.*

Chris signed a few autographs and smiled for a few more selfies while they waited for the cab.

A shiny red cab pulled up and Jordan jumped out into the row of waiting cars to flag him over. They had a quick word about the arrangement and the driver nodded his head and said, "Cool," and the charm began to pour out.

He opened the back door with fanfare and said, "Mr. Burrows, my name is Curtis and it's my pleasure to help you today. Is there anywhere you'd like to go first?"

The men let Meagan get in the car first and Chris followed in beside her, putting an arm around her shoulder. She casually rested her hand on his denim-clad thigh.

As Curtis settled into the front seat Chris said, "Yeah Curtis, first, it's Chris, not Mr. Burrows and this is Meagan, and she is very hungry."

"No problem, man."

Curtis got out his cell phone and before merging onto the road, he lined up lunch.

Chris leaned over and gave Meagan a soft peck on the temple. "Thanks," he whispered.

"Thanks for what?" she whispered back.

"For lining up this weekend. I'm loving this. The town and the people are all fabulous."

"After lunch do you want to see some of the sites?"

"Sure."

"Are you afraid of heights?"

"No."

Meagan spoke loud enough for the driver to hear, "Curtis? After lunch, can you take us up to the gondola? Then to Tunnel Mountain for a short hike. Then, you decide where we should go for a nice private dinner. Something nice featuring the local cuisine on Main Street might be hard to arrange but give it a try. Okay?"

"Sounds like a plan," said Curtis realizing one of them was not a tourist.

The car turned onto the bridge on Banff Avenue to get across the Bow River. Fresh snow had fallen, and elk tracks could be seen trailing across the thick ice from one bank to the other. Meagan pointed out some of the local ungulates as they chewed on low bushes on the opposite bank. One lone male who hadn't shed his enormous rack of antlers for the season yet stood amidst a half dozen females.

"That old buck has lived in Banff longer than most of the townspeople," said Curtis.

"What?" said Meagan surprised. "Is that Alfred?"

"Yeah!" Curtis said even more surprised than her. "He's like 9 years old."

"Try at least 12. I first saw him when I came out to go skiing on Easter Break in first year."

"Whoa," Curtis said, bobbing his head.

"You name your elk?" Chris asked.

"You say that like we are weird or something?" said Meagan. "We only name the notorious ones."

"What's he notorious for?"

"Procreating on Main Street in front of all the tourists," laughed Curtis as he stopped in front of a restaurant. Still laughing he said, "Julie knows you are coming and is holding a table for you. Here's my number, call me when you want to resume your journey."

The door to the Italian pizzeria opened and the warm scent of fresh dough and herbs wafted onto the street reminding Meagan how hungry she was.

The restaurant was packed but as arranged, a lone table for two against the far wall was open. The two sat down and took off their coats and smiled at one another.

A pizza to share was ordered but first, they nibbled on a plate full of calamari to stop the growling in Meagan's stomach.

Chris put down his fork and leaned across the table to talk quietly to Meagan. "You are too much fun to wake up to."

Meagan's mouth was full of squid and she blushed as he continued. "I can't wait for tomorrow morning! Maybe I should..."

Just then the pizza arrived and he had to stop talking dirty. It wasn't something Meagan usually did but it was fun with him. But now she was worried about how to top this morning's escapade.

Lunch went quickly. Meagan noticed a few guys looking at Chris like he was a celebrity, but no one asked for autographs or photos.

As Chris paid for the lunch, Meagan texted Curtis. She noticed there were eight calls on her phone, mostly from her mom. She considered calling her but decided against it. If her mom was that worried, at some point she would call Ben and he would set her straight.

As they waited at the curb, she decided to call Ben.

"Hey cover girl, how's the weekend going!"

"Totally great. You saw the photo?"

"Yeah, what a rip-off! They cut me out!" he said in a mock whine. "Did mom call you?"

"Yes, but I didn't answer any of her calls. Is she mad?" she asked, as she strolled a short distance from Chris.

"I don't know...I've avoided her calls too," he said, through his laughter. "I'm not covering your ass on this one."

"Thanks a lot! That's the last game you're going to," she threatened.

Curtis drove up and Chris waved her over. "If you do get stuck talking to her, tell her I'm back Monday and I'll deal with her then."

"Enjoy your last days of freedom. Oh – and it's a good picture of you."

"Thanks," she ended the call and turned it off. *Shit! I'm in shit when I get home!*

When she got in the car, Chris put his thumb between her eyes and pressed gently. "Quit furrowing that brow."

"You don't know my mom."

"Yet," he said smiling.

CHAPTER TEN

Normally Meagan wouldn't bother going up the gondola at Sulphur Mountain. It was something tourists did, not people who grew up in the area. But she figured it was a quick and easy way for Chris to see the splendour of the Canadian Rockies.

While they had lunch, Curtis raced over and bought their tickets and arranged for a private gondola to the top. They both sat with their backs to the mountain so they could watch the expanding horizon as they went up.

The view from the apex was spectacular and Chris was overwhelmed by the grandeur. He took tons of pictures of the snow-capped peaks against the deep blue sky. When a hockey fan asked if he could have a picture taken with Chris, he obliged but made the man take a few pictures of Chris with Meagan first.

Meagan named all the peaks and explained a bit about the geology and how it was sculpted by plate tectonics and glaciations. Chris was enthralled and took it all in.

Standing in the line to ride back down, Chris was like a boy in a toyshop. "This is fantastic! I don't know how long I've wanted to come here, and it finally happened. It's spectacular."

Curtis was waiting at the base and as planned, fresh cappuccinos were waiting in the backseat as they hopped in.

"Curtis, you are the best," said Meagan as she sipped the frothy drink. Chris nodded at the smiling driver who was watching them in the rear-view mirror. In minutes they were at the parking lot at the trailhead.

"This is an easy trail that will only take about an hour," Meagan said as they got out of the car. She noticed Chris was looking up the steep incline. Then she remembered his ribs and they might hurt with the extra effort. "Chris, I'm sorry. If this is going to hurt your ribs, we can go do something less active."

"Hey, if what we did this morning didn't hurt, neither will this."

He gulped the last of his coffee and seeing a garbage bin, reached to toss the cup but the massive green lid wouldn't budge.

"What the hell?" he said as he jiggled the handle. "You lock your trash cans?"

Meagan laughed and reached to easily open the bin by pushing a hidden lever. "Believe it or not, the bears figured out how to open normal bins."

Oddly nobody was on the trail – just the way Meagan loved it. In the shade of the trees it was chilly but it was pleasing to both of them.

"No colder than a rink," said Chris. They walked leisurely holding hands and chatting more about the mountains, the economy of the town and his upcoming schedule.

At the viewpoint overlooking the hotel, they figured out which room was theirs and decided it was safe to walk around naked with the blinds open. A park bench was nearby so they sat in the sun to enjoy the view.

Chris reclined on the bench with his hands behind his head and his legs stretched way out into the snow. "This is fantastic. How many times have I said that today? How come you don't live here?"

Meagan was dumbfounded by the question. "I don't know why. Dad did enough work here and could afford it. Probably mom didn't want to deal with elk poop on the lawn."

"I gotta look into the real estate here."

"You know what? You can't buy anything here."

"What? Who says?" he said surprised.

"Unless you are a full-time resident, or it's a rental, you can't buy a house here. If you want something you have to buy it east of here in Canmore, out of the national park."

"That sucks."

"Yeah a bit, but Canmore is nice too. I've done a few houses there that are pretty swanky. I'll drive through it tomorrow when we head back."

They both fell silent when she mentioned the end of the vacation.

"Aw, now why did you have to say that?" Chris said in a depressed tone. "I didn't think about hockey all day."

She laughed a tiny bit. "And I didn't think about work either."

Chris put his hand on Meagan's knee, smiled at her and looked into her eyes. "I think we are starting something pretty special this weekend. But do you think we might be doing something that won't work? Do you think we can have a relationship that will withstand the distance? And, how can we do it? I know your career is important and you are establishing a good company. I can't expect you to drop it and move around the continent every time I get traded."

His comments were valid and sunk deep into her chest. Did she let her guard down, sleep with this guy only to get dumped on top of Tunnel Mountain? He wasn't dumping her - was he? She blurted out without thinking, "Are you dumping me?"

"Oh heck! No! Not at all," he said earnestly. "But when you brought up going home tomorrow it made me realize we are going to have a lot of goodbyes."

She didn't want to have the mood go flat so she quickly jumped up and straddled him like she did that morning, but this time there was plenty of fabric in the way.

"Ah yes there will be goodbyes, but just think, there will be just as many - Why…hello there." she leaned down and planted a big kiss on his lips that he took lovingly. She pulled back far enough to whisper, "Hi honey, I'm home."

He wrapped his arms around her and they continued kissing.

As he pulled away, he said. "If you are willing to try, then so am I. We can sit down with a calendar and plan out when we can see each other. If it doesn't work, we will worry about it then."

"It's a deal," she said as she stood up. "Now, we have to high tail it down the path before it gets dark."

The conversation on the way back down the trail was quieter, both of them were thinking about how this relationship was going to work. She was already convinced he was worth running to the ends of the earth for. But she wasn't sure if he felt the same way and that worried her into silence.

Curtis was waiting for them at the bottom of the trail and welcomed them like old friends.

"Hey Chris, did you like it?"

They bumped fists together like cool guys do as they meet on the street.

"Yeah man, you are so lucky. You could climb any mountain any time. I've never been to the top of a mountain and look – today I got to go to the top of two." Chris looked towards Cascade Mountain to the north. "Have you ever been to the top of that one?"

"Yeah, I climbed the icefall yesterday," he said, excited to tell the hockey star about his passion. Chris stood there listening with his mouth hanging open as Curtis told the story, waving his arms and mimicking hitting the blue ice with an axe.

"Climbing a vertical rink? That's fricken awesome."

The three of them climbed into the car and Curtis kept talking about the ice climb. Meagan didn't mind that he was monopolizing the conversation. She was still thinking about their future. Chris sensed she was thinking about their conversation and rested his large hand on her thigh and squeezed it gently. She looked up at him and his warm smile made her feel better. She smiled back.

Unfortunately, Curtis couldn't get reservations at the best restaurant in town but there was room at their hotel's exquisite dining room.

As they stepped out of the car, they thanked Curtis warmly. Meagan was pleased he was such a cool guy and didn't invade on their day. She started to walk into the building and assumed Chris was with her, but he was still talking to Curtis in what looked like a private conversation. Curtis was smiling and nodding his head, agreeing to something.

"Later man," said Chris, as he walked towards Meagan who was standing at the door.

"Anytime Chris. Bye, Meagan," he yelled at Meagan.

She smiled and waved back.

"What was that last bit?" she asked, as they walked towards the elevators.

"What was what?"

"You guys, just now. What were you talking about?"

"Oh, that. He wants an autographed jersey, but didn't want you to hear him asking for something so dorky."

"Aw, that's not dorky. Just wait till he wears it to the King Eddie the first night. His buddies will be so jealous."

They went to their room and the light on the phone was flashing red. Meagan was relieved to find out the message was about the dinner reservations and not her mom tracking her down. They had just enough time to quickly freshen up before heading down to the dining room.

As requested, the most intimate and scenic table was reserved for them. The table was against the window and beyond that was the snow-covered veranda and golf course. The sun had set hours ago but the full moon in the cloudless night sky reflected so much light off the snow, that the trees cast shadows. The host sat them down with a flourish as he snapped their napkins before draping them across their laps.

They sat across from each other looking out the window.

"Last winter I came out with a bunch of friends on a weekend like this," said Meagan, as Chris stared at her from across the small table. "We were staying at the hostel and we cross country skied all day. We had supper and were sitting around the fireplace yakking when suddenly the clouds peeled off the moon and it was like daylight - like this. Someone suggested we go for a midnight ski. Nobody argued, so we all put our skis on and headed down to the river. We skied for hours along the frozen river. A chinook was blowing and the trees were swaying in the warm breeze. It was fantastic. We didn't hit the sack until three in the morning."

"You skied until three?"

"Aw man, that's nothing! Back in my university days, we partied with the elk all night long. That's how come I know Alfred so well."

"Tell me more about the wild days," Chris said smiling, waiting to hear the dirt.

"I just did!" she said laughing. "I'm not telling you anything. I don't want to scare you off with stories from my granola days."

Chris knew he wouldn't hear about it. He looked out the window to see five deer slowly walk across the drifted lawn to nibble on some shrubs. Smiling at the vision he turned back to see Meagan staring at him.

"What?" he said. A quizzical look was on his face.

"What?" she answered back.

"Why are you staring at me like that, do I have salad dressing on my face?"

"No," she said softly, leaning forward and whispering. "I was admiring how handsome you look in this light."

He leaned forward. "If you say stuff like that, I say let's skip supper and see how you look in the moonlight in our room!"

"No way man! I haven't eaten here in years. I'm not moving until I'm fed!"

Chris pretended to wave over the waiter, but ironically their meals were already on the way.

As they finished their dinners, the waiter came up to Chris and whispered something in his ear Meagan couldn't hear. Chris looked up at him rather concerned-like and as he put his napkin alongside his plate the waiter pulled his chair out for him to rise. He said thanks to the waiter then turned to Meagan. "Can you believe it, I left my credit card in the taxi! I hope Curtis is as honest as he looks! I'll be right back."

Chris weaved through the tables and over to the hostess desk where Curtis was waiting.

"Hey Curtis, any luck?" said Chris. They walked out into the hall out of Meagan's view.

"No problem," he said, smiling as he reached into his pocket.

He pulled out a slender long distinctive blue box and handed it to Chris along with his credit card and receipt.

Chris opened the box and inside was a sparkling diamond tennis bracelet.

"Oh man, she's going to flip! This is exactly what I wanted. Thanks, man. You are the best! Here's something for your troubles." He reached into his pocket and gave Curtis an envelope from the hotel room. Inside was enough cash to cover Curtis's rent for a month. Curtis didn't even look inside the envelope; he knew there would be a generous tip. He didn't bother telling Chris he went to Calgary and back for the gift. Meagan would figure that part out.

Chris slipped the box into his breast pocket, thanked his friend again then returned to the table.

"Is the card still hot from all the transactions?" Meagan asked jokingly.

"No kidding. I'll know how honest he is when the bill comes in."

The dishes had been taken away and all that remained was their wine glasses and dessert menus.

"Are you ordering a dessert?" asked Chris.

She smiled and said. "I'd love to, but I swore off desserts a long time ago."

"It's not part of your running diet?"

"Nope, is it part of your hockey diet?"

He shook his head as he folded up the menu. "Nope, but it's fun to look."

They finished their wine and left the near-empty restaurant. Once again, they didn't notice the time fly by.

They walked through the long halls of shops that had closed for the night, peering in at the mountain-shaped crystal figurines in one shop, the mountainous landscape paintings in another and the fine woollen sweaters in another. Chris had his arm wrapped around her and held her at the waist. She wrapped her arm around him but held him gently still worried about the ribs.

Meagan was in heaven. She couldn't remember the last time she had enjoyed the day so much. Especially with the fantastic shower she had earlier. It was hard to believe it happened only that morning and maybe there was more to come.

He must have sensed what she was thinking and said, "If I walk any more, I'll work up an appetite. Let's go upstairs and see what's on TV."

"TV???" Meagan said in horror.

He looked down at her and smiled. "Not."

When they walked into the room, the lights were on low, the fireplace was glowing, and Van Morrison was singing softly from the speakers in the corner of the room. Over on the coffee table was a bottle of red wine already decanted and a tray of chocolates – with a note saying it was courtesy of Darren.

Chris's eyebrows lifted as he saw the layout. "Well, either you have a lot of pull or I've been staying in the wrong hotels all my life!"

He moved over to the table, poured two glasses of wine. With a glass of wine in one hand and a chocolate in the other, he walked over to Meagan who was standing by the fireplace. "For you, my dear," he said, as he brought the chocolate to her lips.

She opened her mouth and he gently slid it in then bent down and kissed her lips. "A sweet for my sweet."

Oh, my goodness! she thought to herself. *This guy is corny and I'm lovin' it!*

Chris had a sip of wine then walked back to Meagan, took her glass and put it on the table. He took hold of both her hands and started to move with the music.

"It's a marvellous night for a moon dance," crooned Van Morrison and they slowly danced entwined in the moonbeams pouring into the room. She raised her nose close to his neck and he tipped his head so his chin would rest on her forehead. His skin was warm and soft. His body felt so right wrapped around hers. Finally, she was dancing with a man who was taller than her. It was a moment she never wanted to forget.

They stopped dancing and Chris looked down at Meagan. "Remember on the hike, we decided it was safe to run around the room naked?"

She smiled a shy grin, "Yeah."

As he started unbuttoning her shirt he said, "Wanna?"

"I can run fast you know," she said, as she started on his belt.

"But I can block pretty good," he said, as he slid her blouse off her shoulders exposing her silk bra.

As he started to undo her pants, she tugged his cashmere sweater up from his waist and kept pulling up, pulling his hands off her pants. She was smiling at him looking him straight in the eyes. As he lifted his arms over his head so she could continue pulling his sweater over his head, she quickly pulled it up to shoulder height and pulled it down over his head like hockey players do in a fight. She had him trapped in his own fight tactics.

"Hey!" came a muffled shout from inside the sweater as she stepped back laughing. "You brat. I'll call for a ref!"

He quickly tossed the sweater to the ground and lunged forward. She suddenly realized she was in trouble and let out a squeal and turned to run. He hopped over the couch like it was a bench and caught up to her as she dashed into the bedroom. A few feet from the bed he leapt at her, grabbed her in mid-air, spun and landed on the bed with her on top of him.

She tried to get away, but her laughter weakened her moves. Finally, she quit struggling and they both laid there laughing at the silliness.

"Give up?" he said, as he held her tight.

"Give," she said huffing.

"Ha!" he said in a mock tough-guy voice. "Puny runner no match for big defenceman."

She sat up and as he tried to sit up, he fell back holding his ribs moaning and laughing at the same time. "I take that back. Puny runner takes down wimpy defenceman."

"Oh no! What did I do? Oh no, did I hurt your ribs?"

Chris flinched a bit as he rolled to get up holding his ribs gently. "I'm alright. I forgot about those things. I think I'll tackle you some other time though."

"You wait here," she said, as she jumped up.

Meagan ran back into the living room to retrieve the wine and chocolates. She set them next to the bed then stacked the pillows at the head of the bed for him to lean against. She handed him a glass of wine then slipped a chocolate in his mouth before leaning over to kiss his lips and quietly saying in a sexy voice, "Puny runner makes big defenceman feel better."

Meagan proceeded to kiss his neck feeling how much warmer he was after their chase. She moved kiss by kiss down to his chest to where his heart thumped loudly. She slowly moved her face to feel the tickle of his chest hairs as they brushed her cheeks. As one hand caressed one of his muscular pecs, she tenderly bit and kissed the other. He put his hands on her shoulders, obviously enjoying the foreplay and the visions of what was to follow. The moon blushed behind the clouds.

Meagan woke to the touch of Chris's hand on her shoulder. During the night she turned to sleep on her side. She had never been much for cuddling all night because she feared whoever she was with would see her sleep with her mouth wide open. Not that she did, but then again, maybe she did!

She turned and smiled at him. It was still dark out, but they needed an early start if they wanted to get him to the airport by noon.

He smiled as he moved her ever-present hair from her forehead. "Now look whose sleeping in?" he teased.

She lifted her head and saw it was 6:05 a.m. "Come on. Five minutes is sleeping in? After how long you kept me up last night I should be allowed to sleep till noon."

"Me? It was you," he protested. "I wanted to come back and sleep."

He put his arm up to shield his face from a flying pillow.

"Wanna go for a quick run? 45 minutes – max."

Meagan was always up for a run. "That sounds great – but you might have trouble getting 45 in. The air is colder and thinner up here. If you aren't used to it, it's a killer. Those ribs might get mad."

As their shoes hit the snow-covered path beyond the parking lot, the streetlights faded, and the pre-dawn glow took over. They didn't talk much, instead listened to the crunch of the snow and their rhythmic breathing. The trail had some hills to put Chris's bruised ribs and lungs to the test. But he said he didn't mind because it was like an extra hard workout.

When they got back to the parking lot Meagan had worked up a glow but Chris was soaked with sweat.

"That was a great run. Thanks," he huffed as he patted her shoulder. "We gotta do that again."

"I'd love to. We'll pencil it in on the schedule," she said as she gave him a little hip check.

They showered together but it wasn't nearly as exciting as the previous morning. They both realized time was not on their side and moved along quickly. They stuffed their bags and got ready to leave the room. As Chris put on his coat, the blue box in the breast pocket slipped out.

"Oh!" he said, as he swooped it behind his back. "Stop everything. I almost forgot something."

She looked up from tying her shoes.

"I want to give you something that I hope you will wear to remember me," he said, as he handed her the box.

Meagan was dumbfounded. She instantly recognized the blue Tiffany's box and knew it was jewelry. "Chris, oh ...oh you shouldn't have. I don't deserve anything."

"Just open it. I think you will like it."

She opened the box and resting on the crushed white silk cushion was the most beautiful bracelet she had ever seen. She caught her breath as the light skipped from diamond to diamond. "Oh, my God! Chris! I can't take this...it's far too expensive." She shut the box and pushed it into his hand. "I can't take that!"

Chris opened the box and took the bracelet out and gently took her hand in his and looped the diamond-studded white gold around her wrist and did up the clasp.

"Meagan," he said softly as he held her hands to his lips and kissed them tenderly. The bracelet rolled down her arm, twinkling as it moved. "I am falling hard for you and don't want to lose you to some handsome carpenter or lawyer. I want you to wear this to remind you that...that, I will be back. The rest of December I am booked solid with games and I promised mom I'd be home for Christmas. They only give us a few days. I want to give this to you as a 'pre' Christmas present."

Meagan swallowed hard and tears started to spill down her cheeks. "Wow," she said softly. "I was so afraid you didn't like me as much as I like you. I've been trying not to fall for you."

"So, you promise not to hook up with a tradesman?" he asked, half-joking.

"Do you promise not to hook up with a groupie in another city?" she asked, seriously back.

"I promise."

"I promise too."

After a kiss, Meagan said, "Thank you very much for the bracelet. I love it and I won't take it off...except when I go over to my parent's place."

Chris laughed. "I have to meet this mother of yours. She sounds downright scary."

"I'll introduce you someday, but I'd stay in your hockey padding for that date!"

Breakfast was a quick muffin in the lobby cafe and coffee was bought to go. By 9:05 a.m., the truck was pointing east.

Meagan quickly drove through Canmore to show him the town and the types of homes being built.

As they resumed the highway drive, Chris said, "Yup, nice houses, but I think I'll find a way to get something in Banff instead."

"Good luck! The only way is to retire there a very wealthy man," laughed Meagan.

"I will," he said nodding. "I'll get something there and my place in The Bahamas. Then I'll have the best of two worlds."

They arrived at the airport with just enough time for him to clear customs, so she pulled up to the curb to let him out at the departure entrance. As he pulled his bag from the back of the truck, Meagan stood on the curb with a lump in her throat. He shut the door and turned and saw her standing there with a hurt look on her face. He put down his bag, walked the two steps and wrapped his arms around her and pulled her tight to his chest.

"Hey, remember what you said on the hike at Tunnel Mountain?"

"What?" Her voice was muffled because she didn't pull away from the comfort of his coat.

"That this isn't just a goodbye." He pulled her head off his chest and continued, "It's getting us ready for the next hello."

She smiled, but a tiny tear dripped from her eye down her cheek. He quickly wiped it away and kissed her strongly.

She put on a brave face and smiled. "You're right. We can do this."

He reached into his pocket and pulled out a hockey schedule. "Here, check and see if my home schedule fits in with your schedule and see if you can spare a few days coming my way. We can either go to The Bahamas or I'd love to show you Boston. Heck, I hear there is a good race there that goes near my house. You could use it as a training run."

She furrowed her brow. "What? The Boston Marathon is what I'm trying to qualify for!"

He put his thumb between her eyebrows and gently pushed on the wrinkle. "I know, Sweetheart. I'm not just a hockey bum," he said, sarcastically.

The lines on her face smoothed out with the smile. "I didn't realize you were teasing."

He kissed her one more time on the cheek and picked up his bag. "Check that schedule and call me, okay?"

"'Kay."

"And, I never have my phone on me so leave a message and I'll call you as soon as I can. Okay?"

"'Kay."

He started to walk away and stopped. "This has been the greatest weekend ever. Thanks."

She nodded and said, "Same for me. I can't wait till we say hello again!"

"Next time I'll make sure my ribs aren't broken!"

The parking guard started walking towards Meagan to get her to keep moving and she got the hint.

Chris smiled and waved, then turned to walk into the terminal. As the doors slide shut behind him she put the vehicle into drive, the new bracelet rolled out from under her sleeve and glittered in the sunlight. As she moved from the curb Meagan said to no-one in particular, "Wait till the girls see this!"

CHAPTER ELEVEN

When Meagan stepped out of her truck at the house, she finally realized how tired she was. Staying up most of the night to frolic with a hockey player was more taxing than she thought.

As usual, she used the office entrance to enter the house and out of habit walked directly into her office to check for messages on the landline or deliveries. As she reached her desk – she stopped short.

Nothing appeared wrong, but she smelt the air. She kept sniffing, turning her head left and right. It was subtle, but it was there. It smelt like stale aftershave. Even worse it smelt like the muck Russell marinates in.

She decided she was over-tired and dismissed the crazy idea that someone had been in her office and who cares, she trusted all her employees. She looked around the rest of the office and didn't see anything to be alarmed about then settled into her chair to finally go through the messages on her phone.

"Meagan, it's your mother." As if Meagan didn't know that voice by now. "I'd like to know why there is a likeness of you on the cover of the newspaper! Call me back."

"Oh yeah," Meagan said as she pushed delete. "Like I want to stick my head in the mouth of a frickin lion. And it was the sports section. Not the whole paper!"

The rest of the messages were far more positive about her cover photo. Most were from her running buddies who were lining up the next run so they could hear all about what she was doing in Banff.

And, that run was the next morning. The sun wasn't warming the air yet at 7 a.m. so arriving at the Y was nasty. Most fair-weathered runners

70

would be scared away but not Meagan's friends. They were congregating in the entrance to the Y. When she walked in, the teasing about the newspaper photo started. Meagan didn't say a word; all she did was smile like a cat. She raised her arm and jiggled the bracelet out from under her running jacket. The voices stopped briefly, caught behind gasps. Then the squeals of delight and giggles of joy filled the room.

"Come on!" she said as she turned for the door, pushing the gaggle in front of her, "I'll tell you all about it on the run!"

The pace was fast as Meagan told them almost everything. She started with the hockey game and how she felt when he got hit, the ride out, the disappointment of him dozing off, the run…she skipped the shower scene, and on into the rest of the weekend's activities. She slowly went over the presentation of the bracelet and the girls moaned in unison when she told him what he said.

It was Lizzie who hit the sombre note first. "Our plan backfired. She found the man to marry, but I'll bet we lose her to the States."

"Wait a minute! I'm not going anywhere. We said we would try this long-distance thing but it's probably not going to work."

Gloria knew the value of the jewelry, "Hey don't be such a dunce, no guy gives a girl a five-grand trinket to just be long-distance friends. He's expecting you to relocate."

"No! We discussed this. Well, not very much. But, he isn't expecting me to relocate."

"Will you?" asked Lizzie.

"We are not that far in the relationship," argued Meagan.

Emma piped in, "I bet she goes."

"Same," said Gloria.

"Same." chimed Lizzie and Robin.

"If I do, it's Boston and he says he has a great place on the route," she said using his line.

They all laughed and agreed she should go and preferably before the next marathon.

"What a bunch of shallow friends you are!" she snapped as they planned who slept on the floor and who got a bed.

The Cottonwood proposal wasn't due for three days but Tuesday morning the final product sat in the middle of Meagan's spotless desk. Every time there is a major proposal, her desk turns into a war zone but as usual, when the project is completed, her desk is cleaned up, signifying in her mind the completion.

She called everyone present into her office to go over the package once more. The two students sat down in the chairs while Ginny, always multi-tasking, stood in the doorway, listening as usual for the phone.

It would be nice to be swamped for once! thought Meagan. Then she noticed Dianne was missing.

"Where's Dianne?" she asked.

Ginny looked around, "She was here. DIANNE!" she yelled.

Dianne emerged from the photocopy room and sheepishly came towards Meagan's little office. Meagan watched her friend slink down the hall and felt a sense of uneasiness. Something was making her start to dislike her college pal but she couldn't put her finger on it. Besides, she was too excited about the finished proposal.

"Okay, let's get started," she said when Dianne finally leaned against the wall in the office.

As she patted the impressive bid portfolio she spoke. "This is the package I'm sending over to Cottonwood. I can't tell you how thrilled I am about the hard work you have all put in. I feel that this is an amazing design. Each hotel will be unique, yet carry some of the same custom, classic lines of the other hotels signifying their connection. I am positive our proposal is unique and that no other company will even come close to our concepts," she told them.

"You guys, if we win this contract,…if we outbid and outshine, like I really hope we will, we will finally have shaken that crummy black cloud from my shoulders. Payroll is not depending on getting this, but it will surely-to-God help! I could even pay myself for once!"

"Now," she paused looking around at the proud faces. "Is everybody satisfied with their contribution? If everybody is happy, then I'm taking this over right now."

The students looked at each other and beamed from the praise from their boss, then turned and looked at her and nodded. Ginny stepped out to answer the phone but yelled back that she thought Meagan should move her skinny ass over to Cottonwood.

Meagan looked at Dianne, waiting for her input. Dianne finally realized the roomful of people were looking and waiting for her. "Oh! Yeah. Um…it's great. I, I think it is fabulous and should finish pretty high." Dianne said in a slightly monotone voice.

Meagan couldn't believe her ears.

"Finish pretty high? Finish pretty high! That's it?" Meagan lost it. "What do you mean finish pretty high? Didn't you put in your best effort? I don't want pretty high. I can't afford to put this much effort into a bid to just finish pretty high. Dianne, didn't you put any effort into this? Have your priorities changed? Are you not part of this team?"

They were both standing now staring at each other over the heads of the students who sat staring at each other not knowing whether they should move or stay.

Dianne suddenly started to suck up to Meagan as if she finally realized

72

her job might be at stake. "Of course I tried my best. I'm afraid you are putting too much hope on this. We seem to always finish near the top and when we do, you come crashing down. Maybe we aren't..." she started to whine, "Maybe we aren't good enough to be bidding on these big parcels. Maybe we should stick with houses and small offices."

Meagan looked at Dianne in disbelief. By now the students had slipped out unnoticed and the two friends stood staring at each other. "I don't want to just do houses and small offices. I am far more capable than that and you know it. My turn will come. I need to find a way past assholes like Russell. Shit! It feels like he is stealing my work."

Dianne started to fidget. "Listen, Meagan, I'm sorry. I really hope we get it. I just don't want you to crumble if we don't, okay?" She put her hand on her friend's shoulder and smiled.

Meagan thanked her and said, "Well, that's that then. I'll take this in and see if we can finish in the top two."

"Do you want some help dropping it off?"

"Naw, I can handle it myself," said Meagan, rather deflated.

"Okay, um, sorry I got you upset," Dianne said softly as she left the office, quickly sliding in behind her desk.

Meagan stood a long time chewing on a fingernail, staring at the pile of papers and rehashing the conversation with Dianne. *Why do I always come in second? Is it a girl thing? Am I too young to be believed? No. This is the one where I am finishing first. This is the best we have ever done.*

She finished convincing herself of her potential, then went to her bathroom to freshen up. Her pale complexion was blotchy from her anger so she caked on foundation and blush to hide it

She stood staring at the reflection in the mirror for a long time and considered the conversation with Dianne. *Maybe she is right,* she thought to herself. *If I don't get this contract, I'll re-evaluate where this crappy little company is going.*

Meagan tried smiling at herself to boost her flattened ego, but it turned into a scowl. She shook her head and slowly turned from the mirror.

When she returned from the bathroom everything was piled nicely on the desk closest to the door. The proposal papers were sealed in an envelope and the thick pile of drafting pages were rolled in a cardboard tube. Dianne and Ginny were standing there waiting to see her off.

"Thanks, guys. I guess this is it," she said less than confidently. Unfortunately, the argument with Dianne knocked some wind out of her sail.

She drove to the Cottonwood office with the music cranked up to bring her out of the frump. She pulled into the parking lot and took the first available stall. Meagan walked to the passenger side of the truck and opened the back door. She tucked the tube under her arm, slung her purse over her shoulder, grabbed the fat envelope and reached to shut the door but the tube slid from under her arm and was heading for the dirty snow at her feet.

"Yikes!" squealed Meagan.

A man swooped in and grabbed the tube before it hit the slush.

Meagan spun around to see the president of Cottonwood holding the tube of blueprints.

"I'm sure you don't want these to get wet," he said, as he smiled at her.

"Thanks so much! That was a near disaster!" she said, as she realized who it was.

"Are you bringing these to Cottonwood?"

"Yeah, we were done early, and I was afraid we would start fiddling with it. This way I thought we'd get Brownie points for getting it in early."

"Yeah, I'm impressed," he said. "Let me help you bring it in."

"Thanks."

They walked into the building and took the project right up to the conference room. There the president introduced himself and extended his hand to shake hers. "I'm Bob Magrath and if I recall, you are Meagan Dunphy. You've done some great work, if I'm still recalling correctly."

"Thank you very much. I am very pleased with this proposal and I hope you like it too. I'd really like to do it for you. I mean for Cottonwood," she added blushing.

"I can't look at it right now with the closing date still a few days away it would be against protocol, but I'm looking forward to seeing it. I've also got a meeting in two minutes. Nice to meet you, Meagan."

"It was nice to meet you too Mr. Magrath."

He touched her on the shoulder, "Please, just Bob."

"Thanks, Bob," she said, grinning as he walked away.

It impressed her to see her bid sitting in such a grand conference room on such a large, glossy oak table. There had to be a dozen boardroom chairs neatly tucked under the table. "I'm coming back to see these chairs filled with smiling board members who want to sign me on!" she whispered as she left the room.

"It couldn't have gone better!" Meagan said as she filled her coffee and told it all to Ginny back at the office. "I hope they don't take long to decide, I can't stand the suspense. I think we have a chance now that he has put a name to the bid. Screw second place!"

"How long do we have to wait?" asked Ginny.

"I hope two weeks. I think they are deciding before the new year."

Christmas came and went. The office shut down for a few days so they could all enjoy the celebrations. As usual, Meagan and Ben rented a big house at the base of a ski resort in British Columbia with a group of friends for some skiing. It was good to get out on the snow and think about other things than work.

On Christmas morning she sat at the top of the mountain for a call with Chris. It was cut short by all his nieces and nephews in the background demanding his attention, but she didn't mind. They talked and laughed. That was all she needed.

But the days dragged on, she desperately wanted to hear about Cottonwood.

Finally, early in the morning of the first Friday of January, the phone rang; it was Bob Magrath, but he didn't sound pleased.

"Meagan, it's Bob Magrath."

"Bob, how nice to hear from you. Have you finished looking over the bids?"

"We have made up our minds, but I'd like you to come into the office and discuss a few things with me," he said, in a very monotone voice.

Meagan paused for a second, somewhat confused by the tone.

"Bob, is there something wrong?"

"I think so and I'd like to talk to you about it before I take the next step. Can you see me this morning?"

"Yes, I can come right now."

"Thank you," he said and hung up.

Meagan stared at her phone. She was puzzled by Magrath's call and was afraid to go see him. Something was going wrong. The contract was slipping out of her fingers.

She grabbed her purse and headed for the door without talking to anyone. Dianne looked up from her desk and saw the look on Meagan's face and she frowned too. She sensed second place was up, again.

CHAPTER TWELVE

Meagan was shown into Magrath's office where five bids and their blueprints were sprawled over a huge table. She figured they were the finalists, and she did notice hers was one of them.

Bob got up from his desk.

"Thank you for coming over so quickly. Please sit down." He motioned for her to sit in a deep brown leather chair, then swiftly shut his office door before sitting behind his desk, void of clutter.

Meagan decided to jump on the situation quickly. "Bob, I don't understand why you have called me here. You don't seem pleased with me."

He looked her straight in the eyes, took a deep breath and started to speak. "Meagan, the day I helped you in the parking lot, I got the impression that you were a hard-working young lady trying to make a go of it in the big world. You seemed dedicated, determined and trustworthy, but after what has landed on my desk, I feel you are a fraud and a cheat."

His voice started to speed up and get louder. "It is absolutely despicable that you would hand in such blatant copies of a competitor's work. It's pathetic that you would submit it on the same bid. Didn't you think we would notice your work duplicates his? I know he was your prof and assumed you would have some influence, but this is pathetic."

He was standing now, waving his arms as he spoke. Meagan sat there dumbfounded by the accusations. Her face paled and her mouth fell open and words wouldn't come out. The tongue-lashing was unbearable.

"Bob...I don't have a clue what you are talking about. Are you saying I copied Carl Russell's work?" she said, defensively and confused.

He looked at her in disbelief and scrunched up his nose. "You can't tell me that you came up with the exact same ideas as Russell who has at least twenty years of experience over you."

"WHAT! I didn't steal his work!" she said, nearly screaming as she stood up.

Bob stormed over to the table of papers and waved his arms again. "Meagan! Look at this and tell me the truth."

Meagan got up and went to the table. Out of the five packages, hers sat closer to another, it had Russell's company crest. Looking at the two side by side she was sickened to see the similarities, if not complete twins.

She shut her eyes as her head started to spin. The cover pages were almost identical in presentation. She started flipping pages in Carl's pile and then moved to the blueprints and artist renderings. They were her designs, colours, styles...everything was hers.

She stepped back and plopped into the chair, shaking her head and barely breathing. What she saw was appalling. "I did not copy his work," she said softly. She bent over to bury her face in her hands.

Neither talked for a long while, and Bob sensed what Meagan was seeing was a shock.

He talked softer this time, in a friendlier manner. "What do you mean? It's impossible that you both came up with the same ideas. The details, the colours...the materials, the theme...it's impossible. The only real difference is in your pricing. His prices are acceptable but yours are far too high. You can't seriously be asking 4.5 million. And, throwing in a transportation cost is absurd."

She lifted her head. "Transportation cost? What transportation cost? I didn't quote 4.5! I submitted 3.2!" she nearly squealed.

Bob went over to the table and grabbed her report and brought it to her. It looked like it was hers. The binder was hers, the paper, the title page, the type, everything except the project costs. Meagan flipped through the prices she knew by heart and knew this wasn't her work.

"Bob," she said finally, still shaking her head, not understanding what was happening. "These are not my numbers. It looks like it came from my shop, but it's not what I submitted. Somebody is screwing me and it's obviously Russell. But I can't prove it."

Bob sat in his chair and leaned way back and paused to think. "Interestingly, Russell's number is 3.2. Why would you suggest your old prof would do such a thing? His career is on the line. How could he manipulate your numbers? Didn't you check your work before you handed it in that day?"

"I did. I did," she said, staring into his eyes realizing he may believe her if she could prove it. Then she remembered the flash drive in her purse. "I can prove it!"

She reached into her purse and pulled out the hard-plastic case she always carries with her. Instead of a safety deposit box or a fire safe, she always kept flash drives with quotes and bids in her purse. It is never out of her sight at the office and she sleeps with her purse in her room. That way if there is a fire, she can grab the purse with the company info in it.

"I have my copy of the final bid right here. I finished it Monday night and printed it off. Then I piled it on my desk and went to bed – with my purse. Can we use your computer?"

He pushed back from his desk and got out of his chair. "I'd like to think you are telling the truth but what you are saying is going to open a can of worms."

"Bob, I've been losing out to Carl on every single important bid since I got out of school. Somehow – I think he is getting back at me," she said, as she slipped the drive into the computer.

"Getting back at you for what?" he asked.

"For not sleeping with him and then for exposing him for trying to blackmail me for my marks if I told. He lost his job at the university because of me but most people don't know that."

Her file popped up on the screen with the proper quote which was almost identical to Russell's. They looked it over, and as she said, there wasn't a transportation fee.

"But this doesn't prove that the one on the desk isn't yours. It just proves that there might have been two copies with different pricing done," he said. "That doesn't prove Russell is stealing your work. His design ideas didn't come off a computer."

"Bob, I guarantee the whole thing came from my office and went to his. Most of the design ideas came from me, not my employees. As a matter of fact, at the launch meeting when the specs were handed out, a busboy bumped into Carl and me as we spoke after the meeting. All our papers hit the floor. When I sorted mine out at home, I had duplicate copies of the architectural guidelines. Do you know if he came for another copy or called in looking for the website? If he didn't get the extras from you, then he shouldn't even know about half the concepts put into the bid. I bet..." She stopped talking in mid-sentence with her finger pointing at Bob.

He looked at her and motioned for her to continue her sentence.

"Oh shiiiit." Meagan moaned. "It's all coming to me now. How can I have been so bloody stupid? I have a mole in my company!"

She gathered her stuff as if to leave. The grief was written all over her body and leaking out her eyes but Bob stopped her and sat her down.

"Slow down. Don't blame yourself for anything yet. I'm not charging you with anything. I have faith in you, that's why I called you privately to see me. I jumped to conclusions and didn't even think that it would be the established architect doing the cheating. I sincerely apologize for assuming it was you. If you have proof of insider knowledge being shared, it has to be reported to the police. This could be a huge offence. Who do you think is sharing your information?"

"I can't believe this, but I think Dianne, my most trusted employee is selling me out," said Meagan. The tears were flowing down her face. She tried desperately not to cry but now that she realized what has been going on right in front of her, she cratered. "I'll go home and figure this out for real. …But now that I think about it, I remember the day I told Dianne that Russell's package wouldn't be complete because of the bump in the meeting room. I felt guilty that I didn't tell Carl about the misplaced guidelines, but not guilty enough to tell him. So, when Dianne questioned my designs that were based on what you required, I reminded her they were expected on the guidelines. I mumbled something about 'stupid Russell' would have mistakes and missed requirements because he didn't have the architect sheets that the specs were on. I remember Dianne looked at me funny and left the room," she stopped to breathe.

Bob sat there and let her continue.

"Now I can see so many other occasions where she and I collided on ideas. Or she paid too much attention to my work. That's why she was photocopying that student's work. She wasn't doing it for Brian. She was taking it to Carl! Oh shit! Oh shit! He was in my office! She brought that asshole in my office!"

Now she was fuming. Her hands were running through her hair, ready to pull it all out. Everything was flooding in and she couldn't stop talking. But Bob finally interrupted.

"That doesn't prove your bid was manipulated. If you printed it off on the night before you brought it in, how did the wrong information end up here?"

She sat staring into space, shaking her head slowly. "I came back from Banff on the Sunday before I handed in the package and I smelt Russell's crummy aftershave in my office. I thought I was nuts and dismissed it. She knew I was going to Banff for the weekend and knew I'd be dropping Chris at the airport Sunday afternoon. I bet that wretched bitch let him into the office! I'll bet they copied the working file off my computer, changed the data then printed out the package. She doesn't know I keep the original copy in my purse. But you're right. How did the cooked books end up here?"

Meagan held her hands over her face then looked up with a wild panicked look. "What am I going to do!" she moaned. "Maybe Ginny is in on it too! She helped Dianne gather everything up and stick it in the envelope to bring it here while I got ready. Maybe she switched it!"

Bob stayed calm through the whole blubbering speech which was rather confusing as to who was who.

"Well Meagan, we have a problem. The way I see it is you seem to be telling me the truth, but I'm afraid you are going to have to prove it. I'm sorry but the Board has already decided to go with Russell. They felt it would be the student stealing the work of the instructor not vice-versa. It sounds like the decision was a mistake. I am expected by my shareholders to have this project up and running. I'll see if we can delay the announcement though as this might get messy."

He reached for her, and as she took his hand to stand up, he wrapped his arms around her and gave her a reassuring hug. As he pulled away, he said, "I don't usually give contractors a hug, but in this case, I think it's necessary."

"Thanks," she said weakly, she was beyond tears now. "I did need that. This was supposed to be MY job — not his. I really wanted to do this one."

"I'm sorry about that. I have to admit, these designs are phenomenal. Maybe if we get this resolved soon enough, we can have his license revoked then you can take over the contract. But I can't guarantee that at all. Now, I think you should stay away from the office for a while. Maybe go home."

"The office is in my home," she said dejectedly.

"Then go to someone's house that you can trust. Grab a big cup of coffee and write down all your thoughts on this. You don't want to let anyone know you have doubts about their loyalty to you, just in case they haven't pulled all the evidence from your office yet. Then hire a lawyer and see what he suggests you do next."

"Lucky for me I have a family full of lawyers," Meagan said.

"Great!" he said as he grabbed the door handle. But before he opened it he added, "I'm not going to tell anyone about this except our lawyer. The other members of the board will be informed to keep it confidential too. Please call me when you uncover things."

She nodded. "I've always hated that man, but I had no idea he was still trying to ruin me. I'm sorry you are involved. I'll try not to drag Cottonwood through this."

She took a deep breath to regain some composure as he opened the door.

As they walked out together past Bob's assistant, their style of conversing changed to polite chit-chat. He even suggested they go for a run someday so she could help him improve his pace.

She stopped dead in her tracks at the elevator. "How did you know I run?"

"I'm a member at the Y too. I've seen you and your pack of gazelles on the trails," he smiled and waved then whispered as the doors shut, "You'll be fine."

As she rode the elevator down, her smile fell from her face quickly. She didn't feel fine at all. She felt like shit.

CHAPTER THIRTEEN

Meagan drove across the city and walked through Ben's company halls straight for his office. She had called on the way over and told him she was coming and that her life had crumbled.

Ben saw her hulking down the hall and came out to meet her. Her scarf fell from her shoulder but she didn't notice. She walked into Ben's arms that wrapped her far better than the wool-blend that fell to the floor did. Ben's assistant picked it up and turned to hand it to Meagan but saw the look on Ben's face and looked away, leaving the scarf on the corner of the closest desk.

They walked into his office as she started to sob. He kicked the door shut and stood there holding his shaking sister for a long time.

Every once in a while, he'd make out a word or two. "Asshole, how could he, how long was he going to do this to me. Prick!" was all Ben could hear through the sobs. He assumed she was talking about Chris.

"Did Chris dump you?" he asked carefully.

She stopped crying and pulled back from his shoulder and looked straight in his eyes.

"What? Oh, geez, that I could almost handle," she said, laughing at the confusion. "Ben, you know why Carl Russell is winning all the contracts over me?"

He shook his head not knowing where this was going.

"Because my BEST FRIEND, Dianne – or maybe Ginny, has been giving him MY work!"

"No way. That can't be! You've been together since second year. You are friends!"

"Obviously not anymore," she said wiping her eyes.

Ben kept one arm around her as they walked over to the mini-conference table set next to the window where the tinted windows let in a diffused sunbeam. He motioned for her to sit down as he grabbed his box of tissues.

The table had been set with a light lunch and a pot of fresh coffee.

Ben said, "Okay, start at the beginning."

As they munched on bagel bites and veggies, Meagan told Ben the morning's event. He listened stoned faced and barely said a word.

She ended it all with an exhausted, "What am I going to do?"

"You mean, what are 'We' going to do," Ben said sternly. "This is a serious offence. That guy is an idiot. You'd think he would stay away from you since you were the one who made sure he wouldn't teach anymore. Doesn't he know you have the resources to put him out of business? Or in jail this time? What an idiot. Not only that, how many other people does he have scattered throughout the city snooping through company files stealing work?"

Meagan hadn't even thought about other companies. She was too busy worrying about her own.

"Okay, so what are we going to do?" she asked.

"Well, I think your pal Magrath has a good idea. Let's clear lunch off here and you write down everything you said and anything else you might think is important. Give me a history of your relationship with Dianne and Ginny. We should consider there may be more than one insider. I don't think your interns are to blame here."

Meagan nodded. She was feeling better now that she had some food and that Ben was taking control.

He stood up and continued talking, "I think you should go back to the office and tell everyone you lost the bid and that you don't know who got it. Shrug it off, give Dianne credit for seeing that you should stay away from the big contracts and then head into your office to start on something new. Being bummed out is fine. I'm going call my best PI and get him tracking Dianne before she leaves your office today. If we keep cool, I have a feeling Dianne will be stupid enough to lead us to Russell."

Meagan stood up and smiled at Ben. "Thanks, so much Benny. I knew you would come to my aid."

"Hey, you don't know how happy I am that it's Russell and not my first guess," he said as he cleared the dishes onto a tray.

"What do you mean?" she asked puzzled.

"When you were blubbering all over my silk tie, I thought it was Chris dumping you. I thought it was the end of my free hockey tickets and bragging rights about Burrows dating my sister."

"You are such an ass!"

She threw a cherry tomato at him. It bounced off his chest, he caught it and popped it in his mouth with a proud smile.

Within an hour she had everything she could think of into a file. Ben had called Joseph Jensen, the P.I., who was already on his way to her office. Hopefully, Dianne hadn't left yet. He also called Ginny and told her a lie about sending Meagan an email with a virus. He said not to let anyone use Meagan's computer for fear of spreading the virus. Ginny fell for his line and said nobody had been in her office all day, so the virus won't have gone anywhere. If the culprit hadn't corrupted Meagan's computer before this day, it would be unlikely she would get to do anything to it before Meagan got back.

Somehow Meagan had to prove the data was tampered with on the Sunday when she was out of town.

As Meagan was about to leave Ben went over the game plan one more time.

"Okay, so go home, be depressed about losing the job and stay in your office until everyone leaves. Don't go looking into the Cottonwood contract stuff until you are alone. Make sure Dianne doesn't sense that you suspect her of anything. Besides, it's just a hunch that it's her. I don't think it's anyone else. Ginny doesn't seem the type. But we have to start somewhere and might as well start with who could gain the most from this."

Meagan nodded. "I suppose you are right, I am jumping to conclusions with Dianne. But really the evidence does point at her."

"Innocent until proven guilty...remember?" he said.

"Yes, I remember," she said as she headed for the door.

"And Megs,' he said slowly. "Even if we prove Carl stole your work, it is highly unlikely that Cottonwood will use the design. I think they'll avoid any involvement with you or Carl."

She just looked at her brother and nodded.

Meagan pulled up to her house and noticed Dianne's car was still there. She took a deep breath and started walking. *I should have gone for a run,* she thought to herself. *Where have I been all this time?*

The office door opened, and Dianne came out.

"Oh," said Dianne, surprised to bump into Meagan.

"Hi, how's it going?" said Meagan.

"Um, good. Where did you fly off to this morning?" asked Dianne.

Thinking quickly, Meagan started to lie, "Ben has a new lawyer in his office trying to buy a house in Mount Royal to renovate. So, he asked me to 'bump' into the guy at the office so I could possibly land some more work."

"Did you?" asked Dianne falling for the line.

"I hope so," she paused to breathe in deep. "I heard from David over at Springer Designs that Cottonwood was awarded. My phone hasn't been ringing, so I guess we blew it again."

Dianne seemed saddened. "Awe Meagan, I'm sorry. That would have been good too. Do you know who got it?"

"Naw, it doesn't matter. It wasn't us." Meagan started moving for the door. "I'm going to pout for a while then start getting ideas together for this lawyer of Ben's. Maybe you are right."

"Right about what?"

"I should stick to the little jobs."

"I didn't mean forever, Meg. We'll get one soon," she put her hand on Meagan's arm to comfort her and it was all Meagan could do to not punch out her nose.

"I'll be alright. My shoulders are getting bigger with every blow. So where are you off to? Are you done here for the day?" she asked, to change the topic.

"I'm off to Flanagan's to see if the beams are the right ones this time. I wasn't planning on coming back today. Do you want me to? It looks like you could use a friend. I could bring back beer and pizza?"

"Thanks, but I'll be alright. I think I'll go for a run later. At some point, I'm going to be angry instead of sad and my sprints are always better when I'm burning something off," she smiled. "See ya Monday."

"Sounds good," said Dianne, as she started to walk to her car.

Meagan didn't wait to see if anyone else pulled out at the same time. She didn't want to be seen doing anything out of the ordinary. Instead, she walked into the office and was heading to her glass enclave. She wished someone at the office was in on the secret because she would have bet the farm Dianne wasn't going to Flanagan's.

As she walked past Ginny's desk she said, "Are the Flanagan beams in yet?"

"Don't you say hi anymore? And no, they aren't in until Tuesday," said Ginny just as rudely.

Meagan stopped and spun around realizing she was an ass. "Sorry. I was rude. We didn't get the Cottonwood gig. I'm bummed."

"You're forgiven. I know and I'm sorry."

"What do you mean you know? You know Cottonwood was handed out?"

"I could hear Dianne talking to someone on the phone."

"Did she say who got it?"

"You don't want to know."

Meagan's shoulders sunk. "Russell?"

"Russell."

Meagan clenched her jaw, nodded at Ginny and turned to go to her office. She went in shut the door, spun her chair so no one could see her face and plopped down. She sat there spinning Chris's bracelet around her wrist. Watching the diamonds sparkle didn't even lift her mood.

Of course, she knew Russell got the contract but the thing that was boiling her blood was how Dianne was lying so well to her. The Flanagan beams, then her concern over the lost contract and then pretending she didn't know who got the job. *How much lying have I fell for! I'll bet she has been sleeping with that creep since school thinking he likes her!*

There is a soft knock at her door and Ginny poked her head in.

"I've got fresh coffee and I saved you the glazed sour cream donut," she said, as she moved towards Meagan's desk with the comfort food. Ginny knew Meagan didn't usually eat donuts, but the sour cream ones brought in by the flooring salesman were Meagan's weakness.

"Thanks," she murmured.

"Are you going to be okay? We'll have other bids come in, and besides, Russell will be so busy on this for so long, he won't be bidding on anything."

Meagan let the chair spin around so she could face Ginny. She took the donut and started chewing. Between mouthfuls, she said, "I'm okay with Russell getting another contract out from under me. I'll survive. That's part of the business. But as I walked into the building just now, Dianne lied three times to me. I've been worried about her performance here lately and now the lies. I'm very hurt."

"It's funny," said Ginny, "she seemed to be trying to help the morning you took the bid over. Remember when you guys argued over big and little projects?"

"You call that help?" Meagan asked surprised.

"No, I thought she felt bad because it was her idea to at least move the stuff to the door and bundle up the proposal."

Meagan stopped chewing. "That was her idea?"

"Yeah, nice eh? Too bad it was a one-time deal."

They both stopped talking, both lost in thoughts about Dianne.

Finally, Ginny looked over at Meagan again with a puzzled look on her face. "Do you want me to start monitoring her actions? I don't mind. If the girl needs to be let go, we should start documenting her actions. I have always thought she spends too much time on calls."

Meagan couldn't believe her ears, Ginny was such a good office manager. "I don't know Gin, she is my friend. I'm sure she will pull out of this," she took another bite to think, then continued. "Naw, maybe you are right. It has been going on too long and because I see her as a friend, I let her get away with it. If you wouldn't mind monitoring her calls and her absentees, that would be great. Plus, if she seems off-target, let me know. Maybe she is hunting for work elsewhere, but putting in time here until a better job comes along."

"Doing nothing here seems to be a perfect job to me," Ginny said sarcastically.

Meagan was reaching to turn on her computer, but Ginny stopped her.

"Don't! I forgot to tell you! Ben called. He said he sent you a virus on an email this morning."

"Awe shit. Did anyone use it since?" she sounded pissed off again.

"Nobody used it all day."

"Good. At least that has gone right. I'll call Ben – he can fix it. Thanks for everything Ginny," she said smiling.

"No problem boss," she smiled back.

Christ, I hope I can trust her. She is good at her job. Thought Meagan has she picked up the phone to call Ben about the 'Virus.'

"Hey, Ben."

"Hey back. How's it goin'?"

"I'm okay. I just bumped into Dianne as she left the office. She lied about not knowing about Russell getting the contract and a few other things. I didn't look to see if Jensen was following her. I hope he is. I'll bet she was trotting off to Russell's place."

"I haven't heard from Jensen yet," said Ben. "He usually calls in the morning to let me know what he found out the day before. He seems to find more stuff at night."

"That's because you usually have him chasing adulteress husbands." Meagan laughed.

"You mean money-hungry cougars."

Meagan laughed at his reference to single older women looking for new money.

"So, I'm starting my computer. Ginny shut if off when you called and said that no one touched it today. Let's hope Dianne doesn't know about the versions list."

"It would be good evidence if it's there," said Ben wishfully.

"Yeah, and get this, Ginny says Dianne was the one to put my bid in the envelope the day I took it over. Ginny didn't touch it."

"Hummmm. Fingers are pointing in one direction, now aren't they?" Ben said softly.

They sat on either end of the phone quietly waiting for the computer to go through the start-up procedure.

"I'm glad you aren't charging me like the rest of your clients. I probably blew 50 bucks waiting for the computer to warm up," she said as she started clicking onto her documents.

Ben harrumphed. "I have a feeling if I was charging you – I'd be making good money on this file."

"Oh. There it is," said Meagan as she opened the Cottonwood file. She clicked on "*versions*" and there before her eyes were the list of dates including the day it was manipulated.

"What does it say?" Ben asked as the line sat dead. "Speak to me."

"– Sunday the 21st at 11:27 a.m., automatic save – it says, then – Monday the 22nd at 8:44 p.m., "FINAL PRINT" – is what I put as a comment. That's the day and time I printed it off."

"Shit, eh," whispered Ben into the phone. Then he went into professional mode again. "This is incriminating, but, okay. Close the file. I'll come there after work and we can print it off together and I'll keep it as evidence. If everyone is out of the office, I think we should look over Dianne's work area and see if she is stupid enough to leave evidence around."

"Okay. I'll dig up something for supper too," added Meagan.

"Sounds good but don't leave the house to get it. I don't want anything happening against us now."

"Okay."

"Give me a couple hours."

She hung up the phone and counted her lucky stars that she could count on Ben. She didn't want to tell her parents about the problem just yet. It would add another chapter to her mother's "I told you so" encyclopedia. Then she started thinking about Chris. *Crap I don't even want to tell him. He'll think I'm an idiot.*

She looked at the Boston game schedule next to her calendar, he was playing in Vancouver. She sighed with relief. "He's too busy to call."

By 5 p.m. the office had cleared out so she went upstairs to dig up some dinner. By 6 p.m. Ben and Soda were walking through the door.

After exchanging salutations, furry hugs from Soda and opening a few beers, Ben took a long gulp. "Ah, that tastes good after a long day at the office. I landed a sweet case today that will prove to be very interesting."

"Really, what is it?" asked Meagan.

"Yours! Ya goof!" teased Ben.

"Oh, haha funny man."

They ate the chicken dinner at the kitchen bar, then shifted their attention to the basement office. Meagan usually liked it down there in the evenings when all the staff had gone home. The computers and photocopiers were quiet and the phone sat still. Meagan frequently did the payroll and mail at that time. But tonight, the place wasn't as inviting. Now Meagan felt betrayed and violated.

They dragged an extra chair up to her desk and she retrieved the file on the computer. Soda wrapped around Ben's feet.

"Yep, you're right," said Ben, shaking his head. "It was definitely used while you were gone. And, you definitely have a solid alibi for the day. But can anyone else come in and use your computer?"

"I guess so, but I don't think anyone else would have done it,"

He clicked on the Sunday version and it popped up with the correct information.

Meagan was hoping the corrupt file was on her computer, but it wasn't.

"I guess we can only prove someone saved the file that day. But it could have been saved onto a stick to be changed. Then, they would have printed it on my copier on my letterhead and bound it, etc. once it was changed."

"Let's print this," Ben said, as he moved the mouse over to the print command. "And I'll take it back to the office to file."

Then he added, "The problem that I can't figure out is, when and how did she switch the proper copy that you made Monday night for the tampered copy she made the day before?"

"I really think she got me pissed off on purpose on Tuesday morning to switch out the copies while I got refreshed," said Meagan. "It keeps going over in my head. I am willing to bet she was planning on assisting me to the truck so she could switch out the files. I just made it easier by going upstairs."

"Hoping to switch it on the way to your truck or getting you so mad that you leave the room is a pretty floppy plan for making the move on such a big crime. Do you think she will come back tonight or over the weekend for any reason?" asked Ben. "We should carefully peek at her stuff to see if she has any incriminating evidence."

"I don't think she will be back. She never has been one to put in overtime — for me — that is," she added bitterly.

Meagan pulled the paper from the printer and Ben stuck it in a blue manila folder. They went over to Dianne's workstation and both stood there staring at it without touching anything yet.

"It's very tidy and organized," admired Ben. "Is it always this neat?"

Meagan thought before answering. It was always neat, but something was missing. She had to think. "Ben. I've been so wrapped up with this contract and with seeing Chris that I haven't been worried about other people's workspace. But it does seem like something is missing."

Ben was still looking. "If you ask me, it's a very sterile desk."

"What do you mean, sterile?"

"There is nothing here to say it's Dianne's desk. No personal effects. Look at that desk," he said pointing at Jennifer's desk.

At first glance, Meagan could see his point. There were pictures of her dog, a happy face stuck to the corner of the monitor, a coffee cup from a radio station and a personalized calendar.

"You're right Ben," Meagan said like a light went on in her head. "Her personal stuff is missing. Usually, there's a picture of us over here that was taken after a hike. Probably her only hike!" quipped Meagan.

She pointed out other missing stuff. "It's like she is only here for a short time. Like she is ready to dash at any point."

"Hummmm," murmured Ben. "That's weird. Considering there isn't a reason yet that she should think she is leaving."

He started pulling out drawers and looking in her wastebasket. There was nothing to suggest she was doing anything wrong. As Ben pushed in a drawer, something white caught Meagan's eye. It was a hanky, all folded nicely. For some reason, she picked it up to smell it.

As she brought it to her nose she immediately withdrew it and squeezed her nostrils shut with the fingers of her other hand. "OH!" she exclaimed. "Yuck! It's his!"

Ben was puzzled. "How do you know?"

She shoved the hankie near his nose. "It's Carl's disgusting aftershave."

His nose turned up and he pushed her hand away. "Ewww. That is cheap! Hermetically seal that!"

They both laughed as she put it back the way she found it and shut the drawer. Ben walked back to Meagan's desk and made notes in the blue folder. Meagan kept looking but couldn't find anything.

She sat down at Dianne's computer and turned it on. She was reaching to push the email button but Ben shouted at her to stop.

"What? It's my property," she said back.

"No. that's okay, just pull the Ethernet cord or kill the wifi so you don't receive any email while you go through it. You don't want her coming in to find email already received."

"Yikes! I wasn't thinking."

She pulled all the cords and turned off the wifi as he suggested and then went into Dianne's email file. She didn't find anything personal but did find some customers wanted better service. *Shit, this chick needs to be fired no matter what.*

Ben walked over to Dianne's desk and was looking over his sisters' shoulder. "Find anything good?"

"Naw. She probably deletes anything she gets that might be secret." Meagan said discouraged.

"Did you check the deleted file?"

"Yeah."

"What about the wastebasket."

Meagan looked down at the wastebasket beside her. "You already did."

"No, not that one," moaned Ben. "The computer wastebasket."

He took the mouse from her hand and started clicking through the "My Computer" icon and worked his way into the "Wastebasket." There was a huge pile of files in there that should have been dumped but obviously Dianne didn't know how to clean up the computer and hadn't set up a maintenance schedule either.

Ben stopped clicking.

"What? Why did you stop?" asked Meagan eager to see what Dianne had dumped.

"I think we better tread carefully here. We should make sure we are not trespassing on private territory."

"What! I don't give a shit if it is private or not. I want to know if she has been selling me out!" Meagan said angrily.

"I know, I know," Ben said calmly. He patted her leg to slow her down. "I think we should take her computer to my office to keep it safe from her this weekend. I'll find out if I have the legal power to open the files or not. Put a different computer on her station for a while. Change out yours and hers. Say that the computer virus seized yours, so you foolishly went to use hers and you carried the virus on a stick and contaminated hers too."

Meagan nodded in agreement.

"Okay. But, can we just look at who the sender was on the dumped files? We won't open them."

Ben thought for a minute and said, "Okay."

They opened the deleted files and found most to be from clients, spam, and people she didn't know. There wasn't any with Russell's name on them.

"Don't look so discouraged. Don't you think he would use an alias?" asked Ben.

Meagan didn't think about that and was uplifted but then she thought about it. "She could use an alias too and for that matter, a Gmail account that wouldn't show on my computer."

"Awe shit. You're right," said Ben dejectedly.

"They both sat there staring at the computer like kids locked out of a toy store. They silently shut down the computer and unplugged it so he could load it into his car. Meagan took her computer off her desk and moved it to her bedroom on the top floor so it looked like both were taken to the repair shop. She shut the lights off in the office and locked the door to the basement and headed slowly up the stairs.

"That's about all we can do for now," said Ben, as they regrouped in the kitchen.

"What now?" she said.

Ben sucked on his upper lip for a while thinking. "Well, I guess we wait and see what the P.I. comes up with. I should have something in the morning. If she is hanging out with Carl as we suspect, we could start a criminal investigation. Hopefully, the emails come up with something. If she doesn't seem to be involved in any way with the guy, we've still got lots of work to do. Maybe we have to look at someone else in the office."

"Naw, the more I think about it the more I'm sure it's her."

Meagan grabbed two beers from the fridge and as she handed one to Ben she continued talking.

"Now that I think about it, Dianne hasn't been a model employee ever.

But she was my friend – so I thought – so I kept believing she would improve. I wanted the company to have this 'aura' of just women working here in a male-dominated industry to prove that it could be done. Boy, I was wrong. I wonder when she started working for Carl? How did he persuade her to steal my work? It seems like I have never won against him. I don't know how come I never figured this out before. Shit, I trusted her too. Did I ever get screwed," she said with a sinister chuckle.

Ben said, "Thing is, I think Carl panicked when he found out he didn't have all the guidelines. He knew he was under the gun to produce and since he had stolen so easily from you before he thought he wouldn't get caught. I think he got greedy on this job. If Mr. Magrath hadn't told you to come into the office this morning, you still wouldn't know why you lost out again. And, you wouldn't notice until the hotels were built and by then he'd hope you would be out of business or too poor to sue. So, maybe it's a good thing you made such a favourable impression on Magrath. If he didn't like you, he would have called the cops first. Even though you put a pile of work into this contract and lost, it may be the one that tips you into the winner's circle. If we nail Carl, you can start succeeding."

Ben started walking toward the family room. "Now, enough work and enough speculating, let's see if we can catch the last period of the game. Maybe that will cheer us up."

It didn't. Boston lost to Vancouver 4-0. Chris spent most of the game on the bench or in the penalty box. When Meagan finally went to bed she laid down and cried herself to sleep. Never had she felt so discouraged. Ever.

CHAPTER FOURTEEN

The cold air hitting her face at 7:00 a.m. was not as refreshing as she had hoped. The wind was icy and blowing hard from the west. She knew her friends were meeting at the Y, but she didn't want to see them. Instead of jumping in the truck to meet them, she ran from the house.

It took about ten minutes before she got comfortable with the shortened strides needed so she wouldn't fall on the hidden ice. After a while, her fingers started to warm up and her stressed-out shoulders began to relax. To stay away from the traffic, she ran towards Sandy Beach where the early dog walkers would be her only companions.

She ran down the steep path ending up along Elbow River just below the dam. Turning north she ran through Elbow Park to look at the elegant homes. Usually finding "For Sale" signs lifted her spirits. Not for herself. There is no way she could afford one of the homes in that neighbourhood, but sale signs meant new owners, and everyone seemed to need to renovate when they moved there.

Meagan started to enjoy the run and made it last nearly two hours. The hills she pushed hard to crest over brought on a pile of sweat and even though it was still very cold, she was soaked. As she turned the last corner onto her street, she saw Dianne's car in front of her house.

Meagan spun on her heels and went out of view of her house. The sweat went cold and she started to shake. She pulled her phone out of her pocket and called Ben.

"Ben! What do I do? She is at my house right now!" she panted into her phone.

Ben didn't even have a chance to say hello. "Do you see a brown Honda anywhere?"

Meagan looked all over the place and sure enough, parked at the end of the lane covered in a lot of snow, there it was.

"Yeah. Is that Joseph?"

"Yeah, he called earlier and had lots to tell, but listen. Go home and don't raise any suspicions. Tell her the computer was contaminated and tell her to go home. Make something up to get her out of there. I'll call Joseph. If he doesn't see her leave in a few minutes, I'll have him call you to see if you are all right. Got it?" he said sternly. "If you are being threatened use my name in a sentence with Joseph."

"Okay. Am I in trouble? Is she going to attack me? What did he find out?" she asked curiously.

"Don't ask now. Go home and get rid of her. I'm not far. I'll be over as soon as I can," he said rushed. "Go!"

She stuffed her phone back into her pocket and took a deep breath. Now she was frozen from the cold and from what lay ahead. She jogged awkwardly with a sense of panic rushing through her frozen veins. The release from the run all but wasted.

Meagan walked up the sidewalk to the house but went around to the lower level to go through the office entrance. As she went down the steps she glanced through the window and saw Dianne standing at her workstation. Her back was turned to the window, but Meagan could see Dianne was talking on her cell phone. One arm was waving and she seemed to be shifting her weight lots. Obviously, she was talking to someone about the missing computer.

It's not like it was stolen, thought Meagan as she watched Dianne's motions. *I did leave a note saying what happened. Am I ever glad I locked the door to the upstairs this time.*

She decided to continue down the stairs into the building to see if she could hear whom Dianne was talking to.

As Meagan opened the door and came in, Dianne spun around looking at her like she was a ghost.

"I gotta go," Dianne said, quickly into her phone. She pushed the end button and shoved the phone into her purse. "What are you doing here?" she said to Meagan, sounding disturbed by her arrival.

Meagan sensed the attitude and said, "I live here. How come you are here?"

Dianne was flustered. "Where is my computer? Why did you take it?"

"Didn't you see my note?" Meagan said as she moved to the desk, picking up the paper. "My brother sent me a virus and unfortunately before I realized what was wrong with my computer, I opened the file on your computer and infected it too. Sorry about that."

"Why did you use mine? Why didn't you use one of the student's computers?" she asked defensively.

"It was the closest. And you weren't here. Does it matter?"

"Now I can't get my stuff off it."

"Don't worry. I took it to the guy who is fixing Ben's and he said he will have it ready by Monday." Meagan said, then added. "What do you need today? You never come in on weekends. I don't recall anything being due."

Meagan stared at Dianne waiting for a good answer.

"I, I. Okay. You caught me." Dianne said indignantly.

Meagan thought for a second that Dianne was confessing.

"I started an email to my mom on the computer yesterday instead of working on the Flanagan's house. I was having a terrible brain blockage so I started a letter and I wanted to finish it off at home and send it."

"You started a letter to your mom?" Meagan asked rather dumbfounded. *Shit, that beats the dog ate my homework excuse,* she thought to herself.

"I know I'm sorry. I should have done something more constructive."

Meagan was standing there shaking her head. *The lies. The stupid lies!* she thought.

Suddenly, she remembered she was supposed to get rid of her.

Meagan started talking sternly. "Listen, I'm sorry the computer isn't here so that you can finish your email. But I have far bigger issues to deal with and I'd rather not have anyone in the office while I sort them out. I'll have the computer on Monday. If I didn't ruin your files, you can finish it then. But right now, I'd rather you left. If it would make you happy, call your mom and charge me the long-distance. Is there anything else you need from your desk right now?" she added.

"No," Dianne said softly.

"Then, I'll see you Monday." Meagan went to the door and pulled it open.

Dianne looked over her desk one more time as if searching for something, but she didn't want to take too much time and raise suspicions, so she picked up her purse and walked to the door.

"I'm sorry you didn't get the Cottonwood contract. I…" Dianne started but Meagan's cell phone started to ring so she stopped talking and said, "See ya."

Meagan shut the door before answering the phone.

"Hello?"

"Meagan?" said a soft middle-aged male voice with a thick accent.

"Yes."

"This is Joseph. Is everything okay?"

"Yes, she is about to leave. Do you see her?"

There is silence on the other end then finally he answers. "Yes. She is getting into her car. I'll follow her and get back to you. Oh, by the way?"

he added.

"What?"

She could hear a smile come into his voice, "I'm not the only one following her."

"What do you mean?"

"Russell has been waiting up the street the whole time."

She could hear his engine start.

"I'll be in touch shortly. Ben will be there any minute."

Meagan stood in the empty office, trying to understand what the hell was going on. She walked over to the desk and pulled open the drawer where the hanky had been the previous night and to no surprise, it was gone.

"I'm starting to think this girl is a little whacko," Meagan said out loud.

It wasn't long before she heard the thumping of feet running down the steps and then Ben burst through the door, frantically looking around.

"She is gone right?" he said breathlessly. His hands were clasped in front of his chest as if he was holding a pistol like a cop in a bad gangster flick.

"Yes," she laughed. "And you knew it!"

"How do you know I know?" he said, dropping his hands and pretending to holster a gun.

"Because Joseph is on the case, he just called me so I'm sure he called you too."

Ben sighed, "Dang, I always want to be the hero and rush in and save the damsel in distress."

"Me? You crack me up," she said, laughing as she locked the door behind him. "Come on upstairs and tell me everything."

"Have you had breakfast or wait," he looks at his watch, "lunch?"

"No, but I'm frozen."

"I actually have food in the car. I'll brew some coffee while you clean up. Then I'll tell you what we dug up."

Meagan ran ahead up the two flights to her bedroom and as she peeled off her wet clothes, she peeked under her bed. The computer was still there. Even though she unlocked the door to the rest of the house to come from the basement she wasn't trusting Dianne at all.

The hot shower stung her cold pink skin but it was a welcomed pain. She jumped out, dried off, slathered on lotion and found some warm comfy track pants and a sweatshirt. An elastic wrapped her hair into a sloppy bun on top of her head. Her nose followed the inviting scent of the coffee coming from the kitchen.

When she entered, Ben handed her a coffee but was busy chatting on her cell.

"Hey, here she is. Good talking to you, man." Ben handed her the phone.

"Who is it?" she asked puzzled.

He smiled, grabbed a muffin from an incredibly tall pile he'd brought and his coffee and headed for the daily paper in the front room.

"Hello?" she asked into the phone.

"Hi to you," Chris answered.

Meagan sank onto the barstool next to her and drank in his voice. She had been afraid to talk to him about the ordeal but now hearing his voice she knew he would help her feel better.

"Oh Chris, you can't imagine how nice it is to hear from you." She leaned her head onto her hand not holding the phone.

"How's it going? You don't sound like your usual peppy self."

"I'm not. The last 24 hours have turned into my biggest nightmare. But first — how are you? We watched the last period last night, but I didn't see you play. You didn't get hurt - did you?"

"Naw, it wasn't my day either. What's the matter with you? Oh, no." he paused and said slowly. "Did the Cottonwood contract get handed out to someone else?"

No answer.

"Oh Meagan, sweetheart. I'm so sorry. Is that it?"

She loved that he called her sweetheart and wished he was there to wrap those massive arms around her.

"Yeah, I didn't get it. But the weird thing is, is that my designs did."

He didn't answer for a few seconds. "What do you mean? They liked your work but not you?"

"Chris, I didn't want to call you about this but it's killing me. Do you have a few minutes?"

Chris answered softly with love in his voice. "Tell me what happened. I'm all ears."

She told him everything, about how nice Bob Magrath was, then wasn't, then was again. How they discovered the errors in his office and then coming home to Dianne's lies and how she and Ben took out the computers and the deception, about the stinky hanky being in the desk then not. How Dianne challenged her in her own office and how Ben is taking care of it all.

She started to cry, even when she said she wouldn't. But through it all Chris listened carefully with empathy, every so often he'd mummer something compassionate to try to make her feel better.

During the call there was a tap at the front door and Ben answered it. It was Joseph. The two men stayed in the front room discussing the latest findings while she continued talking and sobbing on the phone.

After Chris had heard it all there was a long silent pause.

Finally, he spoke. "Meagan."

"Yes," she said through more tears.

"First, I love you. I think you are the most remarkable woman I have ever met. I know you can pull through this. It sounds like you and Ben have a good handle on what has taken place. I think the next step is to introduce it to the crime experts from the police department. Let them take over. Okay."

"'Kay," she whispered.

"Then, once you've got those guys on board, I think it's time for us to take that holiday. The All-Star Break is in two weeks and I didn't get picked to play so I want to go to Eleuthera to check on the house. I want you to come with me. Okay? I'm not taking no for an answer."

She was silent, mostly because she was letting the confession of his love sink in.

"Agreed?" he asked.

"I, I want to do that too," she said through sniffles.

"Okay, I'll get the team travel agent to line things up. I'm going to catch my plane. I'll call tonight okay?"

"Chris?"

"Yeah baby," he said softly.

She paused and swallowed hard. "I love you too."

There was silence again.

"Thanks, I was hoping you'd say that."

She could hear his smile through his voice.

"I'll call tonight."

She put down the phone smiling like a person stuck in the eye of a hurricane. She survived the first wave of terror but the damage coming from the second wave was still on the horizon.

CHAPTER FIFTEEN

As Meagan came from the kitchen, the two men stood up and the doorbell rang at the same time.

Ben walked to the door as he said, "Meagan, this is Joseph."

As they shook hands Ben opened the door and two more men were at the door.

"Ben Dunphy?" asks one.

"Yep, come on in," he said, as he moved to one side.

Meagan stood there watching everything go on.

Shaking hands with Ben, he said, "I'm Detective Derek Whitmore."

"I'm Detective Ron Patel," said the shorter of the two men.

Ben introduced Meagan to the two and they seemed to already know Joseph. Finally, Meagan spoke up.

"Ben, things are moving fast here. What is going on?"

"Come sit down everybody," Ben said as he motioned for everyone to sit in the living room where all the coffee and muffins were laid out.

"Meagan, Joseph found out a ton of stuff last night. And I took the computer and dug through it and also found a pile of incriminating evidence. This morning when you came in, Joseph had already been watching Dianne since dawn. We've been talking and decided it was time to bring in the big guns. So, now we can all contribute to the file for the police."

"Thanks, Ben," said Detective Whitmore. "Believe it or not, you are not the first firm to have concerns regarding Mr. Russell and his ethics. We have at least three other companies who have come forward and registered complaints. We also have your complaint from the University. Ben took the liberties to tell us there might be a connection."

Meagan smiled and gently nodded. She was uneasy with all the people suddenly invading her life and now it looked like her secrets were going to be public knowledge too.

"So," said Detective Whitmore, as he pulled a small recorder from the breast pocket of his suit. "I'd like to tape this conversation if you don't mind. This isn't a formal statement and none of what goes on the tape will be used if this turns into a criminal offence. If we do have grounds for pressing charges, then we will tape your statement for the record. Is that alright with you, Miss. Dunphy?"

All the men in the room were staring at Meagan with serious looks of concern. Meagan looked at them all ending with Ben who nodded slightly to let her know he was with her all the way.

"I guess we should plow ahead."

"Thank you. Now, please tell us your findings from the very beginning," asked Whitmore. "When you are done, we will hear what Joseph found out in the last 24 hours."

Joseph agreed.

Meagan took a deep breath, reached out for a muffin and started to talk. Detective Whitmore asked questions occasionally and Detective Patel asked a few too. She briefly went over what happened in school and moved quickly into what she was seeing lately. The two men kept their eyes glued on Meagan, periodically a pen scratched something onto a pad of paper. It felt like she was the only one talking.

When it got to the part about dating Chris Burrows their attention seemed to sway over to the hockey player for a while, but they quickly regained the focus and asked Joseph for his findings.

"First Joseph, please state your name, business and link to all this," said Detective Patel as he changed the position of the recorder.

"My name is Joseph Jenson. I emigrated from Switzerland about five years ago after spending 24 years in the Swiss army as an espionage specialist. I am now a private investigator and am hired on mostly by law firms like Ben's."

"Okay," says Whitmore. "Tell us what you found out."

"It has been very interesting and I have to say very rewarding. Mr. Russell and Ms. Woods were not suspecting that they were leaving a trail."

Joseph looked straight at Meagan and continued, "I hate to say this but because you were so trusting of Dianne, it made it easier for them to steal your work."

Meagan grimaced as the investigator continued.

"Ben called me around 2 p.m. yesterday and asked me to head over here to watch for Dianne. As I drove, Ben filled me in on the details. I parked down the street and it wasn't long before Meagan drove up. As she walked into the building, I noticed the two ladies talked briefly just outside the door. When Meagan went into the house, Dianne went to her car, started it and before pulling out into the traffic made a call on her cell phone."

"At least she is safety conscious," said Ben.

Joseph nodded and continued. "She took one last look at the house and then drove off. I followed her to Market Mall where she went shopping for nearly two hours. She came out with a few small shopping bags. I did take pictures. From what I can tell it's ladies fashions and shoes."

As he discussed Dianne's shopping spree, he pulled open his tablet and flipped through large images of Dianne going into the mall and coming back. Meagan easily identified the bags and Joseph was right. Shoes and clothes.

"She got back in her car, called someone again then left the parking lot and headed straight back downtown to that fancy condo – the Marquis on 6th avenue. She used a fob to gain access to the underground parking." He showed another picture of her Nissan disappearing into the abyss.

"That's not where she lives," said Meagan confused by what she was seeing.

"You are right," said Joseph. "While I was waiting at the mall, I looked up Russell's home address and that is his building."

Everybody in the room either shifted or moaned. The PI was pulling the case together far too easily.

"That's not where it stops," said Joseph excitedly. "It gets better, worse...depending on your perspective."

The policemen were smiling now. Obviously, they liked the thrill of a chase as much as Joseph.

"I gained access to the underground parking and located her car in stall number 900. Number 901 was empty. So, I waited back outside at the entrance and watched the cars go in for about an hour. At 6:20 p.m., a BMW 6 Series Coupe pulled up driven by Russell."

Again, a photo was displayed. It was Carl wearing designer sunglasses and looking rather debonair as he was photographed waving this fob in front of the reader for the gate.

"I waited a while, then went downstairs."

Ben interrupted, "How did you get into the underground parking if it is a secure lot?"

Joseph stopped talking, looked at the policemen and then continued. "It's my job Ben, don't ask."

The detectives nodded in agreement.

"We don't need to know that Ben," said Whitmore. He motioned with his hand to Joseph to continue.

"I went down to Dianne's stall and to no surprise, Russell's car was in number 901. I went back to my car and called the local pizza company and ordered a pizza," said Joseph.

Everyone was surprised he would tell them his supper plans but they were captivated by the way he was unfolding the events so they didn't question his actions.

"When the pizza came, I grabbed a pizza delivery thermal bag out of my trunk and went to the building as some other people did. Among other neat gismos in my trunk, I have a great little camera that fits in my baseball hat. I slipped in at the same time, thanking the people for letting me in so that the pizza wouldn't get cold. I went to the 9th floor to apartment number 914, that's Russell's door with the pizza and rang the doorbell. I just took some screen grabs to show you quickly how it all went down."

Once again, the pictures were flipping – fast enough to look like an old-time movie but in colour. As he flipped the pictures, the other four people in the room moved closer, hunching over to see.

His hand on the buzzer, then the door opening, then another with Dianne standing there looking at him. The pictures told the story without dialogue. Dianne was in comfortable clothes; not stuff she wore at the office. Obviously, she wasn't visiting for a just short while.

Meagan's heart sank. Ben sensed his sister's pain and put his hand on her back and gently rubbed it. All she could do was smile weakly at him. He kept his hand on her back as Joseph continued with his findings.

"When the door opened, I said, 'You ordered a pizza?' Dianne stood there staring at me like I was an alien, then said, 'No, I don't think so.' She turned and yelled into the condo asking if the person inside ordered a pizza."

The photos showed her head turn as if yelling down the hall. The next picture showed someone coming up the hall, and of course to no surprise, it was Russell, changed into some sweatpants and a tee shirt.

"Russell came to the door," continued Joseph, "like an arrogant ass and treated both Dianne and me like insignificant beasts. He said, 'What the hell is this? I didn't call for pizza, especially from a shit joint like that. Get lost.' As he shut the door on my face, I could hear him reprimanding Dianne for opening the door. I almost felt sorry for her."

The pictures ended with Russell's sour face puckered in the word "joint."

"So," said Joseph with a sigh, "I went back to the car and ate my pizza."

The men chuckled, but Meagan had lost her sense of humour.

"I did stay for a few hours to watch the lights go off in Russell's unit, then I waited long enough to see if Dianne was leaving. Since she didn't, I did. I went home to freshen up and have a rest. I was back on-site by 5 a.m. I checked the garage and both cars were still there. At about 8:15 a.m., Dianne drove out of the garage followed by Russell. I hung back and then followed. When it became apparent that they were headed this way, I turned off and arrived from a different route. I called Ben to see what your routine was and he said you were most likely out running.

"I'm sure they were banking on that too. Dianne parked out front, but as I said to you earlier Meagan, Russell parked down the block. He never got out of his car. Ben called me a few minutes later to tell me you were on your way back into the house and as I hung up, Russell saw you walk up, but did not make any move to get out of his car.

"When Dianne left, she looked at him and shook her head in a firm 'no' gesture then she got in her car and left. He followed her. I don't have shots of this loaded because I waited for Ben to show up and ...that brings us up to current."

No one said a word. They all looked at each other and the photos, piecing together the information.

It was Detective Whitmore who spoke first. "Joseph, I must say, you have added some invaluable information to this case."

Detective Patel cleared his throat to speak, "Yes, I think if Ben hadn't moved out the computers and if Joseph hadn't tracked her, I think this case would be harder to prove. What did you find on the computer by the way?"

He was asking Ben.

"Well," said Ben as he rubbed his thighs with his palms. "I didn't think I would be able to locate anything, but I guess as Joseph said about Meagan being trusting, so was Dianne. I found a way into her private accounts on the computer and dug briefly through her email."

Meagan was feeling sick now and stood up. Ben stopped talking and looked at her.

Meagan realized they were all looking at her. "You guys, I feel like shit. My life is spinning out of control here. Who I thought was my best friend relies on my trust to screw me and my company and now, I'm using her personal files to screw her back! This sucks."

Detective Whitmore stood up too and looked at his watch. "How about we take a few minutes to grab fresh coffee and some air on the deck, then we will go over what Ben has to say."

He reached out and touched Meagan's arm and gave it a tender squeeze. "Meagan, you are right. This is hard to take but when all of this is done, you will be able to pick up the pieces and fly. By the sounds of this, you will not have to worry about either Dianne or Russell anymore."

Meagan smiled at him and he said, "Come on, those muffins are great and you haven't eaten enough."

They followed the others into the kitchen where Ben was already starting new coffee. Detective Patel continued through the room behind Joseph to the deck where they could have a smoke. As the door opened, Soda rushed out and down the steps to where the lawn was buried under the snow.

When they regrouped in the living room, Ben started to tell his piece of the story. He pulled out a few pages of paper printed from Dianne's computer which he left at his home office.

"After I left last night, I plugged Dianne's machine in at home. I called Rowan, a computer geek friend of mine who helped me bypass some of the firewalls."

As Ben went through the secret files, Meagan's head started to spin. She leaned back and listened as Ben read off a few of the emails. It hurt to hear Dianne refer to her as the "Dumb Redhead" or "the Irish Setter" or of late the "Puck Slut."

"Oh, I like this one," he said lifting his head from his notes, "...Ginger and Ice."

Detective Whitmore tried not to laugh and stiffed it by clearing his throat.

Meagan breathed deep and focused on what was at hand. As she spun Chris's bracelet, she made up her mind. No matter what it was going to take she was going to sink those two.

Ben continued to read the emails. "Her emails don't go back further than six months, but it was obvious by the tone the conversations had been going on long before the start-up of Cottonwood. For example; this email refers to 'the Dentist,' and this one refers to a golf club that Meagan won't see the inside of."

Meagan sat up as she heard the contracts.

"You're kidding!" She grabbed the sheet from Ben and started to stammer through her rage. "Those assholes! I gave Dianne Dr. Evans office and we worked jointly on the country club. She worked on them on my paycheque and gave them to Russell!"

"Sorry Megs," Ben said trying to console her. "It looks like anything big you worked on is in here. I have a feeling Russell won many of those."

Meagan sat with her jaw clamped shut.

"Where is your computer, Meagan?" asked Whitmore. "Maybe you can show us the process you use to save your files, so we can confirm that they were manipulated while you were out of the office."

"I'll just be a second, I hid it under my bed."

She got up to run upstairs and as she skipped up the first few steps, Whitmore asked Ben to take everyone down to the office.

Meagan retrieved the computer from behind a pile of clothes under her bed. She lugged the computer down the two flights to the basement. The blinds were pulled, and the two detectives were looking over Dianne's workstation and taking pictures.

Ben came over to her desk and helped her plug in all the cords to get the machine up and running. They talked quietly.

"Megs, are you okay?" Ben asked sincerely.

"Not yet," she said choking back her emotions. His kindness brought on her weakness. "I, I will be though. I think I'm moving from the victim stage to revenge stage. Besides, like Detective Whitmore said, no matter what, these two won't bug me again. Even if I don't prove he stole all this work, I'll expose him and weaken his credibility. I'll start getting contracts again. Probably not Cottonwood though," she ended with a sigh.

As the program loaded, Ben replied, "You'll be better than ever."

The men gathered around and Meagan sat in her chair. She pulled up files, showing how there were changes made on the Cottonwood file on days she wasn't at the office. She started up her tablet and stuck in the flash drive from her purse to show them her private/backup copy. Nobody interrupted and no one challenged what she was accusing Dianne of. The case was becoming very clear.

When she finished up, Detective Patel said, "We need to take this computer and Dianne's and the flash drive in as evidence. Is that okay?"

"Yes, I've still got another laptop and this tablet," she answered then said suddenly, "What do I do on Monday? What do I do with Dianne? Do I fire her? Do we have enough to seal the case?"

Both detectives stood there thinking for a while. Whitmore leaned against the wall and Patel stroked his moustache.

Finally, Whitmore talked to Patel. "What do you think Ron?"

"Well, there are a few options, and we all have to decide which one we want to take. Meagan could fire Dianne. We probably have all the evidence."

"But what are the grounds for firing her? We need a few days to sort all this out before we press charges" said Whitmore.

Patel nodded. "She could let her continue working as if we don't know anything?"

"I could lay her off. I could lay off the whole staff saying that I can't afford them now that I lost Cottonwood?" said Meagan, trying to come up with a solution.

"I'll still follow Dianne's actions," said Joseph. "I'd like to see what she does if Meagan lays her off."

Patel and Whitmore were nodding in agreement then Whitmore said, "Instead of potentially losing the employees, offer a few days off. Say you need to regroup or something. We'll build our case and Joseph can follow Dianne and Russell to see how they handle the shutdown. We should comb through the other computers to see if anyone else is in on the scam too."

Now everyone was nodding.

Meagan nodded too. "That sounds like a good idea. I'll cover the files that are currently being worked on. Then, when you guys are ready, you can let me know and I can bring everyone back."

"How soon do you think you will be ready?" asked Ben.

"I'm going to talk to a few other architect firms who have been making claims about Russell and then get it together. I think Russell will be calling his lawyer by noon on Thursday," said Whitmore firmly.

'Should I call everybody at home tomorrow or wait until Monday morning when they all come in? asked Meagan.

Patel suggested waiting until Monday, so they would have more time before Dianne might get suspicious.

"Plus," added Joseph, "I can watch for Dianne's reaction."

They all smiled. Everybody in the room was on Meagan's side on this case. The culprits were going to be caught this time.

Detective Patel looked at the clock on the wall and said. "I love it when things fall together like this but I've got more important things to do. It's one o'clock already. I have a soccer practice to coach."

"It's winter!" said Joseph.

"Indoor soccer. My 10-year-old plays almost every day and I promised I'd be there this afternoon," he said with a proud fatherly smile.

As they got to the front door and while everyone put on their coats, they went over the plan one more time. The police gave Meagan their business cards with all the numbers needed to contact them. They all assured her they were doing the right thing and the case was going to be easy to put in front of a judge.

As the men were going through the front door, Patel looked at Meagan and added, "Once you tell everyone to leave on Monday, have a locksmith come and change the locks."

"Okay," she said smiling as strongly as she could.

Meagan was hoping Ben would stay behind but the police wanted the computer from his house. He hugged his sister and left.

Meagan shut the door and suddenly the house was silentempty and cold.

So much had been discussed and discovered. She walked around picking up the coffee cups and plates in a daze. Once in awhile she would shake her head from side to side in doubt. The "*why me*," kept coming to her head.

She decided to sit down and write out how she would tell her staff to take the next few days off without letting her frustrations and accusations come out.

About an hour after the men left, the doorbell rang. Meagan looked at her watch. It was 2:30 p.m. "Maybe it's Ben," she said hoping to herself. "It's probably someone wanting to sell me something."

She opened the door and gasped in delight.

Without worrying about the snow on the step she flung herself on Chris.

CHAPTER SIXTEEN

"Oh my God!" she squealed. "How did you get here? I just talked to you in Vancouver! Aren't you supposed to be going to Boston?" she said, hugging him tightly.

With Meagan clung to his neck, Chris moved the few steps into the house. He was obviously pleased his surprise visit was appreciated. "Jez Meagan, that call was four hours ago. I was only in Vancouver! You sounded like you could use some company, so I rerouted through Calgary. Can I stay for a while?"

He was looking into her eyes and holding her in the hug still.

She buried her head in his neck and said, "Stay as long as you want. I can't think of anyone I need more right now."

She lifted her head and as they kissed, Meagan could feel her heart rate slowing down.

This couldn't be happening. It was only four hours since they talked and so much had happened. She let go of Chris and he stepped outside to bring in his stranded duffle bag. She helped him take off his overcoat and just like the first time they met he was dressed elegantly.

She got caught admiring his wardrobe.

"What are you looking at?" he asked smiling at her.

"You always dress so nice," she said smiling back. "Do you ever hang out in like, paint-splattered sweatpants?"

He put his arm around her shoulder as they walked into the house. "Oh yeah, when I'm at home I put on some nasty blue sweats and a t-shirt that's too small so I can scratch my belly as I sit in front of the big screen TV and pound beer and watch soaps!"

"You're lying," she said.

"Definitely. You don't think I have a beer belly – do you?"

They were standing in the kitchen now. She un-tucked his shirt and stuck her hands under the pale blue material and felt his ribs and flat stomach.

"Definitely not," she said as she slipped her hands right around his waist, ending her actions with a kiss on his lips.

"Whew!" he said. "I really think I needed to stop in!"

She pulled her arms out from his shirt, almost embarrassed by her advancement, but he stopped her hands on his warm chest. "How long can you stay?"

"I've got to catch the same flight out as I did last time at one tomorrow. I know it's short but, at least it's a visit," he said with a hurt look on his face.

"Oh Chris, I am so glad to see you, I'll take anything I can get," she said. "Hey, do you need anything? Lunch? Snack? Beer and pretzels," she added jokingly.

"No, I'm okay. But you kinda look like you need some fresh air. Wanna go for a walk? I do have some more casual clothes to change into."

Meagan realized just then she didn't put on any makeup after her morning shower and her hair was still piled like a stack of wire.

"Aw shit, I sat here with four men and looked like this? Listen, you bring your suitcase up to the bedroom and change. I'm going to put some colour on my face, so I don't scare anyone on the walk."

Chris went to the front hall, grabbed his duffle and followed Meagan up to her bedroom.

"Hey, this is nice," he said as his eyes took in the room. Her house may have been on the small side, but that didn't mean she couldn't dress it up. The bedroom was the only real private space she had with the office being downstairs, so she decorated it as her own sanctuary. Soft earth tones covered the walls and a fluffy feather duvet graced the antique bed. The art on the walls were originals by local artists she hoped would some day be famous. Next to the bed was a week-old newspaper, folded open at the sports page where a picture of Chris graced the page.

Chris saw the paper and bent down and picked it up. "Don't you recycle? This game was over a week ago?"

Being caught like a schoolgirl with a crush on a celebrity, Meagan started to blush. She tried to grab the paper out of his hand. "Gimmie that!"

Chris held it high laughing, easily pushing Meagan back. "Got a crush on the hockey player do ya?"

She jumped up to grab it but missed. "No, I was doing the crossword! Gimmie that."

She jumped again but this time onto the bed so she'd have a chance at reaching high enough. Instead of giving her a chance at grabbing the paper,

Chris flung it across the room and pulled her down onto the bed.

"There's no crossword in the sports section." He stared into her eyes then kissed the end of her nose.

Meagan smiled and admitted her guilt. "Okay. It's the hockey player," she paused. "I miss you and with how busy I've been, it's hard to catch you on TV. So keeping a picture of you nearby makes it a little easier."

"Can't you find a better picture than that? I'm a mess! Don't you have any of me on your phone?"

She was stroking his hair now as he continued to lay on top of her. "I don't need one. You are here."

She shut her eyes as he bent down to kiss her forehead, then her nose and then her lips. It was a long slow kiss making her desire him even more. She wrapped her arms around his shoulders and looped her legs around his waist. The kissing continued. Chris moved his kisses from her lips down her chin and onto her neck. Meagan's toes started to wiggle with arousal.

Chris could see she was into what was happening and looked up as he unbuttoned her blouse.

"Still want to go for a walk?"

"Nope. Not now. I'm busy with my hockey player."

With both hands, she pulled his head back to her face and passionately kissed him. His hands worked quickly to pull off her shirt and pants. She tried to do the same to him, but her hands kept mixing up with his.

"You are blocking my moves!" she said laying there in a bra and panties.

"Ha! That's what I get paid for," he said as he stood up finishing off what she had started.

As his shirt slid to the floor, Meagan quickly scanned his muscular body, rubbing her hands over his chest. She was pleased to see no signs of bruising from the previous night's game and was relieved to see his ribs were entirely mended.

Like the snow gently falling outside the window, Chris began lightly kissing Meagan. He was enjoying the pleasure it gave Meagan as he pecked and licked and brushed his lips down her body.

Chris touched her softly, stroking her, making her move into his hand like a purring cat. Meagan leaned her head back into the pillows, moaning quietly as he moved further down her body. His tongue drew circles around her nipples causing them to perk up, so his teeth could teasingly bite them. Meagan enjoyed the sensation and arched her back so her breasts found his mouth easier. He continued to tease her into a sexual frenzy. The ecstasy came in waves. All thoughts and tensions of the last 24 hours vanished as they made love. What was rushing through her body was all that mattered.

Communication was through touch and longing looks as the early nightfall of a wintery Canada descended. Soon, the room was lit by the glow of the streetlight outside her window. They laid wrapped in each others' arms, enjoying the afterglow for a long, long time. Meagan didn't want it to end and obviously, Chris was happy to stay the same way.

But, hunger finally took over and the two rolled out of bed and headed down to the kitchen. As Meagan pulled chicken and vegetables out of the fridge, Chris found a bottle of wine to open. Meagan seasoned the chicken, chopped up the vegetables and threw them all into the oven while Chris told her about the latest happenings in his world.

"The house over on Eleuthera is coming along but it seems to have hit a bit of a snag," he said, as he handed Meagan a glass of merlot. "Things happen slowly over there, mostly because shipping stuff takes forever. But I don't think my project manager has his heart in it."

"What's up? I'd love to help if I can...since I think I won't be doing much else here for a while," she said sarcastically. She had already told him about what went on with the police that morning and was feeling better now that she had someone other than just Ben to talk to.

Chris sat down on a barstool at the kitchen island and grabbed a stray carrot to chew on as he continued. "I was hoping that when I take you there, it would be further along, but I hear it is still sitting as cinderblocks."

"Yikes. Can we sleep in a tent or something?" Meagan asked not knowing what to expect.

"Oh, don't worry about that. There is a small guesthouse built by the previous landowner that we can stay in. It's nice but not very big. Anyway, the project manager is actually one of my old coach's sons. He has a carpentry ticket so I assumed he could handle the job. I don't want to fire him because I feel like I owe it to his dad, but I do want the job done by fall. At this rate, it won't be ready for next Christmas."

Meagan was pulling cheese and crackers out while he was lamenting. As he spoke she could see his concerns. "I feel for you. I try very hard to always keep my projects on schedule for my clients. If I don't get Brent's house done on time, my head will bounce down the front steps."

"He'll do that?"

"No – his current wife will!" she laughed.

Chris nodded, "Good reason to stay on schedule. I'll make threats like that to Mike."

"Why don't you send me a copy of what you are building. Maybe I can help out while we are there. I'd love to see it take shape and get you moved in by the fall."

Chris looked across the counter at her and said sheepishly, "I was hoping you'd be moving in some of your stuff too."

Meagan was flabbergasted by his offer. "Wow! You'd let me bring some of my stuff?"

They both stopped what they were doing. Meagan's cheese knife was lodged in a brick of cheddar and he had a carrot sticking out of his mouth. They stayed motionless for what seemed a long time, staring.

Neither was thinking about long term relationships. Out loud at least. Meagan was hoping it would go that way and so obviously was Chris, but his comment caught her off guard.

Chris raised his eyebrows as if signalling her to say something he would want to hear.

A long drawn-out "Oh" was about all she could muster at first followed by another, "Wow."

"And that means?" he asked, verbally this time.

She put down the knife and walked around the island to stand next to him on the barstool. She slid in between his knees and wrapped her arms around his neck.

"Things between us seem to be moving very fast. I can't believe how comfortable I am with you already. It seems like I already know you."

"Actually, I feel the same way. I really didn't mean to ask you to do that yet, it just slipped out. It just seems right."

"It does, but we have a lot of issues we will have to discuss if we do decide to get more serious. I think I still have a business to run here in Calgary and it's too far for you to commute from Boston."

She paused as the reality of their other commitments sunk in. She started biting her lip, not knowing what she was trying to say. "Do you think we can make this work?" she said, almost afraid of what he might say.

"If it's meant to be, it will work out. Let's not jinx it," he said rubbing her shoulders. "Let's just let it go the way it's going. Let's not worry about jobs or responsibilities just yet. Who knows how long Boston wants me? That might change what you think of me too. What if I get traded to Philly or Toronto or…"

"If you get traded to Edmonton, this whole affair is over!" she joked.

He smiled and laughed at how far she would take the Alberta rivalry. He cupped his hands on her cheeks and said, "Like I said this morning, I love you. I won't go to Edmonton!"

The timer on the oven went off and she started backing away to get to the stove.

"So, we agree to not worry about everything else that we have both been working long and hard for? We won't let silly things like jobs and businesses and hockey trades and hockey careers get in the way?" she said looking at him in disbelief.

He lifted his glass in a toast. "Yep. Why ruin a good thing."

She turned off the timer and lifted her glass to tap rims. As the glasses touched she said, "Agreed. No worries about the future. It will happen the way it happens."

As she sipped her wine, she could see the look on his face. He looked like he would love her forever. She smiled back knowing she wanted to love him forever too and would live anywhere to be with him, even Edmonton.

Meagan woke up as usual at 5:55 a.m. but didn't even lift her head. Instead, she stayed still, staring at the ceiling, listening to Chris's soft breathing. He was lying beside her, rolled on one side facing her. She gently shifted so she could look at him as he slept.

Dang, this guy is great, she thought to herself as she studied his features in the muted streetlight seeping through the window.

His dark wavy hair lay softly on the pillow. She wanted to reach out and touch it but didn't want to disturb him. His bangs were tossed to one side exposing a scar in his thick hairline she hadn't noticed before. She slowly looked down his face, looking for more scars. There was one in his eyebrow, and one on his cheekbone. His day-old beard may have been hiding more. She continued thinking to herself, *I wonder how many more he'll get before he retires from the game? Hopefully not enough to ruin his looks or body for that matter.*

She shut her eyes, committing his gentle face to memory and did something she rarely does. She fell back to sleep.

An hour later, Chris reached around her and pulled her into the warmth of his body. The sensation of waking up in somebody's arms was delightful. She smiled as she opened her eyes.

He gave her a kiss on the forehead. "Wake up sleepy head."

"I'm awake, I'm awake," she said groggily. "I mean I've been awake."

"I know you have. I saw you."

"What? That was at 6," she said, defiantly.

"I know. I was awake too. I just kept my eyes shut."

"Why would you be awake at 6?"

"Hey, I usually stay on Boston time, even when I fly across the continent. It makes it easier."

"Have you been awake all this time? Meagan asked shifting her weight onto one elbow.

"Sorta."

"Aren't you tired? We went to bed at midnight, that would be 2 your time."

"Not bad. But I don't get to see you enough, and I have to admit I enjoyed watching you sleep." He reached up and ran a finger across her forehead. "Besides, it was nice to see your face not look worried."

She blushed. "I have to admit, I did sleep well. Maybe it's because you're here."

He wrapped his arms tight around her, "Yeah, it's that great sex isn't it?"

"So," she said, ignoring his great sex reference, "What do you want to do this morning? Do you need a run, workout, big brunch, do you need to go skating?" she added as a joke.

"Hey, yeah. Great idea! Do you have a pair of skates?" he said, like a schoolboy. "Let's go skating!"

He hopped out of bed and dragged her along. "Do you have skates?" he repeated.

Meagan was hesitant to say yes, but saying no was not an option. By the sounds of his enthusiasm, he would be finding her some skates. "I've got skates, but I'm not very good," she said bashfully.

"Perfect! Now I can be better at something," he said as he reached in his duffle for workout pants. "Is there some outdoor ice somewhere? We can get some pre-breakfast drills in."

Meagan started putting warm clothes on and thinking about the ice in Calgary.

"Oh! We can go to Bowness Park. The lagoon is perfect. And at this time of day, nobody will be there to see me fall. Wait? You have your skates with you?"

"Yup. The rest of the gear travels in crates but I don't want to have my skates go missing so I pack a spare pair in my suitcase. And, it paid off this time!

She found her dusty skates behind her ski equipment. And within a few minutes, they were loaded into her truck.

It didn't take long for them to reach the lagoon. As they drove down the hill into the park, Meagan could see nobody was there. Chris looked over the huge sheet of natural ice and was thrilled by its size.

"Look at the laps we can do!" he cried.

The Zamboni had made its way around the rink, clearing last night's snowfall. He was right; they could do the length of two football fields before slowing down for curves.

Chris had his skates on and was gliding across the ice before Meagan had a chance to untie the knot in her laces that kept the skates together during storage. When she did step onto the ice, Chris was long gone. He had found the channel under the bridge that snaked a kilometre through the rest of the park.

She used the opportunity to practice gliding before he came back.

"Crap!" she said out loud as she nearly spilled, wrenching her back as she stayed upright. "How the hell did I get myself into this mess!"

Suddenly she could hear Chris's blades on the ice, every stride ground into the ice pushing for more speed. She spun around to see him coming straight at her like a bull at a matador. She cringed at the thought of him hitting her. At the last second, he darted to the side and spun around to skate backwards behind her.

"This is fantastic! Do the big guns ever practice here?"

Now he was skating circles around her and it was frustrating her.

"Stop! You're making me dizzy!" she said, laughing as she reached out to stop him.

"Now you know what it's like trying to run with you!" he said sarcastically as he grabbed both her arms to pull her along.

"No!" she shrieked, but it was too late. He was skating backwards pulling her along. She had never moved so fast on skates in her life. He must have seen the fear in her eyes because he slowed right down. Meagan caught her breath. He wasn't even breathing hard as he moved to hold her to his side, matching her skate stroke with his, but doing most of the work. They skated around the rink like a waltzing couple.

"Do you think we could skate like the dancers do?" he said, moving as if to pull her into some contorted figure skating move.

Meagan laughed at his attempt but held his arm tight. "I can't do a triple axel, so don't toss me!"

They were close to the shore where they parked, and Meagan spotted a bench near the edge.

"I need to rest, make a lap without me okay?" she asked.

"Sure," he said, as he sped off.

Meagan sat and admired how smoothly he skated. Each stride took him easily further down the ice. Watching him kept her mind off her woes.

Three cars pulled up and parked beside her truck and five young men spilled out with hockey gear. They walked over to the bench and started putting on skates, not really ignoring her presence, but not acknowledging her either which was fine with her.

The first guy to finish lacing stood up and saw Chris down the ice.

"Shit...look at that guy fly!" he said, in astonishment.

They all stopped what they were doing and looked at Chris.

"Shit," repeated another voice.

"Who is he?" said another.

"I call him on my team if he'll play!" said the first voice again.

"Shit!" said three disgruntled voices. Meagan covered her smile with her mitt.

They stood on the ice as Chris skated up.

"Hey," said the first guy to Chris.

Chris came to a complete stop and said, "Hey, how's it going?"

"Wanna play some shinny?"

"Is it allowed?" asked Chris. No one recognized him with his toque pulled down so far.

"No, not really. We can play until the attendant gets here at 9 a.m. Gotta stick?"

"No, I don't. And really we didn't come to play." Chris said pointing at Meagan. It was like they noticed her for the first time.

"Oh, sorry," said one guy.

Meagan could see they all wanted to play, and she knew it would be fun for them to discover they were playing with a star.

Meagan said, "You can play. It's okay, I don't mind. Do you guys have a spare stick?"

One guy started to wobble up the bank to his car. "Yep."

Chris skated over to Meagan and asked her quietly. "Are you sure?"

Meagan was smiling. "Yes, I'm sure. I can't wait to see these guys when they find out who you are. Don't let them know right away, 'kay?"

He smiled back. "Sure."

The guy with the spare stick handed it off to Chris and the two skated off.

Meagan went to the truck and changed into her boots. There was no point staying in her skates.

The men squared off and a game started up. Chris wasn't trying but was clearly better than any of the younger men. He goofed around a bit but still scored more goals. His teammates were delighted with the stray they had picked up.

It got pretty animated with lots of laughing and shouting. More guys showed up and somehow Chris got away without introducing himself. By the time the park attendant arrived on his ATV, there were two full teams with cheering sections. The attendant sat and watched for a while before calling the game. Chris's team was the winner by a small landslide.

The group of exhausted men skated towards the bench where Meagan was waiting. As Chris handed back the stick, the guy said, "So, can you make it next Sunday? You really picked up the level of play."

Chris shrugged his shoulders and smiled. "Sorry guys, I can't. I'm just visiting."

"Well thanks for the game," said one guy sticking out his hand to shake Chris's. "Where are you from? You play like you are ex-NHL or something."

As Chris reached out to shake his hand, he pulled his toque off, revealing his curly locks. "I'm not ex-NHL yet."

Without the hat they finally recognized him.

"You are Burrows!" screamed one of the shorter guys in disbelief. They stood there staring at him like he was a god.

"Yeah, that's me. Thanks so much for letting me play. That has to be the most fun I've had playing in a long time. It's great when I can play without worrying about a fight."

The guys went nuts laughing and shaking his hand and of course pulled out all their phones. Once again Meagan was the official photographer.

As she took the photos on each phone, one guy said to Meagan, "I heard he had a girlfriend here, man, you are so lucky."

Meagan laughed. "Lucky? This is lucky, standing around a frozen pond watching you guys play before the sun is up? Breakfast in bed is what I call lucky!"

They all laughed, realizing she was kidding. Chris smiled at her, thankful she was so giving.

Chris took off his skates and one of the guys gave him a business card. "If you are looking for a pick-up game again, call me. Unless we're too hungover, we're here on Sunday mornings."

Chris tucked the card in his pocket and put his arm around Meagan. "Thanks again guys, I'll do that. But right now, I think I owe somebody a good breakfast."

Meagan smiled and waved. It was fun to see the delight on their faces and she would have loved to have been a fly on the wall when they went to work the next day, bragging about who they picked up for a game.

Back on the road, Chris patted her on the knee. "Well, where can I take you for breakfast?"

His smile made her smile back. "You love that sport – don't you?"

"Yep, I can't imagine life without it. Now where to for breakfast? I'm starving."

"Let's just hit the grocery store on the way home. I'll grab some bagels and cream cheese. That will be way faster. You'll only have to deal with one adoring fan that way."

Meagan was right; picking up fresh supplies at the grocery store was far faster. They did run into a fan, but eight-year-olds tend not to take up too much of his time when they stare at him.

Back at her house while Meagan sliced fruit and prepared the meal, Chris ran upstairs for a quick shower and to pack. Meagan considered slipping into the shower with him, but she knew it would delay everything and she didn't want to make him late for his plane.

As she laid out the meal, Chris came trotting down the stairs. She shut her eyes and listened, trapping the sound in her brain for lonely days.

They sat at the café table at the kitchen window. A picture on the sill of Dianne and her on the top of a mountain caught Meagan's eye. They had their arms around each other's shoulders, obviously exhausted and by the smiles on their faces, elated with the accomplishment.

Chris saw what she was looking at. "Hey!" he said as he took the picture and flicked it across the room. "I didn't come here to see you get sad. My purpose was to make you happy."

She sighed, "Oh you did, Chris. I don't know how I would have gotten through the weekend without you. I just don't know how to handle tomorrow."

"Call your brother this afternoon and see what he says. Call the detective guy and have him ready to watch Dianne, and..." he took a mouthful of bagel and through a full mouth continued. "Call a locksmith and have him ready to come in at noon," he shut his mouth around the stuff he was chewing and grinned.

She smiled at his wide grin. "Okay smart boy, what do I say to everybody?"

He chewed for a while. Took a swig of his giant-sized milk and said, "Tell everyone you are totally bummed out. Tell them half the computers have viruses and are in the shop, you've got no work coming in; you're tired and want a vacation. And, since you think your mood will affect everyone else's, you've decided to give everyone three days of vacation time, with pay. Then, when everyone comes back on Thursday, they will all be happy, their computers will be clean, and everyone will forge ahead like nothing happened. With that, tell them to go skiing or something."

"And hopefully by Thursday, the police will have sealed the case on Dianne and Russell. And I will start fresh from that day on," she said as strongly as he had. She took a great big bite of her bagel to accentuate her determination. All it did was make him spurt milk as he laughed.

Meagan drove Chris to the airport and as usual, the parting was painful. She tried to be strong on the outside, but on the inside; she was crumbling. Chris could see she was working into a fuss but stayed strong.

"You'll do fine, sweetheart," he said as he held her tight, rocking just a bit. "You have Ben, and the P.I., and the police on your side. And," he paused and looked into her eyes, "You have me."

She shut her eyes and willed the tears to not flow. "I know, thank you. I, I'll call Ben and start planning out tomorrow. I'll call you tomorrow night and let you know how it ended."

"I gotta game tomorrow night. I'll call you after the game. Okay?"

"'Kay."

"Smile, please. A frown doesn't go with your beautiful hair."

Meagan smiled and blushed. She loved that he loved her hair.

"I'll try to watch the game. Don't forget to duck."

Chris laughed and walked into the terminal. Meagan smiled bravely as she watched him disappear through the sliding doors. She took a huge breath of stinky airport air and decided to quit being a victim and to not breathe deep at an airport again.

CHAPTER SEVENTEEN

Driving down Deerfoot Trail, Meagan's phone started to ring. Thankfully it was Ben. She veered onto Memorial Drive and headed straight for his house. When she got there, he was out front playing with Soda.

As she opened the door on the truck, Ben threw a soggy tennis ball through the crack so Soda would leap into the truck.

"Ahhh! Yuck!" A ball bounced off her hand and across the seats. Soda leapt over her, pushing off the steering wheel with her hind paws as she headed for the floor on the passenger side.

Ben came over laughing at the sight. "Haven't you learned how to block yet?"

Meagan was out of the truck now. The dog found the ball and was standing on the seat, wagging her tail and grinding her teeth into the sloppy ball. Ben grabbed it from her and in the same movement threw it across the yard. Soda leapt from the cab after the green orb. Meagan took the opportunity to wipe her dog-slobbered hand on Ben's jacket.

"Yuck!" he said, as he tried to move away.

"Ha, we are even now!" she said laughing.

They walked to the front door and the dog faithfully followed them in, then placed the ball in a wicker basket full of mangled dog toys at the door.

Meagan stared at the dog. "Holy cow, how did you train her to do that?"

"I'm not just a pretty face you know. I can do other things."

"No really, that's cool. How did you train her?"

"Actually, I didn't do anything. She started doing it one day and I didn't stop her. But don't tell anyone else. It makes me look brilliant."

They walked into the kitchen and he grabbed two coffee mugs and then

117

grabbed a third.

"I called Joseph and said you were coming over. He only lives three blocks from here, so he said he would pop by."

The doorbell rang triggering Soda to roar down the hall.

Ben went to the door and brought back Joseph.

Meagan rose to greet him. "Hi Joseph, want a coffee?"

"Yes, thanks. So, how you doin?" he said, smiling and studying her face.

"Well, I'm okay – I guess. I'm glad I've had a bit of time to sort it all out. I think by tomorrow morning I'll be able to handle the group and Dianne. But I'm glad to see you guys. I'd like to hear what you think I should do. Maybe we can work out some scenarios."

They all sat at the table and went over the different settings that could happen. As the sun sank in the window, they came up with a perfect setup they all agreed on.

While Joseph went out for a smoke, Meagan called a locksmith and organized a time for him to come and retool the locks on the house and garage.

Ben watched as she made the call then said, "You seem a lot stronger compared to yesterday. Did you run a marathon or have a spa treatment or sleep the day off or something?"

"Actually." She beamed as she spoke. "Actually, about an hour after you left yesterday the doorbell rang. I thought it was you coming back to check on me. But it was better than you. It was Chris!"

"No way!"

Meagan shut her eyes and dreamily said, "Yeah, way."

"How did he get here? I thought he was in Vancouver and heading home."

"He was, but after talking to me in the morning, he switched his flights and stopped here. I was coming home from the airport when you called."

"So, what did you guys do?" he said then quickly raised a hand in protest. "NO! Don't tell me, I don't want the details."

Meagan laughed. "Don't worry, I'll never tell you any of my sex life. But what was good was to have him here to take my mind off it all for a while. You know what he did this morning?"

"Do I want to know?"

"You will be sooo jealous."

"Okay, what?" he said puzzled.

"He played pickup at Bowness Lagoon with a bunch of guys. They didn't know it was him until the end of the game," she said, laughing as she replayed the imagery in her mind.

Ben screwed up his face in a jealous rage just like she predicted. "What? And you didn't call me?" he said in a high-pitched whine.

"I would have Ben, but it was totally unplanned. We went there to skate and these guys showed up. I could see he was dying to join in, so I sat on a bench and watched."

"You skated?" he said sarcastically, over his rage.

"Well, I tried. And I better keep trying," she said getting serious. "We've decided that we are..."

Ben interrupted, "Getting married!"

"No!"

"Breaking up?"

"No!"

"What then?"

"Don't interrupt and I'll tell you!" she yelled.

He clamped his mouth and dragged his fingers across his lips as if he were zipping it.

Meagan smiled. In all their years, they had never really fought, and she loved that he teased her as if it was a fight.

"Okay," she said, calmly. "We decided that we are..." she paused to find a word that would fit while he stared at her with an impish tight–lipped smile. "...are committed to each other."

Ben let the air burst out of his lips like a bursting pipe. "What? Big deal, a commitment. I wanna see a ring before I start blabbing that he's anything more than just a squeeze."

"Don't tell anyone!" she pleaded.

"I won't. You know I won't."

Joseph walked into the room. "Tell anyone what?"

"That Burrows is..."

"BEN!"

"Her boyfriend."

"Oh," said Joseph. "Who doesn't know that?"

Monday morning, Meagan woke earlier than usual. That's because she barely slept a wink. All night long her dreams kept taking her to the morning meeting and how she would handle it. Some dreams were ridiculous, and others had Dianne flinging files across the room. The last dream had Russell emerging from Dianne's purse and the two of them pointing fingers at her and laughing. The image was too hard to shake so she got up.

She tossed away the idea of a run, thinking the energy would be better spent on the meeting so a long shower would have to do. A run afterwards would clear her head. The first pot of coffee was ready long before the paper would arrive so she turned on the TV to see what was on at that time of day. Nothing. So, she turned it off, leaned her head back and nodded off.

The sound of the newspaper hitting the door woke her from a deep sleep. It wasn't very long but enough to make her feel revitalized. Meagan ran upstairs, got dressed in the blue suit she wore to the Cottonwood meeting, fixed her hair that dried wonky while she napped and came downstairs to have breakfast. Another pot of coffee was set to brew to take down to the meeting. She stood in front of the hall mirror and smiled at herself and said out loud. "I am not a victim anymore. I am taking back my business and my life."

She smiled at herself trying to emulate a confident person. She ran her hands down her jacket to press out the wrinkles and dusted off the lint then walked to the stairs to the basement with the coffee pot in hand.

As she reached the landing, the outside door in the basement opened. Meagan's heart thumped. It was only Ginny. She took a deep breath and realized she better gain better control.

"Hello," Ginny sang out in an overly British accent. "Gorgeous day to be out on the sea, isn't it?"

She plunked her purse down on the desk, slipped off her coat and tossed it on the coat tree, turned on the computer and stuck her coffee cup in front of the pot Meagan was still holding, all in a single motion.

Meagan smiled at Ginny and her ability to do so many things at once. As she poured the coffee she asked, "Still dating the Brit I see."

"Dawling, whatever gave you that idea? Did I tell you he is ex-Royal Navy?" she said with an even thicker accent.

Most days, Meagan would listen and laugh but today was different.

"Hey," Meagan said, seriously as she put down the coffee pot. "I need your help today and I better tell you this fast before the gang gets here."

Ginny saw the look on her boss's face go sour, then noticed the blue suit. She put down the cup and stopped with the accent. "Tell me – I got your back no matter what."

"It's not like I am, er, I mean that the company is broke. You know we are doing fine, but losing this Cottonwood contract has really set me back. I did a bunch of soul-searching this weekend and talked to a few people and am thinking out some options. Because these options hinge on a few details, I think I want the group to take a bit of a breather. I'm not laying people off! I'm just going to give everybody a few days off – with pay, while I sort out the details."

It was a lie, but it sounded plausible. It sounded like a buyout or merge and that's what she wanted. Trying it out on Ginny first was a good idea. When the shoe dropped on Dianne, she would apologize to everyone else.

Ginny asked point-blank, "Are you selling the company?"

"No, I don't think so; I'd rather not say what I'm doing. But I need your help. I'll be telling everyone to go home as soon as they all arrive. I'd like you to back me up, make sure everyone is comfortable with what I say. I don't want anyone jumping ship. I am not firing or laying off anyone and I don't want anyone to send out a resume. I also don't want anyone to leave the office with anything."

Ginny looked around the office and said sourly, "Well I see Dianne's computer is still gone. She can't take that."

"You say that like you think she would."

"Meagan, I don't trust her anymore. I really think she shouldn't be here any longer. She's getting toxic. Maybe there should be a layoff," she added looking over the rims of her red-framed glasses.

Meagan opened her mouth to dig deeper into the comment, but the door opened, the rush of cold air and laughter preceded the design interns.

Meagan quickly changed what she was going to say and said it in a whisper, "Tell everyone not to start anything. The meeting starts when we are all here. When I send everyone home, don't leave."

Ginny nodded and gave a slight salute as Meagan started walking back to her office.

"And...Both my computer and Dianne's are still at the computer shop." She said quickly before shutting her door.

In a panic. she called Ben.

"Ben Dunphy," said Ben in an official-sounding voice.

"Hi, Ben."

"Are you done already?" he asked surprised.

"No. She isn't here yet, but I wanted to look busy. I'm scared."

"Don't worry we are all ready to jump if we need to, but you will be fine. Call me back when you are done. By the way, Joseph is already in place."

"Damn, that guy is good."

"I hope you still think that when his bill comes in."

"Aw shit, don't get me thinking about money or I'm sunk!"

"It will be worth it. Trust me," said Ben.

"I know." She looked up to see Dianne come through the door. "Aw shit, here she is."

"What's she doing?"

Meagan spun her chair around to look in the reflection of the office from the painting on the back wall. She made sure her body language didn't look like she was watching.

"She walked over to her station and is staring at the empty desk... She is gesturing in disgust at Ginny... She hasn't taken her coat off."

Ben interrupted. "You know, you better get out there. If she doesn't stay for the meeting she might jump to her own conclusions."

"Good idea. I'll call you later."

"Be strong," Ben added.

"Thanks."

She hung up the phone, turned and looked at the scene in the rest of the office. Ginny was obviously telling the other three something. Brian and Jennifer instantly looked worried and Dianne still looked perturbed.

"Showtime," Meagan mumbled as she stood up. She took a deep breath and opened her door.

"Hello everyone. Did you all have a good weekend?"

Brian was the first to answer smiling. "Were you down at Bowness Lagoon yesterday morning?"

Meagan looked at him in amazement. "I was! I was there with Chris. How do you know?"

Brian smiled even bigger. "I got a call last night from a friend of mine. He said he played pick-up with Chris."

"Really? Did he have fun?" Meagan asked, grinning as big as he was.

"Oh, man. Did he ever. It's already on his Facebook page. And he's already enlarged the group photo to take to work today to show off to his coworkers. He about crapped when I told him I work for you."

"Or do you mean worked?" said Dianne from across the room. She stood up and was walking towards Meagan in a very threatening way. "What's up with the meeting today? You look like you are dressed to fire people."

Meagan looked long and hard at Dianne. Their eyes locked and there was definitely something very confrontational going on. Jennifer held her breath, fearing the next sentence. Meagan was worried Dianne was figuring things out so she quickly took control in a cheery disposition.

"Geez, Dianne lighten up. Why do I need to fire anybody? I do need to talk to everyone but geez, there are no pink slips. Everybody grab a beverage and come to the table."

Jennifer swallowed and started breathing again. Ginny put the answering machine back on and they all settled into the stools around the boardroom/lunchroom table. Everyone took their favourite seats at the table, but Dianne oddly took the chair at the head of the table which was usually Meagan's. For some reason, her disposition was really rough. Meagan couldn't put her finger on it but decided not to challenge her. At least not yet. She wanted to see what was up Dianne's sleeve this time.

Meagan settled into a spare seat and started to speak.

"I'll make this brief. It's been a long grind working on the Cottonwood project. And you all know we did not get it. I know you all worked very hard on it. I really thought we had a chance on this one. But once again, we were not the bid they took and that got me thinking.

"We are a young company, both in age and experience. I can see why we would get passed over on the big projects. So, over the weekend, in between hockey games," she said smiling at Brian, "I was thinking we need to reorganize. We need to find someone to bring on staff to give us some credibility. I haven't decided if that means we sell or merge, or find a stray designer or architect. But changes need to happen.

"I was talking to a few seasoned professionals and am mulling over the prospects. So, instead of having you all here playing solitaire on the computer while I think this through, I'd like to give you a bonus holiday. So, starting right now, you are on a three-day holiday. I'm paying for it and am assuming to have some answers when you come back in on Thursday morning. Please understand, I am not going to fire anyone. I am actually planning on building the company into something bigger and better, so we can stay in the race with the big dogs."

She looked around at her employees and raised her eyebrows. "Is that okay?"

Brian, Jennifer, and Ginny all nodded in agreement, but Dianne was a thorn.

"Where is my computer anyway?"

"As you can see, both your computer and mine are still at the shop. Turns out the computer geek I took them to had a wedding on Saturday and wasn't feeling up to repairing them yesterday either. He promised to get them back to me by tomorrow."

"There's stuff I want on it though."

"Me too, Dianne, but my hands are tied. What do you need? You are on holidays."

"I still want to work on stuff," she said, indignantly.

"Dianne, if I recall, the Flannagan beams are not due until tomorrow, I can send the crew out on that. And you don't have any pending job bids. And if you did, I could cover for you."

"I still want it. Where is this guy?" Her voice was starting to rise with angst. "There is stuff I want."

"What,...like your resume?" piped in Ginny.

Dianne spun her chair to glare at Ginny. "Watch it, Office Girl!"

Ginny jumped up like she was going to punch her.

Meagan stood up and put her hands out to silence the two. "That! That behaviour will not happen in my office. Dianne, your attitude is despicable. I suggest you gather your stuff and leave. If you decide to apologize to Ginny, you are invited to come back on Thursday."

The two women stared at each other. Meagan had more power and Dianne averted her eyes.

Dianne looked at Ginny. "I'm sorry Ginny. I'm just worried this company is going down and I don't want to sink with it."

She stood up and not speaking to anyone in particular said, "I'll see you Thursday."

Everyone silently watched as Dianne picked up her purse, grabbed her coat and left.

Jennifer quietly asked, "Do you think she will be back?"

"Other than to pick up her Happy Face mug?" asked Meagan.

"Nope," said both Meagan and Ginny at the same time. They looked at each other and smiled sadly.

"I'll freshen our coffee," said Ginny to break the ice.

"Naw, you guys go," Meagan said, as she finally sat down.

The students got up and smiled at their boss, not knowing what to do.

It was Brian who finally got up the nerve. "So, what's going on Meagan? Really, I mean."

Meagan looked up at him puzzled by his comment. "What do you mean?"

Right then, Ginny came back to the table with a few cups of coffee and set one down in front of Meagan. She smiled in gratitude at Ginny and wrapped her cold hands around the mug.

"He means just that," said Ginny as she slid into a chair across from Meagan. "What is with Dianne? Three days off with the promise of continued work when we return sounds pretty sweet. Why did Dianne make it sound like we are going to go down?"

"Yeah. I know she is your friend and all, but why is she so mean to you all the time?" added Jennifer, who never really challenged anyone.

Meagan looked around the table at her employees. She knew she had a damn good group and could probably trust them with her secret. But the operative word was "probably" so she kept her secret hidden.

"I dunno you guys. I dunno. But, don't worry. By the looks of it, the demon on her back is starting to get to her and one way or another we won't have to deal with her anymore. The good thing is, if I do find a new designer or architect, I don't have to worry about Dianne's paycheque anymore. I'd say she has decided to be taken off the team."

She could tell everyone wanted to talk, but the locksmith was coming, and she didn't want them to see him. She stood up and pushed her chair in signifying the end of the discussion.

"Now...," she said with a huge sigh, "If I was handed a three-day paid vacation, I'd get the hell out of the basement! Go skiing or shopping or back to bed. I want to see three happy holidayers on Thursday morning who are eager to work."

She turned and left the table and went back to her desk to avoid any more discussion. Every few minutes she glanced up to see what everyone was doing. The three stood there talking quietly for a few minutes then one by one picked up their jackets and bags. Brian waved and shouted from the door at Meagan, "See ya Thursday, I'm going skiing!"

Everyone waved.

Jennifer took the quiet route and passed by Meagan's door. "Thanks, Meagan. I think I'll go shopping. Are you okay?"

Meagan smiled and said she was fine.

Ginny was the last to leave. She shut down the computers, cleaned up the lunchroom even though no one used it for anything but sitting, then came to Meagan's door.

"Megs?"

"Gin?"

"She is up to something evil."

"I know."

"What are you going to do?"

Meagan paused and thought for a few seconds. "I'm doing it."

Ginny looked perplexed.

Meagan added. "I'm trying to figure out what to do. But I think she is cooking her own goose. I don't think she will show her face here anymore."

Ginny nodded silently. "Are you sorry to see her go?"

"Oddly not. And Gin," Meagan added. "I'm sorry she insulted you like she did. You know you are very valuable to me. You don't think I'm folding the company – do you?"

Ginny shook her head. "No. I know you aren't. I know how much is in the bank. We can stay in business for a long time. And without the dragon, we can last a lot longer."

"So, what are you going to do with your time off?"

Ginny smiled and answered in her silly British accent, "I'm going to ring up my smashingly charming Brit and since the other two took the skiing and shopping suggestions, I am going to drag him back to bed!"

Meagan laughed at Ginny. "Well, have fun! But don't forget to come back to us on Thursday."

"Right-o daw-ling. I'll call if he swoops me off my feet and takes me to his castle on the moors."

Meagan shook her head laughing as Ginny made a grand exit out the door. The office fell silent. Meagan plopped back into her chair and sighed. "Well, that went better than I thought," she said to herself.

CHAPTER EIGHTEEN

The morning was spent organizing what had to be done. She called her tradesmen and the few who regularly pop in were surprised by the lone occupant instead of the usual frenzy of activity. The phone rang a few times; two were for the interns and one was a hang-up from an undisclosed number. She noted that on a piece of paper just in case the police wanted to know.

By 11 o'clock the locksmith had changed every lock including her house locks. In the past, Dianne had used Meagan's house keys and returned them, but Meagan wasn't taking any chances.

After the locksmith left, Meagan sat down to call Ben.

"Boy, it's weird being in here all by myself on a Monday," she said after they exchanged greetings.

"How did it go? You sound calm."

"I can't tell if Dianne is on to us. She was very determined to get her computer back. Thankfully she insulted Ginny beyond what I could tolerate, and that blow-up diverted the discussion away from the computers."

"That's good."

"Yeah, have you heard anything from Joseph?" she asked tentatively.

"No. But that's a good thing. He'll gather a day's worth and get back to me. Where do you think Diana went?"

Meagan thought it out. "Well, she huffed off so that means she will either spend the day at the mall or head straight to Carl's apartment or office."

"Or all three," added Ben.

Meagan was silent.

"Megs?"

She quietly answered, "Yeah." Suddenly she was overwhelmed by the silence in the office. She sat staring at the heap of keys the locksmith left for her employees. She wondered if she needed them.

"You'll be okay. This will work out." Ben was speaking softly and confidently, trying to reassure her over the phone. "We will get this guy and your company will continue to grow."

"God I hope so," she moaned. "Shit I don't know. Why do I bother? Why don't I just shut the door and go work for someone else?"

"Oh Megs, you don't want to do that."

She stood up and started pacing the room. Her heart rate started to rage as she ranted.

"Why not? It would be so easy to just walk into an office Monday morning, hang my coat on the back of the door, grab a coffee that someone else made and sit down to a job that was handed to me by someone else who sweated the bullets. I'd love to have a dental plan, holiday pay, something to leave at the end of the day so that I could go home to my house. Not just upstairs. I'd like to walk away, not worry about it over the weekend, check my bank account and watch it grow every two weeks."

"Are you done?"

"No, I'm pissed off!" she said, waving her arms to no one.

"You don't want that."

"How do you know what I want," she said fuming.

"Because I know you and I know you can not work for anybody."

"Why not?"

"Your attitude would get you fired in a week. You know you can't NOT be the boss."

"Can."

"Can't."

"Can."

"Can't"

She started to laugh, "Can too."

Ben laughed, "You realize, as your lawyer I can charge you 400 bucks an hour to continue doing this?"

Meagan had worked her way to Ginny's desk and now flopped down in her seat. Sighing she agreed. "Okay, can't."

"Feel better?" Ben asked.

"Yeah. It's hard sitting here with no one to bounce this off. Thanks for not charging me for your time."

"Beer."

"Okay, I'll bring beer next time."

"There's a game tonight, why don't you come and watch it with me and Soda. Bring beer and we are even."

"That sounds great, Ben. I'll bring something green to eat too," she added, knowing all he would do is order pizza as usual.

"You can't make me eat it."

"Can!"

"Can't! You're not mom."

Just as he said that Meagan looked up and through the window to the side of the house and saw a familiar head bobbing down the stairs.

"Oh shit. You're right…" she said flatly. "Mom's here."

Ben laughed hysterically. "Hope you live…see you tonight!"

Meagan started rubbing her face. "Why is she here today of all days, why today?"

She knew she had to do some fast-talking. She didn't want to tell her mom what was going on. Out of habit Meagan looked down at what she was wearing and started tucking in her shirt and rubbing the creases out of her skirt. She pushed Chris's bracelet up her arm so it would be stuck under her sleeve.

The door opened and in walked Lorene Dunphy. If there was a course offered in socialite etiquette, Lorene would have a master's degree. Calgary is not known for debutants and families of inherited wealth, but Lorene made it look like she was raised on a plantation of wealth. Most people, however, did not know she came from a standard middle-class upbringing with an average education. That is, prior to entering university.

Her parents hadn't planned for her to go into post-secondary schooling, thinking that working in a shop was fine until Mister Right came along. But what Lorene lacked in guidance from her parents and book smarts, she made up in foresight and damn good looks. Lorene snubbed her nose at the thought of community college and squeaked into university. She took the easiest classes she could find so she could put her energies into the reason she was there. To find a potential wealthy mate. She hung out where the engineers, pre-med and law students would be, wooing the handsome candidates a few years her senior. When she met Duncan, Meagan's father, Lorene sunk her teeth in and didn't let go.

Duncan was a fine catch. Top marks, handsome, well-liked and from a distinguished line of lawyers with a law firm waiting with open arms. Lorene scraped along in her classes but fell into place guiding their future along. They were married as soon as Duncan graduated and as planned, she got pregnant on the honeymoon, thus ending her ability to finish her degree, in what no one ever figured out. She obviously got what she wanted from attending university.

As far as Duncan was concerned, he had found the perfect mate. She was doting, stroked his ego and made him look and feel great. She took control of the household and made sure they attended all the right social functions. Of course, there was a cost involved. Her personal upkeep was expensive and somewhat narcissistic, but she still kept him satisfied.

The kids thought she was a basket case.

Ben and Meagan did love their mother, but she was too controlling for their liking. Ben got off easy being the male offspring; he followed in his father's footsteps and was doing a fine job. The only black mark he had against him was that he decided to step out on his own. He articled at his dad's firm but broke away to build his own law company. Meagan was expected to follow in her mother's footsteps and take a more submissively feminine route through life, and maybe be a lawyer on the side. You, know – be perfect.

Lorene did her best to train Meagan to hunt for the perfect mate. Meagan did try to please her mother and did date Stephan to prove it, but she was too strong-willed to take a backseat. Like Ben said – running marathons and designing buildings was not what her boyfriend or mother could handle, so Meagan broke away from the family and rarely called or stopped by. Her dad understood as did Ben, but Lorene never forgave her. Even though Meagan was brilliant, beautiful and respected by most people in the industry, her mother treated her like a failure. It seemed like the only time she saw her mother, was when Lorene could rub salt into wounds. And by the look on her face, today was going to be one of those days.

Lorene stepped through the door and as she kicked the snow off her designer boots she looked up to see her entrance was received by an empty office – a disappointment for a woman who gages her day on the effect of her entrances.

Meagan was still sitting at Ginny's desk and noticed the look of disappointment on her mothers' face.

She tried to sound cheery. "Hi, Mom. What brings you out through the snow? Is that a new coat?"

Even though Meagan didn't know her mother's wardrobe anymore, she could safely guess it was new. And why skip around small talk when really there was no point talking about the weather with a woman who avoids it. Meagan found it safest to talk to her mother about her favourite topic, herself.

Unbuttoning the collar to reveal another stunning outfit that Meagan had never seen before, Lorene dramatically answered. "Yes, it is new. I just picked it up at Angeline's. I had it tailored to fit properly. I hate buying off the rack at other stores that don't offer customized tailoring. You never look quite right without it."

Lorene was looking at Meagan's clothes. "You aren't still buying at that discount store – are you?"

"Yeah Mom, I am," Meagan responded but wondered how her mother could come in and within a minute insult her about the suit she helped pick out at her favourite designer shop and demand tailoring on something that fit perfectly.

Meagan ran her hand through her hair, tossing the curls over her shoulder. As she walked to the coffee room she asked. "Are you stopping for a coffee?"

"Oh no dear, thank you. I'm meeting the girls for lunch and only have a few minutes."

Relieved the torture would be only minutes long, she grabbed her own coffee and turned back to say. "So, what's up?" Meagan was preparing for three scenarios. First that she would be grilled about Chris, second would be about losing to Carl again and the dreaded third case would be that she heard about both. Meagan was hoping for number one.

"Where is everybody?" Is the first question she asked as if finally noticing the audience wasn't there.

"Oh well, let's see," Meagan said, as she started pointing at desks. "Ginny is stuck in bed today; the students are on a field trip and I think Dianne is out shopping for ideas."

Meagan was pleased with her excuses; all of them were slightly true.

Lorene looked around with a look of disgust and said, "It looks deserted to me."

"Thanks, Mom. Is that why you came?" Meagan couldn't hide her disappointment.

"Sorry, I didn't mean that in a bad way. I mean it's so quiet. You must get a lot done when they are all out," she added, trying to unhurt her daughter's feelings. She quickly changed the topic.

"I really came by to say hello. You haven't been answering your phones lately. Your father and I had a lovely time at the condo over Christmas. You and Ben should try to come to Hawaii at some point. But, I know he is busy with court cases. And, I guess you are too busy with a new love life?" she said, raising her voice at the end to accentuate the love life bit.

"I have been busy. This really is the first time I've been in the office for weeks," Meagan relaxed, it looked like the interrogation was about Chris. "I know I should have called but whenever I had a chance, it was too late to call."

"So, is it true you are dating a...hockey player?" Lorene was looking at her as if she was covered in mud.

"I guess I am. His name is Chris Burrows. I met him a while ago and only see him when he comes through Calgary so really, I don't think it's too serious."

"Who does he play for?"

"Boston?"

"Is he a star player?"

Meagan was seeing where this was going. It's always about money.

"Um, I can't say for sure. He's not a Wayne Gretzky, if that is what you are asking. He's more of a hidden star."

"What do you mean?"

If there is one person who knew less about hockey in Canada than Meagan, it was her mother.

"He doesn't score a lot of goals. His job is to, is to..." Meagan was stuck.

"He's more of a blocker. He stops the Gretzky guys from scoring. He's very good at it too. One of the best in the league," she added.

Her mother nodded in approval. She seemed pleased with the title of best in the league. It was something she could boast about at lunch.

"Well, how serious is this? You aren't planning to marry him or move – are you?"

"Mom, I barely know the guy."

"You know marrying a hockey player would not be a good idea," Lorene said as if she knew this for a fact. "You'd have to give up this career. You'd have to move to whatever city he was playing for. And what is he trained to do after he is let go from the league? Can he afford to be married?"

Meagan stood there dumbfounded. All the blood in her body drained to her feet. She could barely hold her coffee mug. *What the fuck! Is anyone else going to punch me today?* is what she wanted to say.

"Mom," she said softly. "I don't plan to move anywhere. My company – believe it or not – is doing very well and I don't plan to shut it down for anybody right now. He's a nice guy. We have dinner and if he has time, we go for a run together."

"That's it?" Lorene said, staring her daughter in the eyes.

"There's no time for anything else!"

Lorene walked back to where her draped her coat waited and started putting it on. "I just want you to be careful. I don't want you to be sucked in by an egotistical hockey hero and end up having fatherless brats playing hockey in the streets."

Meagan stared at her mother with a threatening glare. Finally, she sucked in a deep breath. "Mom, I'm not going to have any fatherless children. With warnings like that, I'll never find a man."

"If you would socialize with the right people, you would."

That was the last straw. Meagan got lippy, "I'm not hanging out at the golf course or courthouse. As a matter of fact, I kinda like the honky-tonk bar. I'll get me a tattoo, slap on some cheap perfume and head out to find me a trucker. But not just any trucker - I'll get me one driving a semi so the car seats can fit in safely, so we can travel the continent together as one big happy truckin family!"

"Meagan! I don't know why you have to get so snippy! I'm trying to look out for your future."

Oh great! thought Meagan, *Here comes the 'I- did- everything'* spiel she avoided at Christmas.

To Meagan's relief, the office phone started to ring.

"I gotta answer this, Mom," she walked towards her own office to answer it, distancing herself from the conversation. "Don't worry, I'll find someone someday with piles of dough so I can dress snappy like you and hang out all afternoon with the gals, just like you. Okay?"

Meagan waved as she picked up the phone, her mother sadly waved back. She was disappointed she didn't get her usual last word in.

"Meagan Dunphy," Meagan said into the phone with a heavy sigh.

"Hello Meagan, it's Derek Whitmore. Do you have a minute to talk?"

Meagan paused to make sure her mother had really left the office and sat down. Whitmore must have sensed her mood.

"Everything go as planned?" he asked carefully.

"Oh yeah. As far as my employees go, it all went fine. I'm just exhausted because my mother just stopped by to give me my monthly "marry-for-money" lecture."

"Ouch. I bet she didn't tell you to marry a cop, did she?"

"A man in a uniform? Are you kidding? She could explain to the country club that my doctor husband was off delivering babies, but not on shift saving the city! Oh, no...a cop is all wrong, so are firemen, biologists, geologists, salesmen, teachers and her favourite...truckers!"

They both laughed at the expectations.

"Get one of your contractors to drive you past her house while she is out gardening," Whitmore said, laughing.

"No. Better yet, start dating the guy hired to do her gardening," laughed Meagan.

It felt good to be understood. Whitmore's humour was what she needed to shake off her mother's wrath.

Whitmore sighed to calm down. "Okay so, really how did this morning go? Did you change the locks yet?"

"Yep, about an hour ago."

"Good," he paused for a second before continuing carefully. "The techs here did get into Dianne's computer and are going through her files and emails. Do you want to know what we have found so far?"

Meagan shut her eyes hoping for good news. "Yeah, is it good?" she asked, without opening her eyes.

"Depends on who you are," Whitmore said, obviously smug about what he knew. "If you are you, you'd be happy to know the mole has been found. If you are Russell, you better start looking for a new line of work you can enter after a decade in jail. And if you are Dianne, you'd better stock up on stamps, because you definitely shouldn't be trusted with electronic mail any longer."

Meagan's eyes blinked open in disbelief. "Are you serious?"

Whitmore tried to stay calm. "Meagan, this is an open and shut case. There is enough evidence on Dianne's computer to send her up the river. And there is enough with Russell's name on it to pull him into the fire. Not only that, Patel has been digging up old files and already has three other cases where Russell is accused of corporate misdoings. Combine that with the history of sexual misconduct at the university, the man is in serious trouble. At the very least — even with a really good lawyer, he is losing his licence to operate as an architect."

Meagan sighed in disbelief. "This is great. But."

"But what?" asked Whitmore.

"It just dawned on me that I'm potentially sending someone I thought of as a friend to jail. I'm terminating Dianne's career." Meagan suddenly was overcome with the realization, but Whitmore snapped her out of her pity.

"Oh no, you aren't. None of this is your doing. You were duped by these two for too long. By the looks of her email, she has been in business with him since she started with your company. I suggest you look over your books and see when you started losing bids to Russell. I'm willing to bet it starts when she started. I'm willing to bet that this is deeper than just winning the bids away from a competitor. I think Russell is using Dianne as payback to you for ruining his career at the university."

"How did you figure this out so fast?"

"Your friend is not very computer savvy. She never dumped her wastebasket or incriminating emails. She assumed a password to her private account was good enough to guard her illegal activity. And unfortunately, Russell found a gullible stooge. Some of his emails offer her more than the moon. Being on the outside looking in, it's easy to see the deception but look at her. We know she is not the most beautiful or confident girl. A handsome influential man like Russell takes her under his wing...she was willing to do anything, include ruin a friendship that would have taken her further than he ever would."

"I wish she didn't do that," she said sadly.

"It's too late now, Meagan. The damage is done."

"What should I do now?" she asked.

"Let's continue as we decided on Saturday. The group is gone right?"

"Right. I gave them until Thursday morning."

We will continue gathering evidence and probably talk to Russell on Thursday. Do you want to see if she has the balls to come into work on Thursday?"

"Let me think about that. Maybe I should have you here as the 'new architect' that was supposed to be buying into the company."

"That's not a bad idea. I'll call Ben and apprise him of the charges you two should be discussing."

"That's great. I'll see him later today and we can go over the next step. Thanks, so much Derek."

"My pleasure."

Meagan sat down at her desk and squealed with delight. The tides were changing in her favour. At least, for now.

CHAPTER NINETEEN

Meagan stopped at her favourite grocery store on the way to Ben's house. She scanned the warming bins and spotted the seafood cannelloni – her favourite. A quick tour through the produce section found enough vegetables to stock Ben's fridge. It's not that he was afraid of vegetables; he was just too lazy to go buy any. Even though she had told him many times about the benefits of hanging around grocery stores for meeting healthy young women, he wouldn't do it.

Soda was at the door before Ben. Her nose was pressed up against the frosted glass as if trying to sniff out who was on the other side. Meagan could hear Ben's voice as he hurried down the hall.

"Soda! Get down! You're going to scare away the nice salesman," he said, as he opened the door.

"Yeah right," Meagan said. "As if you consider anyone looking for your money nice!"

Ben took the bags and Soda's attention turned from Meagan to the aromatic trail. That made it easier for her to bend over and take off her shoes without a black nose in her face. Her coat ended up draped over the railing as usual.

"Hey, this looks great," Ben said, as he pulled the cannelloni from the bag. "Is it ready to eat?"

"We should warm it up a bit. I'll make a salad. Did Whitmore call you?"

Ben was already heading for the kitchen. "Yeah he did," he shouted over his shoulder. "Come here and I'll tell you about it."

Meagan was already following him down the hall. She couldn't help but admire the fantastic job her team did on the house. Every time she walked through, it boosted her ego. Ben may not be too domestic, but at least he hired the right people to take care of the house.

The kitchen, like many houses in the community, was well appointed. The right amount of granite accented the appliances and richly stained wood cabinetry. She often wondered if he ever stopped to admire the city skyline she worked hard to accentuate in the windows.

Ben was putting the pasta in the spotless oven as he started to talk.

"Whitmore called around lunchtime. He said he had just talked to you. Isn't that fantastic what they found out? Can you believe what kind of snitch Dianne is? I always thought she was a little bit of a lost lamb, but I didn't think she could be so evil!"

Meagan was pulling vegetables out of the bag while he went on. His excitement was fun to watch, even if it was somewhat at her expense.

She found the carrot peeler at the back of the drawer and started peeling. "Derek said I should look at my books and try to figure out what jobs I was losing out on and when. He figures I lost most of the jobs that Russell bid on because of Dianne."

Ben was reaching for the mandatory hockey-watching beer. "He's right. What you need to do is look over your list of job bids. Whether or not Russell won the bid is not important. Your ideas may not have been better than the winner. The point we need to prove is that he stole your ideas. I should probably contact the lawyers representing some of the other architect firms that he won over. He may have a snitch in the other offices."

As he took a swig of his beer to accentuate his statement, he looked up at the wall clock.

"Come on, let's watch *The Man*!"

He handed her a frosty mug of beer as he walked towards the family room and big screen TV that was already cued to the game. Meagan knew the discussion wasn't over, it would resume during intermissions and commercial breaks. If dating a hockey player had done anything it had brought the siblings together. They had always been close but hanging out watching hockey suddenly gave them another reason to visit.

Ben settled onto the couch next to Soda and put his feet up on the coffee table, Soda's head landed on his lap and he proceeded to rub her ears. Meagan sat on the huge leather chair and used the ottoman to prop her feet up. The music for Hockey Night in Canada started up queuing Meagan's heart to flutter. The emotion of the day had pushed her thoughts of Chris to the back of her mind, but sitting down to watch the game brought him to the front. Even though she saw him only yesterday, she wanted to be with him that very second. Now her focus turned to the game and she started to worry about his fate.

Ben was watching her and asked. "How long do you think it will take you to stop worrying that he will get hurt each game?"

"How do you know I was starting to worry?" she asked puzzled.

"I've been watching your face for a long time. You used to look at me with that same look when I went out on the ice."

"Shit, am I transparent or what?" she said, taking a sip of beer.

"It's okay. But when we go to court over this stuff, you gotta have a poker face."

As the end of the first period drew near, Meagan went out to the kitchen and put together the dinner. She was too hungry to sit there and watch. Besides, Chris had a penalty and would be stuck in the box into intermission. She found watching the game on TV somewhat boring. When she was at the games she dictated what she watched and usually her eyes were trained on Chris, but the cameramen were following the plays – not her heart.

Ben came into the kitchen carrying a note pad and sat at the barstools with Meagan. He put the pad in front of Meagan and picked up his fork to eat.

"Okay, here is what you need to do," he said, pointing with his fork to the list hand-written on the pad.

Meagan looked down and saw a huge list of things she had to do. Obviously, Ben had been thinking about the case and wanted to focus on getting things back on track.

He continued to speak as he ate. "You have to use the next few days to pull in all this information. It looks like a lot, but I think most stuff will be easy to find. Your bills for her cell phone, bid packs she worked on that overlapped the contracts he bid on. Give me a list of the ones he won, that you won, that neither of you won but both worked on. Sit down and think about all the confrontations and meetings you've had with him. If you can remember ever discussing Carl in front of Dianne, write it down. I also want you to write down any times you found her missing from the office without good reason.

"I'll bet Ginny can help you with a lot of this, but I don't want you to bring her into the loop until we have made our findings public. I like the idea of having one of the detectives at your office on Thursday morning to serve Dianne with the warrant for her arrest on charges of corporate theft. The other detective will be accompanied by police officers and he will go to Russell's office to serve him on the same charges. Those officers will kick out the staff and seize Russell's files and computers to prove the wrongdoing."

He stopped to take a swig of beer, but Meagan still sat quietly. She was amazed at how fast he was talking and how serious he was.

"We should have these two in court within a few weeks. I don't know what will happen at his office, but your team can pick up and continue working."

"A few weeks?" Meagan was worried. That's when she planned to go to The Bahamas with Chris.

"What's wrong with that?" he said, through his mouth full of salad.

"I was planning to go to Chris's place in The Bahamas."

"Nice!" he said, smiling. "For how long?"

She shrugged her shoulders. "A few days. He's got a few days during that winter or spring break thing they do just before playoffs."

He shook his head and clenched his eyes shut with the reference to the 'spring break thing.'

"Okay, find out those dates for me first, so I can plan around it. It shouldn't be an issue. As a matter of fact, you could use a little fun in the sun. What's his place like? Is it on the beach? Can I go too?" he added, knowing full well the answer.

"I don't know what it's like. He's told me tons of stuff and it does sound great. He says the sand there is soft like talc and pink."

"Pink?" he said, with disbelief.

"Really – it is. The sand is ground up coral and seashells unlike the sand on the west coast made up from ground up mountains."

"Cool. What's the house like?"

"It's not done yet. And he's kinda pissed off about it. The guy running the job is the son of one of his old coaches, but he doesn't seem to be getting the job done so Chris wants to go see."

"I'll bet the guy is sitting drinking rum and smoking pot on the pink sand instead of working," said Ben, as he helped himself to more pasta.

Meagan shrugged her shoulders. "I don't know, but I'll see if I can help."

"Naw, stay out of it," Ben said, shaking his head.

"Why?"

"No, what I should say is – don't appear too eager. Sit back and watch the guy and make notes. After you leave, make your suggestions. If the guy is a jerk, who knows what type of work will get done if the 'girlfriend' made the suggestions."

Meagan nodded. "Besides, I have enough problems on my plate. What could I possibly contribute in five days?"

Ben leaned back on his chair and saw the TV. "Game on."

He headed back to the sofa to plop down with Soda. Meagan cleaned up the dishes and took the note and stuck it in her purse before she resumed her spot on the chair.

Meagan woke early the next morning after a surprisingly restful sleep. She put on her running clothes and went down to the office after a quick stop in the kitchen for a bagel. If she played her cards right, she could have an hour at her desk before dashing off with her running pals. Running, especially with her friends was great therapy. And, it was Tuesday so that meant hills.

She started with phone bills and the client billing charts and stacked them on her desk. It surprised her how time flew by so fast on a chore she thought would be nasty.

As she drove towards the Y, she noticed the flags were flapping. A strong westerly wind was blowing and a quick glance at the temperature gauge confirmed a mild −2C. "It will be a perfect day for a run," she said, to an empty truck.

There standing on the stairs outside the Y was a rainbow of coloured jackets. Everybody was there. Gloria in a blue running jacket lined with reflective tape, Emma in an orange vest and Lizzie in her regular old yellow shell.

"Hey, Meagan," said Gloria, as they came towards her. "Glad you could make it."

"Ya stuck on a big job or something?" asked Lizzie as they simultaneously turned the timers on their watches and started to trot.

Meagan smiled and said, "You guys, this has been the wildest ride of my life and I have no idea where it's going or if it will ever end. How many hours are we running because this might take a little bit."

As they turned onto the running path along the Bow River, her friends stared at Meagan in disbelief.

"Shit," Gloria finally said. "A simple 'I'm fine' would suffice. But hey, a couple hours should clean out your system. Go ahead and spill it."

Lizzie couldn't wait, "It's not about Chris is it?"

"No, thank goodness. He is fantastic and I'm so glad he came along. It's my office. I've got a big problem."

The girls started out with an easy pace to loosen up. Meagan knew she had to be careful of how much she revealed. She loved her friends and knew they would never do or say anything to intentionally hurt her, but they all had husbands they went home to talk to and who knows how much the men folk gossip or where.

As they passed under Centre Street Bridge, Meagan looked up at the stoic lion statues who have graced the bridge for eternity and began her carefully worded story. She decided to give them the Readers Digest version. By the time they looped into Bridgeland she had said enough. They turned to the hills making conversation impossible.

By Wednesday at noon, the piles on Meagan's desk had spread across her drafting table, onto the floor and into the hall. On top of each pile, Meagan left a slip of paper listing the contents of the pile. The phone bills were on the corner of the table with each of Dianne's cell phone bills highlighted. One bill had a red tab stuck to it which made Meagan feel quite proud.

It was from the first year of setting up the company when she sent Diane up to Edmonton to scope out a potential job that in hindsight, she was happy to miss. The owner of the building turned out to be a complete jerk, sending the Edmonton-based company into the poorhouse. What was important was the list of calls Dianne made. Two were to Carl's cell. After that, there were no more calls. Carl must have told her not to call on the company phone. She made a note on the cover sheet to ask the police if they could obtain Dianne's personal cell phone bills from the telephone company.

Meagan went through the expense account and by Tuesday evening she discovered many instances where Dianne had claimed lunch for two when no clients were involved. She bet her bottom dollar she was feeding the creep jobs and food! That pile had many red flags attached including the parking lot stubs. Meagan didn't have time to sort them all out, but she planned to call the parking company to find out the codes for their parking lots. She was willing to bet the parking stubs were not all work-related either.

Meagan made lists of the jobs she bid on, jobs she won and jobs she lost. Then in the last column, she made notes from memory which ones Carl won. She was crushed to see how many he won. Who knows how many others he had stolen, but didn't win. She considered driving by some of the buildings he won to see if any of her designs popped up, but decided that could wait.

Late Wednesday afternoon the detectives came to her door carrying the company computers. Meagan had just finished organizing everything when they came in.

"Wow," exclaimed Detective Whitmore looking over the piles. "Are you moving out or having a garage sale?"

Meagan smiled at him and stood back and admired her efforts. "It's been a very busy few days."

Patel was smiling at her work. He ran his hand across a few piles, reading the handwritten headers as he went along. He picked up the phone bill pile and whistled as he stopped on Dianne's flagged cell phone.

"Nice work, detective," he said to Meagan, as he handed over the pile to Whitmore.

Detective Whitmore smiled and nodded. "You wanna hear what's going to happen tomorrow?"

Meagan took a deep breath making her chest rise. There was no going back. She threw up her arms and said, "Why not. I'm up to my waist in alligators; let's drain the swamp."

The trio moved into the coffee room and sat down at the three end chairs. Patel took a notepad from the side table and placed his pen beside it, ready for notes then started to talk.

After the police left, Meagan put all the computers back where they were supposed to be. She hid the piles of evidence and made a company portfolio up and left it in the coffee room for Detective Whitmore to peruse when he came back as an architect. If she didn't know any better, Thursday was looking to be just another day at the office.

CHAPTER TWENTY

Wednesday night was one of the longest Meagan had been through. Nightmare of Dianne and Russell plagued her sleep again. She gave up and went downstairs to the kitchen to clean out the fridge. Almost everything went into the bin under the sink, because images of Dianne sticking a knife in the mayo jar or reaching into the pickle jar revolted Meagan. New jars of condiments were easy to replace.

At 7:45 a.m. on the dot, Detective Derek Whitmore and another plain-clothed officer entered the office. The other officer quickly took off his shoes, picked them up and along with a laptop slung over his shoulder, disappeared to the second floor.

Meanwhile downstairs Whitmore hid microphones at Dianne's desk, the coffee room and oddly, in the washroom. He wanted to be prepared for any hidden cell phone calls and that's about the only place in the office it could happen. With the spy gear set up, he moved his focus on to Meagan to get her mentally prepared for the day.

Today, he was not a detective; he was transformed into an architect moving to Calgary looking for a company to join. Meagan thought it was odd that on most days, Whitmore looked like a cop in rather cheap brown suits. But today, the corporate blue suit and jazzy silk tie made him look rather downtown-ish. He even made effort to soften his razor-sharp haircut.

"Hello Meagan," he said, with an outreached hand. "Derek White, architect from Winnipeg, looking to invest." His face was deadpan and by the look in his eyes, even though no one else was in the office yet, he expected her to play along.

She took his hand. "Hello Derek, it's nice to finally see you again. I'm so pleased you are interested in my company. I hope you found the financial reports adequate. Is there anything else you need to sway your decision?" she said, as seriously and as unfamiliar as possible. *Gee,* she thought to herself. *Acting is not easy.*

"The corporate reports are fine. I'd like, however, to look over your job listings to see how well you do with your bids. Do you have a listing ready?"

"Yes, I've stacked them in the coffee room; I hope you don't mind using that table. We have such a busy office, I didn't know where else to put them. Besides, it will give you a chance to meet my team."

"Excellent Meagan," said Whitmore. "You are getting the hang of undercover work. I hope this works. Lt. Allan notified me he has already linked into Dianne's computer. Anything she does will pass through his. Let's hope we catch her alerting Carl of your tempting new contract."

"And," added Meagan, with a finger pointing at him. "Let's see if she tells him I'm selling out to you."

Whitmore smiled. "Yeah, I'd love to be in his office for that email."

As Meagan started to ask how they planned to catch Carl, the door opened. Ginny walked in and stopped in her tracks staring straight at Derek. *It's showtime,* Meagan thought as she walked forward.

"Hi Ginny, did you enjoy your time off?" asked Meagan, as she moved towards Ginny who was kicking snow off her boots. "I'll introduce you as soon as you are changed. Is it cold out today? I haven't even been out yet."

It was small talk and rather chatty, but Meagan had to calm down. She walked back to the coffee room while Ginny turned on her workstation and put on her shoes. When Ginny walked into the coffee room, Meagan started the first of many introductions.

"Ginny Strang, this is Derek White."

As they shook hands, Meagan continued her story. "Ginny, I met Derek back when he was in town bidding on Dr. Jensen's office. Neither of us got it obviously, but I called him over the weekend to see if he was interested in joining the two companies together. He's here to see if we have what it takes to make it work."

"Hello Ginny, Meagan says you are the hub of the operations," Derek said, with a warm smile that seemed incredibly genuine.

Ginny laughed, "I'm only the hub when things go wrong. The mud seems to fling into the middle somehow."

She grabbed a coffee cup and was at ease with him instantly.

"So, what's up, Meagan? Are you letting him buy you out?" said Ginny, who never beats around the bush.

Meagan furrowed her brow while tossing her flowing hair over her shoulder in a carefree way. "No, I don't think so. Are you buying me out? Because that's not what we discussed."

"No. I wish I had that kind of money!" said Derek, as the girls groaned about not having enough money in general. "I'd like to strengthen my presence in the commercial scene of Calgary, so I figure it's a good blend with Meagan who is doing more house designs. I don't mean to take away from her efforts in the commercial side, but maybe together we can get us both going on the right track."

It sounded plausible to Meagan. She looked at Ginny and Ginny seemed to buy it. If they can get Dianne to buy it, then they would catch their thief.

After a few minutes, the students came through the door, then they chatted about their days off with Ginny for 10 minutes before Dianne showed up.

When she did arrive, she came blasting through the office door, leaving it open long enough to cool off the room. Oddly she was in a cheery mood. That is - until she spotted Derek and instantly became skeptical. She slowly shut the door and strolled over to her desk to take off her cashmere coat. When Meagan walked by, instead of greeting her friend after a few days off, she tersely requests a meeting in Meagan's office.

Meagan knew it would be about Derek and wanted at all costs to avoid a private meeting.

As Meagan continued to walk she said, "I'd love to chat Di, but I've got to get ready for a meeting in a few minutes that you are all invited to. Hey, my computer works! I didn't lose anything. I stuck yours back in place, but all I did was plug it in. Why don't you check it before the meeting?"

Meagan didn't give her any time to respond, she quickly picked up the closest phone and dialled the YMCA pool schedule recording, making it look like it was an important call.

The diversion worked. Dianne looked down at her computer. It looked the same to her so she started checking her emails that were missed over the last few days.

Junk mail and suppliers letting her know products are ready for pickup flew past her screen and the one upstairs in front of Lt. Allen. The microphone attached to the back of the monitor was so clear he could hear Dianne picking at the polish on her nails.

A few minutes later Ginny called the group into the meeting room so Meagan could introduce Derek. As Meagan stood up from her desk she whispered, "If I pull this one off, I should start working on my acceptance speech for an academy award."

There was a perceptive nervous buzz when Meagan walked in the room. Everyone was worried about Derek who was already becoming fast pals with Ginny on the other side of the table.

Meagan took a deep breath and smiled. Nobody said a word.

"Oh, geez you guys, give me a break. You all look like your favourite aunt died! You better have enjoyed your time off, because it's the last time I'm letting it happen for a long time."

The students both relaxed a bit, but Dianne still sat ridged.

Meagan resumed. "This is Derek (pause) White, from Winnipeg. As you all know, I'm a bit frustrated with how the jobs have been going here. I decided last week that I had to change the luck in this office. Call it karma, Zen, whatever, it needs to shift - or I'd have to shut down.

"Not wanting to shut down, I decided to pull in a top-gun. And that's when I thought of Derek," she said as she waved her hand like a game show hostess at Derek.

"Derek runs a firm in Winnipeg, and I met him a while back when we both worked on a bid here in Calgary. While we chatted over dinner, Derek expressed interest in opening an office here. To make a long story short, since I need some expertise and he needs an office, we've decided to amalgamate our efforts for a test run per se."

She stopped talking; expecting some feedback but nobody said anything. She raised her eyebrows and gestured that she would like someone else to talk but still nobody said anything. "Come on you guys, we are a team here. Doesn't anyone have anything to say?" Meagan pleaded.

The team smells a buyout coming. Finally, Dianne spoke.

"Meagan," she said, without looking up from the nails she was still picking amber polish from. "Can we have a talk without Mr. White in the room?"

Meagan looked at Derek, she was worried about Dianne's motives but Derek stood up and said, "I don't mind if you'd like to talk amongst yourselves. But don't write off a merger just yet, folks. You haven't heard what we have planned."

As Derek left the meeting room, Meagan followed him. "Unfortunately, we don't have any real privacy down here. Would you mind waiting upstairs? The paper is on the kitchen table if you'd like to catch the scores from last night."

Derek nodded and went up the stairs. It was a perfect opportunity to check in on Lt. Allen.

When Meagan sat back down, Dianne was already ranting. "What do you mean merger? He isn't going to merge! He's going to move in and take over. I don't trust him...he looks like a weasel to me."

"What?" said Meagan, in disbelief.

"He is going to come in and steal your jobs right out from under your nose, then he's going to dump us all."

Meagan squeezed her eyes shut. She couldn't believe the accusations coming from someone who was doing the stealing already.

"Dianne!" said Meagan loudly, "I need a mentor. I cannot keep going on like this. He can't steal the jobs – they seem to be slipping away without him. That's why I need him. If I don't have help, we are all at the homeless shelter. And if I recall, we lost that bid too!"

Everyone else seemed fine with Meagan's points. But Dianne continued to lash out. Meagan promised she was not signing any papers and wasn't going to be bought out.

"I promise you will keep your jobs. I promise to be totally transparent with my dealing with Derek. Have I ever gone back on a promise before?"

Dianne was still steaming but realized the rest of the team was not arguing. It was plain to Meagan that Dianne feared Derek would uncover her little scam.

Almost on cue, like Derek knew to come down the stairs at the right moment (of course he knew – he was listening to the wire dangling in the corner!)

When Whitmore entered the room, Meagan explained the group's concerns. He stood there nodding as if he was empathizing with them. What he was really worried about was making sure Dianne got comfortable with him there.

"Okay," he said, standing at the end of the table. "Here is what we will do. A big job is coming up, a new golf course in Winnipeg. They want a clubhouse and bungalows designed. Let's see how we all work together. If we win the bid, I get to stay and we are a team. If we lose," he throws his arms up in the air, "I leave."

Dianne liked the offer and was already scheming to see his departure.

Whitmore reached over to the side table and spread a portfolio out on the table in front of everybody and began the biggest pile of bullshit he had ever told. Meagan was amazed at how well the detective could come across like an architect. He knew exactly what to say, what words to use and how to delegate the work.

Once the workloads were assigned, Whitmore set the bait for Dianne. "Ladies and gentlemen, we don't have much time to do this. We have to have prelims in by the end of next week. Meagan will email the specs to everyone in a minute, so you can get cracking on this job right now. Let's see if we can pull this off. I'd really like to prove to you that we can win a big job right off the bat."

With the pep talk done, the students smiled and returned to their desks. Dianne seemed to have bought into his performance too but wanted to find out more information to feed Russell. As everyone left, she went to get a fresh cup of coffee and started prodding Derek for more about his firm.

Derek wasn't prepared for that. He didn't want to get too far into the lies in case Russell started digging to find out his firm didn't exist. He started rambling on about how many people worked there and how long he'd been in Winnipeg, but thankfully his cell phone started to ring. Derek looked at the screen and smiled at Dianne. It was Lt. Allen's number. "Excuse me, Dianne, coincidentally that's my Winnipeg office calling."

He said hello, and walked off.

Dianne looked like she believed everything and returned to her desk. The email from Meagan was already in her inbox. She opened the email and as promised, the whole project was there in front of her. Dianne smiled and pushed the forward button to an email address called "Mom." Lt. Allen watched it go through. Then she sent another quick note to tell "Mom" the gossip of mergers from the meeting.

After a few moments, "Mom" responded with a simple "Good work, Darling." She smiled to herself so proud of her efforts.

Lt. Allen signed and softly said, "Carl, you are a deceptive old bastard."

Detective Whitmore kept an eye on Dianne. As he studied some drawings he watched as she made the emails to Carl. When Lt. Allen let him know his suspicions were correct and that an email was sent, he decided to let Dianne in on a little secret to see how loyal she was to Meagan. When he saw Dianne get up for a fresh cup of coffee he went in for the kill.

"So, Dianne," he said casually, as he followed her into the coffee room to refresh his mug. "How long have you known Meagan? The portfolio says you have been with the company since its inception."

He poured her coffee as she started to speak, but he made sure it was a deliberate process to hopefully slow Dianne down from returning to her desk.

"Oh, gee. We go back a long way. I think we met in second or third year. We did some dumb gas station design project together," she said, as she scooped in healthy heaps of sugar.

"Why was it so dumb?" asked Whitmore.

She started to laugh as she explained the concept they built. "We wanted to design gas stations that women would want to use. We went way out on a limb and designed new handles for the gas that were lighter, sleeker and less likely to spill. Then we created splash guards to further protect the outfits from spillage."

She laughed again and continued. "Our design was so funny, we went way over-board with feminine touches, putting in extra bathrooms for women with bigger mirrors and powder stations. But the funniest part was, we almost got a perfect score on the project."

"What made you lose marks?" asked Whitmore.

"The prof liked most of our ideas, but thought we went over on the girly touch," she said, wiggling her fingers up near her head. "He figured men wouldn't want to stop at a pink gas station and considering who buys most of the gas in the country, we were eliminating some potential clients. I guess he was right."

"Who was the prof?" Whitmore said as he leaned casually against the counter.

"Oh, you might have heard of him, he's not teaching anymore and has his own firm. His name is Carl Russell. He actually has a pretty good design firm. He always gets what he bids on. It's too bad he was against us in the Cottonwood job. I guess he did a better job."

Dianne leaned her back against the counter to continue talking. She seemed to enjoy the conversation. It was too bad Whitmore would ruin it.

"Russell? Oh, I don't think it's that he has a good design firm that he gets the jobs. I've heard of him, so has the rest of the architectural community across the country. Rumour has it in the association," Whitmore leaned in closer for effect and to say his next sentence more dramatically. "Rumour has it that he steals ideas from other offices."

Whitmore watched as Dianne stopped sipping her coffee. The mug didn't move from her lips for a second. He could see the wheels spinning in her head.

"He doesn't steal them," she said cautiously.

Whitmore shifted his weight from the counter to the door jamb next to him. He wanted to create a barrier so his prey wouldn't escape. "I wouldn't be too sure of that. I've heard that he is under investigation for corporate theft. You know what I heard?"

"What?" she said dryly. She put the coffee cup on the counter as if to steady herself.

"I've heard that he gets to know some of the young architects at the competing companies, usually the young ladies right out of university. Then he gets them to feed him information. Hey, you don't suppose he is using someone here – do you?" he said as if he just thought of it.

"What?" she said again, but with the sound of someone who is really doubting what she is hearing.

"Maybe Jennifer is feeding him Meagan's ideas," he said all excitedly. "I bet she can't be trusted. She probably is sleeping with the old fart and spilling the beans about the office, thinking that when she is done her apprenticeship with Meagan she can walk into his for a ready-made position."

He studied her face as she stared blankly at the floor. She wasn't thinking about Jennifer as much as she was of the thought that Carl had other women doing the same job.

Whitmore looked over his shoulder to see who was watching. "I wonder if Meagan knows about Russell's tactics. I bet she doesn't know. That's why she has been having difficulties. Don't you think that's it, Dianne?"

Dianne's face was red and her eyes were welling with tears. "He wouldn't do that," she whispered.

"What?" said Whitmore, staring her straight in the eye, "Put moles in each company or sleep with more women than just you?"

Dianne's mouth opened to say something, but as the accusation sank in, no words came out. Her jaw moved up and down a few times followed by sad short gasps of air trying to be sucked in.

Whitmore thought she was starting to sway off her heels. He was right. She slumped back against the counter and put her hands to her face.

"No! NO! That's not true," she said, as she tried to regain her composure.

Still acting as a surprised guest Whitmore hands her a tissue. "Gee Dianne, are you okay? You didn't really give away some of Meagan's ideas...did you?"

Oddly, but like the fool she was, Dianne confided in the stranger. She sucked in some air and looked over his shoulder. Meagan was in her office, just like Whitmore told her to do. Her back was to the door so she could see the reflection of what was going on. Meagan studied the faint images hard as Dianne continued.

"Don't tell Meagan, I'll lose my job. I thought he loved me. I don't do it anymore though. I only did it once!" she lied. "It was just a small job. It must be Jennifer now," she added to push the blame from herself. "Please don't tell Meagan I did it. She'll kill me."

Whitmore stood there staring at the pathetic woman in front of him. She had confessed to him so easily. He knew he could probably get more on the spot, but felt there was no need. He knew she was the type to come clean once the chips were down.

He started to speak slowly so she would realize he wasn't joking. As he spoke, he reached in his breast pocket and pulled out his police identification. Dianne's life as she knew it, ground to a halt.

"Miss Dianne Woods, I must tell you that you have confessed to the wrong man. My name is Detective Derek Whitmore of the Calgary Police Corporate Crime Division. You are under arrest for corporate theft."

She stared at his lips in disbelief as he spoke and then stared at the picture on the card to make sure it really was him. Even though Dianne's eyes were swollen with the start of tears, they grew so large when she looked back into his, Whitmore stepped back.

"You lied to me!" she shouted. "You told me you were an architect!"

"How else was I going to get you to confess?" he said calmly.

"You can't prove anything! I made it all up," she said, with shaky confidence.

"No, Dianne. I'm sorry, but I can prove it. The proof is already in police hands. You just confirmed it."

As Whitmore tried to recite the *'anything you do or say'* protocol she budded in.

"What?" she hissed. "What do you mean you have proof?!"

"We have proof you tampered with many files here at Dunphy. We have proof that Mr. Russell has entered this building with you to retrieve information. We have proof through your email history you send information over the internet. We have proof that you stay at his apartment, we have...."

He tried to continue, but Dianne started shouting, "Stop! Stop! Stop!"

She slid to the floor sobbing as Ginny, Brian and Jennifer came running to her cries.

Whitmore put his arm across the door jamb to stop them from coming in. His other hand held up his ID to prove he meant business. "I'm sorry everybody, but I'd like you all to stay back. I just informed Miss. Woods, she is under arrest for crimes she has committed. I'm going to let her regain her composure then we will be taking that classic ride down to the police station."

Ginny stepped back to look in on Meagan who had moved to the door of her office. Their eyes met, but no emotion connected between the two and no words came from either of them.

Meagan couldn't resist. She walked towards Dianne, but Derek still had his arm across the opening so she didn't get any closer to Dianne who was now sitting at the table shaking and crying uncontrollably.

Meagan's mind raced through all the scenarios that had kept her up during the night. She thought of thumping her a good one, or laughing in her face while pointing her fingers or doing a victory dance. She wanted to do all sorts of things to get back at Dianne for all the pain she had caused, but none of it would come out.

Her throat was dry and constricting her airway. All she could do was whisper. "Why Dianne? Why?"

Dianne looked up at Meagan while wiping the bottom of her runny nose on her *dry-clean only* blazer. She stopped. Her nose was at the end of a shiny trail of snot trailing along the tan sleeve. The look on her face turned sour. "Why? You don't know why?"

Dianne regained her strength and stood up with her eyes narrowed to a slit and a strong bitter voice. "You want to know why? I can't believe Miss Smarty-Poo-Pants can't get it. For how smart you are, you are so fucking blind."

Meagan stood there befuddled, as did the rest of the people in the room. For the last few minutes, Meagan was feeling a bit of pity for Dianne, but the emotion was shifting to confusion. Dianne found the tissue Whitmore gave her stuffed in her pocket and was blowing her nose now – still staring at Meagan.

"I can't believe you don't see it."

"See what?" said Meagan, a little stronger this time.

Dianne threw the wet tissue at the garbage can next to the fridge but of course, it missed. Dianne laughed a sickening chortle and sarcastically said, "If you threw that – you would have landed it!" She swallowed hard and continued to rant.

"And that is my point. You have everything. You started out with everything. You don't need anything, but there you are taking it away from the people who have to earn it. You were born not only with money and people who can open doors for you – you also have natural fucking talent. And, every time you flip that goddamn red hair off your shoulder every man in the room salivates! You make me sick!"

Meagan tried to defend herself by budding in. "Dianne, I work for everything, I…"

"Why didn't you just do like your mother told you to do and marry Stephen? By now you'd have a nanny chasing your two kids while you go running with your trophy wife friends at the country club. You'd be out of the way."

Everybody was still standing where they froze. Brian and Jennifer were behind Jennifer's desk, Ginny stood next to Meagan who was still behind Whitmore's outstretched arm. He could have stopped the conversation and taken it all downtown, but he knew Lt Allen was still recording it all and probably enjoying the chat. Besides, these women needed to get a few frustrations out.

Meagan was dazed by the bitterness. Her fight wasn't just with Russell, it was also with Dianne.

"I had no idea you felt this way," Meagan said, somewhat angered. "Why did you hang around with me in school and come to my firm if you hate me so much?"

Dianne chuckled again. "I didn't start out hating you. Like everyone else I started out liking you," she tossed another tissue at the garbage – missing again. Ginny moaned, knowing she'd have to pick it up the dirty tissue.

Dianne continued. "I thought hanging around with you would get me places. I knew people would notice you and maybe, they'd notice me."

Whitmore nodded his head as if to say – that makes sense - then regained his composure.

"I got noticed alright, but just as your damn sidekick. Nobody noticed I have as much talent as you, if not more."

"I knew you had talent, Dianne," said Meagan. "Why do you think I wanted to hang around with you? Or have you as part of my team?"

Dianne's shoulders dropped and her whole body slumped. "You think I have talent?"

"Of course, I do. Who said I didn't?"

Dianne sat back down in a chair and put her hands over her face and took a sad cavernous sigh. "Carl."

"Carl?"

Dianne was sobbing again and from behind her hands she continued to sputter out words. Everyone leaned closer to hear. "Carl told me you thought I was a loser, but he thought I have great talent and that this way we could both get back at you. I'd get back at you because you thought I was a stooge and him…because you had him fired for being friendly to you."

"He wasn't just being friendly," Meagan said bitterly.

"He says he was being friendly, and you took it the wrong way and told your dad. And since your dad has so much pull around Calgary, he had him tossed from the university. He said by pooling our talents, we could bring you down. Then he'd make me a partner at his company and," she stopped to squeeze the sides of her head. "And then I'd get noticed like I deserve."

"Why would you believe him and become so vindictive?" asked Meagan, even madder.

Dianne stood up and started flailing her arms around as she seethed. "I don't know Meagan! I don't know! I guess I'm stupid. He told me he loved me and that he'd take me places. When you are fat and ugly, and a man says he loves you – you jump all over it, because it's probably the only time in your ugly life someone is going to say it. It didn't dawn on me that I was a pawn amongst other stupid hopeless women until this guy told me this morning," she said, pointing her arm like a sabre at Whitmore. "Now I feel like the big fat fool I am."

Whitmore raised his eyebrows and looked at Meagan and after a pregnant pause quietly said, "I didn't know there were other women. I just threw that out to see what would happen."

Dianne spun around and stared at him. "WHAT? You made that part up?"

Lt Allen threw the headphones off his head as the following screech pierced his ears.

Everyone moved away and didn't look while their ex-colleague picked up her bag and coat. Whitmore led Dianne out of the office without much more conversation other than he said he'd be in touch.

Ginny ran upstairs and grabbed some emergency baking out of the freezer to defrost in the microwave. She was surprised to see Lt. Allen come down from the second floor carrying all his listening gadgets. Being a quick thinker, she figured it all out. She gave him some baking and a coffee before heading back downstairs to lay it all out in the meeting room.

As she straightened the chairs and laid out plates, she grabbed a paper towel to pick up Dianne's missed shots, crumpled the paper into a wad and slam dunked it all into the wastebasket. A burst of laughter came from the hallway from Brian. Ginny smiled back and said, "Two points!"

She walked the few steps to Meagan's office to see Meagan sitting at her desk with her head buried in her folded arms on the desk.

"Megs?" she said softly.

"Gin," she said, without moving a muscle. The whole ordeal was an emotional spinout for Meagan. On one hand, she was happy to see her problems being solved, knowing her company would no longer be undermined. On the other hand, however, she was saddened to see what she thought was a friend potentially heading to jail.

"Come for a coffee break."

"No."

"Megs?"

Without moving her head Meagan mumbled, "When do you think she stopped being my friend. When do you think he took her from me?"

Ginny stood there for a while thinking. "I'm willing to bet it was the first time we lost out to Russell."

Meagan looked up. "That was the Evans job nearly two years ago. I should go see that dentist and see what his office looks like."

She put her head back down on the desk without saying anything more.

"Megs."

"Gin."

"Maybe you should call Ben."

"I did, he's already on his way over."

"Then come out. We gotta talk. You'll feel better."

"She tried to sink me," she said, as she raised her head.

"I know. But she didn't." She reached out her hand and said, "Come on. First thing you need is a hug from a true friend."

Meagan smiled weakly and took her hand. Ginny wrapped her arms around her and squeezed tight. After a few tears, they regained their composure. As they headed for the coffee room arm in arm, Ben came rushing through the office door.

Ginny kept Meagan walking towards the coffee room but said loudly to Ben, "It's so like you to show up when the food is on the table. Come on in. We've got a story to tell."

"HA! I've got one that will probably top yours! he said, as he tossed his coat on what used to be Dianne's desk.

CHAPTER TWENTY-ONE

By the end of the day, Meagan was exhausted but in better spirits. No billable work was accomplished, but the team came together and discussed where they had been, where they were now and where to go next. Meagan was amazed by the support the group gave her. Everybody came up with ideas to save the company, expand and grow. That is of course after they had heard from Ben.

While Whitmore pulled the covers off Dianne's involvement, Detective Patel along with two plain-clothed officers and a few extra uniformed police walked into Russell's office to hand him the charges Meagan was laying against him.

As Ben ate the baked goods, he told how Russell denied all involvement. He denied stealing the Cottonwood project, but Detective Patel was ready to catch him red-handed. He asked Russell specific details about the Cottonwood contract and Russell purposely confusing the designs, amounts charged and figures. Russell like all liars couldn't remember anything right.

When Patel asked if Russell knew who Dianne was or what contracts the Dunphy group was working on he played dumb, saying he didn't know Dianne or the firm. Because Patel already knew Dianne had emailed the fictitious Winnipeg job, he demanded to see Russell's email. Russell knew the gig was up. He paused for a long time, walked over to his laptop, picked it up and flung it to the floor – smashing it into a few large pieces.

Patel said it didn't matter what Russell did. The copies were on Dianne's computer, which was the property of the Dunphy company so when Russell accused them of trespassing or wiretapping or any other allegations he could fling, it all fell on deaf ears.

By the time Ben finished telling them how Russell was escorted from the office in front of all his employees, the room was feeling pretty confident.

Meagan was willing to let everyone take the rest of the day off, but Ginny put an end to that idea.

"We are a new team and it's time we started helping out a little more. I'd say it's time for you to take a break. We will pick up where we left off on Friday."

Meagan was taken aback by the vote of confidence. "Well, this does feel good. I guess I'll go check out The Bahamas without worrying about the office."

Everybody was quick to groan that she was taking advantage of them a little too quick, but they all went back to work, happy to know the office was cleared of double agents.

Meagan stayed in the office and worked into the evening. A home reno project came in and Meagan wanted to get the bid out as soon as possible. She decided to bid at almost a loss, just so they would get it and feel more confident.

When the phone rang, she was surprised to see it was already 11:30. She eagerly reached for the phone after she saw who was calling. "Chris," she said softly without even saying hello. She cringed when she remembered he had a game that night and she missed it entirely.

"Hey babe, how'd your day go?" Chris sounded tired, but he sounded good.

"Oh, I guess if I were a hockey player, I'd say I took it on the boards pretty hard. Butt I stayed clear of the penalty box. How about you? I'm sorry, but I forgot about your game tonight," she said, with regret.

"You missed me on TV?" he said sarcastically. "What could be more important than drinking beer with Ben and watching me play?"

"We had our own brawl today. The good news is it looks like it's the end of the lying and stealing," Meagan said, sounding relieved.

"Man, that is so good to hear," he said warmly.

Meagan spent a few minutes telling him the highlights, then stopped almost mid-sentence because of the silence at the end of the phone.

"Chris?"

"Yeah," was the soft response.

"Why are you so quiet? Did you get hurt today?"

She couldn't see it, but she could tell he was smiling while he talked. "I'm just thinking how good it will be to go to Eleuthera without this hanging over your head. It will be nice to see you smile."

"Well, I'm not out of the woods yet. I still have to make a living and prove to myself that I wasn't losing the contracts on my own. Maybe I can help out on your beach house to get some spending money."

Chris laughed, "Hey, don't expect anything other than rums on the beach and relaxation because that's all I have planned. We only have a few days and I want to make the best of it. If you want to look over the house while I sleep in the afterglow of great sex – then that works for me."

They were both laughing and started making plans for the vacation. It was looking like Meagan's life was finally taking a path she felt good about.

Time crept by like a slow blizzard. Meagan was incredibly busy - which should have made the days go by fast but, it didn't. She juggled the workload that Dianne was doing along with her own bids. There was also a lot of work to do with the detectives and Ben before she could jet away. And, most important – she picked up her pace and ran more with the girls.

The day before she was to leave, Meagan went running in the predawn light with Lizzie who was always keen for a run. As they rounded the corner onto the path from the YMCA the westerly wind hit them full force.

"Holy shit! Isn't winter over yet? This is cold!" shouted Meagan through her scarf. "Did you check the temperature on the way down?"

"Yeah, don't worry, it's only -17."

"Yeah, but the wind chill is taking it way over the threshold."

The two bent their heads into the wind and settled into their stride. If the temperature were below -20 Celsius, they would have moved indoors to the treadmills, but that was always seen as a last resort. After a few minutes, they would warm up to the task and start talking. Until then, they paced along nicely.

Meagan always enjoyed it when this happened. Even though it was frightfully cold, they were out there, helping each other along. The moisture in their breath instantly created a crust of frost on their scarves that covered their nose and mouth. People driving by though thought they were nuts. Yeah, probably they were.

"So, Megs," said Lizzie, as their stride slowed. "Excited about the trip?"

Meagan laughed. "That's an understatement! I can't wait to go. Hanging out on a hot beach with Chris is going to make this run even sweeter. Maybe we can go for a run there."

"Meagan, just relax will ya? He isn't looking for exercise, he needs to rest. That's what this break is, isn't it?"

"Yeah, I guess so," huffed Meagan as she pulled down her scarf. Even at -17 C her face was too hot to cover anymore.

"I hate to be blunt, but this may be your chance to prove to this guy that you are the right girl and to see if he is the right man," Lizzie said in all seriousness.

Meagan stole a glance at Lizzie. "What do you mean – right girl, right man?"

Lizzie chose her words carefully. "Meagan, this guy is cool. From what you say and how you say it, it looks like he could be the match for you. But you have to be careful. Where is this going to take you?"

Meagan fell silent as they went under the 10th street bridge. The ice from the Bow River was pushing up in large burgs onto the path making footing treacherous. Concentrating on her future and her footfall at the same time was almost too much for Meagan.

"Where it's going to take me? What are you talking about? I want to put Dianne and Carl behind me and grow my company. I'm not going to give it all up now and dash off to Boston, just in case he likes me."

Meagan lost her footing on a patch of blue ice but regained it with a pun. "I have to watch where I'm going, you're right."

They ran silently for a minute and then Meagan opened up as the reality sunk in like the day in the kitchen when they talked about commitment. "What am I going to do, Lizzie? What if he is the man? I really do like him – but I've got a company to run. I have to prove I can do this."

Lizzie glanced sideways at her friend.

"Who do you have to prove it to? Your dad? Your mom? Your employees? Good God, you don't need to prove anything to us. If it's you – you have to prove it to, you better be careful that in proving you are a success to yourself, you don't push out a chance of true love," said Lizzie.

She continued to lecture her pal, "You have proved yourself in many ways. And who's to say that you can't set up in another city? It's not like you are dependent on the Calgary economy, buildings have to go up everywhere," she added with a chuckle.

They crossed the river on the suspended path under the bridge at Crowchild Trail, marking the middle of the run and the chance to put the wind behind them. They loosened their jackets and their cheeks instantly felt the reprieve from the stinging cold.

Lizzie continued talking since Meagan was still lost in thought. "Maybe you should think about moving to a different city anyway."

"What! Why?" Meagan said surprised.

"Maybe you need to brush Carl and Dianne right out of your system. Who knows what will happen once they are charged. Carl can afford the best lawyers in town. I wouldn't be surprised if he gets off with a slap on the wrist. Don't worry about Dianne, she'll sink like a rock and won't bug you again."

"I never thought of that," Meagan said softly.

"If Carl gets off easy, I have a feeling he will still haunt you."

With the weight of the world firmly planted on their shoulders, the women continued to run toward the warmth of the Y. Meagan knew Lizzie wasn't trying to hurt her feelings. It was just a bit of reality, that's all.

CHAPTER TWENTY-TWO

Heading to the airport the next day, Meagan was still thinking heavily about what her friend said. Lizzie was right, she did need to make some choices about her future. When the ticket agent gave her a first-class seat because that's what was listed on the ticket, Meagan smiled inwardly and decided to quit thinking and enjoy the ride for the entire trip.

The flight went without any hitches. The man seated next to her tried to flirt, but when Meagan politely asked about the woman and kids on his laptop screen saver, he stopped asking about her plans in Boston and got to work on his game of solitaire. On the approach into Boston, Meagan had her head swivelled to watch the landing. It was her first time flying into Boston and as she scanned the view, she hoped it wasn't her last.

Meagan hoped Chris would be at the airport, but she knew that was impossible. He told her a car would be sent to get her because, by the time she reached the arena, the game would most likely be in play. Still, as she came through the security doors, she searched for a friendly face. One of her all-time teen fantasies was to rush into the arms of a handsome man waiting at the airport with a single rose in his hand. Yeah, she knew that was corny.

There was a friendly face waiting for her – but it wasn't Chris. A handsome young man in a black suit stood in front of the crowds holding a sign "Dunphy."

"I'm assuming you are looking for me?" Meagan said, smiling as she walked towards the tall, chiselled man. Meagan is by no means a short gal but this guy still towered over her.

He looked down at her and said very professionally, "What is your first name please?"

Meagan was stunned by his cold demeanour. "Ah, it's Meagan. Meagan Dunphy?"

He stopped holding up the sign and smiled at Meagan. "Thank you, Ms. Dunphy. We can't be too sure. Other drivers have gone all the way downtown with freeloaders."

"Oh. I never thought of doing that myself. How clever. I'll remember that for the way home," said Meagan.

He quickly looked at her in surprise.

"I'm kidding!"

The driver took her bags and asked her to follow him to his car. A gleaming black Lincoln was sitting directly in front of the doors and its trunk popped open as they walked towards it.

"This is our ride, Ms. Dunphy."

"Wow. Is this your own car?" she asked as she stepped into the spacious back seat.

He laughed. "I wish."

He pulled the car out of the loading area, but then pulled back to an empty curb and parked. Meagan was confused but he explained.

"I just wanted to get away from the loading zone. The commissionaires are a crabby bunch that write the tickets before you see them coming."

He reached over to the passenger side of the front seat and picked up a large box and handed it back to her. Then he handed her an envelope that was tucked in his breast pocket.

"These are from Mr. Burrows. He asked me to give them to you long before we reached the arena. I will be staying at the game and will drive both you and Mr. Burrows back to his house. That way you don't have to worry about your luggage. It'll be safe in the car."

She reached up and took the box and envelope. As she started to open the envelope, the car moved away from the curb and into traffic.

Inside the envelope was a note and two tickets to the game. The note said:

Hello Meagan,

I am so excited to know you will be in the stands tonight. Thankfully it isn't a Calgary game so you can cheer for me without worrying about flying beer cups. I hope you like the gift in the box – I'm looking forward to seeing you wear it tonight. As for the second ticket. You can offer it to my cousin, Scott. He's the one driving the car.
Love ya, Chris.

She read the part about the gift again and thought twice about what it might be and whether or not she should open it yet. She looked up and saw the driver watching her in the rear-view mirror. "Are you Scott?"

He smiled, "Yes, ma'am."

"Will you be my date at the game?"

"Yes ma'am."

"You have to quit with the ma'am stuff then – save it for my mother! Call me Meagan please."

"Okay, and you can call me, Sir!" he said, laughing at his joke.

After a few minutes, he looked back again and said, "Aren't you going to open the box?"

"Naw, I thought I'd save it for later."

"Better not," he warned.

Meagan got the hint. If Scott knew what it was – then it wasn't sexy lingerie. She peeled back the paper and opened the box. Wrapped in tissue was a tailored Boston jersey – #28 with Burrows plastered across the shoulders. She smiled.

"I think Chris wants to make sure you know exactly who you are cheering for."

"Yeah, I get the hint," she said laughing. She took off her jacket and sweater and pulled the jersey over her head and tossed her wavy hair over her shoulders, nearly covering his name. The jersey fit beautifully over her blouse, a little large but not huge and baggy like she feared.

As she reorganized herself the car pulled into the VIP parking lot of the arena. Scott hung a parking pass from the rear-view mirror and opened the window to talk to the attendant who tried desperately to see who the guest in the backseat was. Meagan started to flush and suddenly realized she was a spectacle. HIS girlfriend has arrived.

As they parked, Scott tossed off his suit jacket and put on his own jersey. Feeling overwhelmed with the whole evening ahead of her, Meagan decided it was nice to have a new friend come along to the game.

"I'm glad you are going to the game with me, Scott," she said, nervously as they walked to the building.

"I don't mind at all. Wait until you see how good these seats are!"

Scott was obviously thrilled to be going to the hockey game. But it didn't matter to Meagan if it was a chess match with monkeys. All she wanted was to be wrapped in Chris's arms again.

As they walked into the arena, Meagan looked at the scoreboard. Ten minutes of the first period had already been played and Boston was down by one. She didn't care about that either. She just hoped Chris hadn't been in a fight.

Scott knew exactly where to go and led her down the stairs to the fifth row. Two seats at centre ice were empty in a sold-out crowd making it easy for Meagan to figure out where they were headed. As they sat down a beer and a coke showed up.

"I pre-ordered," said Scott as he handed her the beer. "Cheers. And welcome to Boston."

They clinked the plastic cups and had a sip each. The play on the ice stopped and the players moved off the ice for the commercial break. That's when she finally saw Chris gliding effortlessly across the ice. He always looked so big when he was dressed in his uniform. The pads covering most of his body, the few inches of height from the skates and the helmet all added to the super-sized-ness. He was already looking at her and smiling that sexy soft smile that always made her want to gently cup his smooth cheeks in her hands and pull his lips gently to rest on hers.

She smiled at him and his smile grew bigger. He nodded and she nodded back. Then as quick as the greeting started – it stopped. Chris sat down on the bench and refocused on the game.

Meagan glanced sideways at Scott, but thankfully he was preoccupied with the man on the other side so he didn't catch the eye contact. She wouldn't have to explain herself.

Scott spent most of the game talking to the opinionated man which was fine. She spent most of the time just watching Chris. She tried to not be looking at him when he was off the ice so she didn't get caught watching him all the time.

The game-ending horn blared, and the crowd stood up deflated. Boston lost to Toronto 3-1. Chris didn't score and more importantly, didn't take any hits.

"It'll be about 45 minutes before Chris comes out of the locker room, how about we wander the concourse for a while and count how many pictures have him in them," suggested Scott as they joined the throngs leaving the seats.

Meagan shrugged her shoulders and said, "Sure. How many pictures are there?"

He just laughed. They rounded a corner after counting three photos with Chris in various poses and came to the front entrance they didn't use. It wasn't how many pictures really, it was how big.

Meagan's mouth dropped open in disbelief. Huge banners were draped from the three-story ceiling. Each banner was at least 30 feet tall and had the hockey card mug shot of each player. There – far larger than she would ever imagine seeing him, was Chris.

"Shit," she said, as she peered up at him. "His nose is taller than me!"

"Yeah," said Scott. "Just think of how big his – um" he cleared his throat and quickly said, "Hands. How big his hands would be!"

Meagan laughed and blushed as did Scott. They quickly resumed their walk after Meagan got a photo in front to send to the girls.

After half an hour of finding 37 photos, they came back to the dressing room door and were met with a mob of hockey fans.

"Oh, rats," moaned Scott as he leaned against the wall. "I was hoping this wouldn't happen tonight with them losing."

"What?" asked Meagan, looking at the crowd.

Scott explained as players intermittently came out the door. "Usually it's after they win that the crowds are this big. There is always someone here, looking for autographs and approaching the players with public appearance appeals. See the young ladies over there?" he said, pointing with a nod of his head at a few beautiful girls primped to cosmetic perfection. "Those are the chicks waiting to stalk the players. They don't care about the game or the guy. They, well, you know."

"Yeah, I know. There are buckle bunnies in every sport," said Meagan, as the girls perked up as a few players moseyed over.

"Buckle bunnies?"

"Oh, that's a rodeo term. It's what cowboys call the girls chasing them. If you see someone like them wearing a big buckle…well, same thing."

The door opened and a few more players came out and behind them all was Chris. Some young boys swarmed him for autographs and as he signed hats and jerseys, he looked around for Scott and Meagan. When he saw them, he smiled and said to the group, "Last one, my friends. I've got someone very special waiting for me."

He signed three more because of the loud moans emitted from the kids then briskly walked over to Meagan, dropped his duffle with a loud clunk and gave Meagan the hug she was waiting for.

"It's so good to see you here!" he said like a schoolboy. "Did you enjoy the game? Sorry, we didn't win. Has Scott been nice? He didn't make you stare at the banners and count the pictures, did he?"

Scott started to protest but Chris continued, "Scott does that to every relative that comes to town. How many did you count this time?"

"Thirty-seven," Meagan said laughing.

Chris laughed even louder. "Thirty-seven! Geez, Scott. Did you run around with photocopies and nail them to the wall. Thirty-seven – damn that's a lot."

He wrapped his arm around Meagan's shoulder and they started walking. Scott dropped back a few feet to resume his role as the driver, dragging along the duffle.

By the time they reached Chris's house, they had finished the chitchat about the plane ride, the weather in Boston, where he lived and ordered Chinese food. What they didn't get to do was kiss and talk as lovers, because Scott was in the front seat and there was not a privacy screen between the front and back seats.

The car entered a posh old neighbourhood. Enormous oak trees lined the boulevard. Set well back from the curb were stately homes. Unlike Calgary, where garages dominate the front, these streets had back alleys where the garages hid. Some houses had single lanes leading to the side of the house. Scott maneuvered the car into one such lane.

Meagan looked at the house in amazement. "This is your house?"

"Yeah, why not?"

"It's so huge and beautiful, but it doesn't seem like you," she said, trying not to sound critical or surprised.

He looked at it with a critical expression on his face and said, "Yeah, it doesn't look like an NHL goon's house. You're right. Truth is, it's okay. I got it from a guy who left the team. He wanted out and I didn't have anything, so I bought it cheap. So far it's paid off," he added, with an approving nod.

"Let's go in," he said, as he reached for the door. Scott was already waiting on Meagan's side.

"I'll bring the bags in, Chris," Scott said, as Chris rounded the backside of the car.

"Sounds good to me. Let's see, we need to be at the airport for 7 a.m. Will you be ready, or should I wake you up?"

"No. I'm good. I'll be ready."

"As the two started to walk for the front door, Meagan said, "Why would you suggest waking him up?"

"Oh," he laughed. "Scott lives in the basement suite. He didn't tell you?"

Meagan smiled back at Scott. "He doesn't release much information until he has to."

"Oh yeah, another thing," said Scott. "You know when you asked me if this was my car?"

"Yeah."

"It's his," said Scott, pointing at Chris. "He owns it. I rent it from him and drive all sorts of clients around. It's pretty good work and keeps me sober on weekends."

"Yeah," said Chris sternly. "And that keeps Auntie Jane happy too! I just don't know what I'll do when you finish university."

Scott headed around to the back door while Chris led Meagan up the front steps.

Meagan was amazed at how beautifully it was designed and decorated. Definitely built in the 1940s, it was either a damn good replica of a Greene and Greene design or an actual house done by the architects themselves. As she took her coat off, she slowly spun around admiring the art, the colour schemes, the furniture and how it melded with the woodwork.

He interrupted her thoughts. "I didn't do any of this. Don't even think I have any talent past the rink!"

"It's fabulous though."

"Thanks, when I finish paying for it all, maybe I'll admire it too."

Meagan looked up at the sparkling chandelier as she laughed and as her glance came down it rested on Chris's face. She thought about how great he looked at the game and without thinking any further, she took two steps towards him and lifted her hands to his face to cup his freshly shaven chin in her palms. He rested his chin in her hands and tipped his face to kiss her. Meagan's mind swirled. Kissing Chris was all that mattered. She was in love.

Five in the morning is very early, especially if your body's clock is set for two hours west. When Chris nudged Meagan to get out of bed, she was surprised to see he'd already dressed and made coffee.

"I thought you'd need a kick-start this morning," he said, as he sat on the side of the bed holding a mug of dark coffee. Meagan stretched and sat up with a huge yawn.

"Oh," she said, covering the yawn. "That was rude."

"What? The way I woke you?" said Chris.

"No! That yawn in your face. I nearly swallowed a pillow with that one."

He handed her the cup and pulled the covers away. "Come on, we'll dawdle on the beach this afternoon."

She took a sip and put the cup down and headed for the bathroom to freshen up. She didn't want him waiting.

Ten minutes later, they were loading their bags into the trunk again. Scott looked just as weary.

All three stayed up too late eating Chinese food and laughing. Scott had hilarious stories about Chris when they were kids and she loved hearing about the pre-pro hockey player. By the time they hit the hay; neither was looking for anything other than a goodnight kiss.

"Even the seatbelts in first class are nicer!" said Meagan, as she leaned into his shoulder as they settled in for the flight to Nassau.

Chris smiled and wrapped her arm around his and kissed her nose. "I am so happy to be off the rink for five days! That's four days of being with you. Are you going to be able to stand it that long?"

Meagan smiled back. "Heck, I'd spend a month in The Bahamas with anyone just to get out of my usual winter wonderland. I think I can take a few days with you."

They were leaning in for a kiss when a fan noticed who was on the plane.

"Hey!" said the short man wearing a weathered Boston ball cap. "Now I see why you didn't play any better last night. You were thinking about her instead of hockey!"

Before Chris or Meagan could say anything, the man continued down the aisle. Meagan was offended by his remark and Chris could feel her body tighten.

He patted her hand gently and after thinking for a few seconds he whispered some words of encouragement. "Meagan, I'm sorry. I'm sorry, but this type of interruption will always happen in Boston. Some fans are great. But others take the game seriously and think they need to coach us both on and off the ice."

"But he was rude," she protested.

"Yep, but you know what? You have to shake it off. It's not easy at times — especially when a bald dork in a bad hat blames you for the loss. But you have to be very, very civil. Don't let anyone get you riled up because that's when somebody with a camera catches you doing something the tabloids will pay for. And another thing, since I'm giving you the fan appreciation lecture, please don't say anything to the media other than cheery stuff. They'll try to get cozy and to be a friend. But never ever trust them. Some are nice, but some will use an ice cream scoop to carve out your heart."

He was serious. Ben had warned her, and it was finally sinking in. There was now a third party in their lives she had not considered. She looked back at him with a stern face and nodded.

"It's stupid, but I never thought about you as a paparazzi target. I'll try to remember the source the next time someone is obnoxious. And, don't worry...I'll just tell the boring stuff about us to the inquiring minds at the rags."

Suddenly, the man was back with a felt pen and the hat in his hand, "Can you autograph this for me? I'm a huge fan."

CHAPTER TWENTY-THREE

Stepping off the plane, Meagan could feel the warm, humid air and drank it in with a big deep breath. The concourse in the Nassau airport was bright and breezy with oversized pictures of beautiful Bahamian children enjoying the water and wrinkled old people working with baskets. Both the kids and the old people were smiling toothless smiles.

"Oh," she moaned, "This air is worth the flight alone. I can feel my skin gulping in the moisture."

Chris laughed, "Yeah, by the end of the week any worry lines will have disappeared."

Just past the customs booth stood a tall man dressed in a baggy Tommy Bahamas golf shirt, sloppy khakis shorts and flattened flip-flops.

Chris walked directly to him and shook hands and hugged. "Dan, the flyin' man – how's it going?"

"Totally good, Goon-man. Totally good," he said back.

"Dan, this is Meagan Dunphy of Calgary. She is my guest and I think you'd better get used to seeing her around."

"Ah," said Dan as he grasped her hand, pulling her in for a peck on the cheek. "How you stole Goon-man's heart is a story you'll have to tell me someday."

Meagan laughed at his instant friendliness. "I guess so."

"Dan is my inter-island pilot of choice. He has a charter company that pops me over to Eleuthera quicker than the big companies."

As Dan picked up a bag he said, "Only if we do less talking in the airport. Come with me."

They followed Dan out of the building to a rusty old Nissan truck.

"Jump in Meagan," Dan said, as he tossed the bags in the back and walked around to the driver's seat.

The three squished into the cab for the short ride over to the charter terminal. No security stopped them. They zipped across the tarmac and parked next to a Cessna Caravan.

Dan could tell Meagan was surprised at the lax security.

"Everybody knows everybody here. They know I'm not a drug smuggler." He points at an airplane across the tarmac. "It's those guys they watch."

Meagan looked at the airplane he pointed at. It was exceptional compared to the rest in the lineup. "How do you know they smuggle drugs?"

"Not too many charter companies spend money on retractable floats. We don't need to land in secluded bays like they do."

"Is smuggling a big concern here?" she asked as he stopped the truck.

Both men laughed at her honest question. Dan answered in two words. "Big. Time."

As they got out of the truck Dan continued. "The Bahamas is one of the drug gateways to Miami. Huge ships will bring it in this far and then high-speed boats or little planes like that will mule it over to South Florida. The ocean can be pretty shallow around The Bahamas and the sand on the bottom is constantly shifting. You should see how many shipwrecks there are of those drug runners. It's getting to be a mine-field of ditched boats out there."

Meagan took one last look at the sleek plane and thought to herself how naive she is. *And here I thought it was for sightseeing.*

Dan's plane was a six-seater with plenty of cargo space. Meagan hopped into the second row while Chris rode shotgun next to Dan.

The engine roared and the plane popped into the sky. Meagan thought the view was spectacular from the commercial flight, but this stole the show. Because the flight was only going to take 15 minutes, Dan didn't bother taking the plane too high.

"I like to take it high enough to miss the masts on the ships in the harbour. I like freaking out the naked sun-bathers as I buzz by," laughed Dan, as he banked east.

Meagan could see the magnificent Atlantis Paradise Island Resort. From the air, it looked extravagant.

Dan looked back at Meagan and saw she was admiring the resort. "Hey Meagan, tell Goon-man if he truly loves you, he should take you there instead of his shack on the beach."

Meagan smiled at his joke. She could tell they were friends, and no harm was meant.

'Hey Fly-man, keep that up and I'll start using my own plane," threatened Chris.

The two men kept talking, but Meagan tuned it out. She was busy watching the bottom of the ocean go by. Dan was right, you could see clearly to the bottom and the channels were very visible.

The colour of the water intrigued Meagan and she couldn't stop staring at the changing shades of greens and blues. Sailboats drifted along with long shadows cast on the ocean floor. Once in a while, she noticed dark objects on the sand, but they were not distinguishable as rusting drug runners.

As the water got deeper, she could see submerged islands or bands of reefs.

"We are following the island down from the top," said Dan, over his shoulder at Meagan. "This is Current Island coming up on the left. Not too many people live on it, as the only access is a shuttle across Current Cut to the north island."

"What's a current cut?" asked Meagan.

"Current Cut is a deep channel between the two islands where the tide surges through. It's quite a phenomenon. Cutting through there when the tide is right cuts hours off a sailor's journey. Sailboats will moor and wait for the tide to turn to take advantage of the free ride, but all sorts of ships cut through there. It's a great dive spot too. You can walk to the other side of the island and put on your snorkel and jump in. All you have to do is float with the tide to see everything below you. It's pretty strong; if you look closely you can see the standing waves."

Meagan saw the cut as they flew over it. "That sounds so cool. Is it easy to do?" Meagan was getting excited at the thought of new adventures.

"Oh yeah it's cool, but if you are floating east, you can't miss the corner of the island or the tide will take you for a very long ride."

Chris saw the horror on her face. "Don't worry. It's not that bad. A strong swimmer can get to shore. You can swim – can't you?"

She paused before answering. "There's a reason why my water polo team referred to me as 'the rock' but I can float if I have to."

Chris smiled. You'll be fine. If we have time to do it, I'll make sure the tide is heading into the gentle Caribbean side and not the Atlantic."

Meagan smiled weakly and returned her gaze out the window. Uncluttered beaches stretched across the horizon and the best part, there wasn't a tourist in sight.

As the plane came in for the landing at Governors Harbour Airport, Chris scanned the parking lot.

"I didn't see Mike. Did you?" Chris said to Dan, as the plane bounced once on the rough landing strip.

"Jeez no, Goon-man. I guess I was preoccupied landing an airplane. Do you want me to circle so you can look again?"

"No. Sorry dude. I forgot that it's technical to land this thing. You do it so well."

"Actually, I can do this airport in my sleep and I didn't notice him either." Chris looked at his friend and realized the scolding was just for effect. "We can call him when I park this puppy."

Chris turned to Meagan. "Mike was supposed to be here with the Jeep. Don't worry, we won't have to wait too long."

Meagan thought the look on his face disagreed with what he said. Mike, as she recalled, is the guy in charge of the construction of the house. And the same person that seems to be taking too long to get the job done.

"Maybe he got stuck in traffic?" Meagan said sarcastically.

Dan burst out laughing and said in his most convincing Bahamian accent. "Ha, she be feeling the island ways before she even touch da sand."

With the Cessna parked in the faded yellow painted square number 42, Dan started dialling Mike's cell phone. Meanwhile, Chris and Meagan grabbed their bags and walked towards the small squat building at the side of the runway.

Two men dressed in American Airlines blue uniforms sat on broken chairs tilted back against the building, only their heads were able to reach the shade cast by the short eave. Big double doors were propped open with cinder blocks, creating a breeze for the crowd of people slumped on the plastic chairs in the waiting room. By the time they got through the doors, Meagan was feeling the heat and sweat beaded at her brow.

"I can see why those guys don't move. Christ, it's hot here!" she said to Chris, who was showing the same symptoms.

"Don't worry, you'll be loving the heat in a day," he said, with a warm smile.

As they walked through the building, Meagan noticed many of the Bahamian women stared at Chris like he was a god. Yeah, he's tall and handsome, but it's not like he was the first pale white guy to walk through the airport in five seconds flat. Five seconds because the building is that narrow.

It wasn't until they were in the parking lot when Meagan noticed the taxi drivers were staring at her. As she lifted her thick hair off her neck to cool down she said, "Chris?"

He was looking for the Jeep but turned to see what the concern was. "Yeah?"

"Why are those guys staring at me?"

He looked past her shoulders to see at least five dark men smartly dressed in worn out, but clean suit jackets and almost matching pants. He smiled as he bent to her ear and whispered, "It must be your red hair, it really is an anomaly here. And, you are kinda thin."

"What?"

Chris laughed quietly, "Yeah, a lot of Bahamian men prefer their ladies a bit heavier than you."

"Oh great! I'm a skinny freak with red hair!" laughed Meagan quietly.

"Hey, Goon-man!" It was Dan putting away his cell phone as he walked out the door. "I found Mike. He was tossing a few brews at Ronnie's on Cupid's Cay and was surprised we had already landed."

"Already landed?"

"Yeah, he thought the weather was going to delay us," added Dan.

They all looked up at the cloudless sky. Chris looked at Dan even more pissed off. Meagan decided to keep her mouth shut.

It was only 10 minutes until a blue topless Jeep blazed into the parking lot with a sudden stop in front of the two.

"Chris! Dude! I'm sorry man. I totally screwed up," said the 20-something guy driving the Jeep. He sprang from the door-less opening to retrieve the bags.

"No problem," said Chris, smiling at the young man. "This is Meagan."

Mike stopped what he was doing, giving Meagan a chance to look him over.

Unfortunately, she wasn't impressed.

He stuck out his hand to shake hers. "Meagan, nice," he said melodically as he looked her up and down. "I mean, nice to meet you. Have you been to the islands before?"

"No," she said, as she wiped the sweat from his hand on her pants. "But so far I am really impressed."

With everything but you! she added in her head. For someone who was supposed to be a professional, he didn't look the part. Mike looked like he spent too much time polishing bar tops with his elbows. His feet were filthy as were his dungaree shorts. His T-shirt was faded, full of holes and stunk, but then so did he – like stale booze. He was handsome – as in was. Meagan could tell that he'd come from a pleasant-looking gene pool, but he obviously wasn't cleaning his end of the pool very often. His hair was dull from neglect, as was his skin. His teeth which were probably capped due to hockey mishaps were stained and chipped. Meagan shifted her weight to get into the backseat of the Jeep to avoid more dialogue.

They pulled onto the Queen's Highway and headed south towards Governors Harbour, Chris's place would be another eight kilometres beyond the town. Even though the road had a fancy name, it was still only two lanes with pits and potholes causing the best drivers to swerve. Mike, with one hand on the wheel and the other waving at oncoming cars, carelessly hit every hole.

The wind whipped Meagan's hair in swirls. She kept grabbing and finally had most of it captured. She didn't mind. The moist air and the smell of the sea were washing away the tension and fatigue, and the lack of trust she had for the driver.

A tight corner to the left and the town suddenly appeared. Meagan drank in the sight. It was exactly as she thought it should be; a scattering of brightly painted houses, tall trees, kids and dogs running freely. Mike slowed down as they entered the town.

A lone gas pump marked the busiest place in town. Behind it, a market with windows plastered in faded cigarette ads, public notices and Bahamian flags. Across the street, painted in sunshine yellow was the police station. A policeman in a uniform, made of fabric looking far too heavy for the heat, walked out the door as they passed. He stopped walking and stared at the Jeep as it drove by.

Meagan waved as she had to the children, but the policeman didn't wave back. He wasn't looking at her. He was looking at Mike – hard.

She put her hand back in her lap and studied Mike again. The policeman obviously didn't like Mike.

Meagan tried to listen to the conversation, but between Mike changing gears and the wind picking up intensity, she could only catch a few words.

"Slow," "...delays," "...not my fault and it is under control," was about all she heard, but she watched his body language which looked uncomfortable.

Something's not right, she thought to herself. Mike must have felt her untrusting vibes. He looked at her in the rear-view mirror with just as much distrust. She smiled at him to try to shake it up, but he didn't see. They were slowing down to turn into what was supposed to be her dream home to come.

The dirt lane was narrow and it was obvious the foliage was trimmed only when larger vehicles caught straying boughs in the frame or side mirrors. Meagan loved it even though it was overwhelming. The privacy felt wonderful to her. She looked forward through the whipping branches to see an opening filled with the blue of the sea. As they continued down the lane and as they broke through the trees, the sea grew bigger with a beach showing on the horizon.

The men jumped out, but Meagan was mesmerized by the view. It was stunning. Like someone staring in the flames of a campfire, Meagan's eyes were trapped by the calm vast view.

Chris extended his thick hand to help her out of the backseat. "Well?" he said smiling proudly. "Do you like it so far?"

Meagan was speechless. It was beautiful. The cove wasn't overly large. It was deep enough for boats to come in, but shallow enough to keep the waves from sweeping away the pink sand.

"Pink!" That's all that could spill from her mouth. "Pink!" she said with school child delight. "It's really that colour."

Chris laughed as he wrapped his arm around her shoulder, walking her over the sparse grass to the beach. "I told you so," he said in a mocking voice.

She bent over and scooped some perfect Caribbean sand in her hands. "I know you said that, but it's so much more beautiful in real life. And, it's incredibly soft!"

Chris smiled the *I-told-you-so* smile.

She kicked off her shoes and socks. "That feels so good."

Chris tossed off his shoes and followed her to the shoreline where she stood in the edge of the waves. Meagan stood staring out at the sea, following the horizon to the jagged uplifted rocky limestone outcrops, then followed the trees and beach to the dock until she was finally looking at Chris. She wrapped her arms around his neck and planted a hot kiss on his lips.

Pulling back just enough to look him in the eyes she said. "This is by far the best place I have ever set foot on. I don't care if the house is an outhouse – I love it!"

He grinned. "I'm so glad you like the view. But, I am afraid of what the house is looking like. Do you want to see it?"

"Of course I do," she said, smiling back. She did glance at it as they drove up, but wasn't going to pass judgment just yet.

They turned around and Chris started to tell her his dream about the location. His passion for what he wanted was woven in his voice.

"I've spent most of my life on or around ice. Quite frankly, when my knees give out and they don't renew my contract, I hope the only ice I touch for a year is in my drink."

Meagan laughed at his joke but didn't interrupt.

"I love my job. I love hockey, but...," he shook his head. "It's going to get harder to pull out of bed to go to the rink at 4 a.m. So, I wanted to build something that would be the ideal retreat. Something far from the ice, far from the smelly locker room and far from the crowds.

"I wanted to build a home now that will be good for my future. I want the design to accept people with sore knees, so guys like my buddy, Gordo can visit without moaning as he heads to bed or down to the beach. I want it to be fun for a family to come to and enjoy forever. I'm thinking of today and planning for my retirement," he paused, smiled and laughed. "Shit, that sounds like a frickin' retirement commercial!"

Meagan was smiling at him and agreed with everything. She was visualizing herself there for the long term and feeling the lump grow in her throat.

"Well then," she said, as she cleared her throat. "Let's look at the blueprints and see if a wheelchair ramp can be added on for this Gordo guy."

"Not so fast," he said, pointing at a small house she hadn't noticed before. "That is the guesthouse of the future, but right now, it's our little beach cabana. Let's start there."

Mike had already disappeared into the construction, leaving their bags beside the Jeep.

The guesthouse was set off to the left of the main house at the end of a trail surrounded by hedges of hibiscus trees and bougainvillea. The different shades of pink slowed Meagan down. She had to admire them.

"Don't worry, those things flower all the time. They'll be here tomorrow," said Chris. Meagan quickened her pace and caught up.

The house was beautiful from the exterior. It was a two-story and had the classic hurricane-resistant sloped roof covered in flat tiles. Big windows faced the beach with huge shutters rolled ready for trouble. The plaster was a pleasant dull yellow, a typical colour for The Bahamas, blending nicely with the beach and the sea. It had a wraparound veranda facing the ocean and away from the main house. Deck chairs and a big soft chaise lounge created an inviting conversation pit.

"Why do you have it wrapped in bug nets?" asked Meagan as they stepped through the screen door. "I don't see any bugs."

"Yet," said Chris. "Sadly, there is one drawback to this island and it's the sand flies. Have you ever seen one?"

"Ummm, 'fraid not."

"That's because you don't. They are like those no-see-ums over on the mainland. They come out at dusk and before you know it, your ankles are covered in bites that itch all night."

Meagan hated bugs and liked Calgary because of the lack thereof. "I'm good with the screen. You can still see through."

"Don't worry though, there is still some deck without screens and I plan to do the half and half treatment on the main house too."

He opened the door to the house, and they stepped into the coolness of the air conditioning.

Meagan set down what little she carried and scanned the living room and even though the furnishings were rather dull and worn out, she saw the potential for a feature in Beach Homes Digest.

Chris started rambling on about the house. "The furniture isn't exactly what I want here, but I didn't want to spend time or money on good stuff until I was finished the big house. I figured I'd bring over a crate from Florida all at once."

"Sounds smart," she said, to an empty room. Chris was already walking into the kitchen and talking about its shortcomings.

"Same thing here. The stove isn't what I want, and the table is a joke."

Meagan walked in and fell in love with the design. "The cupboards are beautiful and the fixtures are great," she spun around taking it all in. "This is one really nice guesthouse. The stove is fine. Why would you need a better one in the guesthouse? I'm assuming your guests will join you most times in the main house for dining."

He paused and nodded his head. "True. But, what if my mom comes for a month? If I'm not here, I think she'd be more comfortable in a smaller house. I'd like to put in a ...."

Chris stopped talking and stared at Meagan. "What?"

Meagan grinned back. "What - what?"

"Why are you staring at me like that?"

"I'm not staring. I'm...I'm admiring you away from the rink."

Chris blushed and came to stand in front of her. He easily lifted her up and sat her on the cold granite counter. Meagan parted her legs and he stepped closer so she could wrap her legs around his waist. He kept his hands on her ribs, slowly moving them up to cup her breasts in his hands as she ran her fingers through his hair. He bent forward and kissed her mouth passionately. She relaxed under his touch.

Like in the movies, footsteps thump up the steps and the outside screen door creaks like it should, warning them of an intruder.

"Chris!" came a shout from the entrance. "Chris man, where you be?"

Chris slid his hands off her breasts and smiled as he stepped back. Meagan hopped off the counter and tried to look casual leaning against it.

"Rolly? Heeey," shouted Chris, as he walked out of the kitchen. The deck door finished slamming and the house door silently opened as Chris greeted the visitor.

Meagan could hear the men talking like long lost friends. Their laughter rolled into the kitchen. Instead of ruining the conversation, she opened the fridge to get something to drink.

Empty.

It was empty except for ketchup, hot sauces and other condiments.

Meagan was perplexed, but not for long. The screen door banged again and Chris and Rolly followed their voices into the kitchen. Both were carrying boxes of fresh food.

"Ah, you must be the Mrs?" said a handsome tall dark man with wild smoky hair.

"Ah, ease up there Rolly," Chris interrupted. "I haven't worked my spell on her yet."

Meagan laughed at Chris's uncomfortable situation and stuck out her hand.

"Naw, I'm nobody's Mrs. I'm just Meagan."

His strong hand enveloped hers in a warm handshake. "Well," he said, with a laugh in his voice. "Sorry for jumping the gun, Miss Meagan. When you do decide to marry the lug, call me. I got the perfect place for a wedding. I've married dozens of women there."

Meagan's face dropped, but both men laughed.

"He's a Justice of the Peace." laughed Chris. "Geez man, how often do you use that one?" referring to the joke.

"As often as I can," he said, as he walked towards the door. "I'll bring in the rest. Your butter isn't in this lot and it's no good dipping lobster in a puddle in my car."

Rolly moved swiftly out of the room, still chuckling about the marriages.

Meagan started lifting food out of the box. "That guy is a J.P.?"

Chris took lettuce from her hands, "Yep, and a teacher, a taxi driver, a deliveryman and um, a contractor and a great guy to have as a house sitter. I just email a list of stuff I want, and he comes within a few hours of me getting here. Good huh?"

He twisted the top off a cold bottle of beer and handed it to her, then got one for himself.

"Hope this tides you over until I've got the lobster ready."

Meagan scanned the boxes.

"It must be in the next load."

"Nope, it's fresher than that."

"Where is it?"

Chris finished a big swig of his beer and pointed out to the bay with the bottle. "Out there. We gotta go dive some up. We should skip the house tour and go now, while the tide's out. That way, we have three less feet of water to dive through."

Just beyond the mouth of the cove, Chris turned the motorboat a hard left and searched the shore for something.

Meagan looked over, but all she saw was the scrub trees hugging the shore. "What are we looking for?" she shouted over the engine.

Chris pulled back on the throttle and the boat puttered out a little further before he stopped the engine and dropped anchor.

"A marker. There is a tree I look for and when I see it – I stop the boat. I've always had good luck on this reef for lobster, so I keep coming back."

Meagan looked overboard and through the waves, she could see straight to the ocean floor.

"It's not too deep," she said.

Chris was already getting out a long metal spear and some unique work gloves designed for working with fish.

"Naw, most of the water around here is only 10 feet or so."

"Really?" said Meagan in amazement. "Do boats crash on the reefs at low tide?

"Sure. There's a boat on the other side I'll show you."

He handed her a set of fins and a mask.

"A boat?"

She was astonished but didn't let that stop her from stretching the tight fins over her toes and slap snuggly on her heels. She was getting scared but was keen to see a shipwreck.

He continued to organize his gear, while he filled her in on the ways of the high seas.

Chris was ready to slide over the edge. "Come on, I'll show you."

He popped over the edge and waited for her to slither in.

"Are there sharks?" she asked, while her feet tested the water.

Chris grabbed her ankle with his free hand and pulled gently. "Don't worry I've got my trusty harpoon to protect you."

She jumped in but didn't hear if there were any sharks to deal with. She really didn't want to know.

The boat was anchored about 10 metres from the face of the coral reef. Meagan was amazed at how clear the water was and how vibrant the colours were. She slowed down to admire the fish and Chris stopped too.

As he tread he pulled the snorkel from his lips. "Don't worry about sharks, there aren't that many in these waters to worry about. Come on, the boat is over here." He realigned his snorkel and mask and waved for her to follow.

Just beyond the top of the reef, lying on its side was the boat. It was a brilliant red slim speed boat that was probably worth a fortune. It was eerie to see something that represented noise and action sit so still. Meagan didn't know how long it had been there, but obviously long enough to have algae and small organisms start colonizing it.

Meagan circled the boat, looking at the great hole in the bottom where little orange and white fish darted in and out. She wondered about the riders, they must have been thrown out.

Movement out the corner of her eye caught her attention. It was Chris, diving down and poking his gloved hands and metal stick into crevasses in the limestone. She watched as he methodically poked, went back up for a breath then dove back down to continue prodding. Suddenly within a flurry, he stabbed into a hole with his weapon and a lifeless lobster came out of the hole pierced onto the skewer. Even through his mask, Chris looked pleased.

Meagan felt a little sickened but continued to watch the cycle until he had two lobsters lined up like beads on a necklace on the skewer. He pointed in the direction of their boat and she followed him back.

While holding onto the edge of the boat, Chris tipped the skewer into the back. The clunk of the lifeless lobsters could be heard from where Meagan treaded, removing her mouthpiece to talk.

"Are you done? That's how easy it is?" she said, as he swam over to her.

He smiled warmly and kissed her on the shoulder. "Yep. That's the big hunting expedition of the day. Did you want to try it?"

"Oh, no," she said, shaking her wet head. "I don't think I want to reach into a dark hole in a reef like that. It's okay – you be the great provider."

"Come on then, let's take a quick swim around the reef. I'll show you some more stuff, so we can work up an appetite."

He put his snorkel back in his mouth, reached for her hand and they swam together.

Meagan felt comfortable with Chris leading the way. Once in a while, he'd point at a fish or a coral or some creepy creature. He pointed ahead of them at a few large, long fish drifting with the current near the sandy bottom. Chris pointed at their mouths and even though Meagan was a prairie girl, she could tell they were barracudas looking for the lobsters Chris had impaled.

They circled the reef slowly and by the time they reached the boat again, Meagan was in love with the ocean. Chris was right, she was going to enjoy being with him in The Bahamas.

CHAPTER TWENTY-FOUR

Next morning, Meagan woke with a start. The sun was crowding the room with rays — a sight never seen in Alberta's notorious dark winters. She sat up and looked at her phone beside the bed. It was only 5:45. She looked the other way and saw an empty lair where Chris slept. The smell of coffee permeated the room. She smiled and laid back down.

"It's only 3:45 my time. I think I deserve to go back to sleep," she said to the sun, as she rolled away from the light. She smiled to herself as she thought about the previous night that included delicious lobster, wine, candles and of course, great sex on the deck. She scratched the middle of her back where a sand fly had bitten her and decided one bite was a small price to pay. Her eyes grew heavy and she fell back to sleep.

The next time her eyes opened, the room was different. Chris had been in and shut the blinds. A coffee sat on the nightstand next to her phone glaring with the rude time of 9:15.

9:15! Holy shit! I never sleep this late, no matter what time zone, she thought as she grabbed the coffee. *Crap! It's cold. He's going to think I'm a lazy oaf.*

As she stood to get dressed, the sounds from the yard stopped her in her tracks. It was Chris in a heated discussion with Mike. Meagan walked closer to the window to hear what the big deal was, but it was hard to catch it all. She peeked through the blinds hoping that would help.

Chris was ranting about something. His voice wasn't loud, but his body was. Arms gestured with power bursting from his waving hands. Conversely, Mike had his fists buried in the same ratty shorts she saw him in yesterday. His shoulders curled under the outbursts from Chris. The two men stood staring at each other, then Chris put his hand gently on Mike's shoulder and they walked towards the unfinished house. Meagan was amazed at his demeanour. Obviously, he was upset with the building, but he still showed kindness.

"Not me," Meagan whispered to herself. "That guy is playing games with Chris. But not me."

Meagan swiftly got dressed in a pair of shorts and a light T-shirt, tied her hair in a ponytail and trotted down the stairs into the kitchen. Chris left out a delicious array of fresh fruit and bagels, so she quickly made a fresh pot of coffee and settled in to eat.

It was almost an hour before Chris walked up the path to the house. Meagan watched him from the deck with her second cup of coffee. She didn't think her appearance at the worksite was welcomed yet, so she decided the deck was safe.

He smiled at her when he noticed her sitting in the chair they both occupied the night before.

The screen door announced his arrival with an alarming shriek. He stepped in far enough to let the door snap shut, then leaned on the jamb.

"Well," he said, crossing his massive arms across his chest. "Aren't you the lady of leisure?" There wasn't a hint of the frustration he was expressing before. Maybe they sorted things out far from earshot.

Meagan smiled sheepishly as she started to rise. "Can I get you a coffee? I made a fresh pot."

"Naw," he said, as he gently pushed her back into the cushiony sofa. "I'll grab one and be right back."

A few minutes passed and he was back with a tray crowded with food and coffee. He set it on the side table and crawled into the seat with her and wrapped himself around her, nuzzling her neck and biting her earlobe. She giggled and kissed him back.

"Did you get enough rest? I figured it had been a few long days, so I'd let you catch a few extra zees. Or is that a few zeds in Canada?"

She laughed, "That was very nice of you. Thanks. I promise to get up with the rooster from now on."

The sounds of construction thumped through the air and Chris's body tensed. He reached for a chunk of mango then his coffee.

"So, when do I get to see the fancy shack?" she said cheerily. She thought it would be best not to acknowledge the morning discussion.

Chris leaned his head back and shut his eyes. "Ugh."

"Ugh?"

"Ugh."

Meagan waited a minute and carefully asked again. "Somehow I'm sensing that the project isn't going as planned."

"Yep," he said, without moving.

He opened his eyes and turned his head at the same time as he rested a warm gentle hand on her thigh.

"I know I have to be patient. Mike is a good guy and he needs the break. I told his dad I'd let him run the show. But this isn't what I brought you here for. I wanted to show you my dream home and how far along it was. I wanted you to see what might be in store should you take up my offer of a long-term game plan.

"Instead, I've brought you to a mess. I don't think any progress has been made since I was here three months ago. Permits that were supposed to be nailed to the wall have not been acquired and approvals are missing. Supplies are not ordered, there's no brick for the walls," his voice started to rise as he vented. "But the frickin' shingles are lying in a heap, *'in case they get that far!'*... Shit."

"Approvals and permits?" Meagan didn't want to sound alarmed, but nothing gets built without those in Canada. "Why don't we spend a day getting them done. Is there an office in Governor's Harbour where we can stop in at? It would be a good excuse to see some of the island."

She eagerly stared at her boyfriend.

He paused for a minute. "Naw, I gotta let Mikey do his job. He can do it. I told him what has to be done in the next few days. Let's see if he just needed some guidance. Okay?"

"His dad means a lot to you, doesn't he?"

"Yeah, it's for Coach," he said, as he got ready to sip at a hot coffee.

"Alright. I'll keep my busy nose out for a bit, but I want to look at it today to see how it's going. If he's doing shoddy structural work, I want to put a stop to it. If he can't handle the job, can I come on? I don't want him making the steps too steep for Gordo. I'll do it for free," she added cheekily.

"Free?" he laughed. "You might have a deal!"

Within the hour, Meagan was pouring over the blueprints on the kitchen counter. What she saw on paper was a dreamy home. She had to quit daydreaming about what she wanted and focus the details laid out in front of her. Oddly though, many of the features were ones she would have requested or desired. *Maybe we are meant for each other?* she thought.

The plan was simple, yet stylish. It was sleek, open and inviting. Walls were kept to a minimum, using stub walls to allow the natural light to sweep through the structure.

The main floor was designed for entertaining with large open spaces and vaulted ceilings. A chef would drool over the layout and size of the kitchen. Interestingly the dining room was a screened-off area out on the side deck. A novel idea she thought.

Meagan flipped past the electrical drawings to the page for the second floor. Two bedrooms and an office filled the space. Each had its own bathroom, but as expected, the master room was the feature room.

Two steps down out from the master bedroom and facing out to the cove, was a huge veranda. Glass railings were sketched in to make sure the view from the bed was not obstructed. The steps down would also help. The bathroom was as big as the spare bedroom with a huge walk-in clear glass block shower. The blocks coiled like a conch shell. The soaker tub was raised with low windows that opened to the deck.

Meagan was absorbed in the drawings and didn't hear Chris come into the room. He watched her study the plans.

"Well? Do you want to see if it measures up?"

"Oh!" she said, with a start. She stood up from the bent-over posture she took on to read the prints, sighed and said, "Chris, this design is spectacular. Whoever created it did a splendid job of optimizing the space."

"Thank you," he said, with a grin.

"This is your design?"

He bobbed his head shyly. "I drew it on a napkin and a guy in Boston did up the design. I think he did a good job."

"It's great! Let's go see if Mike is doing it justice. I haven't spent much time on it, but at first glance, I know there are a few structural things that need to be done correctly or they get redone. And we don't want a redo — do we!?"

She rolled up the plans and kissed him on the cheek as she headed for the door, but he grabbed her by the elbow.

"Hey, hey hey...not so fast," he said, with a cautionary tone.

She looked at him puzzled as he pulled her in tight as if to stop her from moving.

"Please remember in The Bahamas," he paused to draw in a breath. "In The Bahamas, they work at a different speed than in Calgary or Boston. It's hot here. So, people, projects and things move slower. Don't be critical, okay?"

Meagan tried not to be offended by his warning but felt bruised by it. "I wasn't going to go in and crack whips."

He slid the blueprints out from under her arm. "How about, while the workers are there, you pretend to be nothing more than a visitor that knows nothing about architecture or load-bearing walls or electrical code stuff. Just be a hockey player's sweetheart who loves him very much."

He looked like he meant it, so she relaxed and said, in a candy-coated sweet voice. "Okay Poopsie. But when they pull out of the driveway..." her voice dropped — "Bam! I pull out the blueprints. Deal?"

"Deal."

They strolled to the front of the house, chatting softly about dinner plans at the local bar and grill. When they got to the front of the house, Chris started to talk about the house and the layout and the purpose of what he had designed. He kept Meagan's attention easily as he poured out his passion for the house.

"The ocean and all the oxygenated air sweeping across the beach is important. I want to capture it both in sightlines and airflow," he said, as he waved his arms as if bringing the air to his face.

Mike came through the door, laughing. "Hey, Boss! Good thing the air is free - cause that view sure as shit ain't!

"Hey Meagan, sleep well?" he continued as he danced down the steps.

Meagan smiled warmly. "Hi Mike, I did. Thanks for keeping the construction sounds down for me."

He laughs. "No Mon, I didn't keep them down for you. We just work quiet here. Did you come to see your dream home? Is he gunna let you change anything?"

Chris made a grunting noise, while Meagan answered. "I signed on the dotted line that I'm not allowed to girly it up. If I don't want a rink in the dining room, I'll have to live in the guesthouse."

Mike gestured for Meagan to go into the house. "Whew, that means I don't have to rip out the locker room then!"

Meagan was smiling as she entered the house and kept it plastered on her face as long as she could. If marks were to be handed out, she'd give him about a 50. To the untrained eye, it was messy but fine. But being the honour student with top marks in all of her classes, she knew way too much.

They maneuvered through the main floor, where the living room would be, the dining room, the bathroom and finally into the kitchen where plumbing and electrical were disasters.

Kitchen cabinets were already hanging on the walls, but most of the drywall hadn't even arrived.

"Mike," she said nicely. "Why do you have cabinets hung, but nothing behind them?"

"Oh, that's what we do to keep the snakes out," he said, in all honesty.

"Oh," she said, looking around for snakes not knowing what to believe. She stepped away carefully.

He got the reaction he wanted.

Meagan smiled at the workers as they moved through the house. There were at least six guys on the job. Two Haitians were moving drywall, three Bahamians unloaded lumber out back and one other American named Dave, the foreman sat on a sawhorse smoking a cigarette.

Within two minutes of purposely asking Dave a bunch of first-year trade school questions, it was quite apparent he didn't know the difference between a finishing nail and a concrete spike. Meagan was getting worried. *This guy is no foreman!* she thought as she walked into what would be the master bedroom.

She leaned against walls and counted off space and found walls wiggled and much of the building wasn't square. Something had to be done immediately or Chris would be wasting a mountain of money.

Chris could see that her mind was already working on reworking the house. She caught him looking at her and she quickly replaced the concern on her face with the look of pure joy.

Walking up to him, she wrapped her arms around his waist. She could feel his heat through the shirt. "This is going to be a great house, Chris. Your design is great," she ended the sentence with a kiss on the edge of his jaw. She didn't want to piss him off, but what she was seeing was a job for a demolition man.

"Why don't we take the boat out and find a beach to have lunch on?" Meagan said quickly. She could feel his tension and she was afraid she was the cause.

As they walked back through the house, Mike walked past with a load of lumber. "Did you decide on the colours for the bedroom? I thought you'd like to decide that."

Meagan looked at him and wondered for a second if he really thought of her as someone so simple.

"Naw, not yet. I'm still thinking about that load of shingles out front. Do you know if they are up to the current code? If the shingles aren't rated for 240 kilometres per hour, oh excuse me – that's 150 miles per hour in American, then they will peel off and become projectiles and leave patches of the wood roof susceptible to the rain and rot. Speaking of rot, what about termite prevention? None of this wood looks like it was pretreated, and it is close to the soil making entry easy for the pests. So, no. To answer your question, the colour of the bedroom walls is not high on my agenda."

Leaving the two men staring in disbelief, Meagan walked out of the building and back to the guesthouse. The screen door got in the last word.

They packed a hamper full of food, beer and wine and a blanket in almost utter silence. She knew Chris had every right to be mad at her but decided to leave the discussion until they were on the water. If he wanted to yell at her, he wouldn't have to worry about other people hearing.

Chris navigated the boat past the reef at the entrance to the cove and out onto rolling soft water. The sky was clear again and was a stunning backdrop to the green sea and pink sand. He kept his eyes on the ocean. His jaw was clenched. Meagan was getting very worried that she just tossed away a perfectly good relationship. She gently touched his arm and he looked over at her.

"Please stop the boat."

"What?" he shouted back.

"Stop the boat!" she said, loudly this time.

Chris pulled back on the throttle and the roar of the engine quit. The boat rose with the swell of the wake then relaxed on the calm water. He didn't look at her at first but put his hand gently on her leg. Suddenly Meagan realized his frustration wasn't with her.

"Meagan, I'm so sorry," he said softly.

"Sorry? Sorry for what?" she questioned. "I'm sorry I lipped Mike off at the end there. You asked me not to say anything and I did. I'm sorry."

Chris looked up at her and smiled warmly. "Oh, you don't think I'm mad at you – do you? It's Mike's shoddy work that I'm upset with."

He stood up and went to the back of the boat and took two beers out of the cooler, opened one and gave it to Meagan. She took a drink of the ice-cold beverage and realized just how damn good a cold beer can taste when you are hot. Chris opened the other one and took a thirsty swig.

"I watched you go through the house and I watched where your eyes went. When I looked at things from your perspective, I realized how crappy the house is."

"It's not that bad," lied Meagan.

"You're lying," he said laughing. "I can see through your sunglasses that you are lying."

She smiled, conceding her guilt. "Okay, I'm lying. It is in a bit of a bind. But we can fix it," she paused and looked him in the eyes. "I can fix it."

He took a long drink, looking back at his cove. "I can't fire Mike. I can't," he said softly.

"You won't. He'll just have to work with me."

He looked at her. He looked at her long. He pulled off his sunglasses, then he lifted hers to the top of her head and touched her warm cheek with the hand that had been holding the cold beer. The feeling was refreshing and Meagan's cheek leaned into the coolness. He kissed her lips softly.

"But. You'd have to spend time here. What will happen to your business in Calgary?"

"Business? What business. I'm sure Carl's escapades have ruined me in Calgary. What little work my office has, they can handle. With me away, they can actively pump out their resumes without getting caught," she said, but only half-joking. In the back of her mind, she visualized an empty office upon her return.

"You don't have to stay here really," he said, with a slightly more enthusiastic voice. "We can go over it with Mike, get you drafting a schedule in the next few days, then you can come back in a month or so to begin working in earnest. You could do a week on and a week off sort of thing." He stood up, excited with what was coming to his head. "Some weeks you could stop in Boston. We can see more of each other this way!"

Meagan grinned as she watched him pace back and forth. Two strides and he'd pivot, two strides and he'd pivot again. She started to laugh as the boat rocked. He stopped at the edge of the boat and looked at her.

"What?"

"What back," she said, laughing.

"What are you laughing at," he said, as he started to laugh.

"You are pacing in a dinghy!"

He looked around him and realized what she was saying. In typical hockey player fashion, he grabbed the back of his shirt behind his neck and pulled it off over his head in one swoop. Then he dropped his shorts.

Meagan's eyes popped out in surprise.

Chris pumped his arms once and tossed himself off the boat in one mighty backflip. His pearly white ass mooned her as he flipped.

She didn't do a backflip, but her skinny pale ass was soon to follow.

CHAPTER TWENTY-FIVE

By the time they returned to the house, they had polished off the beer, ate all the food, drank most of the wine and made wonderful passionate love on the blanket under the searing hot sun on a deserted beach. Naked, they drew in the sand fresh ideas for the house. Only when the sound of another engine entered their ears did they decide to put on some clothes and make the trek home.

"Do you think we should talk to Mike tonight with regards to my involvement?" Meagan asked as she sliced vegetables for their dinner.

It was already dark out, but there were still lights on at the worksite. Meagan figured it was Mike making a good show for the boss but not exactly working.

Chris rolled a carrot around in his teeth as he pondered her question. He walked around the counter to take a better look through the window at the other house.

"Naw, I think I better sleep on the idea. He might be pretty upset with the change of command."

The next morning Meagan woke with the sunrise. She rolled over to see Chris was still beside her. She didn't wake him or move. Watching him sleep was one of her favourite rituals. She scanned his jaw for more cuts, but it was fine.

A car door clicked shut in the distance. Most ears wouldn't have heard the noise, but Meagan knew it well from when her ex-boyfriend would try to sneak in after an all-nighter with the girl he finally moved in with.

She slid out of bed and moved closer to the window without being seen. She couldn't see much, but there was definitely someone there. She slipped on her running clothes and tiptoed downstairs and out the front door. She was going to push the screen door open, she stopped in her tracks. Her fingers pried it open just enough to squeeze through without it creaking. She didn't know if anyone else paid attention to squeaky doors, but she knew it would blow her cover.

Meagan didn't know what she was looking for and suddenly felt like an idiot, so she quickly ran towards the shore to pretend she was out for an early morning run on the beach, which was actually a good idea considering all the food and beverages she had been consuming.

After 10 minutes of being chased by high tide waves, Meagan gave up running on the sand. She didn't want to ruin her runners in the saltwater, so she ran up towards the houses to head for the highway. As she passed the main house, Mike came out of the door.

When he saw her his face brightened into a huge smile. "Hey Red, you start early."

She cringed at the nickname but didn't bite back. Instead, she slowed to a walk and stopped her watch timer.

"Hi back, Mike. I didn't know you started this early either. Why are you here now?"

He stepped down the first step and sat down. "Everybody starts early in the Caribbean. If you didn't, you'd waste away in the heat. My guys should be here in 10 minutes. We usually start at 7 o'clock."

Meagan figured he was telling the truth and thought she should lighten up on the guy. She walked up the steps and sat down beside him.

"Mike, I'm sorry. I feel I owe you an apology," she said, without looking him in the face. "I think I snapped at you yesterday when we were inspecting the house."

"I didn't think you were so bad. But it did get me thinking. What do you do for an occupation?" he asked cautiously.

She looked at him and said. "I'm an architect. I design and construct houses, offices and lodges. I have my own company."

His eyes widened, but he quickly regained his composure. "An architect! Why didn't someone tell me? Now I feel like such a fool. I didn't think you knew anything, so I treated you as if you didn't need to know details. I would have explained things better if I'd known you'd understand."

Meagan smiled at him. "I understand quite well. I'm not just a mop of red hair," she added as she pushed stray curls from her sweaty forehead.

"Gee," he said, rather sheepishly. "Too bad you live so far west. I'd invite you to come and contribute to the building, but you must have way too much to do there and it's so hard to get here. But don't worry, I'll get 'er done and you'll love it." He patted her on the leg and stood up to walk back into the house to end the conversation. A car with a loud loose muffler was pulling down the driveway with Mike's crew.

"Actually Mike, I think I do have the time to help out. I think I'll finish up a project I'm working on then be back to help out."

She watched his body involuntarily jerk at the mention of her coming back.

He stopped and carefully turned around. "Really? When?" he said, slowly and with caution as if to control an urge to blow up.

Meagan stood up and bounced down the steps as carefree as she could. "I don't know. A month maybe? How about I come back over in an hour or two and we go over the work schedule together to see where I can fit in?"

"Ah, yeah. Sure," he said stiffly. "Bring the boss too."

As she walked back to the guesthouse she murmured to herself, "You must have way too much to do there and it's so hard to get here. But don't worry, I'll get 'er done and you'll love it! I'll show you – you asshole! I don't know what you think you are doing but it sucks. I'm going to barf!"

She pulled on the screen door and it screamed. As it slammed she spun and glared at the hinge and said, "When I get back, I'll oil you first!"

She stomped into the kitchen for her morning brew.

Chris's eyes popped open to the sight of an empty bed as the door and her stomping feet echoed through the house. He quickly tossed on his shorts and T-shirt and bound down the stairs to see Meagan. Her back was towards him and she was talking wildly with frantic gestures to herself as she looked out the window at the main house.

"Megs?" he said sweetly. "Is there a problem?"

She spun and looked at him. Her face was red with embarrassment and her hair – reacting to the humidity was spraying from her head like wild rusty springs. She dropped her arms that were in mid-swing.

"Um, I, didn't get far on my run. The waves were too big. I didn't want to get my shoes wet."

"Did you bump into Mike?"

"Yeah," she said strained.

"And?"

"Chris, please understand that I am not a confrontational person. I like things to go smooth and I usually don't start arguments and to be honest, I rarely win them. I don't like to get on people's bad sides. But Mike, I don't know what it is about him. He asked what I do for a living and I told him honestly. Then I said, I'd maybe come back to help out." She paused to catch her breath.

"What did Mike say?" he asked slowly.

"It wasn't what he said," she said, with a confused look on her face. "It was what he didn't say and how he didn't say it."

Chris snorted a laugh. "What?"

"He doesn't want me here, but I don't think it's my expertise that threatens him. I don't get it."

Chris picked up the coffee that was brewing and brushed off her concern. "Naw, like any man, he doesn't want a woman as a boss. He'll get over it. If he didn't put up his fists, things will be fine."

He took a swig of his coffee and headed back upstairs. "I'm going to brush my teeth. I'll race you to the other side of the island."

She saw her fears were dismissed. And felt like a fool for thinking Mike was up to no good.

"If you want a real race, you mean top to bottom not across!" she yelled at his disappearing back.

All she could hear was him laughing hysterically as he trotted up the stairs. He knew she could probably do the 100-mile distance. "Across is fine," he shouted.

Meagan and Chris stayed away from the construction. Not to avoid Mike, but to see a bit of the island. Chris had roamed almost every inch of every beach and now wanted her to see what was in store.

Heading up the bumpy highway through James Cistern and Gregory Town, they were met with a one-lane bridge over a skinny arch of limestone. Chris pulled the car to the side of the road and said, "Come take a look at this. This is the bridge I told you about on our first date. It's amazing that we actually drive over this thing."

Meagan jumped out of the Jeep and walked in the hot breeze with Chris.

"The island comes to its narrowest point between the north and the south islands right here," he said pointing down. "On that side to the east, is the deep blue Atlantic Ocean. Look how dark it is."

She looked over the edge. The dark blue water was a good 80 feet down a sheer cliff, smashing against the rocky steep shore.

"But this side," continued the geography teacher as the walked a few metres, "it's the Bight of Eleuthera; shallow, calm and peaceful. This is where the sailors looked through the arch they called the Glass Window. I think I bored you with the details on our first date. This is where the islands meet. When the wind is howling like a hurricane, the waves surge hard enough to push cars off the bridge. One hurricane actually pushed the bridge off its mooring."

Meagan was shocked by the power of the water. As he talked about the forces, she watched the angry waves surge in and out of the small opening.

"Your place is on the Atlantic side - but it doesn't seem this scary," she said.

"Yeah, there are definitely spots you want to avoid – like here," he said, as he walked back to the Jeep. "I picked the cove so I would have some protection from the waves and weather."

They continued driving through the little town of Bogue, not far from there was the tip of the island to the town of Current.

"I like this town. If I could have found a place here, I would have bought it. There's about 100 people – including all the snowbirds and the only store in town is Rosie's. She usually doesn't have much other than canned stuff and sodas but it's enough to keep her busy."

Chris spun the steering wheel and they pulled off the narrow main street and parked next to a nondescript faded pink building where the door was pinned open with a cinder block.

He turned off the engine. "This is Rosie's. Let's see if she's got any Coke."

The candy case was on the right as soon as they entered the store. Meagan looked in at the candy doing its daily ritual melt in the hot sun. The Christian pamphlets scattered on the glass top did nothing to prevent the chocolate from melting.

"Hey, Miss Rosie," Chris said, warmly as he walked towards a little Bahamian lady bent over a new box of cans near the back. She stood up and squinted at the tall figure in the sun.

When his shadow blocked the light, her face lit up. "Mr. Burrows. It has been far too long. Are you well?"

The two hugged gently and walked arm-in-arm to the front of the store.

"Of course, I'm fine. And you? Is anyone helping you in the store these days?"

"Oh, I got help coming and goin' all the time," she said, still admiring Chris.

"Hey Rosie, this is my girlfriend, Meagan. She's from Canada."

"Oh, maybe you know Linda."

Meagan was shaking her boney, yet strong hand. "Linda?"

"She's from somewhere in Ontario and married Bob. Where are you from?"

"I'm from the west, Calgary."

"Ummm," said the lady through a soft, thin smile. Meagan could tell she didn't care.

"Mr. Burrows, how long you here for this time?"

"Oh, just long enough to pick up a few Cokes," he said, as he opened the rusted cooler.

She laughed. "No dear, on the island?"

Chris looked at his watch and looked at Meagan. "Gee I guess I'm, er we are heading back after tomorrow. I'm back to work on Monday."

Meagan quit listening and went outside to see the town. It was very small. From the door, the land dipped so she could see over the rooftops to the teal-coloured water. Most of the houses were proudly kept, painted in soft washes of pink, yellow or blue. A few houses were totally wiped out, only beat-up foundations told the tale of the power of hurricanes.

Chris and Rosie walked together out of the building still talking.

"You should take Miss Meagan to see if she knows Linda," she was saying, as they stepped into the sun.

Chris smiled at Meagan. "Yeah, if they don't know each other they'll want to, but I better save that for another visit. We got lots of miles to see still."

He gave Miss Rosie a peck on the cheek and the smile crept across her face again.

Meagan waved and got in the Jeep.

Chris put the bottles of pop in the back, and they drove down the road to the right.

"You don't drink Coke," Meagan said.

"Nope. But she doesn't know that. I use that for an excuse to see her."

They drove two minutes and were out of the car again, but this time it was the end of the island.

"This is the cut," said Chris as they looked across a narrow channel towards another island. "That's Current Island that you saw from the plane."

Meagan scanned the water between the islands, and it was raging like a swift mountain river. A sailboat was bobbing through without its sails up, taking advantage of the current.

"We'll have to come back and snorkel this. If we get in on the east side, we ride the waves into the calm water, but we'd get out about here. Underneath is a fantastic array of sea life, drifting with the current.

"How deep is it out there?" asked Meagan, as she looked towards the dark water. She remembered Dan warning about a long float.

"Not bad right away. As a matter of fact, in low tide, you have to be careful and not ground out in a boat. Just like Dan said. And if you do get stuck out there, there are some shoals you could stand on and wait to get rescued. That is — if you are tall enough to cling to it through high tide!"

Meagan was looking at the water and how strong the current was. She decided they would ride the waves to the west where the water looked more like a Caribbean resort advertisement.

Chris kissed her on the cheek. Don't worry, it's not that bad. Once you get to know the water and its habits then it isn't so scary. These people would shit their drawers if you plunked them into an Alberta blizzard. You just gotta respect your surroundings."

For some reason, Meagan couldn't stop looking out to the dark water. "I can shovel my way out of a blizzard, I don't know how I'd get out that!"

On the last day, before the searing sun crested the trees, Chris took Meagan for one last run and brought her back on a winding path through an orange orchard behind his property.

They eventually discussed house details with Mike who seemed enthusiastic about Meagan coming in exactly a month to collaborate. Chris was thrilled with the thought of the two of them working on the house together. He had regained confidence in Mike, and he knew Meagan could move the project along. He couldn't wait to call his old coach to tell him Mike was doing a great job.

"I have to thank you for taking on this project," he said, as he brought fresh drinks out to Meagan where she sat on the veranda looking out at the dark beach.

It was another beautiful night and their last. A bit of a breeze was coming up off the water and the waves were loud as they slapped the shoreline. A full moon was hidden behind the clouds.

Meagan smiled as she took the glass from his hand. He sat down beside her on the swinging chair and wrapped his arm around her and continued to speak.

"I know you don't think Mike can do the job and frankly I was worried too. But now with your guidance, I know it will turn out perfect. And this way," he said, as he squeezed her shoulder, "You will get the house you want too. Our home. Cool!" he said, taking a drink.

Meagan was overwhelmed with it all and started to well up with emotion. Life was moving in weird ways lately. She sat quietly hoping the tears wouldn't spill. When she turned her head away the eyelash dam gave way. One huge tear tumbled down her cheek and splashed on Chris's forearm.

Meagan quickly wiped it off his arm and tried to dry her eyes, apologizing the whole time.

"Oh, Chris. I'm sorry," she said, between sniffles. "I thought I was stronger than this."

"What's wrong?"

"Nothing. Oh, nothing at all," she stammered. "That's just it. This is all good. It's all good, but my life at home sucks. Everything is moving so fast. Look what has happened to me in the last few months. I, I am barely making a living and can't figure out why. I meet you, I find out the competitor is swindling me, I fall for you, I find out he's using my best friend, my company tanks. I end up really falling for you. You bring me here and it's beautiful and I really start to really, really fall for you and now you tell me like it's my house to build the way I want…but my business is

still tanking. Life with you is paradise…but I need my company to work…
I need…"

She was going to continue, but Chris couldn't stand the tears anymore
and she was starting to hyperventilate. He put their glasses on the table and
wrapped her in his arms as tight as he dared. She quit talking and melted in
his heat. Her breathing slowed down, and the tears stopped. They stayed
intertwined for a long time. He slowly stroked her hair.

The only sound was the waves.

"Are you okay now?" he asked quietly, as he kissed her forehead.

Slowly she said, "yeah."

"How do you eat an elephant?"

She pulled back to hear him better. "What?"

"How do you eat an elephant?" he asked again.

She thought for a moment and could not see where this was going.

He answered, "One bite at a time. Now, don't let the situation with
Carl bring you down. You will get through this. He will be punished. You
can rebuild. But you cannot do it all at once. One bite at a time."

Chris smiled at her and wiped the last of the tears off her face. "Okay?"

She smiled back and took a big breath, then leaned forward and lightly
bit his nipple through his shirt. "I'd rather bite you!"

The conversation deteriorated right there.

Chris quickly picked her up and swiftly took her to the chaise lounge
where he placed her gently on the soft pillows. It was their last night
together probably until playoffs were done and neither of them wanted to
waste another minute.

The moon pushed the clouds away to get a better view of the couple as
they enjoyed the foreplay based on the suggestion of biting. They giggled
and the moon glowed brighter. Chris's body shone blue in the light as he
moved on top of her to make love. Meagan wanted to shut her eyes and
enjoy the warmth, but the image of his muscular body above her added to
her excitement. He cupped her breasts in his hands and bent down to bite
the nipples. He looked her in the eyes and they both laughed. His body
moved with the rhythm of the waves, Meagan arched and rocked with the
motion.

The lovers were happy to lay in the moonlight and listen as the waves
continued to make love to the beach.

CHAPTER TWENTY-SIX

The next morning was overcast. *A perfect day to leave the perfect holiday,* thought Meagan as she quickly showered and packed. Her suitcase was loaded with shells to share at the office and her carry-on bag now included a tube with a copy of the blueprints. Her little DSLR was loaded with hundreds of pictures she planned to use for reference when working on the design.

While examining the house and taking pictures, a few details glared at her - like the odd room in the back of the crawlspace that was not on the blueprint. There were windows at the back, but they were bricked in. She didn't say anything to Chris. She didn't want to alarm him. Instead, she would come back and address the situation herself.

She finished her coffee and tidied up while Chris went next door to the worksite. She knew a housekeeper would come to clean up and remove the excess food, but she didn't think it was proper to leave a mess. It wasn't long before the horn on the Jeep beeped for her to come out. She quickly grabbed her bag and dashed through the screen door. It screamed its farewell one last time.

Again, Meagan enjoyed the drive in the backseat. She sat holding a crossbar with one hand and the other restrained her hair from dancing in the breeze. The two men chatted in the front while she watched the sights go by. She was pleased with how much she knew of the island already, but then reminded herself that it's hard to get lost on a one highway island.

Pulling into the airport, she could see Dan already prepping the plane. He saw her looking and waved. Letting go of her tangling hair to wave back was a bad idea. It flew up like a copper-coloured banner, whipping in the wind.

Mike stopped the Jeep like a hockey player hitting the boards. Meagan's hair flung forward in a heap. As she tried to sort it out, Mike looked in the rear-view mirror and laughed at the sight.

"You have the craziest hair in the world, Red!"

She wanted to lash out with a personal insult but thought better of it. "It's this dang humidity! I didn't think it could get any worse. Next trip, I'm bringing a toque!"

The airport was noisy with the commercial planes revving the engines. Chris helped her out of the back seat while Mike unloaded the bags. With a few bags, Chris headed towards Dan who was already talking to him. As Meagan reached in to retrieve the tube, Mike quickly grabbed it, "I've got it!" he said bluntly.

She slipped her purse over her shoulder and headed towards the plane, but when she turned to look back, Mike was following with a single bag, no tube. *Shit, he is weird and really up to something,* she thought to herself.

She kept walking slowly towards the plane until he was close enough to outmaneuver him. As he started stuffing the bags in the cargo compartment, she ran back to the Jeep and looked in the backseat. Her tube wasn't there. She looked in the front and to her surprise, he'd stuffed it as best he could under the passenger seat.

Meagan pulled it out and quickly popped the lid. The blueprints were still there. She didn't know how he could have stashed it so fast or why but still wanted to confirm they weren't disturbed.

Mike could see her walking back with the tube. "Oh, hey, sorry man. I was going to bring that in a second load."

He reached to put it in the cargo for her, but she held tight. "I'll keep it this time, Mike," she said strongly. "I don't want to have any reason why I can't get my work done before I return."

"Ah, yeah, about that. When do you think you will be here? I mean, like exactly? Cause really, I don't need you. I was just trying to please the boss when I said you could help."

The noise from a commercial 737 increased to a deafening howl as it started to wheel away from the airport. The other two men were on the opposite side of the plane so Chris couldn't see or hear what was going on between Meagan and Mike.

Meagan stood there staring at Mike and he back at her. Even through his sunglasses, she could sense the seriousness of his statement beaming from his eyes. His jaw was clamped shut; she could see his pulse pounding though a vein on his temple.

"But I want to help," she said, smiling to see if he would relax. "It will be fun to participate in what I hope will be my house too."

He didn't lighten up, instead, he leaned closer to accentuate his point. "I don't want your help."

Meagan started to take in a mighty breath to lash out at him, but Chris came up behind her.

"Let's go!" he shouted while sticking his hand out to shake Mike's. "Meagan will be back next month to give you a hand. You guys will have a great time."

Mike smiled at Chris, but when Chris turned to get into the plane, he slowly shook his head back and forth at Meagan with that same evil glare.

"See you in a month, Mike. I'll send the changes before I come," she said, just as firmly and stepped into the plane.

Dan saw the whole conversation and felt something wasn't right, but let it go. He latched the backseat door after Meagan crawled in and watched as Mike walked back to the Jeep. Not once did Mike look back. He started the Jeep and blasted back onto the pothole infested road. Dan looked at Meagan. She was looking out the opposite window avoiding everyone.

They flew straight to Miami, skipping the airport in Nassau so Meagan could fly direct to Calgary while Chris could go direct to Boston. The goodbye on the tarmac was rushed as Meagan's flight was loading at the next gate. Dan rushed over to the baggage handlers to load her bags while she and Chris ran into the building so she could load the plane properly. At the gate, it was a quick "It's been fun...gotta go." And "We'll talk tomorrow."

When she sat in her first-class seat she looked out at Dan's little plane and waved goodbye and settled in for the flight. Reaching into her purse to grab a stick of gum, her hand found a small brown envelope with her name on it scrawled in Chris's writing.

She opened it to find a sheet of paper and a rolled-up piece of tissue. The note was brief.

"I'd rather be on the plane with you – but we know that's impossible, so please wear this necklace and think of me on your way home. Love Chris."

She loosened the tissue carefully, expecting something glamorous like the bracelet but instead a tattered, white hockey skate lace threaded with a few seashells fell into her hand. She had to cover her mouth with her hand to stop from laughing out loud. It was rudimentary, like a grade school art project, but she instantly loved it. It was from Chris and made for her and that was all that mattered. She strung it around her neck – tucking it under her shirt. Laughing to herself again she said, How *do I explain that my millionaire boyfriend made it and not a three-year-old!*

Waking up to the sound of the wind howling outside her bedroom window brought her back to reality swiftly. She woke up way too early for the time zone and decided to forgo a run in the snow for the chance to catch up in the office. When she got home at midnight, she came through the front door to avoid the office. But now it was pulling her through the house, past the coffee maker and into the basement. She stood at the bottom of the stairs holding her mug close to her chest in one hand with the other resting on the dark light switch. She feared the room would be emptied by creditors.

She flicked the switch and the glare of brilliant LED bulbs blasted through the room igniting any surface that would glow back.

Meagan sighed. Her shoulders dropped back into place. Everything was there. The desks, the drafting tables, copiers, computers, and the best sign of all – the recycle bin was overflowing. They've been busy!

She walked to Ginny's desk. You'd think she had quit for how tidy it was, but her military training was still in her blood. Over at Jennifer's desk, it was the usual uncontrolled swirl of paper. A new picture was on the wall of her and Brian. "A budding romance I'd say," she presumed out loud.

Meagan sipped her coffee and turned to look at Brian's desk and it was loaded with work. She could see new files in his in-basket. "This is weird," she said, as she turned back to walk into her office. "It's like jobs have poured in." She stopped at the door to look at her desk. It was piled neatly with files and mail. She walked around the desk and put her coffee on its coaster and sat down, still staring at the files.

"Mail or files. Mail or files," she said, out loud as she looked back and forth.

"Files."

She flipped through the headers. St. Francis church – bid. Maloney house – bid. Lindsay house – bid. Parker house – awarded. Zoo café – bid. Laggins renovation – awarded.

"What the heck! I should leave town more often!" she squealed, as she settled in to read the files.

The muffled rattle of keys at the door and the dull thud of someone putting their weight against it to break the frost that glued it to the frame broke Meagan from her study. She looked at the clock on the wall. 7:52 a.m.

"Holy cow," she said, as she looked from the clock to what she was wearing. It was too late to dash upstairs. Ginny was blowing in along with a gush of frozen air.

"Hey, Boss! A lovely welcome we have saved for you," she said loudly, as she removed her outerwear at the door.

Meagan got up from her desk and pulled her housecoat tight as she came out of her office.

"Ginny! Shut that door!"

Ginny gave it a mighty shove and it slammed into place sending a new wave of frosty air through the room and straight up Meagan's housecoat. As she shivered and danced, Ginny walked across the room laughing at the sight.

"Well, what do you expect? You left right when the work started piling in. Did you see your desk?" she asked, obviously proud of what had happened.

"It's phenomenal! What happened? No, wait. Don't tell me," she looked at the clock again, the others would arrive soon and it was bad enough that Ginny was looking at her in that beat-up old rag. "Let me get dressed. You guys can fill me in when I look presentable. I can't wait to hear."

Meagan ran up the stairs. Ginny followed, but only to the kitchen. Knowing her boss, she knew she hadn't eaten. The replenished stash of frozen muffins came to the rescue.

It only took Meagan 15 minutes to get dressed and head back downstairs. Halfway down she could smell the blend of fresh coffee and warm muffins rushing up to greet her. She stopped running down the stairs to listen to the laughter coming from the basement.

She came around the corner and everybody stopped talking and looked at her. Meagan stood there grinning. "This is great. This is all I needed," she said to them all.

The four of them pulled up chairs and Meagan kept smiling.

"Well," she asked in anticipation. "Who wants the talking stick first?"

Ginny couldn't contain herself and poked her arm into the air like a first grader. "I'll start. I'll start!"

She opened her tidy binder with section headers sticking out all down the side.

"First, welcome back."

Meagan nodded. She didn't dare speak. She wanted the suspense over with.

"We decided with you and Dianne gone, we had to prove that we could do the job quite fine, so Brian and Jennifer hit the pavement. They reopened a few files that had just been closed and requested the chance to resubmit. Also, being that spring is around the corner...well not today, but soon...more businesses want to get jobs awarded and started."

She flipped the binder to the first chapter and continued to talk and talk and talk. Brian and Jennifer added in when needed but Ginny handled the meeting like a seasoned pro.

When she closed the binder, Meagan sat smiling.

"This all happened in less than a week? Who are you and what have you done with my office manager?"

They all laughed.

It was Brian who spoke up. "We didn't realize how depressing or controlling Dianne was while she was here. We didn't realize how much she controlled the meetings or the direction of the conversation until we had a meeting after you left. Being that she was supposed to be the head contract bidder, we always sat back and let her lead. Who would have thought she was up to so much evil?"

"Yeah," added Jennifer. "It's been cool making the bids. I just hope we didn't bid too low."

That same thought had been pulsing through Meagan's brain the whole time they were talking, but she held back that thought. "I'm sure you did fine. I'll look them over and I'm sure Ginny didn't let them go out without eyeballing them. If you are all done, let's get back to work."

"No, there is one more thing," said Ginny, raising her hand again. "This is what we have planned. What are you going to do? Are you staying here?"

"Oh. Do you mean me and Chris or what?"

Ginny nodded. "Chris."

"Well, this is awkward — but no worse than talking to my mother I suppose," she took a deep breath. "I saw what is supposed to be Chris's house. The location is absolutely the most beautiful place on earth. But I have my doubts about Mike, the guy who is supposed to be handling the contract. The guesthouse we stayed in was fine. I don't think he had anything to do with it, but the big house is something Popeye slapped together. I was planning on going back in a month to help, but I don't know how I will fit it in with all this work you lined up.

"Besides, I think he is trying to run me off the site. I don't know why, but I think he is up to something other than building the house and my presence will ruin it," she added, lost in thought and staring at the table.

The three looked at Meagan and each other. Finally, Brian broke the silence.

"Um," he said, as he raised his hand to speak while looking at his boss carefully. "Who said we wanted your help? We can handle these for a while. It would be best if you gathered up your stuff and headed back to Eleuthera sooner than later. You can stop a bad building from continuing, see what this Mike guy is up to and then come back and help us when we need it. Two of these contracts don't start for six weeks."

Meagan looked at Brian, then Jennifer and then Ginny who was nodding with agreement.

"You've got a good point. Thanks, Brian," she said, still with a furrowed brow. "I'll see what Ben has lined up for me with Carl. If I can go back in a few weeks to sort it out, that might be better."

"Besides," said Ginny, as she got up to leave. "By then those damn tan lines will have faded and you'll need new ones."

Meagan laughed. "Can I tell you about how much fun it was?"

They groaned "NO!" and left the room.

Jennifer poked her head back in, "Okay, kidding. Tell us at lunch. I do what to hear about it!"

Talk about getting back into it! Meagan was swamped. The bids for the zoo café and the Lindsay house were awarded that morning and that brought her load up to five, including the house for Brent and luckily with that crazy wife of his, that would always be a going concern…until the wife got everything and dumped him that is. By noon she was on the phone with Ben.

"Where the hell have you been!" was the greeting he gave her.

"I was in The Bahamas. You know that!" she said in defence.

"I know," he said in a whining voice. "I just wish I got to go too. Was it fun? Are you married yet? Am I an uncle?" came the rapid-fire questions.

"Ack" she cried out! "No. NO, I mean yes, it was fun and no and no to the other two. I'm not married or prego – Good God! How about you?"

"I'm not pregnant either," he sighed jokingly. "I've been too damn busy with the mess you left behind."

"I left a mess?" Meagan asked concerned. "What did I do?"

"It's what you started!" he said. "We need to talk about your screwball professor. What's for supper? Hey, it's game night. You bring pizza and beer. Soda and I will warm up the TV."

The line went dead.

"I guess I'm bringing pizza," she said, to no one and feeling slightly deflated as she hung up the phone.

Doesn't anyone want to know how much fun I had?

A small feta spinach for her, and a "meat lover's meat overload" for Ben balanced on top of a case of beer as she headed up his front steps. It sickened her to buy it, but it was his favourite pizza.

She tapped the door with her toe which started Soda into her frenzy blasting down the hall. She couldn't help but laugh at the nose rubbing against the smoked glass as if trying to smell through it. She figured with that dog's sense of smell, Soda smelt her from the corner.

"Hey Megs, nice tan," said Ben, as he took the pizza and beer. Meagan bent down to pet Soda, but the retriever followed Ben like a starving hound. She followed Ben into the kitchen and looked at the clock.

"Can we talk business now or do I have to wait for intermission?"

"Eat first. I'm starved," he said, as he stuffed a hot slice in his mouth. The cheese was too hot and slid and slopped onto the counter. "Awe crap! I guess that will be your piece, big girl," he said, as he scraped the cheese on top of the kibble in Soda's dish.

Meagan handed him a knife and fork to use, but he frowned. "Oh come on! You really don't think I can eat pizza with a freakin' fork? That's just too civilized!"

Meagan shook her head and placed a dainty piece in her mouth and continued to enjoy her slice. Ben begrudgingly took the cutlery and sliced off a bite and started to eat – and talk.

"So, as soon as you left town, the media caught wind of the story and ran it on the front page of the city section. I've got it saved for you. When that hit the newsstands, shit hit the fan. Other girls that were used by the creep came forward from other companies, as did the architects."

He took a swig of beer and smiled while wiping his face. "Megs, I've got a class action suit out of this. All those guys have come to me to compile the charges. We can nail this guy on so many counts. There is no way his legal team can get him out of it. I am going to get so much business out of this! It's awesome!"

Meagan sat with a bewildered smile on her face. She couldn't believe the thrill he was getting from it all. Obviously, being a lawyer was the right occupation for her brother.

"This is so cool Ben," she finally said, while he attacked the cooling pizza. "I wish it wasn't because of me though. I wish I wasn't part of it all. I'd rather be standing on the outside looking in."

"Will it make you feel better that I will make so much money from the other plaintiffs that I won't have to bill your company?"

"Really? That's awesome, cause I really don't know how I can pay for your services," she said relieved.

"You wouldn't pay anyway silly! I'm suing that guy's ass off. We will have everything come out fine."

Meagan's eyes grew. "What? I get to sue him?"

"Shit yeah! And stupid Dianne. And Cottonwood can sue too. That's something else we need to talk about," he said, as he looked at the clock. "But that will wait until intermission. GAME ON!!!"

She laughed as she slid off the barstool following him into the den. "You are sooo Canadian! Game On."

CHAPTER TWENTY-SEVEN

Saturday morning, Meagan was running around the Glenmore Reservoir with her friends. It's a pleasant 16 kilometres of trails weaving through a residential area, past a local heritage museum and through a protected wildlife park, where everything from chickadees to moose are spotted regularly. The girls used the time to relax and talk about work, the stock market, the world and the latest in the local news. And, the local news that week was all about Meagan.

"Hey," said Gloria as they dipped into the trees, "I saw Ben on TV. He looked really good. He sounded so articulate. He's good at his job."

"Thanks, I'll tell him you saw him," Meagan said, without commenting on the case. She knew they would ask if they wanted.

They wanted.

"So?" said Emma, "What gives? Are you alright?"

Meagan sighed, "Yeah. Deep down I know I'll be okay. It's a little overwhelming but I'm surrounded by good people. Look at my team, they have jumped up and taken all the responsibilities on. And are doing a great job, I might add! Then there is Ben; like you said, he is all over this too. Then there are you guys. I can't tell you how important the runs are. You all know the venting is as important as the run."

Emma said, "Actually I read an article the other day that said guys don't know what they are missing. It said, woman chat to each other about emotional things without being judgmental. But when guys get together, they talk about hooks, bullets, carburetors and football. Nothing emotional about that.

"Oh sorry, Megs," she added. "Speaking of sports, how is your hockey player away from the ice? Can Chris talk about anything other than the game?"

Meagan didn't take Emma's comment as an insult. "Actually, you guys, he is really a deep guy. I am stunned. I was worried the trip would prove to me that we were not compatible."

There was a pause, but Gloria couldn't wait, "And...?"

Meagan took a sideways glance at Lizzie, who was looking back at her and smiled. Lizzie had been waiting to hear the news more than anyone.

"Oh yeah. I think we can get along just fine for a long time."

Lizzie gave her two thumbs up and smiled.

Gloria grabbed her left hand in search of a ring, saw it was empty. Along with Emma, she started tossing bullet fast questions.

"No ring?"

"No ring."

"Did he propose?"

"No."

What's wrong with him?"

"Nothing!" laughed Meagan.

"Are you moving to Boston?"

"No."

"Is he moving to Calgary?"

"Hell no!"

"Is he good in bed?"

Meagan sputtered and laughed, "Yeah. But he's better on the porch!"

They all gasped then laughed with her answer. They didn't expect that.

"Stop! Enough!" she finally said. "You are getting far too personal. Here it is in a nutshell."

Meagan slowed the pace down slightly. She told them about how pretty The Bahamas was. How nice the people were and how fantastic the water was. She went on about diving for lobster and the crazy water at Current Cut. Then she started in on the house and she lost her buoyant chatter and got serious about design flaws and inconsistencies.

"You guys, I'm telling ya, that house would never pass an inspection here. It will take one hurricane to blow it over. That Mike - does not know what he is doing - and it worries me."

"Did you tell Chris it's unstable?" asked Lizzie.

"I did and he knows it, but he won't do anything. He gets mad at Mike, but because Mike is his favourite coach's son, he feels he owes it to the coach to give him a chance."

"Why don't you go fix it?" said Emma.

"I do plan to go over in about a month and help out."

"But by then he might have the doors hung upside down and the windows in sideways," cautioned Emma.

"I'd go back now and fire the kid and get the job done right," said Gloria as they rounded the corner near the hospital. All talk stopped as they ran past the green gown-clad smokers who were dragging their IV poles to the path where they were banished to smoke.

"I was told that by one of my interns this week, but I don't think Chris would like that."

"How long has Mike been working on it?" asked Lizzie.

"Quite a while. And that's what also sticks in my head. How can it take sooo long? I wouldn't be surprised if he is up to something."

"What could he be up to other than gouging Chris?"

"Running drugs," said Meagan seriously.

"No! What makes you say that? That's a pretty strong accusation," said Gloria.

"I know it is, but he is very weird. He is determined to not have me come back. He tried to hide my roll of prints when I was leaving."

"So?" laughed Gloria, "That's not a drug runner!"

"No, I know. But he has the kitchen cupboards hung without the drywall in. He gave me a lame excuse that it keeps the snakes out. Then, down in the crawl space, there are more boxes of cabinets. How many houses is he suppling cabinets for? Also, I noticed there is a room at the back of the crawl space, but it is not in the blueprints. And, I find it odd that an oversized dock was put in first."

Nobody talked. They kept running and thinking through what Meagan was implying.

Finally, Gloria said it. "You have to go back now."

CHAPTER TWENTY-EIGHT

Three days later, Meagan was walking out of the airport at Governors Harbour. She decided too many people were telling her the same thing she was trying not to tell herself. She had to prove Mike was either a poor general contractor or running drugs or both. She thought long and hard about telling Chris what she wanted to do but since his schedule was so busy with the push on for the playoffs, she figured it would be best to show some initiative and go on her own.

As she stood at the curb considering her ground transportation options, the old guy who brought the food drove by, did a double take and stopped the car.

"Why if it isn't Miss Meagan, all by herself. Where is the boss?" he asked, as he spilled out of the car to walk over and shake her hand.

"Hello, Rolly. What a wonderful coincidence to see you here. I came by myself this time."

"Well, why didn't Chris call me to line up the groceries? There won't be anything to eat. Did you call Mike to comes for ya?"

Meagan smiled inside at the island way of speaking. "I didn't call Mike, I was going to get a cab to take me to the house. I didn't want to disturb him."

"Well hon, that won't do. I be takin you to the store and then to the house. We can't have you hungry." He smiled warmly, as he placed her suitcase in the backseat. "Come on, let's get you set up."

They drove to the store well below the speed limit. Cars and trucks pulled out to pass while Rolly chatted about the island and asked her questions.

"So how long you going to be here this time Miss Meagan? Are you going to help fix up your house?"

Meagan laughed at how he fondly calls her Miss Meagan, "Ah, it's not my house Rolly, but I do want to see it finished properly. I am slightly concerned that Mike may not be lining things up just right. I don't know if you know that I am an architect." She tried to say it without sounding snotty.

"I knew you were some-ting like that. I saw you looking at the house like you knew what you were doing. I could tell you was lookin' beyond paint and bathrooms. I'm glad you are here. That might get that lazy loaf moving faster."

Meagan quit looking out the window and looked at Rolly in amazement.

He smiled. "Mike ain't up to no good. We all know that here, but the boss don't know it."

"What do you mean he ain't up to any good? Are you a carpenter or an architect too?" she asked.

"No ma'am. I think him and his workers are soaking Mr. Chris for a lot more than what the work is worth. When me and the wife come over to check on the guesthouse there isn't any work going on. Nothing for days on end. But he be there. I think they are using the place for parties and what not. That's why the wife and I go so often. We want to make sure the parties don't go into the guesthouse."

They pulled into the grocery store parking lot and went into the cool store. Rolly didn't have air conditioning and used the warm wind to cool down the car. By the time Meagan entered the store, she was soaked with sweat.

Rolly grabbed a shopping cart and started putting all sorts of food in the basket.

"Don't worry, Miss Meagan, I know exactly what to be getting. I'll just put it on Chris' tab."

"But I don't need all that!" she protested.

"I seen how skinny you are. You gotta put some junk in that trunk."

Even though Meagan tried to put the snack food and the processed cheese products back, Rolly kept putting them back in the cart. Meagan gave in graciously.

Just because he buys them doesn't mean I have to eat them, she said to herself.

It had been less than two weeks since Chris and Meagan left the house and Meagan did have high hopes the house would have shown signs of development, but as Rolly's car pulled in she could see nothing much had happened. And even though it was only 3:30 in the afternoon, nobody was on the site.

"Wow, good thing you are here, Rolly, I assumed Mike would be here with a key to let me in the guesthouse, but I was wrong," she said, without trying to show how discouraged she was.

Rolly stopped the car in front of the guesthouse and they both took her bags and groceries into the house. As usual, the screen door screeched.

"At least you're glad to see me," she said to the door.

Rolly helped her put food away then they both looked for the keys to the Jeep. Finally, they went out to the carpark that was shaded from view to find the Jeep wasn't there either.

"I gotta go past Mike's house anyway, so I'll take a look and see if he is using it. We'll get it back where it belongs, so you got something to drive," said Rolly, as he headed for his car.

"Thanks, Rolly. I appreciate your help. I'm so glad I bumped into you at the airport. I don't know what I would have done. But you know what? I think I'd like it best if you didn't announce that I'm here. He will find out soon enough. And, in the meantime I can study the house without him hovering over my shoulder," Meagan said.

"Sure. Sounds fine. I'll call or come by tomorrow. My phone number is on the wall next to the phone if you need anything," he said, as he put the car in reverse. "You be okay by yourself?"

"Of course, Rolly. I live on my own in Calgary. I think this is far safer than that!"

"You put my number in your cell phone right way."

"I don't have a plan here so I'll just use the house phone. I'll be fine."

He smiled and nodded then pulled away.

"Shit I hope it's safer!" she said, through her smile as he drove away.

Meagan looked at her watch and at the sky. She had about an hour before the sun would set and figured it might be her only chance to snoop through the basement. She ran into the house and grabbed her work camera from her purse and ran across the yard. Oddly her heart was racing.

"Calm down silly," she said to herself. "You are not going to find anything illegal in here and then you will look really stupid."

Meagan walked through the front door and noticed a pop can was still on the porch from before. A few boards had moved, and a wall was semi-plastered. In the living room however, there were new cabinet boxes.

"What the hell?" she said quietly. "This house is not going to lack in storage space!"

She popped open a box top and sure enough, there was a brand-new oak cabinet. Not the same as the ones hanging in the kitchen, but a cabinet.

Something behind her came crashing to the floor. Meagan spun around muffling a scream. It was Mike. He was staring at her. His tool pouch lay in a heap at his feet.

"Oh Mike!" she said, "Where did you come from. You scared me!"

His lip curled like a protective dog, "More like where did you come from?"

He walked over closer to her and she took a step back from the boxes.

"I didn't have any work in Calgary, so I thought I'd hop on a plane and come back to help out. I hope you don't mind. I've got some great ideas that I think Chris will really like."

"Don't you think you should have called first?" he demanded.

"I am sorry. I don't have your number. And with Chris so busy – I didn't want to bug him. I thought we could surprise him by getting the house closer to being finished."

"My schedule says it is coming along as planned. You people that come over here and think everything has to rush. Nobody works fast in The Bahamas. It's all about savouring the experience."

He was staring at her, locking his eyes on hers, trying to overpower her. But Meagan wasn't about to retreat.

"Okay, I'll try to savour it with you. When you are done here, why don't you come to the guesthouse for supper? We can have a beer and discuss the ideas I thought would work." She was backing towards the door slowly waiting for his response. He kept staring at her like a creep. Then he suddenly changed.

"Food sounds good."

"Great. I'm happy. If we are going to work on this together, we might as well cooperate from the start," she stepped closer and put out her hand to offer a truce. He reluctantly took her hand in his and gave it one pump.

Meagan smiled. *That's a start,* she thought. *I won't get killed as long as I keep his belly full.*

"Oh," she said, turning back to ask a question. He was still staring at her but it was rather leering this time. She chose to ignore it. "Where's the Jeep?"

"I let Henry use it to take his wife to work. He'll bring it back in a few days."

He picked up his pouch and headed for the stairs.

"Few days?"

"Yeah, don't worry 'bout it. It ain't yours," he said, as he started to climb.

Meagan went back into the guesthouse and into the kitchen to start making some supper. As she reached for a beer, the house phone rang. She stood there staring at it for a few rings wondering if she should answer.

"Hello?" she said politely.

"Is this the lady of the house?"

Meagan smiled and sat down on the closest barstool while cradling the phone between her shoulder and her ear, she cracked open the beer. It was Chris.

"No," she replied. "There is no lady of the house."

"You must be the sexy redhead then?"

She giggled. "How do you know I'm a redhead?"

He laughed in a low voice, "Because only redheads sound this sexy."

They both laughed.

"So, what are you doing way down there? I just called your office and they said you ran off to The Bahamas. You went without me," he said, rather sadly.

"Oh, I'm sorry. I didn't mean to disappoint you. I came down to surprise you with a Valentines gift of helping out."

"Hey honey, I can't come down there now, we are in the hottest part of the season."

"I know! That is exactly why I came. I went home and my staff was doing such a great job without me, they sent me down here to see if I could speed up the process. I was hoping to have the house closer to completion when you win the playoffs," she paused, but didn't get any response that she was hoping for – like *Gee thanks! You're the best!*

"Chris?"

He was silent for a few more seconds. "I guess that is good. I was hoping if you were going anywhere, you'd come here. And I was hoping you'd come for playoffs. It's not every day you play for the Stanley Cup and to have you here would be special."

"Oh." That had never crossed her mind. "Oh Chris, I'm so sorry. I didn't think about that! Do you want me to come now? Or wait for April? I haven't started anything."

"No, it's okay. Not yet I mean. Actually, this is fine. You are closer to Boston this way. You could come next weekend."

She smiled, "Yeah, I'd love that. I might have tan lines for you to trace."

"You said you were there to work," he said sternly as if he were the boss.

"In all seriousness, I do plan to work. Chris, I'm not feeling very confident with Mike."

"Don't worry about him, he's doing fine," he assured her. "He'll probably pick up the pace with you there."

She had a swig of her beer and set it on the counter. "Chris, I'm not sure. In the time we haven't been here, only one pony wall has been plastered and I find it odd that there are more cabinets."

"Meagan," he said flatly.

She paused, "What?"

"He's fine."

"But I think he is up to no good," she blurted out. She wanted to tell him her fears of drug smuggling, but he stopped her again.

"Meagan, the guy is fine. He can do the job." He sounded terse this time, so she dropped it.

"Okay. Mike said he'd stop by for supper and we'd go over everything and I'll work like a redheaded busy bee and take pictures of the progress and come see you next weekend."

"That will be perfect. If we keep up this winning streak we should be solid going into playoffs. Hopefully you'll be sleeping with someone on the way to the cup or ....be sleeping with a loser."

"You won't lose!" she protested into the phone. "You can't!"

"Why not?"

"Because you can't afford my renos if you lose."

They both laughed and continued to talk small talk, but under it all Meagan was working it over in her head. She'd take photos alright, but it wouldn't be just half plastered walls. She was more determined to show Chris that as Rolly said, *"Mike ain't up to no good."*

When Meagan got off the phone, she put together a healthy salad and got the meat ready for the barbecue. All the time she kept looking out the window to see if Mike was coming. She waited. And waited. And waited.

The lights were still on at the house, but she hadn't seen any movement for a while. She looked at her watch. "7:40. There is no way he is still working."

Meagan grabbed two cold beers and headed to the house.

She purposely made noise as she walked up the steps so he'd know she was coming.

"Hey Mike?" Her voice echoed through the brightly lit house. No answer.

"Mike? You still working?" she yelled again, directing it upstairs.

No answer at all. She walked around the main floor, as she went up the stairs calling his name again, she bumped into the carpenter's belt he left halfway up the stairs.

"Well, poop. I've been stood up," she said as she reached the second floor. She walked to the veranda attached to the master bedroom.

It was a clear night and the stars were putting on their best dazzle. There was no moon to be found. Meagan stood for quite a while looking at the view of the bay of dark water and out to the ocean. Looking at it gave her a chill. Alone it wasn't inviting, especially when she thought of the full moon on their last night. She smiled at the memory of Chris and her on the porch.

She turned back into the house, flicking work lights off along the way, except for one. She kinda liked the idea of at least one light on. She decided not to push her luck of poking around and left to eat her salad by herself.

By 11 p.m., she was exhausted. Even though it was only 9 o'clock in Calgary, she had taken the red-eye the night before and was feeling the sleepless flight. She drifted off quickly, but her night was fitful. She was too hot and tossing the covers off and on, dreaming of pirates and boats slipping into her harbour, and soft voices that turned into the waves whispering as they slipped up the beach.

Meagan woke to the sun and its heat pouring through the shade-less window. Daring to look at the clock she saw it was 6:00 a.m. "Oh, man. It's only 4:00 a.m. my time."

She poured out of bed determined to be ready to greet the workers when they arrived.

Waiting for whoever might show, she walked down to the dock with a big mug of black coffee. The sound of her shoes seeped into her head bringing swirling bits of her dreams. Snippets of voices and thumping shoes didn't make sense.

As she stepped off the dock, she noticed marks in the sand just above the high tide. She was startled when she realized what it was. There were drag marks and multiple footprints. She followed the marks with her eyes to the house.

"Crap! I wasn't dreaming. There were visitors during the night."

She ran to the house under construction, lunging up the stairs two by two and went through the door.

Everything was the same. The boxes were exactly where they were the night before.

She looked around and seeing she was alone, took the chance to go down to the crawlspace. It was dark down there with only the light from the stairwell oozing down the short flight of stairs. At the bottom she could see a tiny seam of light seeping out from the top of the door to the storage room that she questioned that was absent in the blueprints.

Meagan swallowed hard. She flicked on a trouble lamp and slouched so she wouldn't crack her head open on a floor joist as she walked through the stored construction material. Her hair kept snagging on nails hammered through the floor far from the joist they were intended for.

She stopped in her tracks.

The deadbolt was hanging ajar!

Oh crap! Do I open it? There could be dead people in there! Or worse! Live people! she thought to herself. *It's now or never.*

She swallowed hard and slid the lock out of the loop and slowly opened the door.

The light burst out of the room like it wanted to escape. There were more cabinet boxes piled to the ceiling. She put down her mug to have both hands available and carefully pulled the lid on one box without a taped lid.

Big bags of white powder were stuffed into the box.

"I knew it! That bastard!" she whispered.

She tried pushing it to see how much it weighed, but it didn't shift. Peeling back the top bags she found out why the box was so sturdy. The cabinet frame was still in the box adding strength. She looked around the room and figured at least 20 boxes were in there.

She checked her watch. It was 6:45, the crews, if they actually worked, were supposed to be there before 7. Thankfully she had stuffed her little camera in her shorts that morning. She moved quickly taking only enough photos to prove her point. She folded the lid back the way it was and retraced her steps out of the basement.

As she hit the landing, she could hear a car coming down the driveway. Running to the other house was out of the question, they'd see her. She flew off the steps heading the other direction, running as hard as she could to be as far from the house as possible before they would see her.

Shit, for a marathoner, how come I'm so out of breath, she thought as she slowed to walk as if she was out for a morning stroll. It was as if nothing out of the ordinary was going on —except her heart pounding like a bass drum in her throat.

With her back to the house, she slipped the SD card out of the camera and put it deep in her pocket. She picked up some rocks and twigs and started throwing them into the trees as if she was clearing the beach. Instead of a rock, she threw her camera into the trees. *I don't need that in my pocket when I go back,* she told herself.

The workers congregated out front and Mike was in the middle of them all. One guy pointed at her and they all turned. She waved and Mike slowly waved back. Instead of hurrying, she started doing stretches and yoga – anything to give her a chance to think out her next move. Somehow, she had to get the pictures back to Chris. If she wasn't so cheap and bought a data plan for her phone it would have been easy.

No, not Chris, she thought to herself. *I'll send them to Ben. He will take me seriously. Chris will get mad at me for not trusting the shithead and say I made it up.*

She suddenly looked out to the ocean with a sinking heart. A wave of self-doubt washed over her like a tidal wave. *Maybe Chris is in on this? Maybe that's why he isn't thrilled with me coming here on my own. Naw, he's got his hockey career on the line. He wouldn't do that.*

She picked up more rocks and shells and threw them into the foaming tide. *I think he values his relationship with the old coach more than he values ours.*

With that thought, her stomach flopped. She stepped away from the tide zone, far enough to sit on dry sand and stared out at the waves. In her sulking, she didn't notice Mike walking towards her.

"Hey," he said in greeting. "Sorry I forgot to come over last night. I didn't think about it until just now."

She looked up at him and thought he was sincere. "Yeah, no big. I hadn't made anything special."

Meagan looked back at the ocean.

"Did you turn the lights off last night?" Mike asked sweetly as if trying to find out when she was over there.

She didn't look at him, she was welling up with tears, "Yeah. I went over at about 8 p.m. to find you and just left the one on. Is that okay? I thought one was a good idea."

"Did you go over this morning?"

She pulled her knees up under her chin and buried her face. Her hair cascaded, tenting her shoulders and head. A muffled "No." came as she started to cry.

Mike paused, "You okay?"

She wiped her eyes and stood up. She realized she was in grave danger and had to stay focused. Even though her relationship was tanking she had to get out of there alive.

"Yeah, I'll be fine. I had a bit of an argument with Chris last night and have come to the conclusion I shouldn't be here," she started waving her arms in exasperation. "He says you can do it on your own. You say you can do it on your own. I shouldn't barge in like this and think I should take over."

Her arms stopped flapping and fell to her sides. "I'm sorry."

Mike was taken by surprise and stared at her. "Okay, um, are you leaving then?"

She looked at the bay one more time, at the dock, and over at the houses. The workers were still standing around the truck.

"Yeah. I'll go back and see if I can get a flight today. If not, tomorrow."

As they started to walk towards the houses, the so-called foreman, Dave started walking towards them with his cell phone held next to his ear.

"You can't do it sooner?" he was saying into the phone.

They stopped walking as he ended the call.

"What's up?" asked Mike.

"The wind picked up at Glass Window."

"Aw shit," said Mike. "Are we hit?"

"Yeah mon, the whole south island went out."

Meagan was stumped. "What's out?"

Mike turned and looked at her. "This is why it takes so long to get a job done. The power goes out when the wind picks up at the bridge and knocks the lines down." He turned and looked at Dave. "For how long?"

"They say no more than eight hours."

"Yeah, same old story, they'll sit in the fucking truck until their shift is almost over and then put another fucking band-aid on the line and call it fixed."

"I'll send the boys home," said Dave, as he walked away.

Mike turned to Meagan, "You can still phone the airport. I'll take you there."

Meagan didn't say anything— she walked back to the house as if totally dejected. Mostly it was an act to get out of the jam she felt she was in, but still, she did feel like her life with Chris had ended.

She stepped up to the screen door and gently pulled it back and it moaned instead of screech.

"Wow, door," she said to the door. "You feel my pain."

She walked over to the phone and checked the numbers listed on the wall for the airlines. She only had to call one to find out no flights could leave until the power went back on.

With a banana in one hand, and a coffee in the other Meagan settled into what used to be her favourite chair on the porch.

This sucks, she thought to herself. *I've got evidence in my pocket, but no way to send it to Ben. I can't win.*

She sat for a while feeling sorry for herself, summing up all the bad stuff that had happened lately.

"Shit, if it isn't Carl ruining me, it's me ruining me! Why don't I just keep my great ideas to myself," she said to no one, as she walked up the stairs to gather her stuff. She looked around and shrugged her shoulders. "I barely unpacked."

She looked out the window at the construction and shook her head. It was quiet over there. Most of the trucks were gone, as were the workers. *I could have made that the best house on the island. This really REALLY sucks! They are all assholes,* she thought as her anger took over from self-pity. Out loud she said, "Screw Mike and screw Chris. I'll get the pictures off to Ben and let the chips fall where they may. Maybe I'll be back for the court case."

Meagan went to the computer workstation in the kitchen, turned on the computer using the battery supply and slipped the SD card into the port on the side. The pictures popped up and were pretty darn convincing, they proved the drugs were in the boxes, in the basement of Chris' house. She regretted throwing the camera, but knew it was a risk to keep it. Mike obviously was worried she was over there this morning. She flipped to the last picture and her blood turned to ice.

"Oh shit! Oh no! OH NO!!!"

Not only did the pictures show the drugs, in the corner of the last photo was her brown coffee mug. And it was still there!

And even worse, a truck came barreling down the driveway and stopped at the house.

CHAPTER TWENTY-NINE

"I am so dead!" she whispered as she quickly opened her email. The server was down, but she could get the email ready.

She pulled up Ben's address and typed "Is my red sweater in your car?" When they were teens, that was the code words they used in front of their parents for *"I need to talk to you right now!"*

She frantically started typing.

"Ben, I can't go into it. I'm in big trouble. REALLY Big. Check the photos. That's Chris's basement. He didn't believe me, but it's true. I think Mike knows I know!"

She dragged the photos into the text.

"A boat came last night and I think another will come. call for hel-"

She froze. There were voices, loud voices. Her heart started racing even faster. She stopped typing and pushed "SEND", pulled the SD card and tossed it into the drawer. An error message came up alerting her there was no service. It said;

"Do you want to resend when service is available?"

As she pushed the "Yes" button, the screen door shouted out a shrill alarm as it banged against the wall. Someone was running into the house!

Meagan jumped up from the computer as Mike charged into the room. Without warning he slapped her across the face, making her tumble backwards across the room.

"You bitch!" he screamed as he grabbed her arm, yanking her to her feet. She tried struggling but he had a strong grip.

"Mike! You are hurting me. Stop that!" she tried to pry his grip, but he shoved her again and she fell against the counter.

"What the fuck were you thinking?! You are so fucking dead now! And so am I! I tried to get you to keep your nose out of it all. But you just don't get it," he reached out to hit her again, but she blocked the hit and pushed him away.

Meagan ran for the door, but it was announcing another arrival. She stopped in her tracks and a huge man dressed in a loud floral shirt grabbed her by the hair as she tried to spin for a different door.

She screamed out in pain as he twisted his fist into her curls. All movement in the room stopped. The door was a silent witness.

"Well Mike, what have we here?" said the intruder, as he held her head close to his.

"She was snooping Al. I found her mug in the room."

"Snooping were ya? Did you take any for yourself?"

Meagan was so scared and could barely speak. "I, I didn't mean to snoop. I'm an architect. I was checking to see if the foundation was correct. I didn't mean to see anything. I promise not to tell. Honest."

The big man laughed and calmly ran his figure tips up her arm making both her and Mike cringe. "You won't be telling nobody nuthin."

He sniffed her hair then pushed her back at Mike. "Take her to the basement. When the boat comes tonight – she goes with it."

Mike didn't say anything he twisted her arm behind her back and pushed her through the door. The groan of the hinge masked the sound of the radio coming back on, the fridge generator kicking in and, the ping of the computer sending her message.

As they stumbled across the yard, Meagan tried desperately to reason with Mike.

"Please Mike, don't do this. Please, you can still get out of it. You can save me and that will get you an easier sentence," she was using everything she could think of, but it was no use.

Mike kept his jaw clamped shut only opening it to say, "Shut up bitch," every few feet.

He dragged her down the steps into the basement and pushed her into the room full of cocaine and shut the door. Meagan heard the deadbolt click. Through the wall she could hear Mike. "You are so fucking stupid!" His fist slammed into the door and Meagan screamed into her hands as she covered her face in despair.

She pulled her hands away, *Wait!* she thought to herself. *The light is on. Power is back. Oh God, I hope Ben got that email. I am so cooked.*

She looked at her watch, it was 3 o'clock in The Bahamas, so it was just after lunch in Calgary. Ben would be getting back to the office. He knows to pick up her emails when the secret code is on it. That is — if he comes back from lunch and isn't in court for the afternoon.

Meagan sank to the floor and hugged her knees that were again pulled up to her chest. She rubbed her face and the back of her head where "Big Al" pulled on her hair.

It was shortly after 6 p.m. when voices crept through the door jamb. Men were coming down the stairs into the basement. Meagan stood up. "Please be cops! Please be cops!" she whispered silently.

The door opened and five nasty looking men all carrying an assortment of guns were staring at her.

"Yeah," said one slowly as he leered at her. "Yeah, this will be a sweet ride."

"Just get her out of the way, dick-face," said a smaller man. "You can do her later. Right now, we got to work."

A third guy motioned with his gun for her to move out of the way so they could lift the boxes.

Meagan thought about dashing for the stairs, but the one guy kept his eyes glaring on her and his finger on the trigger. More voices boomed outside, but she couldn't make out the details. A large engine rumbled in neutral at the dock.

It wasn't long before Mike came down the stairs and looked at her sadly, shaking his head. "Man, oh man, this isn't the way it was s'posed to go. I'm really sorry, Meagan. Really sorry."

Meagan's mind was racing, "What are they going to do with me? Come on Mike!"

Mike pulled some tie-wraps from his pocket and wrapped one around her wrists behind her back. Then he told the gunman to take her to the dock and when they were on the boat, to do the same to her ankles. Meagan glared at him with loathing in her eyes. If it was the last time he saw her, it would be a haunting memory. Half of the boxes were still in the room, but Mike locked it up and followed them up the stairs.

The sun was already setting as they walked onto the dock towards a nice 50-foot-long Sealine yacht. The boat was designed to cruise with people, not awkward boxes and that's why Meagan assumed some of the boxes were left behind. She was hoping Ben had already alerted the authorities, so they'd be caught red-handed but as she scanned the peaceful bay, no one looked like they were there to help her.

Most of the guys were already on the boat as Meagan stepped onto the back deck. Her escort sat her on the back bench and tied her ankles as instructed. He smiled up at her as he did it. Meagan wasn't sure what was behind the smile, but didn't want to ask.

Al and Mike talked as they slowly walked towards the boat. When they got there, Al turned to her and said, "Ever swam with the sharks, Red?"

They all laughed, except Mike. He turned and walked away with his phone to his ear, hopped into a car with a few other guys and drove off.

The yacht slowly moved away from the bay. Meagan looked back at all the lights left on in both houses. She laughed to herself about the wasted energy. *Like they care.*

As soon as they were beyond the reef, the guy at the helm put the throttle down and it started to plow effortlessly through the waves. After about 20-minutes, the boat stopped, and they drifted. And drifted.

Meagan counted heads – one driving, one standing beside him, two underneath in the hold pouring rum and sampling the cocaine. The two at the helm kept watching the dark horizon as if waiting for something. Once in awhile, they'd start the engine and relocate the boat, then they'd drift. They never explained themselves to Meagan, but she figured they were waiting for another boat to arrive. So was she, but most likely not the same boat.

Hours drifted by.

The two from down below kept coming back up with rum for the other two. Meagan couldn't hear anything, but every time the guy who was eyeing her earlier looked at her, his gaze got more focused. He was pounding down the rum like a bad movie pirate and staring at her.

Suddenly the guy driving picks up a cell phone and has a quick chat with someone. He tosses the phone down and thrusts the boat back into the waves. They were obviously on the way to meet someone.

The wind was whipping through Meagan's hair tossing it all over her face. The leering man came over and gently moved it off her face, holding it in his hand for a long time.

"That is the most beautiful red hair I have ever seen. Many a man would want to have you for his own." He leaned down, and his wretched rum-soaked breath poured over her face. "And I will have you!" His tongue dragged up her check. Then he stood up laughing and walked over to the group and they all laughed at something.

Oh shit, I'm going to be sick! was all Meagan could think. She scanned the horizon which was now completely dark. *Where is a moon when you want one? I'm dammed either way. I can get raped then tossed to the sharks or... toss myself to the sharks.*

Just as she decided her fate, her pirate came back. He knelt in front of her. He reached for her breasts and slowly started caressing them as he giggled sadistically. Meagan tried to squirm away, but it was impossible. There was nowhere to go.

He continued to laugh and as he tried to work her shorts down, he realized he needed to cut off the twist tie at her feet. He stood up and went to the men, they stopped talking and looked at her and laughed. One guy handed him a blade that shone from the dashboard lights. Meagan thought she was going to die.

He came back and bent over her to cut the ties. As soon as her feet were free, Meagan recoiled her legs and pushed him as hard as she could. He was caught off balance and teetered toward the other side of the boat. Meagan jumped to her feet, lunged at him and ducked.

She caught him in the gut with her best impression of a football tackle. The boat bounced on a wave at the same time and both of them fell off the stern. His head hit the little deck at the back, but she did her best to dive away aiming as far as she could away from the boat.

She held her breath as long as possible and kicked as hard as she could to get away from the captor.

Meagan tried not to gasp as she surfaced, but her lungs were aching. She spun around and around as she caught her breath. The boat kept moving away!

She could hear the guy in the water yelling for help and for them to stop, but they couldn't hear. Besides, they probably thought he took her into the stateroom to finish his business.

It was awkward with her hands behind her back, but Meagan did her best to swim as far from him as possible. She could hear him frantically call for her now, knowing the boat wouldn't come back.

"Red! I'm sorry. Help me! I can't swim. Red!" He was crying and under any other situation, she might help him, but it was every woman for herself now.

Finding lights on the horizon, she laid on her back in the rolling waves and started to kick. "Please Ben, read your email," she said in desperation. "I really need you."

CHAPTER THIRTY

It was about 5 o'clock when Ben got back from a day in court. He tossed his coat on a spare leather chair and sank into the chair behind his desk. He looked down his list of emails. He sighed when he saw the endless list scroll under the mouse. He was about to close the computer when he saw the red sweater subject line from his sister.

"What?" he said as he dragged the mouse down to click it open.

His eyes bugged out as he gasped for air. "Holy shit, Meagan! You got enough troubles here!"

He called her cell, but it went straight to voicemail. Then he pulled out the list of contact numbers Meagan had left him and called the guesthouse in The Bahamas and of course got no answer as the boat had left an hour ago and drug lords don't usually answer someone else's phones.

He called Chris's cell. "What night is this??? Crap! Chris has a game."

He called Detective Whitmore who was surprised to hear Meagan had new troubles. Ben forwarded Meagan's email to Whitmore and turned on the TV in his office to find the game. Chris was on the ice.

He muted the tv and went online to find out the phone number for the Boston arena head office. It took a ton of persuasion, but he finally got someone to understand this was a life and death situation and that he needed to talk to Chris right now. "Tell Chris it is Ben – and it is extremely serious. Lives are at stake!"

The office assistant ran through the concourse and pushed through the 'Players and Management Only' door. She ran down to ice level and got the attention of the assistant trainer who took the phone to the head trainer who handed it off to the assistant coach. Every time it was handed off the message grew from life and death to plain old death. The assistant coach handed it to Chris and said, "There is a guy called Ben — it's important." The look on the coach's face startled Chris. It was hard to hear over the cheering crowd.

"Ben?"

"Chris! It's not good, you gotta go now!"

"I'm in a fucking game Ben, what the hell are you saying?"

"The drug smugglers have my sister."

"What! Hold on!"

As Ben watched on TV, Chris jumped up and pushed his way off the bench and towards the hall into the locker room. The team manager tried to stop him, but the assistant waved him off and leaned into his ear to explain the urgency.

Chris ripped his helmet off and it crashed to the floor. With the phone back up at his ear he talked to Ben.

"Wait! Start this again. What are you saying? What smugglers?"

"I got an email, my machine received it at 1 p.m., I didn't get out of court until 5. It says she found the drugs in your basement. She said, Mike knows she knows. She sent some pretty incriminating photos. She says you didn't believe her! Chris! My sister is missing because of this!" Ben was shouting into the phone now. "What can you provide the police about the people working on your house?"

Chris' head was spinning. He wasn't listening. All he could think was he might have got the love of his life killed. "How can this be possible? Ben, I'm so sorry."

He stopped in his tracks. "Ben?"

There was silence on the other end of the phone.

"Ben," he said again. "You know I had nothing to do with this. I love your sister. We were planning to get married."

"Were, Chris? You ARE planning to marry her. She better not be dead. And you better not have any knowledge of this operation or you'll head to jail and not marry her come hell or high water!"

Chris continued walking down the hall into the locker room. The office assistant followed him at a distance carrying his helmet and gear that he kept dropping.

Ben and Chris came up with a plan while Chris peeled his uniform off keeping one hand on the phone. He eventually handed off the office phone to the assistant and grabbed his cell to call Scott. She sheepishly asked if there was anything the team could do to help. He smiled and gently pushed her out of the locker room. "Wait here please."

When Scott finally answered the phone, Chris told him to pull the car up to the loading dock. He figured the media already noticed he left the bench and will be hounding him at the door.

"I'll get the guys to let me pull in. That always works," said Scott as he dashed up the aisle.

Then Chris phoned Dan in The Bahamas.

"Hey Goon," Dan said as he picked up the phone. "Why aren't you on the ice?"

"I got big problems Dan and I need your help. Do you know anyone up here that can fly me to Governors Harbour right now?"

"I know guys that can fly you to Nassau, but nobody can go to the out islands in the dark. The runways shut down and everyone goes home. What's up?"

Chris took a deep breath, "Dan, Mike has been running drugs out of the house. Meagan tried to warn me…but I didn't believe her. Now she is missing."

"Holy shit, man. You start heading for the airport. By the time you get there, I'll have someone ready to fly you to Nassau. I'll be here waiting. As soon as there is a speck of daylight, we will fly to Eleuthera. Okay?"

"Yeah, it's the best we can do," he said, slowly under a wave of emotion.

"Chris, we will find her. She is a tough chick. And she'll beat the living shit out of you when we find her, but – man, you deserve it."

"Thanks. I know. And it will most likely be the last time I see her too."

"Don't worry. Get going. I'll call you as soon as I get a plane."

Chris grabbed his duffle and shaving kit from his locker and headed for the door, but two large men in dark suits were coming through with the assistant on their tails.

"I'm sorry Chris, they wouldn't stop," she said in a panic.

Holding up badges they introduced themselves as detectives from the DEA. Apparently, Detective Whitmore made some calls.

Chris looked at the badges and then over at her. "Thanks, Cheryl. These guys are here to help me."

Her eyes darted from Chris to the detectives. She started to open her mouth, but Chris stopped her by holding his hand up. "Cheryl, a friend of mine is in trouble. Please don't say anything to anybody about these guys. Tell the press I hurt myself in practice and can't play. Then go to the loading dock and tell Scott the change in plans."

Chris looked at his watch, "A plane will be ready in 30 minutes at the airport – can I fill you guys in as we fly?"

Meagan couldn't see her watch, but she felt like she had been bobbing in the waves for hours. Every time she looked towards the shore it seemed no closer.

"What way is the tide going? Come on! Give me a break!" she cried out loud in a panic. She stayed vertical for a while, whip kicking the eggbeater like she learned in water polo. *Who would have thought I'd need this skill again?*

Suddenly her foot bumped something soft. She went stiff. Nothing came to bite, so she put her toe down again. It was sand. A shoal.

Meagan put both feet down and relaxed a bit. The water was chest height. She sighed. *I am so tired. This is not the answer, but it sure helps.*

Her arms were tired and numb from being tied behind her back. Her wrists were rubbed raw from the plastic. She tried to pull her butt through her arms like Houdini, but even with how skinny her butt was, there was no way she could do it without dislocating her shoulder or drowning. She decided to rest as best she could and think about what to do next.

Her mind was racing. *What if Ben didn't get my email? That means I really am alone. Crap! What if he doesn't get the email at all? That means nobody has any proof those guys were smuggling the drugs. Not only do I have to get to shore, I have to get back to the guesthouse and get that card. If Chris finds it, it will be a year from now and he probably won't look at the images. He probably doesn't even have a camera. And if he's in on it, he won't be turning in the evidence on himself.*

Stopping on the underwater sandbar gave her body a rest, but it also let the chill of the water in. She started to shiver. She tried pacing on the sand hoping she could stay there while the tide receded, but the waves would knock her over. And, if the water is receding, that means she would be fighting the current to get to shore.

"Aw shit. This sucks," she said aloud. "I'm cold. Someone frickin' find me! God. Damn. It!"

She looked at the shore and walked as far as possible on the sand towards it then leaned back into the waves. She was determined more than ever to make it to land, to find the photo card and to get on with the rest of her life. As she laid back into the waves, she angrily shouted at the silly sliver of a moon that finally showed up.

"I am going to get to shore. I am getting the photos, I am leaving Chris. I am leaving Mike. And, I'm leaving goddamn Carl in my past!" She chanted over and over with every kick. Then it changed to, "This. Is. Why. I. Run. Hills. Every. Week. This. Is. Why. Fucking. HILLS. ARE. MY. FRIENDS!"

She stopped shouting and kicking for a while and went back into the whip kick, so she could wiggle her numb fingers. In the distance, she could hear the breaking of waves. She strained to see, but it was too dark and she kept tipping and bobbing with every wave. To her delight, little lights on the beach were getting bigger.

"I must be riding in with the tide! This is good! This is good!"

She resumed floating on her back towards shore. She knew there was a big chance she would be smashed on the exposed limestone that walled much of the island but hoped there was a chance for a nice soft landing on the pink sand.

"Is landing on a beach asking too much?" she shouted at the moon.

The noise of the waves got louder and louder. She kept going towards them until suddenly she was lifted and thrust towards the shore on a gentle surf wave. As the wave died out, she flipped over to see where she was going and smiled.

"Beach! Thank you, Mr. Moon."

Meagan kept reaching with her toes to find the sand and eventually it rose up to greet her. She stumbled in the shore waves that would catch her feet each time they receded and fell numerous times, but finally thumped in a heap on the hard sand above the water line.

Panting, and smiling up at the moon and the stars she laid there for a few minutes. *Hallelujah! The swim part is over.*

CHAPTER THIRTY-ONE

Rolling over onto her knees and shoulders, she righted herself to stand up. She scanned the shore. *I either need a knife to fall from the sky or a sharp piece of limestone.*

She looked around and realized she knew where she was. Looking left and right, she remembered. *This is the beach we drew out ideas on! I'm not far from the house. But that's impossible. Oh, I get it. Not only was I floating, I was drifting too. The waves actually helped me go back towards the house.*

Meagan walked to her right where she knew there was some exposed rock. She turned back to a prickly outcrop and rubbed the tie wrap against the rock. If she could see what she was doing, she probably would have stopped. The rock was ripping at the wrap, but also at her skin. Her arms were so numb she couldn't feel the pain or the blood.

Suddenly her hands broke free and her shoulders slumped forward. The shock that rushed through her body was excruciating. She fell to the sand and moaned as the feeling came back. Like the tingling of a foot that fell asleep, both arms tingled and surged with knife-like stabs. She looked at her wrists, even under the pale moonlight, she could see the mess.

"Ouch! Now I look like I've tried to kill myself!" She squeezed her wrists to stop the bleeding and looked at her bloody watch. It was 2:31 a.m.

"I know the road runs parallel with the beach. I can run along it until I see that path we took for a short cut back to the guesthouse," she paused. "Christ, now I'm really nuts. Why am I talking out loud?"

She went back into the water to rinse the sand off and writhed in pain from the salt flushing through the raw mess that used to be her wrists. It was too much pain, knocking her back onto her knees. She crawled out of the water and stumbled for the back of the beach. Her legs were still wobbly from the water.

The sea grapes were prickly and impossible to break fresh trail in. She paced the rim of the trees looking for a trail that every bay had. Eventually, she found it and headed inland. Her hair and T-shirt would snag on bushes and the thorns scratched her legs and arms, but she was beyond feeling pain. Endorphins were pushing her now.

At the road, she turned left and started to run. Her shoes were full of water and she was weak from fighting the waves for so long. A slow slog was all she could muster.

She heard an engine coming towards her, so she jumped back into the trees to avoid being seen. *You could be someone handing out a million dollars, but I'm betting not.*

When the car was long gone, she came out of the trees and resumed her journey.

It took almost an hour of trotting and walking before she found the path Chris and taken her on. She turned and started to run with earnest desire to not stop until she reached the house a mere 300 metres away.

With a final 100 metre sprint left, a man dressed entirely in black jumped out of nowhere, grabbed her and fell with her to the ground.

His hand clamped firmly on her mouth to block a scream. She tried to fight but was weak and gave up. *Shit. I quit,* is all she could think as she stared at the man whose face was covered in black paint. He sat on top of her and pinned her arms with his legs sending bullets of pain through her body. She screamed in pain, but it was muffled under his gloved hand. With his other hand he put his finger to his mouth signalling her to hush. She relaxed, but tears were streaming from her eyes. The pain was searing. She screamed in her head, *Get off me! Get off me!*

He reached in a pocket and pulled out a badge. The ID quickly flickered in the light. She didn't know what law enforcement he was – but he was on her side. She nodded and he got off.

Meagan was trying not to cry out loud. She showed him her wrists where the shiny blood flowed from the open wounds. She could see the pain in his eyes.

He reached for her and hugged her. Then with a calm controlled whisper, he spoke into her ear. "I am Agent Cooper DEA, I am so sorry for hurting you. I'm glad to see you alive. Stay here. We are about to move in on the scene. You are safe with me. Okay?" He stayed pressed against her. She nodded but didn't let go. Her body needed his warmth. It felt good. He could feel her shaking and kept holding her until she could hear a voice in his earpiece.

He pulled away only far enough to push a button and talk. A thin mic was wrapped around his ear to his jawbone.

Agent Cooper whispered, "The beagle is secure."

A voice said something. And he replied, "Affirmative."

She could hear him and thought, *I'm a fucking beagle?*

He smiled at Meagan. Under all the black paint she could see he was not only handsome but sincere. She smiled back thinking, *Well, Maybe I haven't sworn off men entirely.* She shook her head. *What am I thinking!!*

He offered her a compact bottle of water and she eagerly drank it all.

He moved back against her ear. "Don't move until I do. Follow me as quietly as you can or roll in a ball and stay put. We don't move until we see action. I am here to stop escapees from running up the path," she nodded against his ear and he continued, "This may get ugly."

She nodded again.

He moved into a crouch and resumed his stakeout position. It wasn't long before the sound of a motorboat slipped into the bay. She recognized the sound as the boat she fell from. She wanted to tell Cooper but kept her mouth shut. He probably knew more than she did.

Both houses were still lit up like Christmas casting a glow for about 10 metres and then the darkness of the night took over. If there were any other agents out there, Meagan didn't see or hear any of them.

The boat docked and men came from the house carrying or dragging the boxes. Al was there shouting for them to hurry.

Mike came out of the house asking questions. She heard her name but couldn't make anything else out. From their vantage point, the guesthouse blocked some of the view.

Suddenly hell broke loose and happened far too fast for her exhausted head to process.

Floodlights from every angle lit up the scene. The guys on the dock dropped the boxes and reached for their guns. Bullets sprayed from every direction.

A man came running up the path and Cooper stood up and cold-cocked him. The man hit the soil like a sack of sand and laid motionless. Cooper quickly tied his hands and feet. Meagan looked at their runner and realized it was the short guy from earlier that day.

Agent Cooper grabbed Meagan's hand and pulled her back behind him. More shots were fired, windows in the big house were shattered and bullets lodged into the walls. A man on the dock screamed as he fell into the water. Others tried to get into the boat for an escape. A huge coast guard boat beaming enormous floodlights came into the bay, blocking all access. From the lane, big black SUVs spit gravel as they filled the yard. More agents dressed in black and carrying rifles poured from the SUVs, shooting as they bolted to hide behind piles of wood, cinderblocks, and the useless asphalt shingles.

The smugglers were outnumbered.

"This is the US Coast Guard," boomed a voice from the boat. "Drop your weapons and put your hands behind your head."

More bullets were fired, Big Al fell to the ground.

Meagan was in shock. *This isn't happening for real is it?* is all she kept thinking. She stayed hidden behind Cooper waiting for the noise to stop. Eventually, she rolled into the tight ball as he suggested. It was too much for one day.

After a few minutes of people running around yelling things, the voice on the boat said, "Site secured."

Agent Cooper turned around and bent down to Meagan. His black hat had been removed to show a head covered in spikey blond hair. "Meagan, are you okay?" he asked gently.

She looked up at him. "Has it stopped?"

"Yes, we won," he said reassuringly.

He gently put his hands under her armpits and helped her to stand. He didn't want to hurt her arms again.

"How did you know it was me when you pulled me to the ground back there?" she asked, between sobs that overtook her body.

He was pulling his coat off as she asked and put it around her shoulders. As he lifted her hair he said, "How many redheaded women do you think are running around in the dark down here?"

He reached into the side pocket of his utility pants and pulled out a roll of gauze. "I would have done this sooner, but the white is like a beacon."

He wrapped her wrists as men ran past to pick up the guy Cooper had left on the path. "Now, let's introduce you to the Commander."

He put his arm around her and helped her through the weeds and down into the light. She didn't think she needed the help, but it felt good. And she knew he'd get bragging rights this way.

People were everywhere, all over the lawns, on the dock, in the guesthouse and the main house. Some were covering the dead smugglers while others took pictures of the scene. As Agent Cooper and Meagan approached a group of men they stopped talking.

Agent Cooper introduced Meagan to the Commander.

"It's a pleasure to meet you, Ms. Dunphy. Where have you been? You look like you were dragged behind a train."

"I have to say it's been a long day," she said, with a weary smile. "Would it be okay if I went inside, got changed and grabbed something to eat? Then I can explain everything."

The man in charge smiled and said, "That's just fine. Cooper?" he said, turning to the agent. "Stay with her and start getting details."

"Yes, sir."

They walked over to the guesthouse and as they walked up the steps, Meagan noticed the screen door was ripped from the hinges. Its job was done. It didn't have to announce any more arrivals.

Cooper led the way up the stairs and checked every nook and cranny of the room while Meagan looked at herself in the bedroom mirror. The Commander was right. Her hair was a rat's nest of sand, salt, twigs and leaves. Her face was bruised from where Mike had hit her, and her complexion was blotchy from exhaustion. She went into the bathroom and tried to lift her shirt over her head but couldn't get her arms up. "Oh no," she whispered. "This is awkward."

"Agent Cooper? Are you still there?" she said softly.

"Yes, is something wrong?"

She could hear him come closer to the door. She pulled it open. "This is really not right, but I'm beyond modest at this point. Can you help me out of my clothes and into the shower? My arms are so stiff, they won't go any higher," she said, as she raised them less than chest height.

"Um, I um, just a second," he pushed the button on his mic, explained the situation and requested a female agent. "Oh. That's no good. Well, um, send Derby up. He will witness that I followed her requests with tact and discretion."

Agent Cooper started the shower. When Agent Derby got there, they created a screen with towels. Cooper reached around and took off her clothes. A towel was wrapped around her body, so he could reach into the shower to wash her hair. Sand and seaweed fell to the shower floor. When her hair was clean enough, the men left the bathroom so she could rinse off. It was the craziest setup, but the most refreshing shower of her life. Her wrists stung, but it felt good to wash away the last 12 hours.

Refreshed and in comfortable dry clothes that were easy to slip on, she came down to the kitchen where Cooper and Derby had laid out food.

"Wow, you guys are great! You save lives, you are spa attendants and can cook! Are you married?"

Both guys laughed. Agent Cooper came over and took more gauze out of his pocket and applied some antiseptic lotion before rewrapping her wrists. This time she noticed he had a ring on. It didn't matter – she was still sworn off men.

Meagan went over to the drawer and pulled out the SD card and handed it to Cooper. She saw her computer was exactly where she left it.

"I don't know if you need this, but here are the pictures from the basement. Did my email get through to Ben?"

"Yes, it did and that was great thinking. It was because of Ben that the DEA and the Coast Guard were put into action so fast," said Cooper.

Suddenly Meagan thought about Ben back in Calgary, "Did anyone tell Ben I'm alive?"

Cooper nodded. "Remember when I whispered into my mic? He was notified instantly. He'll be waiting to hear from you."

"Did anyone tell Chris I'm alive?"

"Yes, and if you are interested, he is clear of all of this. The poor guy was interrogated the whole evening and is clear of all wrongdoing. The smuggling was all Mike's idea," said Cooper.

The three of them sat down at the table and as she talked and ate; they ate and took notes.

When she got to the part about falling off the back of the boat, Derby stopped her mid-sentence. "Wait. Someone fell off the boat with you?"

She looked sadly at both men. "Yeah."

"Oh," Derby said. He got up from the table while he talked into his mic and left the room to report the man lost at sea. A few minutes later he came back with the Commander and a few other men, who sat down at the table and joined in the discussion and the meal. What was going to be a week's worth of food was polished off, including the chips and junk food Rolly tossed in the cart.

As it does every day in the Caribbean, the sun popped up over the eastern horizon far too soon. The Commander looked at sunlight kissing the tops of the palm trees and saw it as a signal to leave. As he rose, all the men followed his actions.

"Ms. Dunphy, I don't know if anyone has told you this yet, but your efforts brought down the biggest smuggler in the Caribbean. Al Taylor has been sneaking cocaine into Florida for years and because of you, he has been eliminated. Thank you."

Meagan was dumbfounded. "What about Mike?"

The commander shook his head from side to side. "He is in pretty deep water right now."

"Wow," said Meagan, "landing the guy in jail is not exactly how Chris had intended on paying back his coach."

"Ms. Dunphy," said the Commander, "You are free to return to Calgary today if you feel inclined. When we need more information – we will be in touch."

"Thank you," she said. "I think I'll do that."

As each man walked past her, they hugged her gently trying not to touch her swollen arms. Each complimented her on her amazing efforts in the water. When Agent Cooper came up, she stopped him by struggling to put her hands on his chest.

"Agent Cooper, thank you for saving my life."

He seemed surprised. "Saving your life? I bout broke your arms. How could I have saved your life?"

"If you hadn't tackled me and shut me up, I would have barged in on the smugglers AGAIN – and this time, I'm sure they would have finished me off between the eyes." She reached up as best she could and touched his cheek with one hand and kissed the other.

He hugged her and looking at Derby said, "If only everyone we help was so appreciative!"

The men filed out and suddenly Meagan was alone.

She walked down the steps and watched as her agent's utility vehicle left the yard. There were still people there working quietly behind yellow tape on the crime scenes like they do in the movies. The whole place was a mess, but she didn't care anymore. She walked over to what was going to be a beautiful house and up onto the veranda. It was in ruins. Beyond the yellow tape across the door, she could see all the boxes were gone and the place was riddled with bullet holes and broken glass.

She turned and walked down the steps and back to the guesthouse without looking back.

She called the cab company to have someone pick her up. She was done with the house. Done with Chris. And done with The Bahamas.

CHAPTER THIRTY-TWO

Meagan dragged her duffle down to the porch and went back in to make a pot of coffee. The dispatch said his driver would be 40 minutes and she didn't want to sleep until she was on a plane. Her arms were killing her, but she did the best she could to clean up the dishes and turned on the dishwasher. She would call Rolly from the airport to let him know there was still a little food in the fridge and to apologize for the horrific mess.

As the dishwasher changed cycles, she heard a car pull into the yard. She looked at her watch that was scratched from rubbing on the limestone, "Holy cow! He said 40 minutes – that was like 10!"

Meagan turned off the coffee maker and dumped what had brewed down the drain. As she rinsed out the pot, her back was to the door.

"No coffee on the deck today?"

It was Chris and behind him, Dan. Neither man looked like they'd slept.

She stared at Chris. Emotions swirled through her body.

It was Dan who talked first. "Hey, Meagan. You okay?"

Tears were welling in her eyes. "Ah, yeah Dan, thanks. It's been a long race, but I finished."

He didn't move from behind Chris. He could feel the wall of tension around her and knew to leave. He smiled, waved, and walked away.

Chris didn't move. He stood there staring at her with so much sadness in his eyes, but Meagan was not going to fall for it. She swore in the ocean she was done.

She took a deep breath. "I have a car coming in 20 minutes to take me to the airport."

He swallowed hard, nodded and softly said, "Okay." His eyes were misting over. "Are you really okay?"

She stared at him in disbelief.

"No. Of course not!" she cried out. "What do you think? While you were chasing a fucking puck, I was beaten, nearly raped, tossed into a pitch-black ocean, listened to a man drown, floated like a tied up piece of driftwood for EVER! Was dumped on a frickin' beach by crazy waves, ripped my arms open on limestone – tell me that's going to heal pretty!" she said, as she held up her wrists to show the blood-soaked gauze.

Tears streamed down her face as she continued to seethe, "Then I was taken down by a massive agent, then watched three thugs get killed. All because you wouldn't believe me," she stopped to breathe through her sobs then shouted, "No! I am not fucking okay!"

Tears rolled down Chris's face as she ranted. When she was done, she slammed the coffee pot back into the machine and tried to head for the door.

She needed to pass him, but he gently put out his arm to stop her. She wanted to rip it from his shoulder but stopped without touching him – that would make her crumble and she didn't want that to happen. She wanted to leave.

"Please move," she whispered.

"No," he whispered back. "I really have to talk to you. You can leave and never come back because that is what I deserve, but please, listen to me."

Meagan didn't move. She shut her eyes trying to stay strong and not cry, but she was exhausted and could not control her emotions or her eyes. Tears dribbled down her cheeks.

He took her silence as a yes and started to talk, quietly at first, but he gathered his strength. He had to. It was his only chance.

"Meagan, I am so sorry. I had no idea this would happen. I would never, ever have put you in a situation like this. From the minute we met at the Y, I knew I wanted to hold you and love you for the rest of my life. Did you know Ben called me in the middle of a game last night?"

She looked up when he mentioned Ben.

Chris wiped his eyes and his dripping nose on his shirt. "The phone was handed to me on the bench. Meagan, I walked out of the rink without even thinking about the game. When Ben said you were in trouble, my world crashed at my feet. I didn't know just how much you meant to me until he called." He choked back some tears but continued.

"I'm sorry I didn't believe you, but I grew up with Mike following my every move. He idolized me. I was his hero. I fell for that. I was suckered in by Mike and my own ego. I didn't think he could possibly do something as crazy as smuggle drugs. I believed he was like his dad, an honest hard-working man. My blind faith in him almost cost you your life. I will never forgive myself for my poor judgment. I can never ask for your forgiveness.

I know I don't deserve it. When the agent confirmed you were alive, we were at Dan's in Nassau waiting for daylight so we could get over here. I was so relieved to hear you were okay. I knew at that moment you probably didn't want to see me ever again."

He stopped for a second. "Meagan?"

She looked up at him. This was killing her. His tears and raw emotion were creeping into her heart. He looked her straight in the eyes with his sad teary eyes.

"I love you very much. You are the best thing that has ever happened to me. If you leave me now," he paused, he could barely talk. "...I understand. I can live with that. If you had died, I don't think I could carry on."

Meagan kept looking at him, studying his face and thinking over the scenario.

Somewhere from the deepest part of her exhausted waterlogged brain, a glimmer of rational thinking took hold.

A little voice shouted in her head. *What is my problem! It's my ego in the way now. This is the best man in the world and I'm making him suffer. He did not do anything wrong. Exactly!* she answered the voice. *He didn't inflict this pain. He is a victim in this too.*

The feeling of relief washed through her body and she gave in to the exhaustion. She reached for his hand and said, "It's not your fault and we can talk about this later. But right now, I'm really tired. Will you hold me while I sleep for a while?"

His body sagged with relief. He wrapped his arms around her and said, "Sure baby." He kissed the top of her messy hair. "Sure, for how long?"

She snuggled into his body as hard as she could and whispered, "Forever."

ACKNOWLEGEMENTS

It all started simply enough. A handsome man ran past me, flicked his hand in that nonchalant "hello" a runner would do then ran out of sight. I told a friend about it and she challenged me to write a novel based on that single encounter. Who knew such a juicy piece of fiction was waiting to be told!

I'm forever indebted to Angela Saclamacis and fellow author, Sophie Torro for lighting the fire under my butt and making me push "send." You two are inspirational, may your inkwell never run dry.

To people along the way like Claire Harper, Barb Martowski, Lisa Monforton and my daughter Bonnie who read copies or listened to me go on and on, thank you. I'm done now.

To my pack of running friends – a million miles of gratitude.

Thanks to Jeff Wearmouth and our kids, Clay and Bonnie for being the best people I know. Clay I'm sorry I burnt your finger with the molten sugar that one Christmas. But you have to admit, the Croquembouche was worth it. And Bonnie, I did not mean to leave you behind at the gas station in Canmore when you were ten. I should probably find the man who saw what was happening and thank him for the frantic waving.

Jeff, you are my rock. Without you, I'd probably be living under one.

ABOUT THE AUTHOR

Joanne resides in Calgary, Alberta and calls the Rocky Mountains her backyard. She is an avid runner with a drawer full of T-shirts and finisher medals from marathons from around the world. Chasing the family on bikes and skis is another passion.

Sometimes she uses her science degree but usually she is looking for the next travel adventure to write about for leading Canadian publications. Combining her love for the mountains, The Bahamas and running was a perfect way to tell the *Ginger and Ice* story.